MANGATA

MOON

GW00778086

By Jacqueline Freeborn

THE BOOK CHIEF®

IGNITE YOUR WRITING

Published by The Book Chief Publishing House 2024
(a trademark under Lydian Group Ltd)
Suite 2A, Blackthorn House, St Paul's Square,
Birmingham, B3 1RL
www.thebookchief.com

ISBN: 978-1-0686981-9-4

Book Cover Design: Deearo Marketing
Editing: Laura Billingham
Typesetting / Proofreading: Sharon Brown
Publishing: Sharon Brown

Published by The Book Chief

Narrative Comparison

Where 'The Fault in Our Stars' Meets 'The Notebook':

Step into 'Mangata Moon', a novel that beautifully intertwines themes of love, loss, and redemption, much like John Green's 'The Fault in Our Stars.' Relive the emotional intensity and romantic drama reminiscent of Nicholas Sparks' 'The Notebook.

If you're moved by stories that explore the complexities of love and the relentless passage of time, 'Mangata Moon' is your next must-read.

Jacqueline Freeborn's debut novel weaves a tale of emotional depth that combines the best elements of romantic drama and emotional literary fiction, offering a profound, thought-provoking journey into the heart of human connections and the beauty of life's fleeting moments.

Table of Contents

—

—

Dedication

Mum

For your endless love, support and belief

1

Life

"Gratitude, connected and completeness"

I have never feared death. From the moment we take our first breath of life we know the inevitability of its arrival, that moment of silence, darkness, void of everything, everyone – flat lined.

And now it is here, I hold on to every bit of life I have left, so I can remember everything, everyone, before I end.

My eyes can no longer see, yet they are full of colours, faces, moments, a kaleidoscope of memories focusing rapidly, then gone just as quickly. My life rewinding fast, so fast, no time to hold on to the images and memories, but I know they are forever etched within my soul.

The smell of freshly cut grass, egg and cress sandwiches, roast beef, our sweet, sweet lovemaking, newborn life, and most of all you… the taste of you.

I feel your lips upon my face, our last kisses, your soft caresses, the last touch. My heart fights bravely and valiantly to keep me with you. It is beating so fast, and echoing so loud within me, that I cannot hear you, and for the first time, I am fearful.

Faster and faster, louder and louder, until the beat becomes one deafening, excruciating monotone. And then it just stops, no warning or slowing… it just stops.

As the finality of me diminishes, I hear your voice whispering to me. The last words, "I love you Rosie." And as I lay, empty of life, your voice fills the voids, before death takes hold, cushioning my journey from the life I had, the life I loved, into the next.

Sound is the last thing to let go. I can still hear your sobs. I wish I could still feel the tears that I know are falling from your eyes onto my face, still connecting us. Your voice fades, the cries are no more; I am already falling, and I know all that I was has gone, and so has the structure and familiarity that the gift of life bestows.

Where and what am I?

2

The Letter - September 1994

"The infinite power of words"

He felt it as though the whole world had been turned up with the click of a switch. Suddenly, with no warning, it was just there. An indescribable feeling, exposed, raw, and he thought this must be how a new born feels at the moment of birth, thrust uncontrollably away from the safeness, warmth, and tranquillity of inside, into the harshness of the new world on the outside. The awakening, seeing light for the first time, the touch of another being so sudden the change that every part screams as lungs inflate and feel the coolness of oxygen, fuelling the start of life.

Slowly he reset. His eyes re-adjusted and the multitude of colours and the brightness that had exploded in front of him diminished. But the orchestra of noise still hummed in his ears, like listening to the sound of the ocean on the shore, except the crash of the waves never retreated, just smashed, and smashed again and again, until just as quickly... silence.

"Charlie...Charlie." Jake was staring intensely and concernedly into the face of his friend.

Charlie blinked.

"Woah mate, what happened? You got me worried there. You scared the shit out of me!"

"I dunno." Charlie replied, "feel like I am on the bloody sea. Everything went woozy, and floaty just for a moment or two, like being reborn."

"It was more like 5 minutes. You just went into some sort of trance. Like a sort of seizure, but without all that flailing around shit, I really expected you to froth at the mouth, your eyes disappearing into the back of your head. You were like a zombie mate. My hearts beating like my bleeding drums Charlie boy. That's just not right, dude. Dead man sitting, that's what you look like."

Jake continued. "You need a beer or a spliff. Always find it helps when shit happens to me." Jake lit his cannabis spliff, took a huge intake of breath, filling his lungs with its contents, and handed it to Charlie as he breathed out. Charlie shook his head. "Take it, you look like death, not reborn, get some life back in you, I swear this stuff heals everything.

Anyway, now you've clarified you haven't had some sort of stroke, what does re-born feel like?"

Charlie sat back on the sofa. His head was still swimming and the world was still slightly out of focus. "It's like I was inside out. I could hear the rush of my blood being pumped out of my heart, like the sound of a waterfall crashing. The whole world felt out of synch. It still feels like that. Everything feels raw. I am tingling all over." Charlie shuddered.

"Jeez Charlie boy, get a pen and paper and write that stuff down. I read somewhere that all the geniuses Mozart, Gershwin, even Sting, had these out-of-body experiences, and then the words and music just exploded from them. Make us rich Charlie Boy. Don't waste an out-of-body experience. I've been waiting for one for years!"

Jake handed him a beer, and at the same time he gave him the pen and paper. Charlie waited for the volcano of genius to erupt, but the molten inspiration stayed calm, and although he had felt the earth had moved, there was certainly no spark about to ignite.

That was Saturday and ever since, something had remained, loitering within him.

As the days passed, its presence preoccupied him more and more until its familiarity took hold of him, and as much as he tried to shake it off, deny it was there, the stronger it became. He felt his mood darkening, as he couldn't eradicate it. The memories of her started to suffocate him again, just as they had done before. For so long he had lived under the pretence that he had managed to block her out, but his self-protect button had just been annihilated and he didn't know why, until Friday that is.

The letterbox rattled and, as always, Rocky ran to the door, snarling ferociously, belying the big soft, sloppy lump of a beast of a dog he was. He was the only thing Charlie needed in his life, so the emptiness hadn't devoured him after he had left her.

"What have we got today Rocky, any brown ones? Always piss on those boy. Nothing good came out of a brown envelope." Rocky jumped on the bed with the agility of a Russian floor athlete and dropped the saliva sodden post on his chest, tail wagging, eyes bright. Charlie flicked through the envelops and found a couple of brown ones still intact.

"What did I tell you about these, boy?" he said as he threw them on top of a mountain of unopened post in the corner of his bedroom. A pile so big it was starting to become a bit of a fire hazard. There it was.

He recognised the handwriting on the small white envelope and his heart skipped a beat as he held his breath with the shock of seeing his name written by her. The way the letters flowed with such fluidity, he felt they could float off the edges of the paper, so full of grace and softness, and he knew his life would inevitably change if he opened the envelope. She had come back. He stared at the envelope, reluctant to open it.

He could just throw it unopened onto the pile in the corner, but that sweet smell of her had already left the envelope and infiltrated his nose, getting into his system so quickly, unstoppable, clawing at the thick brambles that had wound their tendrils around his heart, stopping anything or anyone from touching it again... until now.

"Christ dude!" Jake was sitting on the worn brown leather sofa, crossed legged lotus style, his usual position when smoking a spliff, which was most of the time. "Who'd have thought, after all this time?"

Jake was Charlie's best friend, well, if truth be known, his only real friend. He was his shadow, always there beside him, he always had his back. He was the only who had stuck by him, guided him through the dark torments that had haunted him after he had left.

He reminded Charlie of Shaggy from the cartoon Scooby Doo. Everything about him was long and lanky and his arms and legs never seemed to work in synch, it was a wonder he managed to walk and function, but that seeming lack of co-ordination had not affected Jake's surreal ability to play drums and percussion like no-one else he knew. In fact, Jake could turn his hand to almost any instrument and within hours, he'd have mastered it. Charlie wondered why he'd chosen drums, and he surmised it was the only way he could release the pent up energy and emotions suppressed by the amount of drugs and booze he shoved into his body. His boundless raw talent, totally unrealised by his laziness annoyed the shit out of Charlie, but fair dues to him, no matter how much cannabis he smoked, and alcohol he drank he'd never let Charlie down when they were on stage, or in life.

"Hey maybe it was her that caused that weird crap on you? You know, I always thought she was some sort of witch.

17

You used to call her that... white witch, do you remember? She turned your heart black Charlie, cold and black. Wow, you got that pen? I think I'm gonna have an episode. Sting watch out."

He inhaled the spliff, holding in its potency for as long as he could, gently exhaling, filling the room with its sweet aroma, pen poised for genius to flow.

"Nah, it's gone," he said disappointedly. "So, what you gonna do dude? What exactly did the witch's note say? Has she put you under her voodoo spell again?"

Charlie tossed the envelope over to Jake, hoping by sharing its contents, it would dissolve the impact it had had on him.

Jake reached out to take it from him, looking over his shoulder as though someone was watching and whispered, "Are you sure, dude? I mean, I don't want her to witcherty pitch her stuff over me man. I've got my own magic here and I don't want her messing with that."

Charlie leaned over and took back the envelope. Jake may be his best friend, his confidant, but the words she had written by her hand were just for him and he could not share the intimacy of the act of writing them with anyone. He imagined her slender small fingers guiding the pen to create the words; words just for him.

The aroma of jasmine and rose attached to the words she had written, would not be contaminated by the stink of

Jake or his cannabis, and while Jake lost himself in the oblivion of dope, Charlie opened the envelope again and read the contents for the tenth, or was it twentieth time.

"Charlie,

I hope this letter finds you well, and that life is treating you well. The years have passed so quickly, yet it feels like forever since you went. How does that work, Charlie?"

He knew exactly how many years, months, and days since he had seen her face, and even though he had managed to erect an artificial and somewhat feeble defence around his heart, his internal calendar had not stopped ticking, counting his emptiness and loneliness even if his consciousness had tried to forget.

"I do hope that the medicine of time has healed the darkness you had, and that life is more joyous and fun. I do not write to open any wounds that may have healed and believe me, I have started this letter too many times over the years, only to throw it unfinished onto the fire. I do not want to re-ignite any pain for you Charlie, but I need to see you. I wouldn't write and ask if there was any other way.

A first love is a true love, of that I am sure. It stays even if it is buried away deep to be forgotten. I do not know if you share your love with another, what I do know is that the lightning bolt that struck the night we met, tuned our hearts to beat as one until the end of time, no matter where we are, or the distance we have between us.

Please come, I do not want to hear your voice until I see your face, so please do not call.

As always Charlie, I wait for you to return. Write and let me know when you are coming.

Yours always,

Rosie x"

Not even "will you come" because he knew she knew he would. The lightning that bound their hearts together all those years ago had struck again. The date on the letter was Saturday. Maybe she was a witch after all.

"Rosie

I should say, it's lovely to hear from you after all this time, but I can't. I knew you were coming back; I felt it before your letter arrived. I am content with my life and I really do not want you back in it.

I will be there Friday.

Charlie"

I knew he would come. He's been waiting all these years unaware, his pride and his pain trying to lock me out.

Forever, he had said as he walked out of the door 8 years ago, but deep down buried beneath the mountain of anger, devastation, and sadness, I knew forever was for us to share. Time and distance didn't diminish us, it just separated us.

"You only live once," he had said to her. "Actually, we live every day, but we only die once," she had replied.

The memory of when he first saw her was imprinted into him, every muscle, sinew, and cell. It was like a photographic negative hidden away in the recesses of his mind in a pocket of darkness, hoping the years would obliterate it.

But it was always there, and sometimes the temptation was too much. Even though he knew the sharp pain of recollection would pierce his heart so deeply, he just could not help taking it out of its envelope of time, holding it up to the bright sunshine and returning to the moment his heart had stopped, just for a millionth of second, and tuned itself to hers.

Charlie knew going back was like opening Pandora's box, but the pull from her was too strong. His anger rose. "Witch," he muttered to himself.

3

The Return

"To go back or to come back"

The familiarity of the landscape caused Charlie's heart to beat a little faster and his breathing to deepen a little as the noise of urban life disappeared behind him. In front of him was a place he had worked so hard to forget and eradicate any memories. His ability to do this had, for most of the time, brought him some peace except for when he woke before the sun had risen, covered in sweat, shaking, curled in a ball in the centre of his bed, his cheeks wet from tears as he dreamed about her. Over the years, the dreams had lessened in their frequency, but they always came back, the imprint of the past permanently etched into every inch of his being.

He knew the way there intuitively. The open countryside and the winding roads pulling him back with such strength he felt that if he took his hands off the steering wheel, his foot off the accelerator and closed his eyes, he would still end up there.

He could already smell the saltiness in the air, gull cries escorting him back, signalling his return.

In the distance, he could hear the sound of the sea as it crashed onto the cliffs, regular and rhythmic like the beat of a drum.

The wind blew through the leaves on the trees like notes from a violin as nature formed a natural orchestra so intense it overwhelmed him, causing him to shake and breathe so fast he felt as though he would pass out. He slammed on the brakes to bring the car to a sudden halt, causing rubble from the country lane to spray across the grass verge.

Damn her, why had she bothered him? She knew he would come if she asked him, but why ask him after seven years? Seven years without her and now he was going back. He had wanted to ignore the letter when it arrived, pretend it hadn't come, but he knew he would open it and with just one sheet of blue paper that contained no more than 100 words, he'd opened up Pandora's box.

He rested his head on his hands on the steering wheel for what he felt was just a few moments, but by the time he raised his head the sun was already starting to lower. He looked at his watch. He'd been there almost an hour. He looked towards the horizon and saw

the vastness of the North Sea as it touched the Northumbrian coastline, the undulations of the waves seemingly beautiful, gentle, and calm, belying its coldness and ruggedness.

This magnificent but unpredictable sea was just like love, beautiful, and wonderful on the surface, but underneath uncontrollable and destructive.

Charlie turned the ignition of the car and continued on his way. A wooden, weather-beaten sign indicated that Hefring was only one mile away, one mile until he would see her face again.

It was about six thirty when Charlie's red Ford Cortina pulled onto the gravel of Claymore Cottage. His drive through the tiny village had already evoked memories of that September when they first met.

Ghosts and shadows of bunting lined streets, the smell of fresh doughnuts mixed with fish and chips came to greet him with each corner he turned.

The cottage was situated about a half a mile away from the village. The sharp right-hand bend off the main coast road that led directly into the long rising drive way concealed the house from sight, but it also enabled it to have the most magnificent views over the sea, as well as a bird's-eye view of the harbour and the

chimneys and rooftops of the rows of connected houses that formed the streets of Hefring.

The hawthorn hedges were still there on either side of the driveway and the sound of the tyres on the tiny stones was still incredibly familiar, as though he had not been away at all.

The lowering September sun cast long shadows from the silver birch trees behind the hedges as his car stopped outside the house, joining two others already parked there.

He recognised one as Frances's old green Fiesta and he guessed the other blue car, a mini, belonged to Rosie.

The almost permanent state of nausea that had been with him since the letter had arrived increased and he breathed in to keep down the half-eaten stale sandwich he had managed to eat on the journey. His heart raced as he knew the slightly ajar oak door was all there was between him seeing her again.

All the pent up anger he had felt over the past few days gave way to a huge sense of foreboding as he walked towards the door. There was no sound from the house. The window to the left of the property was open and a white net lace curtain flicked in and out of the frame.

Charlie pushed open the front door. He gave a very light knock as he entered the hallway. As he did so, he looked behind to ensure there was an escape route back to the car if he needed it, back to the comfort of his pre letter life.

But Charlie knew there was no escape, that the house had already got a grip on him, that there would be no turning back and he had to face whatever was in front of him.

The house was still, silent. All he could hear was his own internal body organs fighting to gain control over what was happening. His heartbeat started to slow down, but this only increased the sound of it thumping against his chest. The familiar smell of the house, a mixture of jasmine and beeswax, consumed him.

They say smell is the strongest sense to evoke memories, and the familiarity of it all brought with it a flurry of images from the past, their intensity so strong they caused him to stumble forward onto the red-tiled floor. He closed his eyes, listening to the sounds of this place, the sound of the sea in the distance as the waves sang a chorus of shhh, shhh, shhh as they gently lapped the sand. The sounds of the house welcomed him back as the beams that held up this old house seemed to mutter his name. This was her home, not his.

Against the backdrop of his memories, he heard laughter and singing, a voice so sweet and clear, a child's voice coming from the back of the house. He edged forward, walking towards the curved wooden staircase in front of him. To the right was the lounge. The door was closed, as was the door of the dining room straight opposite. Directly in front of him, just to the left of the staircase, the back door was wide open, revealing a very colourful back garden.

Both doors to the house, the front and the rear, were directly aligned so that when you stood on the drive, and if both doors were open, you could look down past the garden and see The North Sea.

This had always been a fascination for Charlie, and he appreciated the wonderment and insight of the builder who had designed and constructed this house. It looked as though the house had outstretched its palm to touch the sea and coastline.

The garden was just like a traditional English garden in a novel or gardening book, full of shrubs, flowers, and trees with a huge expanse of lawn, and a constant hum of insects and birds. He remembered this as though he had only been gone a few days.

The kitchen door was to the left, just before the back door. It was open and just as he walked past to head towards the garden, he heard a voice shriek.

"Oh, my God…Oh, my God." A woman was holding the door frame to steady herself, her hand on her mouth as she tried to regulate her breathing.

"Charlie?" The woman said in astonishment.

"It's me Fran, I'm so sorry if I scared you." He took hold of her arm to steady her. "I did knock at the door. It was open and so I just came in. I probably should have waited."

He looked down at the small woman, her hair bundled in a bun at the back of her head.

"Charlie, Christ Charlie," she continued. She looked directly into his eyes and touched his face very gently.

They were both silent as they looked at each other, taking in the subtle changes of ageing that life had etched into their faces before she put her arms around his waist, her head in his chest, and he felt her start to shake and sob.

This tiny but strong, steadfast woman who Charlie had never seen show one ounce of fear or foreboding before, felt like a broken, limp rag doll as he held her tightly to prevent her legs from buckling.

It confused him, and he was starting to feel scared. As Frances's cries began to subside, she stood back from him and he saw a face so full of sadness and sorrow.

The singing in the garden stopped as though it was tuned in to Frances's voice and muffled sobs. She composed herself and took a white handkerchief embroidered with daisies from the pocket of her apron and wiped away the tears that had fallen from her melancholic eyes; her look moved from Charlie to the open door. Charlie had expected an angry or stern Frances, not a saddened one, but that sadness was concealed in an instance, as a huge smile spread across her face and a child's voice said,

"Aunt Frances, are you sad I could hear you crying?" The child was running from the garden but stopped as she saw Charlie with his arm still around Frances's shoulder.

"Who are you?" A tiny voice asked.

"It's okay, Neave, it's okay. I was crying because I was overjoyed to see Charlie. You don't know Charlie, but he's a very, very dear friend and he's come to visit, so don't look so scared."

"I'm not scared of him. I was just scared because I thought you were crying and I don't like to see you sad."

Frances looked down at the happy small child, who was staring intently at her. She knew she was trying to fathom out whether she was telling the truth. Her long wavy blonde hair was full of bits of grass and she turned to look at Charlie. He took a huge inhale of breath; it was just like looking at Rosie. She had the palest of blue eyes, so open and innocent, and they were staring directly into his.

"Hello friend, my name is Neave." She said, her eyes not leaving his.

"Delighted to meet you Neave, my name is Charlie."

"I know that Aunt Frances told me. Why are you here? Are you here to see Mummy? Are you the Charlie she whispers sometimes when she's asleep? Because if you are, you will make Mummy very happy to see you."

Charlie felt his heart warm to this tiny human who was the mirror image of Rosie. Anyone who could warm his heart had to be someone special. The anxiousness that had consumed him since the letter arrived was forgotten for a moment as he recounted her words…Mummy will be happy. He was angry with her for sure, but that was OK. this child had actually said she still whispered his name.

Maybe the wrath of an abandoned woman wouldn't be coming his way, even though he knew it was justified.

The child continued to talk.

"Are you Mummy's friend?" She continued.

"Yes, I am her friend, well I hope so."

"Well, I don't see how that can be because friends see each other every day, well almost every day like my mum's best friend Annie, so I don't know how you can be that good friends cos I've never seen you before."

"Leave Charlie be Neave, he has driven a really long way to come and visit us and I'm sure he needs a cup of tea, so why don't you go back into the garden and play again and we can talk later after Charlie has had his drink. It'll soon be time for tea and a bath."

"Are you staying for tea? You can have a sleepover if you like, my friends have sleepovers."

"Neave off you go into the garden. You can chat to Charlie later. Charlie is invited for tea and if he wants to, he is more than welcome to have a sleepover. Off you go…"

She pointed towards the open back door. Neave tipped her head to the left as she smiled at Charlie before running out onto the lawn and disappearing into the shrubbery and bushes at the end of the garden.

Charlie just didn't know what to make of it all. When he had left all those years ago, he never imagined he would return and if he did, he did not expect to be welcomed back. That being said, Frances had always been a person who had never held grudges and always tried to look for the positives in everything. A lot of time had passed and the old adage, time is a healer, might have worked with Frances even though it certainly hadn't for him, but he needed to keep his guard up as he had left her niece heartbroken and that had been unforgivable.

"I'll make tea," she said as she held open the kitchen door, waiting for Charlie to walk through.

"Where is Rosie?" he asked very tentatively. "She wrote to me and asked me to come. Did you know that?"

"Come, take a seat Charlie, there is lots to catch up on."

Little had changed. He took a seat at the round pine table with its six slightly battered chairs in the centre of the room, surrounded by a mish-mash of different

coloured kitchen cupboards. Green gingham checked cotton curtains still at the window. The memories came flooding back.

Rosie with her white blonde hair held up with pins, wisps falling down her neck, her standing at the sink filling the kettle with water, wearing a white Rolling Stones tee shirt and cutoff blue Jean shorts hardly long enough fully cover the cheeks of her backside, laughing as she looked at him, the sun's rays haloing her beautiful face.

"Charlie …..Charlie." Frances's voice pulled him back from his memories. "I'm sorry I can't remember. Do you have sugar?"

"No, no thanks, not now," he replied.

"Teas and coffee were yours and Rosie's speciality. Have you still got that tea shop? What's it called Driftwood Café?" he asked as he drank the hot tea, and before she had time to reply, he continued, "Do you know she served me coffee in that tea shop before I came in that day and met you?

She annoyed me with her chattering." He said with a smile on his face as he relived the moment, "God, I was a bloody arrogant prick then."

"Only then?" Frances asked, almost teasing, but it had serious undertones as though she wanted a straight answer.

"I'm not the same. I hope I've lost some of that arrogance. I lost lots of myself when I was here…."

"We all change Charlie. Don't be so dismissive of your arrogance. It was actually that, that pulled her to you, your overly confident manner. She told me you were immature and self-centred, but there must have been something else she saw underneath all that, otherwise she would not have given you the time of day." Frances replied.

He looked up at her, his thick dark hair still almost covering his eyes and Frances knew why her niece had fallen in love with this man.

———

33

"Thanks for the kind words but I was a prick, and you know it, it's just that you're too polite just say it." He waited for a while for Frances to answer. "You could disagree, you know," he continued.

"Well, you know Charlie, there is something in my makeup that prevents me from telling a lie, an untruth, no matter what it is, so I will refrain from disagreeing, and yes, you were a prick, as you put it." She said, that familiar lovely smile returning.

Charlie smirked and thought how time did change us. Frances would never have said prick. In fact, he'd never ever heard her swear or curse before now.

The warm tea was taking effect, and he started to relax a little, curiosity as to why he had been asked to return, replaced some of the anxiousness, and Frances was being more than polite, she genuinely seemed pleased to see him.

"So where is she, Frances? What was so important that I had to drop everything and come down here and see her? It wasn't an easy decision to make to be honest, and I was disappointed and really upset to get that letter after all this time." The smile went from Frances's face, the selfish 'it's all about me' Charlie was, unfortunately, still there.

"Mmm, I guess it wasn't easy for you to come back and it wasn't easy for her to write and ask either Charlie, as I am sure she'll tell you. It's not for me to discuss."

"And the child's father won't mind me being here, and isn't he upset that Rosie still speaks about me?" He asked cheekily, oblivious to how much he had already upset her.

"The child has a name, Charlie. It's Neave, and her father hasn't ever been part of her life."

He registered that she seemed upset that he had not remembered Neave's name.

Charlie suddenly felt as though someone had kicked him in the gut. His head was trying to do the maths…he left seven, almost eight years ago… was the child his?

She couldn't be. She was only about five. He shook his head to dismiss the thought.

"You'll see Rosie this evening Charlie, I have prepared the attic bedroom for you. I'm assuming you are stopping, as there is lots to catch up on."

He hesitated.

"It feels more than a little uncomfortable being here Frances, I can't deny that, but I guess I will have to stop over to wait for Rosie as it's a three-hour journey back."

The me, me, me of old was still in there, Frances thought, more interested in himself and his feelings than that of a woman who had fallen to bits when he had left. Much had happened over the years, and Rosie had eventually picked herself up and built herself a wonderful life. When she had been blessed with Neave, the loneliness that had haunted her was overridden by the love she had her for the child.

Frances had not wanted Rosie to write to him, but she had insisted.

Frances had hoped to meet a more mature Charlie, one that was less self-centred, but leopards don't change their spots and that is why she had pleaded with Rosie to leave him be. One part of her was delighted to see him, because Rosie, and she herself, had really loved him and they had had some really wonderful times. Frances had always known he wouldn't stay with them.

It was first love, a holiday romance, but when he did go, Rosie was so low for so long that she had wondered if she had suffered from the type of melancholy you read in a Bronte novel, a broken heart, never to be repaired. Neave had changed that, and the sensitive, kind, happy Rosie re-emerged, never to be overshadowed again.

Charlie drank his tea and took himself off up the stairs to the attic bedroom, stopping very briefly outside the closed door of her room. It had been theirs when he had lived there.

He continued up the narrow spiral staircase and pushed open the very old creaky door. He guessed it was the original one, as there were lumps and chips out of the wood, probably over 200 years old, and it had one of those metal latches as a handle.

The tiny attic bedroom was full of boxes and toys piled up against the sloping recesses of the room.

A small single wooden frame bed covered in a very old handmade quilt was in the centre of the room and to its left was a smallish window that didn't quite shut right. It was a very quiet room; it felt like a room you went to if you wanted to escape and hide from the world. Charlie could hear the distant sound of the sea from the gap in the window and muffled voices and child's laughter from way down below in the kitchen.

He threw his holdall onto a tattered chaise longue, to the right of the bed, and turned on the bedside lamp, which immediately cast shadows onto the sloping walls. He felt as though he was surrounded by dark faceless beings watching over him, which unnerved him somewhat. He had never felt anything but love and warmth and security in this house, but there was an anticipation creeping back into him, a sort of fear looming and he didn't like it. He liked to be in control and, not knowing why he was there as well as not having seen Rosie, he felt exposed to the unknown. He knew this feeling evoked the very worst of him and he realised he must have sounded very rude to Frances earlier, telling her he couldn't stop long when this had been his home and they had welcomed him into their family with such ease.

It was a bit weird that Rosie wasn't there, but he assumed she must have had a late night at the café and she would be home soon, then all would be revealed and he could bugger off back to own life.

He laid on the bed; it was comfy, and he fell asleep almost immediately. The stress of the last few days had exhausted him. His dreams came quickly, a vivid living tapestry of memories, colours, sounds, feelings, rushing over him like ghosts and ghouls.

Rosie at the kitchen sink, Rosie dancing on the table, Rosie laughing, running barefoot on a deserted beach, Rosie's wails and sadness, his happiness, joy, and rage swirling round like a tornado and just like Dorothy in the Wizard of Oz he was sucked into it.

He tried to scream, but it was as though his voice had been stolen and all that came out was an array of indistinguishable sounds.

Charlie woke up in a sweat, his mouth dry from trying to call out. The shadow army was darker and stronger now and it loomed above, looking down upon him. He sat up and rubbed his eyes, initially unsure of his whereabouts. The rows of photographs of Rosie and Neave on the wall, along with family, all of whom he'd never met, brought him back to reality. He was in her house. He looked at his watch, 7.40 p.m. The sun had almost set.

He sat at the edge of the bed, his hands in his hair, and muttered to himself.

"What the fuck am I doing here? Why on earth did I come?"

He contemplated sneaking out of the house. The dream had left him feeling anxious. The hot anger had been a much more amenable friend than the cold feeling now taking hold of him. Being fearful of something you can see is really bad, but the fear that manifests from something intangible is by far the most terrifying, and this fear, this unwanted gut wrenching feeling, was getting stronger and stronger. He felt totally out of control. He just needed to get away. It had been the wrong decision to come back. Nothing ever good came from looking back, never mind actually going back.

What was he doing? He needed to get out of the house, this place that held his long forgotten demons.

4

September 1984 - The Beginning

"The point in time or space at which something starts"

It was dusk. The setting sun cast shadows that transformed seagulls on the wind into huge pterodactyls, fading as they soared away into the orange and crimson of the evening sky. The sea glistening like a blanket encrusted with millions of tiny diamonds, twinkling on the waves as they licked away at the soft pale sand. Tranquillity, calm and peace, just what Charlie loved laying in the sand dunes hidden away from the busyness of life. Laid amongst the blades of sun-baked grass was a place Charlie felt he belonged, at home, a place where he could be alone. He couldn't really describe to anyone the feelings he had when there was just him. It was his little piece of heaven on earth.

He wasn't one for sharing or closeness. "Mon beau loup." Cecile had called him.

"C'est parce que, you are like a lone wolf, watching, looking, listening, mais sentiment n'est pas importance... feelings are not important. You like being alone, happy with who you are, and you will let no one touch your heart."

He had loved her 'Frenchness', romantic, mysterious, much older than him. She was the one who had awakened the enchantment of lovemaking, shown him the thrill of touch, the warmth of intimacy.

At eighteen years old Charlie had actually thought she was the one, but twenty years older and much wiser, Cecile had known better and, of course, she was right. She had known solitude was his love. "Mon Lou-Lou" she would call him, the recollection of her words always warmed him and made him smile.

Charlie learnt from this passage into manhood, that he would never experience love the way others had, the way it was described in books or in the words of a song. He did however love the company of women; he revered the softness of their skin, the plumpness of their breasts, the small arch in the curve at the end of the spine as it gave way to the voluptuous roundness of their backsides, every woman different but wondrous in their own right.

He loved the way he could make them relinquish any inhibitions, the moaning and sighing until the moment of complete and utter abandonment took hold of them, and just how beautiful they looked when they let everything go, in fact he adored this more than his own coming.

Charlie wasn't saddened by his inability to love, he actually felt quite lucky, blessed even, for he had come to the conclusion love was actually just a journey to pain, unimaginable pain that would arrive sooner or later, in that one or the other would leave taking with them endless guilt, whilst the one left behind faced irreparable heartbreak.

If not this, then death would eventually take one before the other, leaving devastation, sorrow, and indescribable loneliness. He did love lovemaking; he loved chocolate digestives; he loved a peachy backside and the look in a woman's eyes as she came. He just had never been in love, not even with Cecile, so yes, he felt blessed. He never wanted the torture or responsibility that being in love brought.

The only thing he was in love with, which provided him with more satisfaction, completeness, and devotion than anything on earth, was his absolute obsession with music.

Charlie lost himself in music and no-one, not even Cecile, touched his heart like the notes and sound of music did. He was indeed a lucky man as music would never bring him heart ache, just joy, satisfaction, and contentedness.

Charlie was enveloped in a warm blanket of one of the many sand dunes that stretched for miles along Mangata beach. He could hear the distant sound of the sea as it approached with the turning of the tide, the long grass swaying rhythmically in the warm breeze. Natures ballet and orchestra, his ear picked up the sounds of the composition created by Mother Earth. Notes erupted in his head as the formation of a melody started, and he tapped them out with his molars in doing so, carving a place for them in his memory until he managed to capture them on paper.

To anyone watching him it would have looked as though he was sleeping, motionless except for the tiny movements of his jaw as the notes took shape and patterns formed like the murmuration of starlings as they twist, turn and swirl in a magnificent evening sky performance. This is how sounds and notes came to Charlie, with such grace, beauty, and harmony. He just had to be patient and wait for them for them to formulate, and a song would emerge. It was almost there when…

"What the fuck!" Charlie shouted as he sat up, spitting out a mouthful of sand particles that had interrupted the birthing of a song from a crescendo of his creativity. He was face to face with the huge, hairy face of an enormous beast of a hound, dripping dog saliva from its jaw, the same saliva Charlie was also wiping from his own mouth.

"I am so sorry," he heard a voice say. He could hear her voice but couldn't see her, the brilliance from the low fading sun blinding him. Charlie shielded his eyes from its radiance as the dog straddled his body, dropping even more wet mouth juice slop across his face as he did so.

"Lou-Lou!" the ET like shape shouted.

Why was she shouting him? Why was she talking to him? Not only was he completely slimed, he was also equally completely confused. How did she know about Cecile and Lou-Lou? It was their private thing, never shared with anyone. The beast was looking down at him.

He held himself steady with his hands whilst it continued to frolic all over him, its elongated tongue creating yet more gunge as it proceeded to lick his entire face.

The shape was but a blur as the brightness of the sun continued to frame her. The beast took no notice of her protestations and demands to stop and continued to share the contents of its mouth with him. The shape lunged towards him shouting "Lou-Lou!" as the dog thrust itself forward in what Charlie perceived was a serious attempt to mount his head and bang him. His perceptions confirmed when the ET like shape said, "I am so sorry, oh my God, I am so, so sorry".

She fell forward in an attempt to grab the beast's collar, which she managed to do. The beast, seeming to know that this action would cause a cessation of its humping, tried to climb over Charlie's head, causing ET to replace the beast's previous position, her legs straddling him as she struggled to restrain its amorous antics. The beast was too strong and ET had to let go of its collar. It bounded away across the dunes, no doubt looking for another unfortunate victim to fulfil its sexual requirements.

ET, one foot on either side of Charlie, collapsed in a heap at his side, a mass of multi-coloured floral cloth and hair, reminding him of images of witches who go puff and disappear, leaving just a residue of clothes behind. A head appeared, well a ball of hair was all Charlie could make out, spluttering and spitting, and once again he was covered in gob fluid that didn't belong to him.

The whole episode had taken but a few moments and, despite his trauma, Charlie's mind had instantly gone into song mode. He already had the title of what would surely be a hit … "Share your spit with strangers" …or maybe not.

He still couldn't see her properly, her face was totally hidden by a mass of long blonde curls, and before he had caught sight of the features beneath, she stood up, and shook another ton of sand from her locks covering him once again.

"Oh my God, you look like my dog, there's no wonder she made a beeline to you…she's only a pup, well adolescent really, all those hormones and all that, and she humps…not sure what all that is about…" she continued to babble, "but honestly you really are a human version of my dog, it's unreal."

Something that resembled a dog and someone who was obviously a witch had stepped big time into Charlie's no-go zone, his personal space, uninvited and unapologetic, insulting him at the same time. No way did he look like that slobbering animal, and how dare she say that after she and her beast had assaulted him?

"Woo, woo, woo," Charlie heard himself say as he tried to push himself backwards on his hands in retreat, the dry soft sand seeming to engulf his attempts, as he

simultaneously scanned the immediate area, for signs of the slobber beast who might return at any moment.

"What the fuck!" he continued in protestation. "First your bloody freaky oversized, oversexed sloppy-mouth hound attacks me, well actually worse than that, it sexually abused me, then you literally throw yourself at me. They say dogs are like their owners. I guess that's where she sodding well gets her friskiness from, and if that isn't enough you tell me I look like her.. A word of advice, not the best way to get my attention. Think you both need some lessons in sexual etiquette if you ask me."

There was a moment of silence, no movement except she cocked her head to one side, just as a dog does when it is trying to suss something out. He still couldn't make her face out. All he could see was a shape surrounded by light, another beast in human form. She definitely must be a bloody witch, he thought. She had him at a disadvantage, she could see all of him, and he didn't like that, and then as suddenly as she had appeared, she was gone, purposely kicking a mound of more sand into his face, running away in the direction the dog had gone a minute or so ago.

Charlie laid back in his warm sand hammock, waiting for the peace and tranquillity to return, desperately trying to recall the notes he'd had in his head, a

masterpiece almost complete before the witch and the beast had interrupted him. But just like the swallows, you only get a moment to capture them before they are gone. "For fuck's sake."

"Be with you in a min," Rosie shouted as she heard the familiar ding as the café door shut.

It was almost time to close for the day and she was just about to throw away the last of the chocolate cake and lemon meringue. "Some cake left if you want it. I was just about to get rid of it. You can have it no charge."

"Nah, just a coffee," was the reply.

"Sugar and milk?"

"Two and a just drop of milk – nice and strong if you don't mind."

"Not good for you, all that caffeine at the end of the day."

"I'm a night owl!"

Rosie prepared a mug of strong, sweet coffee and brought it to the table of the last remaining customer in the Driftwood Café. He was totally engulfed in his own thoughts, head down, scribbling on a small notepad, his whole body rhythmically moving, his fingers tapping on the green spotted tablecloth, in tandem with his sneaker clad feet.

"Thanks," he said without looking up at her, absorbed totally in his own inclusive beat party. His hair, black with streaks of almost grey blonde from summer sunshine, and the strong square jaw looked vaguely familiar to Rosie. She cocked her head to one side as she waited for her curiosity to translate into revelation as clouded memories became sharper and focused. It was him, the rude, arrogant dune weirdo.

"Unbelievable, still as rude," she muttered under her breath as he reached for his mug, not lifting his eyes from the notebook, the pages full of scribblings, musical notes, words, and symbols, a real hieroglyphical mess as far as Rosie could make out. Her mischievousness kicked in and with all the restraint she could muster, she refrained from pushing his chair back, straddling him, and licking his face. Instead, she just stared at him. He did actually look like her dog, Lou-Lou a Siberian husky. His thick dark hair was unruly and wild, his eyes were green, although she could not see them, she remembered how piercing they were, surrounded by a thick mass of long dark lashes, all in all features far too pretty to be wasted on a man.

Despite his prettiness, he still of course had all the traditional traits of a bloke that Rosie had experienced on the few times she had been in a relationship. She had become bored very quickly with their child like petulance and self-obsession with their own importance. It was always all about them and their lack of ability to see beyond their own feelings and needs was quite hilarious. Her most recent relationship, well if could she call it recent, it ended almost 6 months ago; she finished up being more like a mother to Rob, who was 10 years older than her. She had been attracted to him as she had hoped men actually did mature and become less selfish with age, but her hopes had been shattered as their relationship slipped into her worrying about him not having enough food in, or whether he had bleach and washing powder, whilst he really did believe he was being benevolent allowing her to sleep over.

She, of course, was privileged and damn lucky to benefit from his extensive sexual experience, as well as his amazing cock — all his words, of course.

She shook her head to try to shake away the memories, but unfortunately Rosie seemed to have the ability to store all her experiences with uncanny accuracy, vivid colours, and details, as though they were life films stored in the archives in her head that she could instantly replay.

She looked down at the 'loup'. He was still shaking his head as though listening to music and without thinking, she stroked his thick dark mane of hair, just as she would Lou-Lou.

"What the fuck?" his word jolting her from this unconscious momentary action. She stood back. She knew she had the advantage over him again as the lowering September sun streaming through the shop window blinded him for the second time.

He shielded his eyes, putting his arm over his face, trying to focus. He couldn't see her, but she could see him, the man-wolf. She was still bemused by his uncanny resemblance to Lou-Lou.

"Sorry," she said. "You had some sand in your hair. I thought it was going to sprinkle in your coffee."

"What is it about this place?" he replied angrily, "Doesn't anyone know anything about personal space and customer manners?"

"And of course you know everything about politeness and gratitude, don't you?" she replied. "We are closing by the way, so you need to vacate like now. You are so engrossed in your, whatever that mess is on that notepad, that you are oblivious to the fact we shut fifteen minutes ago."

"Well excuse me for being a customer and maybe you should put a sign in the window – Manhandling and fondling of customers is included in the service!"

"Hmmm…why is everything always about men, even the bloody English language? Why is it manhandling, not woman handling or even person handling? I know why, because men are so self- obsessed that all words have to be all about them." She didn't shout or raise her voice, just delivered her statement in a very calm way, which infuriated him even more.

"Well, in case you haven't noticed, I am a man, and I have been manhandled, and even worse, I have had a lecture on feminism," he emphasised 'man' as he spoke. "All I wanted was a quiet cup of coffee, like I wanted a quiet time on the beach. This is the second time this week some bloody woman has interfered with me without me deriving any pleasure whatsoever, I might add."

Rosie rolled her eyes at the sexual innuendo, a popular and annoying part of male conversation. "This mess as you refer to it, is creativity which has once again been stunted," his hand were flailing around his head and she couldn't suppress a smile as he continued to remind her of Lou-Lou, uncontrollable, a bit of a nutter but cute at the same time.

"How dare you laugh at me!" he said, taken aback by her indifference to his protest. "I am a musician!" he declared.

"Well, George Michael, as I said before…we are shut, so it's time to go-go." And with that Rosie walked back to the shop counter as the man-wolf huffed and puffed as though getting ready to blow the place down, collected his messy notes and stropped out of the café like a sulking child, slamming the door as he left.

"Dick," Rosie muttered as she cleared the table, but she couldn't help smiling as she did so.

5

Hefring

"Goddess of The Waves"

There was a buzz and sense of anticipation throughout the small village of Hefring. An invisible thread of excitement connecting every house, shop, business, child, adult, even the trees and flowers seemed brighter, as a gentle warm breeze danced through them creating the familiar hum of nature's September song.

Rosie loved this place tucked away on the Northumbrian coast. She loved the wilderness of its landscape, almost uninterrupted by human interference. Miles and miles of sandy beaches fringed with wild grasses and dunes, undulating like a natural roller-coaster of bumps and grooves. Tall trees edged the dunes, guardians and protectors of its beauty and magic.

Hefring was a tiny village hidden between the crevice of two hills that met and gave way to the sand and pebbles the North Sea washed up.

The buildings were constructed from the natural grey stone, almost camouflaging the dwellings, merging them into the natural landscape.

Fishing was still at the heart of the community, although in recent years the village had seen the development of cafés, restaurants, and a few small family hotels, as visitors found this cosy little place and came in trickles to observe and experience the vast expanses of rugged coastline - a sanctum for nature to share her riches.

Its history was full of myths and legends of Vikings. Stories passed down from generations of how the Viking Sea God, Aegir, had rewarded a great Viking warrior for hunting and slaughtering a mythical sea dragon, a Kraken, which had attacked Viking boats as they invaded England. He had rewarded them with the gift of one of his seven daughters of the waves, Hefring, meaning the lifting one, and she carved out a safe cove for the Vikings to land and to settle.

The shape of the cove resembled a hand and fingers as though Hefring herself had literally clawed a way into the landscape to provide a place for the Vikings, a place with rich soil for farming and a sea so bountiful of fish that they would never go hungry again.

Rosie imagined she found remnants of this past time as she explored the coastline. Pebbles that resembled teeth from the Kraken, glass made smooth from the waves, were eyes of the sea monster and of people lost at sea. Pieces of driftwood washed up on the shores, beaten by the powerful northern waves so much that they often disintegrated into dust as she tried to pick them up. To her, these were remnants of wood from Viking boats that had landed on the shore hundreds of years ago.

Hefring was the place Rosie had taken her first breath. As life was given to her, it departed from her mother Kathleen, who had died in childbirth at the very young age of seventeen, a life never lived and Rosie was determined to live life for both of them.

She had been brought up by her mother's sister Frances, Aunt Fran, and despite never having looked into her mother's eyes nor felt the love of her embrace, she felt as though she knew her and was connected to her through the stories Frances told her about Kathleen. Their home was full of photos of her, drawings and sketches her mother had drawn, and her mother's favourite soft bear always sat in a rocking chair keeping watch over her until she fell asleep.

The rocking chair had been one of Kathleen's favourite places where she would sit for hours on end rocking and singing to herself, an imagination that had no boundaries. Frances often told Rosie her mother's stories, one of her favourites being that the rocking chair was a small boat riding the North Sea, rescuing ancestors from the Daneland as they tried to avoid the fate of the Kraken.

Rosie, like her mother Kathleen, was fascinated by history and the lost secrets held in every grain of sand, every blade of grass and every mound of earth. Kathleen had sworn she could feel the heartbeats of the thousands of souls who had lived and died on this land, and Rosie often felt that same connection to those no longer with them.

The primitive etchings of a small child, the tattered edges of paper that held the stories she had written, the collection of 'treasures' she had collected from the shoreline, all these things ensured that Rosie always felt her mother's presence. It had given her the sense of belonging that every child needs, knowing who they are and where they had come from.

Rosie felt her mother's love every day and a connection that could not have been stronger, even if Kathleen had been able to physically love and care for her.

Rosie's most treasured possession was a crocheted pink, blue and lemon blanket Kathleen had made whilst she had been carrying her.

As a child, Rosie had told Frances she was part of her mother, and when Frances had asked her to explain, Rosie had told her that Kathleen had grown her from herself, so this meant she had to be part of her mother. What a child instinctively knew, science provided the evidence, she had her mother's cells, blood, and DNA, and whilst their home gave her the physical reminders of Kathleen, Rosie could feel her spirit running through her veins and in her heart, feeling her influence her thoughts, actions, and decisions.

She felt her mother was always with her, guiding and protecting her, encouraging her to live life to its fullest as she knew all too well that no-one could predict when the end of life would come.

Above her bed was a watercolour her mum had painted. Frances had said it was her self-portrait, a silhouette of a woman, her belly full of life not yet born, long hair caught on the wind against the backdrop of nature's wilderness, the dunes and the coastline Rosie loved so much. When Rosie closed her eyes as she stood looking out at the North Sea, she could feel her mother's embrace in the wind, like soft

chiffon wrapping itself around her, that same feeling that comforted her as she fell asleep at night.

She had only once asked Frances about her father. Frances had said she didn't know his name, she had never met him, nor seen his face, but that her sister Kathleen had loved him unconditionally. Her mother had told Frances he was a spirit from the past who had come to her from the sea, bestowing her with the gift of the seed of life, ensuring everything that had lived in the past would continue to be part of life to come.

Rosie imagined her mother meeting her strong Viking warrior as the white horses from the sea brought him to her at dusk every night. They would lay in the grass looking up into the darkness of night, the stars of souls departed smiling down on them.

As she grew older and gained the knowledge of how life was made, she created an image in her mind of a shooting star across a cold December night whilst her parents made love on the sand, protected from the cold by the deepness of the dunes.

—

She imagined the love her mother and her Viking warrior father had had, hoping that one day the spirits who had brought them together would give her the opportunity for the same unconditional love and passion. She was getting a little

disheartened though, as her experiences to date had only revealed that men on the whole were mainly shallow, selfish, totally preoccupied with themselves and actually not that interesting at all.

September was a special time in Hefring, and Rosie loved it. An annual festival was a time to celebrate nature's gifts to humanity. It was a time when most of the people in the village attended the tiny church located just outside the village to sing together and share home-made food gifts. The Viking history was even captured in the stained-glass windows of the church and when the brightness of the sun shone through the multicoloured glass, it cast images of a sea dragon being slaughtered by the hand of God as lightning struck. The preciousness of this land and its ancestry was respected and loved by generations of families whose bloodline could be seen, carved in the many headstones in the church's graveyard.

For hundreds of years, there had been very little exodus from the village. It was only recently that young people had started to leave to go to university or to take jobs in the ever growing nearby cities.

Newcastle seemed to be stretching out its tentacles consuming the land and emptying it of people.

For Sale signs had started to pop up as folk died and their children did not have the inclination to return and live in family homes. Many of these had become holiday homes for the wealthy in the cities. With this came other changes that could never be undone. The passing down of skills, traditions, and land from family to family, cracking permanently what had connected generations. Creating divides that once opened, would never re-connect again, like cracks of a fault line in the earth's core.

September was magical in that it brought back those had migrated to the townships and cities to join in the celebrations. They brought with them new friends and relatives to stay over and share in The Festival of Mabon, a festival that continued to connect this little town with its Viking past.

Mabon, which celebrates the harvest, is also a celebration of balance, balance between night and day, light and dark and man's precarious relationship with nature, a reminder that balance is essential for harmony and togetherness.

For four days in September Hefring was full of market stalls, bunting, dancing, music, and song and despite the community having a strong Church of England following, and Mabon retaining its pagan name and origins, it was a time for all beliefs to come

together to celebrate, share and enjoy the partnership between nature and humankind.

Rosie loved every day of the festival, each day bringing something different. Friday night was the start of festivities with the traditional harvest festival at the Church, followed by a procession of floats and people weaving through the narrow streets finishing at the harbour where the Vicar of the Parish said a prayer to give thanks to God for nature.

Pagan leaders were also given time to share their thanks before all the horns of the fishing boats moored in the harbour blasted out to signal the start of the festival. Friday was a time to celebrate the unison of humankind and earth, of man and woman, of families and friends. Friday celebrations were about the togetherness of family, friends and neighbours and saw great gatherings on the expansive sandy beaches, picnics, and storytelling. Children and adults alike sharing the fruits of mother nature and looking for treasures buried in the dunes until the sun set.

For those who did not venture to the beach, the carnival atmosphere flowed amongst the houses, pubs, and cafés. Fairy lights, candles, and flowers woven round fences and gates as neighbours shared food and drink.

Crafts and memorabilia for sale, as well as freshly made cakes, pies, and local honey mead, as stalls filled the tiny market square.

It reminded Rosie of one of those old Hollywood musicals full of wonder and gaiety, totally devoid of reality but everyone wanting to be a part of it.

Rosie took in as much as she could as she made her way over to The Driftwood Café to help Aunt Fran with the surge of customers that were no doubt flooding through the doors. Frances had opened the café as Rosie started school, and although she didn't spend much time serving these days, she would be there to help Rosie over the festival weekend.

Rosie ran the café, and though she had an offer to go to Newcastle university to study English literature she chose instead to remain faithful to Hefring and stay in the town, despite of her aunt's gentle encouragement to leave and go out to see what the world had to offer.

Rosie had not been persuaded by the lure of student life, endless partying with immature people, and taught by lecturers who had spent all their lives in the closeted world of academia.

Her experience of education and her beloved English language and literature had been tarnished when so-called experts, teachers, pulled apart the heart

and soul of stories to find meaning. This wasn't the purpose of literature as far as Rosie was concerned. Stories were meant to be fantastical, mystical, taking the reader into their own unique imagined creations, landscapes, characters formed from the words of the writer; no one's imagination is the same, so trying to standardise and intellectualise sentences, paragraphs and pages felt so wrong to her.

Instead, she put her creativity into the little café, giving a facelift to both the interior and exterior, renaming 'Frannie's Food' to 'The Driftwood Café', transforming it into a thriving hub for people to meet and enjoy the homemade pies, cakes and baking delicacies Aunt Fran baked.

The place was also full of well-read books, on bookshelves that covered every inch of the walls. It was Rosie's idea. She named it 'The Enchanted Library', as she believed words brought wonder to those who read them. The books were free to anyone and the only ask was for each reader to write inside the book cover, words that described what the story had given them.

Whether this was happiness, encouragement, enjoyment, whatever feelings were evoked, and, of course, that they brought them back for others to do the same.

It was a clever idea as it brought a regular flow of local people, including many children, who, when returning their books, bought a drink and a cake and then spent time discussing the stores they had read.

To Rosie, this was a far better way to pay homage to the thousands of hours and creativity invested by authors than the clinical dissection of academia.

6

Frances

"Courage, determination, compassion and kindness"

Frances was pleased to see Rosie's arrival at the café. She was beginning to feel a little overwhelmed as a party of twelve had just sat down.

In her usual smiley way, Rosie took their orders and started preparing three pots of tea for them, humming away as she did so. Frances couldn't be more of proud of her, this petite young woman who was just at the start of her adult life with all that it had in store for her. Despite her tiny frame, she had such strength of character, a strong will, and an almost ferocious streak when she felt the need to defend someone or something.

This was definitely a family trait, not bowing to conformity and challenging injustice. Frances remembered her own parents, her father a doctor, her mother, his nurse, giving food parcels to families who had too many young mouths to feed.

In those days when women had very little influence or power in the world, she had seen her mother and heard tales of her grandmother using their persuasiveness, emotional intelligence, and human relationship skills to make sure the voices of the poor and sick were heard.

Frances, now in her mid-fifties, had witnessed societal and economic changes, seen technological revolutions that were progressing at an alarming rate, and she would be the first to acknowledge that women had never had so much freedom, but she was certain men would never give up their stranglehold control of the world and share it evenly with them. The fact women started to believe that they did actually have some power was, in fact, just like the story of 'The Emperor's New Clothes'. The hype took over reality.

It was all a veil of pretence and clever marketing, and even though Margaret Thatcher was the country's first female prime minister, Frances had been disappointed as she saw none of the strong female traits she had hoped for, more of a man in female guise, with immaculate hair, and more handbags than Frances could ever imagine. Someone who seemed more preoccupied with herself - another male trait - than leading the country.

This pre-occupation with power and control, Frances had concluded, was likely to be driven from the unconscious male psyche as she believed deep down they were actually fearful about the power of women and so they subdued it on every level in society.

Religion, for example, wasn't it Eve, the very first woman, who led Adam astray using her seductiveness? And even in the work of Shakespeare it pervaded, as three witches and a manipulative queen evoked ruthless ambition in Macbeth and needless bloodshed in the pursuit of power. The unconscious embedment that women are the ultimate curse of men had silently and insidiously contaminated the minds of both men and women, perpetuating the myth that men are the strongest and most suited to positions of influence and power. The myth, in a very covert way, reinforced by stories since the beginning of time.

This needed to change. The fact that Rosie, like many other young women these days, questioned this and rebelled against blind conformity, gave her hope that someday there would be parity in the way the world celebrated and valued the uniqueness and differences between men and women.

Whenever she had tried to engage in conversation with other women who frequented the café about her thoughts, she could tell by the disdain in their faces and the dismissive comments they made, that they thought it was because she was a spinster and that in some way she was bitter and anti-man because she had never married.

So, she chose to keep her thoughts to herself, sharing only with Rosie as they conversed over dinner, and although Rosie concurred with most of Frances' thoughts, Frances also knew that Rosie was a romantic in denial.

The stories of the love affair between Kathleen and her Viking lover that had helped Rosie in her childhood had implanted in her the notion that someday she would find her very own version of a warrior and that true love did exist somewhere. Frances didn't want to crush her dreams, but she felt deep down that sooner or later the candle of hope Rosie held would extinguish and Frances would have to hold her hand and her heart through it. She could almost feel the tinges of the inevitable heartache and sadness in what was to come in the pit of her stomach.

She recalled their last discussion about whether the act of sex was contrition and a way for a man to take control and power over a woman through the act of penetration, or whether the power of consensual sex was held by women. Rosie had argued that because a woman could say no and regardless of how much a man tantalised her, if she said no, then sex would not take place, then ultimately, the power of sex was with a woman.

Conversely, a man could try to say no...but the majority of men could not suppress physical arousal, even if in their heads they wanted to say no. She had continued the thread of her point of view by concluding that this was the ultimate reason that men feared women and tried to always control them because they had the power to control the thing that drove most men: sex. Although men never consciously linked both, it was just their egos that led them to believe they were stronger and the strongest always had the right to power, but power and strength took many forms.

Rosie was her child, even if she hadn't had the privilege of creating her. She had been with her since she had first opened her eyes, and she was immensely proud of the woman she was becoming.

She had initially been disappointed that she hadn't chosen to go to university, her teachers equally so, but at the same time she was relieved as she couldn't imagine a day not seeing that beautiful face, nor engaging with that fascinating mind of hers. She had decided to give the café to her as she felt the responsibility of it would give her a purpose; she didn't want to see her drift aimlessly and say yes to the first man that showed her kindness and pretend love, get pregnant and be trapped before she had experienced life.

That was two years ago and since then Frances had watched her mature into an extraordinary young woman. Her emotional intelligence advanced beyond her years. She had embraced the transition from the comfort of childhood into the uncertainty and at times bewilderment of adulthood, learning that self-responsibility is balanced by excitement of the freedom to make your own choices and live by the rewards or penalties of those choices.

She had become a very confident, free-spirited young woman, forming her own views of the world, led by the values Frances and Kathleen had given her.

Frances knew Rosie had had boyfriends, and she was certain she had also had sex, but they had never discussed it.

The way Rosie had expressed her views on sex during their latest discord indicated to Frances that this was so.

She had also witnessed subtle changes in her niece over the past twelve months, the way she spent more time choosing clothes, brushing her hair, adding mascara to her fair eyelashes. Frances had also found packages of the contraceptive pill in her bedroom. Unlike many other parents who thought losing virginity was a bad thing, Frances was not upset by this. She viewed it as the start of Rosie's enlightenment about her own femininity. The discussion they had the other night comforted her, as she felt sure Rosie would not let the love of any man devour her spirit or control it.

Frances made herself a cup of tea and took a slice of lemon meringue into the back of the café leaving Rosie to weave her magic with customers, as the café filled with happiness and laughter.

She shook off her shoes to give her feet a rest, sat on the very worn but comfortable armchair and, with the chatter from the front of the café in the distance, reflected on the fact that although she had not had a traditional woman's life, she hadn't experienced most of what her friends had in marriage and pregnancy but she didn't feel that her life was any less rich.

Fate intervened when she herself was younger than Rosie, and her life path took a turn she had never expected.

Kathleen had always said she would have a girl and had chosen the name Rosie as soon as her belly started to swell.

Frances had asked her many times how she would cope if the child was a boy, but Kathleen always used to laugh and say it was the Gods will that she had a girl so that in time her daughter would also be able to carry life and the ancestry of her Viking lover would live on. The story Kathleen told about a mythical Viking spirit laying with her in the dunes used to annoy Frances, and she would challenge her and demand to know the name of the father of the unborn child. She pressed her so many times to reveal him, saying he needed to acknowledge his child, that he needed to step up to his responsibilities emotionally and financially, but Kathleen was adamant she didn't know his name because he was a spirit. Frances used to wonder why she wouldn't reveal his identity and just stuck to this story.

Kathleen wasn't like other people. In years gone by, she would have been revered and respected as a healer and seer, or possibly burnt as a witch. The locals either loved her, or were suspicious and avoided her.

Rosie was the image of her mother, both beauties with almost white blonde hair and the palest of blue eyes. When it became clear Kathleen was pregnant and unmarried, many of the women in the little town feared her lover was their husband, or worse still, that Kathleen had whored herself to one of the tinkers, travellers or musicians who frequently passed through the town. The sexual revolution of the sixties hadn't reached Hefring.

In the end she gave up asking and just accepted the stories Kathleen told were all she would ever discover.

69

Kathleen's story telling had always been an intricate part of their lives.

She was incredibly artistic writing stories, poetry, sketching and painting, and their home became an extension of Kathleen's imagination as her art adorned the walls of the cottage and her words filled endless notebooks that cluttered shelves and filled the drawers. She could even turn her hand to embroidery and crochet. Furniture and beds in the house were still covered in the blankets Kathleen had created. When Frances was in the house on her own, she often heard the sweetness of her voice as she sang around the house. She had always been a child who lived in her own world, and this continued into her short-lived adulthood.

Frances had been an only child into her teenage years. She could remember the day she had noticed her mother's belly growing and her father patting it lovingly, a smile on his face. She had known this wasn't middle aged belly fat on her slim and elegant mother and remembered feeling quite disgusted, repulsed, and embarrassed that her mother at the age of forty-five, and this was seriously old to a fourteen year old girl, was actually still having sex and was pregnant. Her father had picked up on her feelings and when he had told her that the room she had as a playroom was going to be the bedroom for her new brother or sister, Frances became very resentful and sulky. Her father had reprimanded her for her selfishness, telling her that many of the families he cared for lived in houses much smaller than theirs and the children usually had to share a bedroom with many of their siblings.

70

She needed to be grateful and appreciative of the things she took for granted, grow up and be prepared to help her mother with the baby once it was born.

Frances remembered hiding her feelings of anger and resentfulness, thinking she would leave home as soon as she could so that she did not have to share anything with the child.

That all changed the minute she laid eyes on her sister, and all those feelings vanished in an instant when Kathleen curled her tiny hand around Frances's finger. Her parents told her she could choose a name and Frances didn't know where Kathleen came from. She didn't know anyone of this name, but that is what she chose. She became Kathleen's shadow, always there, comforting, feeding, and caring for her. She took her everywhere with her and she remembered the first time Kathleen walked barefoot on the sandy beach and the sheer delight she had as she ran through the dunes. It was always Kathleen's favourite place, where she was happiest and most content. On the days when her mother couldn't settle her, Frances would take her to the beach. She never knew if it was the sound of the sea, or the wind that always blew even on the warmest summer days, but Kathleen's sobs would subside, and she would calm herself.

She was a child who had never taken to schooling. The teachers said she never concentrated and described her as being 'backwards'. Her father used his standing in the local community and the respect he had as the local doctor to avoid her being sent to a so-called special school.

He insisted she would catch up on her learning as they all would help her, that her problem was that she preferred to spend her time in the outdoors rather than

in a classroom. She was more absent minded than most, but backwards she was not. Kathleen's idiosyncrasies and her different ways became just part of life in the village.

Frances was twenty-one when her life's dreams and expectations for the future were shattered into a million pieces. Her mother and father died in a car crash on their way home from Middlesbrough during one of the county's worst ever snowstorms.

They were having their evening meal with Kathleen chattering away as she always did when the police arrived and told them.

Frances's stomach still knotted in anguish whenever she thought about this evening, even after all these years. The whole village had turned out for the funeral and Frances had been faced with a decision that changed the course of her life. At the age of twenty-one, she had been old enough by law to take legal responsibility for Kathleen. The only other choice being for Kathleen to go into the care system and taken away from the stability and familiarity of her life in Hefring. It hadn't really been a choice, but Frances knew at that moment she would never marry. No man would take on responsibility for a child who wasn't his, especially a quirky and unique child like Kathleen.

She had become a spinster the moment she made the decision to care for her younger sister.

Initially, she had much support, neighbours offering to take care of Kathleen whilst Frances met with friends or when shopping, but she wasn't an easy child and didn't respond well to changes in routine. She struggled to adjust to life without her parents, retreating deeper into her own carefree world of make believe and stories. People were always kind to them both and everyone in the village knew Kathleen as she spent her out of school days exploring the beach, the harbour and streets in the village, her sweet singing a recognisable sound in the community. Their sympathy for this unusual child whose parents had died morphed into genuine fondness and care.

This was fine while Kathleen was a child, but as adolescence took hold and her body started to change into that of a woman, men's heads would turn, not to listen to her songs but to admire and lust after her beauty and innocence.

By the time Kathleen had left school at fifteen, the mood of the village had changed towards them. No longer was she seen as an orphaned child, she became a threat as women became jealous and wary of her beauty, seeing how their menfolk looked at her.

Frances had seen this, and it had hurt her deeply, as all the promises they had made to support them both after their parents' death just fizzled away. Fortunately, Kathleen never picked up on this, as she only saw the best in people.

When Kathleen became pregnant at the age of sixteen, Frances had been incensed that someone in the village had betrayed them, probably someone she knew taking advantage of this precious soul, pretending to be some sort of Viking spirit just so he could take away innocence to feed his sexual need. What upset her even more was the fact that he had managed to worm his way into Kathleen's world of Vikings and folklore, manipulated her so much that she truly believed her lover was the son of a Viking god. How could anyone take advantage of another living soul in such a perverse and cruel way?. Frances was sure the father was someone who knew her and every time she went into the village she used to look directly into the faces of all the men she saw, trying to recognise any fleeting moment of guilt they had in their eyes. But they all looked guilty, as all of them had no doubt fantasised about being the one that had taken her. The women became cold and distant from them both, twisting things, blaming Kathleen for having seduced one of their men. As if that had been possible.

Frances recalled that Kathleen must have been in labour for a couple of days before she had noticed. She spent most of her days and nights wandering on Mangata Beach, the place she where she said her lover would return when her baby was born.

Frances had seen blood on the sheets of her sister's bed when she returned home as the sun set on a cool September evening. She had called the midwife who arrived within the hour and not long after had asked Frances to call the doctor. Rosie was born on the 4th of September at 9.50pm.

—

Kathleen died at 10.03 p.m. after holding her daughter for only a few short minutes. And so the cycle began again as the doctor gave Frances the tiny baby whilst tears flowed down her face in grief at the loss of her beautiful sister. Her role as surrogate mother and guardian to yet another young life had begun.

She had looked into the tiny infant face, eyes so bright, not a squeal or cry. Rosie had been the only name this child could have had, her cheeks the colour of the deep pink roses in the garden, roses her father had planted for her mother after Kathleen had been born.

Destiny for Frances was to be a mother again without feeling the ecstasy of lovemaking, nor the wriggle of life growing in her womb.

She had vowed she would give this child all the love a biological mother would give and that Kathleen would always be an integral part of their lives. She was grateful for all of Kathleen's creations and keepsakes in their home, treasures, and memories for this little bundle of life to be surrounded by the wonder of her mother.

The tragedy of Kathleen's death actually affected the village quite hard and a collective sense of guilt for how they had behaved towards Kathleen hung over the congregation at her funeral.

Rosie grew up without knowing either of her parents. She had many similarities to her mother, but equally, as many differences.

In appearance, Rosie was Kathleen's double, long white blonde hair and the palest of blue eyes. But her body was much stronger and athletic than her mother's and Frances often reflected on Kathleen's claim that Rosie's father was a Viking warier. She certainly was fearless and an adventurer, but she also had her mother's kind nature and the ability to connect to people and charm them. She became a very much loved child, excelling at school but preferring nature, the sea, sand dunes and outdoor life to studying.

She had the same ability as her mother to create stories; she loved reading and teachers were always telling Frances she had so much potential if she would just apply herself and knuckle down to learning. She also spent much time on the beach, like Kathleen, scouring the coastline, picking up debris washed up on the shore and transforming it into beautiful works of art. This creativity certainly came from her mother, as had her tendency to cock her head to the left when she was contemplative. Frances had told Rosie endless stories about Kathleen and she hoped it had been enough to ensure the child didn't feel lonely or lost without her true mother.

"Aunt Fran, are you OK back there? You are awfully quiet." Rosie's voice jolted Frances from her reveries.

"I am, just taking five mins."

"It's been more like an hour…you sure you are OK?" Frances could her hear the concern in Rosie's voice.

"I must have dropped off," she replied, "I'm getting old my dear," and with that she squeezed her swollen feet back into her shoes and returned to the front café to help Rosie clear away as the last customers said their farewells.

7

Mabon

"When Darkness and Light Harmonise"

Rosie woke to the distant sound of the sea from her open bedroom window. She could smell and taste its saltiness, a familiar wake up call for her as she always slept with the window open regardless of the weather. It was Saturday, the best day of the festival, and she felt a surge of excitement and anticipation of what the day would bring.

The book she had been reading as she had fallen asleep was open page down on the pillow at the side of her, Wuthering Heights, one of her favourites. She was re-reading it to strip away the memories she still held when she was forced to examine every single word in preparation for her 'A' level in English Literature, which took away all the beauty in the story. She wanted to connect with the qualities of the characters and actually lose herself in the plot, becoming absorbed in the excitement, the passion, the love and tragicness of this outstanding novel.

Mr Jackson had advised her to keep her poetic, romantic ideals to herself and concentrate on what was needed to achieve the 'A' grade he knew she was capable of.

She had fared better in sociology as she loved studying human interaction with society and should she have gone to university, it would have been a tough choice between literature, sociology or even psychology, as relationships also fascinated her.

She had been brought up as a Christian, attending church every week and Sunday school as a child. She adored the stories and fables, but as she got older, her naturally inquisitive mind started to question meanings and purpose behind the stories. She concluded they were devised to persuade and influence people to be compliant, to achieve order and stability, or to dispel fears and offer an explanation for the unexplainable.

She was intrigued by the notion of balance, that for everything good there was an equal possibility of the opposite. Good versus evil, God and the Devil, and despite her Christianity, she did hold a fascination for other beliefs, especially the origins and purpose of them. She knew her Aunt Fran had some concerns about all this. Rosie did often question the notion of fate, whether a blueprint for your life was made prior to birth by some great power.

But today wasn't a day to dwell on questions that could not be answered. Today was the second day of the Mabon festival and Saturday night was by far the best. Singers and musicians took to the stage that had been constructed on the car park in the centre of the town. Rosie would have a full day at the café, but Aunt Fran had offered to close up so she could come home and get ready for the evening celebrations.

It was going to be a great day. Lou-Lou was already licking her face, letting her know it was time for the day to start, time for her early morning walk.

The warm rising sun was still on its daily mission to consume the coolness and darkness of the retreating night. Its warm rays were displacing the fine sea mist that hung over Mangata beach as they arrived for their morning walk.

Rosie sat amongst the sand dunes as Lou-Lou ran and played with whatever she could find as a playmate, a broken stick, a curled up sleepy crab or just the spray of sand she created herself as she ran in circles trying to catch her tail. This beach was special to her, the place where she was conceived, the place she felt connected to her beautiful mother and her father, whoever he had been. She had laid down in every dune on the beach over her lifetime, imagining it was the actual spot they had been lovers, her place of origin.

She had researched its place in history. Its name was an old Viking word which put some sense into her mother's story. Mangata she had discovered wasn't easily translatable, but she had found two possible meanings and she loved both. The first meaning is the trail of light left on the sea by the moon, which she imagined must have been why her mother had believed she saw a Viking spirit coming from the sea. Rosie had spent many nights sitting in the dunes when the sea was calm, the full moon shining on the dark waves, its reflection creating a path of light to the shore, and she understood why the Vikings gave it its name.

The other descriptor, equally difficult to translate, was that it describes the specific feeling of falling in love, and of course this resonated with her so much, the name of the place where she was made paid homage to love. She was a romantic at heart and despite knowing her mother's story made no sense whatsoever, that she had clearly found difficulty living within reality, Rosie adored the notion she was the daughter of a Viking spirit. This place was sacred too.

The beach wasn't popular with other people. Most preferred the less dramatic and less wild beach to the north of the town that was filled with deck chairs, multi coloured beach huts, snack bars and ice cream vendors, and that was why she had been startled to find a moron

of a bloke, illegally squatting in her dunes, contaminating it with his presence and rudeness. Seeing him the following day in the café where he was even ruder was bizarre, and she hoped that if her life was being led by fate, he was just an unfortunate coincidence and they would not cross paths again. She had to admit to herself that he was sort of handsome, but that wasn't enough to balance out the miserable grouch he obviously was. She had wasted enough time on him, and she wasn't going to allow him to ruin the day by taking up anymore of her time. It was approaching 8:30, and the sun had almost eaten the cool mist to reveal what was promising to be an absolutely beautiful day.

As she sat in the soft sand, still damp from the night, she reflected on how much her life had changed over the past couple of years.

She had been released from the shackles of a school uniform and the restraints of constant studying. She felt as though she had shed her childhood skin like a snake does when it outgrows it. Her whole body, mind, and soul felt newly born, alive, full of anticipation of what life would offer her, the adventures that would come her way, and the excitement of the unknown. It felt like all of her senses had been re-tuned and she was touching the world and everything in it for the first time.

She only had a small circle of friends whom she had known since she was a primary school. Anita Neets was the one who had gone to university studying biology. She had always been the sensible one, the one who had always taken stock and had prevented them from getting into trouble at school.

Annie was the tall, skinny, quiet one who over the past twelve months had somehow morphed into a leggy blonde supermodel who now turned the heads of every man she passed. She worked at the bank in the village on the High Street. It had never been so busy since she started, but Annie had shown no interest in any of the men who turned up to open new accounts or move their money from other banks, just to grab fifteen minutes in her company. She remembered how cruel they had all been at school, calling her 'twenty niner' as she had remained flat chested and boy-like in her appearance until she left school.

Jeanie was the petite, pretty one who had attracted all the attention in secondary school. She had matured so much earlier than the rest of them.

She had an incredibly huge bosom and leant back when she walked, which the whole of their class had scientifically attributed to the size of her breasts. She was now engaged to Phil, who was a Joiner at Taylor's builders, where she had worked for the past three years

as a receptionist since leaving school after her 'O' levels. Although the four of them had been inseparable in their childhood, it was Annie and Rosie who had remained firm friends with Neets at University, and Jeanie besotted with Phil, getting married and having babies.

Rosie was looking forward to spending festival time with Annie later that day. They would meet and get ready for the festival together at Claymore Cottage. They had already agreed they would celebrate nature's relationship with the world by braiding their hair, adorning it with September flowers and become hippies for its duration. Neets might join them, but she preferred to have her head in a book. She was obsessed with medical science. She didn't want to waste precious time on frivolities she had told them; she wanted to find new ways to fight diseases and save lives.

Rosie did share some of her passion and understood her obsession with science, but she had observed the shortness of time between when a woman has freedom to explore and enjoy life and when life becomes consumed with caring for others, husband's and children and she, Rosie, wanted to extend that time so she could live and love life to its fullest.

She had seen the sacrifices Aunt Frances had made, and she'd often wondered if someday, someone, maybe Neets, would discover a hidden R gene, the R of Responsibility, within the DNA of just females, that awakens when women give birth, or they become a mother. The R was responsible for fatigue. Consuming fun, abandonment, and carefreeness. The 'I' becomes a 'We' overnight and even though the umbilical cord is cut, that act of disentangling two separate lives, strangely builds a stronger bond than anything on earth, protecting, guarding caring, a pure unconditional love that subsumes everything else. She wasn't ready for her R to be released yet.

Her stomach groaned, reminding her that it was time for breakfast.

"Lou-Lou, come on girl, time to go," Lou-Lou of course ignored her until she was almost out of sight, it was the same routine every day, part of their morning game, until Rosie reached the top of the hill when Lou-Lou would always bound past her racing her home.

8

Valhalla

"The Hall of the Fallen"

The September hum of anticipation that had consumed Hefring since the start of the festival had been replaced by the noise and chants from the large crowd that stood in front of the stage in the village car park. Saturday night, 'Music in the Park' was ready to kick off.

Charlie's heart was beating far too fast, his hands fidgeting, full of nervous energy and excitement, fuelled by the chants and chatter from the crowd. This is what he lived for. He never felt so alive as when this adrenaline was pumping through his veins.

He always hung back for just a few extra minutes so that his whole body was consumed with anticipation, excitement, fear, he couldn't distinguish between them, but the combination was like rocket fuel to his performance. He started to jump to pump up the energy, as he nodded to the D.J. who was waiting to announce them.

"Hefring, are you ready?" the D.J. shouted down the microphone, the crowd responded with cheers that almost drowned out his announcement...

"Welcome to the stage…Valhalla…" he held onto the 'a' for a few moments as Charlie and his band entered the stage, waving their arms and punching the air as they did.

It looked like the whole village and many more too had crammed into the car park to see them and Charlie drank up the energy they had, overloading his system already crammed full of his own. Now there was no hint of nervousness, just pure excitement.

"Hefring," he shouted down the mic, "Thank you". He knew from experience that any preamble dulled the energy, so this was all he said. The crowd roared even louder as the bass drum started a deep, slow, rhythmic beat. Charlie picked up his guitar from its stand and began gently plucking at the strings. The crowd quietened until there was no other sound except Charlie's guitar and the drumbeat. The notes enchanting, casting a spell on the whole audience. He could almost see the notes weaving through them, capturing and connecting them in music, their heads nodding simultaneously to the rhythm against the crimson and orange of the evening sky.

In the distance, the sound of thunder could be heard. Dark clouds hung over the North Sea as nature

added her voice to the music. Charlie loved this quiet opening. It always took everyone by surprise.

Instead of the sound of electric guitars booming out rock, Charlie gently played his guitar to the shallow beat of the bass drum and sang a ballad in such a deep and soulful way that it seemed to hypnotise everyone in front of him.

"To the sun and the moon, the stars, and the earth…

We bask in your treasures, we worship your worth…"

The tone of his voice, the words he sang, the haunting blend and simplicity of drum and guitar transfixed the whole crowd, whose faces were being shadowed by the onset of the night.

He waited for a few moments before he continued, feeling the power he had over them as they hung onto every note and word.

"But all of the riches and beauty you show is nothing compared to the love I bestow."

A bright flash of lighting ripped through the evening sky and, for a moment, shone a spotlight into the dark blur of the crowd, lighting up the most exquisite face he had ever seen. An angel reaching out

to him, imprinting herself into him, and then just as quickly she was gone as the thunder rolled and she was lost in the sea of bodies swaying in his music, all oblivious to what had just happened, waiting for him to continue…

"When I first saw your radiance shining so bright

That beautiful face, lost to the dark of the night"

His head was racing. How could that be? Did he imagine it with the atmosphere from the crowd? Had he got carried away with the magic of the moment and the words he had written?

He shook his head to bring himself round and back to reality as the base guitar added to the beat, building the song, the keyboards kicked in and Valhalla exploded from lullaby to rock; the crowd exploding with them as he sang,

"Thor, God of Thunder, lightning, and sea

Find her heart and bring it to me."

This is what he lived for, the power of music to evoke the abandonment of everything for just a short while, freedom from all the stresses and worries that life brings, enriching, nourishing, and re-energising the soul.

An hour and a half and two encores later, Valhalla sat on straw bales at the back of the stage, exhausted, sweaty, but euphoric with their performance.

The much promised thunder storm never materialised, it had headed off over the sea but the dramatic effect it had on the start of the show had been awesome and Charlie had concluded that the face in the crowd had been a figment of his imagination, caught up in the moment. He peeled off his sweat sodden shirt and threw it into the back of the van that was parked at the side of the stage. D.J. Jack had continued with the music, but already people had started to disperse.

Jake took out the spliff he had pre rolled, lit it, and sat on the grass, legs crossed in his usual lotus position.

He inhaled deeply, held his breath, and then slowly blew out the smoke.

"What a fuckin' gig!" He said. "It's like we were proper rock stars, famous and all that," he continued, a smile taking over his entire face as the effects of the drugs and the gig took hold.

Gazza, the bass player, opened a tin of beer as he said to Jake, "Why do you need that stuff? Surely being on stage gives you more buzz than that shite." It was a statement rather than a question. "An audience like that is the best drug ever."

"Man, it's just like the icing on the cake, that's all."

"So, what's the cherry then?" shouted Steve, the keyboard player, as he wiped the sweat from his face with a towel. "It's got to be the women," replied Gazza. "Be sure to get a few after a gig like that. Music seems to get the sex juices flowing in the all the hotties, and I saw a few before the gig so hopefully we're all gonna get some cherry tonight."

Steve looked at Charlie in admiration and said, "Sheer genius that mate the opening song, taking it right down like that, you had them in the palm of your hand and then that fuckin' thunder and lightning when you were singing about Thor, swear to God Charlie you have something special mate to get the Gods and nature to sing to your tune."

Charlie smiled.

"And that, my friends, is why we are all gonna get laid tonight," Gazza said, "Because Charlie boy here has put a bleeding spell on them all."

"Gazza, is that all you think about?" said Jake.

"Sex and Music and Rock 'n' Roll, so much better for you than that stuff Jake," replied Gary.

"It's sex and drugs and rock 'n' roll and don't be so pious mate," continued Jake.

"Woo hoo, fuckin' pious…you been doing that Guardian crossword again?" replied Gazza. "Private school boy thinking you are a shit load better than us comprehensive kids."

"Charlie went to private school too. Seems to me it's you that has got the problem and the hang up, not us," replied Jake.

It was always the same after a gig, instead of getting rid of the pent up energy, it just seemed to accelerate and there was always some sort of fracas. It was harmless banter though, and Charlie had become accustomed to hearing it. It was just a continuation of the night's entertainment.

He walked round to the front of the van, opened the door, and pulled out a clean shirt that was hung on the mirror. He shivered and realised how dehydrated he was.

He must have lost about 40% of his body fluid during the gig and he needed a beer.

He could still hear the familiar band banter; the different personalities, talents and artistic expressions that were almost a perfect blend on the stage, but more difficult off. But Charlie wasn't going to let the childish bickering dampen the aftermath of a super gig.

He knew it was his presence on stage that made the difference between a good gig and a brilliant gig, but even he had to admit that this one had been exceptional.

He reached for a can of lager from the six-pack on the front passenger seat. Despite him having performed for hours, Charlie felt as though he'd been plugged into an electric charger. His body and mind were still buzzing. The image of the face he had imagined in the crowd seemed to be etched into the back of his eyes, and he couldn't rid himself of it. It was there in front of him. He rubbed his eyes to clear and erase it, but when he opened them, it was still there, staring right back at him through the window of the van.

"What's in this bleeding can?" he muttered to himself.

"Probably lager or beer," the image replied.

"What the fuck! Are you real?" His hand stretched out, touching her hair.

"You are a crazy man," the face replied, a face that took hold of him. He was unable to look away.

Her eyes, the palest of blue, seemed to be pulling him towards her. Her fine, almost white blonde hair full of fresh flowers looked to be floating around her face. He was feeling slightly spooked by her presence.

"So, Valhalla," she continued, "Do you actually know what that means?" Her voice was surprisingly slightly husky.

"Erm some sort of god I think, or something from Star Wars maybe, I dunno, I just like it. Why are you asking? You were in the crowd tonight, weren't you?"

"How else would I have known you called yourself Valhalla? You might be able to crack out a tune, but I'm doubting there's much between those ears," she replied, a slight smile on her face.

"Wow, sneaking up on people and then insulting them. Is there any reason you are here, I mean except to spook the shit out of me and insult me at the same time?"

"Touchy and sensitive as well as talented, I wasn't insulting you, just teasing."

He felt unbalanced and certainly not in control of the situation, which he didn't like. He pulled himself together and brought forward the cocky macho man he was more familiar with.

"How did you do that back there, blackout everybody else's face so I could only see yours? Are you some sort of white witch or something?"

"I'd like to think so. You've got me sussed." This time she laughed, which relaxed Charlie a little.

"I'm Rosie," she said. His eyes were transfixed on how her mouth pouted ever so slightly when she said her name.

"A whole lot of Rosie," he replied.

"Are you saying I'm fat…a whole lot of me?"

"Obviously not," he retorted, looking her up and down. "I meant the song."

"Well I never knew you had written a song about me. I hope it's a good one."

"I didn't write it, it was AC/DC. Don't tell me you have just been to a rock concert and you haven't heard of them. They are rock gods!"

"Nope, never heard of them."

Charlie started to sing "Wanna tell you story… about a woman I know…When it comes to lovin'…she steals the show."

She cocked her head to the right, smiling as she did so. "Carry on."

"Nah, that's as far as it goes. We will leave it there as otherwise you'll be accusing me of implying you are something else that clearly you are not."

"Fat, think you've already thrown that one at me," she responded.

"No, not that."

She raised her eyebrows. "Tell me, what's next?"

"She ain't exactly pretty," Charlie sang.

"Ok stop right there, I've heard enough," she laughed. "So, what exactly am I then if I 'ain't exactly pretty? If you were to write a lyric about me, what would it be? "

Her brazen flirting actually floored him again. He was off balance, and didn't like this unfamiliar feeling. She sensed it, but instead of going in for the kill, she softened her voice and said,

"So Mr Singer, Mr Valhalla, you have me at an advantage." Charlie felt the opposite. She, this Rosie woman, was completely in control of the conversation.

"You know my name, I'm a whole lotta Rosie…what should I call you?" The sweetness in her tone helped stabilise him.

He held out his hand, and she took it in hers. The softness of her skin, the gentle but firm hold around his hand sent a shock wave through his body and he just couldn't fathom what was happening to him. He composed himself.

"Well Rosie, I am Charles Henry Shafton, or Charlie to my friends, so I will leave it up to you what you chose to call me."

"Hello Charlie," she said smiling, "And now we have established that we are friends, maybe I could have one of those cans," she said, pointing at the five remaining lagers in the van. Charlie could hear the continuing saga that was playing out behind the van with the others, but it was all in good humour. Constant piss taking was just part of band life.

"Sure," he said, pulling the ring of the can before handing it to her.

"Charlie boy," he heard Gazza shout, "Who have you got back there? You're one hell of a fast mover pretty boy."

Charlie turned to see all of them looking over at him and Rosie. "Cheers," Steve said as he raised his can. "Happy fuckin'," and they all started to laugh. Usually Charlie would laugh back and say something like, "Don't be envious, you grumpy shits," but he just felt embarrassed. He shook his head at them, handed Rosie the can, and said,

"Probably better if we leave them to it," pointing to a grassy embankment a few yards away. "I am so sorry," he apologised. "It's just band banter."

The embankment marked the parameter of a small remembrance garden that had a plaque with the names of men from the village who had died in two world wars.

"Any of your relatives?" Charlie asked, wanting to change the subject matter from shagging.

"No, none. I never knew my father or my grandfather and grandmother both died in a car crash when my mother was four!"

"Jeez!" Unsure what else to say, he laid down on the incline, his hands behind his head, looking up at the night sky.

There was a full moon and the heavy dark clouds that had made their presence known earlier in the evening were still loitering, blanketing the majority of the stars out of sight. There was very little breeze, but the evening was becoming cool and he felt her shiver slightly as she laid down on the grass at the side of him.

"You cold? I'll get my jacket."

"I'm fine. I like being outside and love looking up at the night sky. Makes me feel alive," she replied.

Away from the background noise of the disappearing crowds, he could hear her voice clearly for the first time. It sounded familiar somehow. He couldn't work out how, but everything about this woman was strange. She just wasn't the type he would ever be attracted to. She looked like a modern day hippy, a tree hugger, flower talker, and she definitely wasn't a rock chick. How could anyone not know about AC/DC but she was alluring, there was no doubt about that.

"So, do you know about Valhalla?" She asked him again.

"You seem a bit obsessed with it," he replied, "but I think it's something to do with Vikings. Their heaven maybe…how am I doing? Magnus Magnusson… my specialised subject is Vikings."

"I doubt very much you would get through to the finals of Master Mind, but I would give you half a point. It's more of a special place of sanctuary for all the departed, those worthy of Odin's affection and respect, those who had been honourable, honest, and true in life. It's a place where their souls dwell for all time."

"You want a job?" Charlie asked, not taking his gaze from the night sky.

"I have a job already, but curiosity has got me. Tell me what you had in mind."

"Song writer maybe, your words tell stories and have a flow about them. That's a gift all song writers want. Maybe we should co-write call it 'Sanctuary for the Souls' or maybe rock it up at bit AC/DC style and call it 'Death Chamber'."

"I'll consider it," she replied playfully. "Would that mean we would have to work together?"

"Afraid it would, I could write the music."

"I am sure you could. The hieroglyphics just flow from you!" she replied.

Hieroglyphics. The word echoed in his head. Someone else had referred to his music as hieroglyphics recently.

He sat up, racking his memory before turning to her, looking down on her face, trying to fathom why this beautiful, enigmatic, intelligent woman was familiar to him.

"You don't remember do you?" she said, looking straight into his eyes. "We have bumped into each other before tonight Charlie, more than once, well actually the first time it was more humping than bumping and it was my dog, Lou-Lou."

He just stared at her, his eyes darting left and right as the memories quickly coming into focus of that huge beast licking his face, thrusting against him, with the silhouette of its owner hovering above him like a celestial being.

"You!" he exclaimed. "You and that bloody dog. Good God."

"And then again in the Driftwood Café, my Café."

His forehead wrinkled in puzzlement as he tried to recall seeing her again.

"Strong black coffee, no sugar, no milk, and definitely no cake. Apparently, I sexually MAN…" she emphasised the word man, "handled you twice…lucky you," she said.

He put his head in his hands, as the images came flooding back, the sound of her familiar voice, the tilting of the head, the fine flowing hair.

The sun had blinded him on both occasions. He remembered how arsey he had been, because on both occasions she had interrupted the final notes of his song, the song he had opened up with that evening. It was all too much of a coincidence for someone who didn't believe in coincidences and for a fleeting moment, he did consider that she was some sort of stalker. It was after the incident in the café that the opening verse had come to him, and just before he sang it, he had seen her face in amongst a crowd of hundreds.

"You can show your face, Charlie, I have seen it before, but guessing you just hadn't seen mine?"

"Well, in fairness," he responded, "and in my defence, I was being attacked by the horny hound and if you remember, you did throw yourself at me." he sounded a tad angry, he didn't know why.

"No, no, no Charlie, I didn't throw myself at you. I fell over, but you were that angry you wouldn't listen to me, and it seems to me that I am making you angry again."

"I'm not angry!"

"Really?"

"I'm not angry now, a little bit confused to be honest. I was angry then because I was writing a song and I have to find a place of solitude where there is only me and then I just have to wait for the sounds and notes and words to come. I was almost there and then, wallop, you and your dog jumped right in the middle and everything scattered."

He stopped, realising he was rambling. Calming himself, he continued, "and then you did it again…you touched my hair, you told me I looked like your dog…"

"You do. My dog is beautiful. She's uncontrollable, a free spirit, has the greenest of eyes and she is so lovable when you get to know her. And yes, she is a she. She's going through the experimental stage, you know. Shall I be a male or female?"

Charlie was unsure how to respond. Was she suggesting he was those things? He knew he was attractive to women. His list of one-night stands and the odd few women he had chosen to see for a few weeks, (all had thought they were the one that could have caught him, tied him down, filled him full of the pain of love, but none of them had), was testament to that. This woman he had known for only a short time was affecting him like no other, not even Celeste. He

did not reply, just laid down once again at her side.

"I too have a place I go to, a place where I can be on my own, because I need my dream space too. It is really special to me. It is the place I go to try and connect with my family. It's the place we humped and bumped into you, Mangata beach. It rarely gets visitors, so Lou-Lou finding you there snuggled in the dunes was a shock. You have shared my special place, the place where I was created Charlie. It is the place I go to, but no-one knows where I go to when I am there, my dreams, my hopes, my sanctuary." Rosie said, a faraway look in her eyes.

"You really should think about writing songs, what a line that is – It is the place that I go to, but no-one knows where I go to when I am there, my dreams, my hopes, my sanctuary," he replied. She didn't respond.

"You are so different to anyone I have ever met, Rosie, and I am feeling more than a wee bit out of my depth here. Usually after meeting someone after a gig…" he paused, "Well, just saying I am not used to still having my trousers still on."

She laughed.

"Well I'm not sure if that is an insult or a compliment, Charlie boy," she said, "But I am awfully pleased you've not dropped them yet."

"It is actually a compliment, I think," he replied, "And to be honest I intend keeping them on tonight."

"And why is that…don't you fancy me?" she said coyly.

"I dunno, I really don't know because you clearly know just how hot you are. Maybe it's because I would like to see you again."

There was a silence between them, not an awkward one but more filled with anticipation.

"Can I kiss you?" he asked softly.

"No-one has ever, ever asked me if they could kiss me before Charlie. Blokes just normally think they are irresistible and pounce, so a bit of a first for me too."

With that they both sat up. He cupped her tiny, delicate face in his hands and very gently kissed her. It felt like nothing else he had ever felt, like he was melting into her. His common sense defence was screaming for him to back off, to walk away, but he just knew he couldn't.

They continued to talk, sharing stories, revealing things about themselves with such ease.

The noise from the town and the festival gave way to the quietness of night and the when the only thing that could be heard was the distant crashing of the waves on the harbour wall, Rosie said,

"It's time for me to go home. Early start at the café tomorrow, Charlie, but I have had a lovely evening. Thank you." They had only had the one kiss, enjoying the conversation that freely came. She had calmed him and it was only when he was calm that he realised just how uncalm he usually was. It was a strange feeling, not suppressing. He took her hand to steady her down the grass.

The car park had cleared of everyone. The stage was empty. Instruments, amps, and speakers had been dismantled and put back into the band's van.

"Shit," said Charlie, "I never helped the guys dismantle the gear. I will get earache for sure tomorrow.

They might forgive me if I told them you were a great shag and, to be honest, I doubt they will believe me when I tell them we have talked for hours, I am not a great conversationalist."

"I beg to differ. Your conversation skills are impeccable as has been your chivalry," she replied.

"For fuck's sake, please don't share that with anyone. I have a reputation to maintain," he joked, "But if my conversations are that interesting, then how about we resume them tomorrow? Maybe I could come by and sample that coffee of yours again and you could take a break and join me?"

"That sounds great Charlie. If you come for 10, I will do you one of our fantastic bacon and egg breakfast sandwiches."

"There is only one 10 o'clock in a musician's life and it has p.m. after it not a.m., but for you little white witch, I will make an exception. Where do you live? It is past midnight, and I need to keep up my chivalry and ensure you get home safe."

"Mmm, not sure how I feel about chivalry to be honest, but thoughtful of you to offer. Being a witch, no-one would bother me and I know this place like the back of my hand."

"Well then…A demain," Charlie said. "Until tomorrow."

"Bien sur, mon loup," she replied, taking his breath again as this was just how he and Celeste would say their goodbyes…maybe she wasn't kidding, maybe she was a white witch. She blew him a kiss as

she left and disappeared into in the dimly lit narrow streets.

It had been a very strange night indeed, he thought as he returned to the B&B. Fortunately, Jake was snoring like an old man when he snuck into the room, so no ribbing until tomorrow. She was still in his thoughts as his head hit the pillow. His insomnia didn't make its usual appearance, and he drifted off into a very deep sleep.

9

Driftwood

"Where the spirits of ancestors dwell"

The doorbell tinkled as it opened, it was 10.15, Rosie looked over to the door of The Driftwood Café, hoping it was him, but it wasn't, it was an elderly woman with two children, "Probably still in bed, or found someone to shag," she muttered.

"What was that dearie?" Frances said.

"Nothing Aunt Fran, was I just thinking out loud."

"Well don't, it's confusing. You know my hearing is getting worse. I thought you said bread with a rag, made no sense whatsoever."

Frances had noticed that Rosie seemed much more pre-occupied than usual this morning. Initially, she thought it must be because she was tired after getting home so late, but she wasn't grumpy, just not quite her bubbly self.

Her concentration was a little off, and she seemed to be attuned to the bell on the door; every time it chimed, she looked up with a huge smile on her face that disappeared as customers walked through the door.

"Rosie, the man in the corner in front of the window, can you take him this mug of coffee and chocolate milkshake for the boy, please?" Frances continued. The café was about half full and as Rosie weaved through the tables with the coffee and milk shake, she overheard snippets of conversation between the customers.

"He's not worth it…don't play with the sugar…that band was brilliant…why don't you and Mummy love each other anymore, do you still love me?"

She stood for a moment, not wanting to interrupt the conversation the man and his son were having. They were both so immersed they were unaware that she was standing at the side of the table until she coughed to let them know she was there. The man looked up at Rosie, a mixture of embarrassment that she had overheard the conversation and also sadness and anxiety. She smiled at him.

"Chocolate milkshake I presume is for you and a cup of coffee for dad. We have a special offer on today," she continued, "Free ice cream for all boys and their dads today, so what's your favourite? Would it be chocolate?" she asked. The boy looked at her with very sad eyes, "Well come on then," she said, "Let's go and get some and what would daddy like?"

"A scoop of hindsight and forgiveness if you have those, please," he answered.

"Actually, I do," she replied, "Camouflaged as mint choc chip if that's okay?"

"Sounds perfect," the man said.

Rosie took the little boy's hand. He must have been about six years old.

"What's your name?" she asked. "My name is Rosie."

"It's Nicholas," the boy replied.

"Well Nicholas, I must say you have a fantastic dad bringing you here for milkshake on a Sunday morning. Are you here for the festival? There are some great rides and games, face painting, football competitions, fabulous things for little boys just like you."

"I wish Mummy was here with Daddy too. They don't live together anymore. All my friend's mummies and daddies still live together, and mine don't." His little sad face really touched her and tears started to well up in her eyes.

"Are you good at keeping secrets Nicholas?" she said, looking down at his huge brown eyes. He nodded. Rosie bent down, so that she was looking into his face.

"Well Nicholas, can I share my secret with you?" He nodded.

"Well when I was little like you, I didn't have a mummy or a daddy," Nicholas's eyes opened wider, somewhat confused.

"You see that very lovely kind lady just there making those sandwiches?" she pointed at Frances, who waved and smiled back at them both.

"That is my Aunt Frances, who had to be both my mummy and daddy."

"Why didn't you have a mummy and daddy?" he asked, looking genuinely concerned and confused.

"Well I'm not sure really. I think I'll find that out when I'm a grownup."

"But you are a grownup," Nicholas said. Rosie looked at her hands and then put them on her face.

"Why goodness me, you are right, I think I am a grownup, I must have forgotten," she smiled at him and he smiled back.

"Don't you miss your mummy and daddy?" he asked

"Well not really, because I never knew them, but I too sometimes felt sad when all my friends had a mummy and a daddy, but as I got older, I realised the love my Aunt Frances gave me was just the same as the love my friends got from their parents. It isn't where love comes that is important, what is important is the love itself.

And you Nicholas, still have the same love from your daddy and mummy even if they can't live together anymore, so try not to be too sad because they both love you just the same, probably even more. Grownups can be weird. That's why I try and forget I am one." He squeezed her hand a little and his eyes looked a little less sad.

"Your daddy looks a bit sad too don't you think?" He nodded. "Does ice cream make you a little bit happier?" He nodded. "Do you think ice cream could make daddy a little happier?" He nodded again.

"Well I think if you took daddy's ice cream to him with a huge smile and then gave him the biggest hug you could, then I bet you could also magic a smile onto his face. The magic thing about smiles is that they spread."

His face broke out into a huge smile and it seemed to Rosie that the sun had just shone much brighter, as she smiled back.

"You see," she pointed at her face, "You have a super duper magical smile, you've put a smile on my face. I think that you probably have the most magical one I have ever seen. Are you ready to spread that magic to daddy?"

He nodded and very carefully took the dish of mint choc-chip ice cream and walked over to his father with a very huge smile. One of his front teeth was missing, which just added to the magic of the moment.

"Daddy this is happy ice cream, it makes people happy and even though you and Mummy don't live together anymore, you can still be happy, and I have a magic smile, Rosie told me that if I smile my magic will make you smile too." He proudly gave the ice cream to the man with a huge smile, which did release the tears Rosie had managed to keep back. The man took the ice cream, put his arms around him, and squeezed him tightly.

"It's happy ice cream Daddy, why are you crying?" he said, confused.

"Well Nicholas, sometimes we grownups cry when we are happy, and your ice cream and your magic smile has really made me very happy, look I am smiling, these are tears of joy."

"Grownups are strange, just as you said Rosie," Nicholas said, looking back at her.

The man looked at Rosie, and silently mouthed "Thank you" to her as she wiped away her tears with the back of her hand. She had been so engrossed in the conversation between Nicholas and his dad that she hadn't heard the café door tinkle open and she hadn't been aware Charlie had been standing right behind her, listening to the whole conversation. She turned to leave them and bumped straight into him.

"Charlie!" she exclaimed. "You started me. I didn't know you were there. Are you trying to get me back for last night?" she joked.

Charlie's eyes were also brimming with tears. This woman stood in front of him was like no one he had ever met. How was she so wise, so knowing, so caring at such a young age?

"Are you okay Charlie?" she sounded concerned, totally oblivious to the impact her kindness had had on him.

"Yeah, sure I am. It's a bit windy today and my eyes are still struggling so open at such an unearthly hour of the day."

She smiled at him with that beautiful, enigmatic smile.

"Pleased that you are here, take a seat and I'll come and take your order," she said.

She was in work mode, a busy little bee very different to the serene, calm woman he'd been with only a few hours before.

She was still adorned with flowers, they covered the very traditional apron she had on. Her hair was tied up in a loose knot on the top of her head and a few beads of sweat had pushed out a few strands of blonde hair which rested at the nape of her neck. It was the first time he'd seen her neck, so slender he didn't know how it was strong enough to carry that beautiful face and head so full of knowledge, sweetness and, of course, the insightfulness in abundance that he'd just witnessed.

Charlie walked towards a well-worn sofa on the other side of the window.

At the side of it was a very low, rickety wooden coffee table.

"Am I okay here?" he pointed

"Sure is, that is the VIP area," she smiled

"VIP, I like that," he grinned and jokingly said, "Did you make this table?"

"Actually I did," she replied.

"Wow, a woman of many talents aren't you Rosie?"

"It's made of driftwood that I picked up from the beach and that's why this is The Driftwood Café."

"So not only are you only a potential songwriter, you are also a child counsellor and a carpenter, I am in awe," he feigned a bow.

"Have you been eavesdropping and listening to me Charlie? That's very rude."

Charlie saw a frown starting to appear on her face, and she looked genuinely upset.

"No, no Rosie, I had just entered the café and I was just standing there. I actually thought you'd see me and then I realised that you hadn't and I thought I couldn't move or make a noise because it would have interrupted and spoiled that special moment that you created for that little boy and his dad."

"Honestly, I'm not a sneak. In fact, I'm probably the absolute opposite of that, a straightforward sort of guy. Say it as it is and I respect privacy tremendously," he replied apologetically.

She cocked her head again, just as she did when she was in the dunes, whilst contemplating how to respond.

"Okay then, take a seat. I believe you. It's a strong coffee isn't it? And what would you like for breakfast? The menu is on the very special handmade brilliant table in front of you, and we also have some specials on the board behind the counter."

"I can't read them from here," Charlie replied. "What are the specials, and why the special?"

"Well they are special because I've infused them with a concoction of local spices and spells," she stopped to see if he was listening as he seemed to be distracted, maybe drifting off into his hieroglyphical world of notes again.

"Yep, I'm beginning to think you do have some sort of 'witchiness' inside you."

"I thought you were back in your mythical world of notes and songs and weren't listening to me."

"Quite the opposite. I was actually listening to you your voice. It is mesmerising and sort of puts me in a trance."

He grinned at her, his green eyes catching the sun's rays that were beaming through the windows, making them appear to twinkle. He looked directly into her clear blue eyes and Rosie felt her cheeks burn a little; it was her time to feel unsettled and not fully in control.

"You are such a sweet talker Charlie boy, but all that patter won't work on me," she replied, trying to bring back control in the conversation.

Knowing he still had the upper hand, he patted the sofa and said,

"I beg to differ and so whilst I have you listening to me, why not take a break and join me in this VIP spot, and I will buy you breakfast!"

Frances had been observing with interest the interaction her niece was having with the young man.

She couldn't hear the conversation, but it was clear they had met before from the flirtatious behaviours from both and the pink tint to Rosie's cheeks. Was he the reason she had come home so late last night and why she had been so fixated with the café door? She walked over to them both.

"Good morning," she said. "What can I get you? I've not seen you in here before. Is it your first visit? Are you here for our fantastic festival?"

Charlie looked up at the mature woman, who spoke.

She had a really genuine welcoming smile, a few creases around her eyes and the top of her lips, with a white peppered grey hair that was cut short around a very happy round face. He guessed she was about fifty years old.

"Well I visited last week, but apparently I was a little rude to Rosie here, so she's invited me back as a VIP guest so I can make amends and see if my behaviour can improve."

He certainly had the patter, she thought, and with those good looks, she could see why Rosie was blushing.

"So you are a VIP guest are you? Sorry I didn't catch your name, are you famous?" she asked.

"I'm Charlie and no not famous yet, but hope to be some day". He held his hand out and Frances wiped whatever was on her hands on the front of her apron before she took his.

"Well very pleased to meet you VIP Charlie. I'm Frances. So what can I get you?"

"What would you recommend?" he asked

"He needs something infused with a lot of humbleness definitely no ego as he's already full of that and tell him to take his boots off before he eats so he doesn't put his size tens in it again," Rosie said

Frances stared at her for a moment. She hadn't heard Rosie speak like this anyone else. She knew her niece really liked the young man sat in front of her.

"I recommend a full English breakfast for you Charlie, you look a bit peaky and Rosie, why don't you take your break and I'll bring you dippy eggs and you can join your guest."

"Dippy eggs," Charlie mocked. "What's dippy eggs?" he laughed. Rosie looked mortified.

"I think I will just have toast please Aunt Fran," she turned and pulled a face at her, which indicated to Frances to just go before she made things worse.

"Ok dearie, toast and strawberry jam it is. Sit down Rosie, I can manage for a while," and with that she left them. Charlie patted the sofa once again and Rosie sat beside him.

"Only teasing," he said. "I like dippy eggs too, they were my favourite when I was a kid."

The intended fifteen-minute break ran over by more than an hour. Frances watched Rosie and Charlie chatter, laugh and flirt with each with such ease, and she saw Rosie as the young woman she had become, not the child she had raised. She was truly a beautiful person, not just physically, but in her ways too. She had a natural empathy that Frances had never witnessed before in anyone so young.

Of course she was biased but observing her from a distance, watching her with this young man, Frances felt that she was in the process of letting go of her little girl, who had never been blessed by parents, nor grandparents in fact no other family except Frances, but they had a bond that even the most loving, caring parents could not have surpassed. Frances watched as she observed the start of her niece's first young love.

She would probably get her heartbroken as most young women do, although Frances herself had never felt the excitement of that love and then the earth shattering pain as it ended. She had only read about it in books. A summer romance maybe, Charlie certainly wasn't a resident of the village and she hadn't seen him before, maybe he was there on holiday, or visiting for the festival, she just hoped that the heartbreak that would inevitably follow when he went back to where ever he came from would be short-lived and didn't shatter Rosie's precious heart into tiny pieces. There would be others and then eventually she would meet her lifelong soul mate and perhaps bring Frances a grandchild.

Frances shuddered at the thought of anything happening to Rosie as it had her sister Kathleen and her parents. She felt as though she would never get over or live a life without Rosie in it.

But Charlie didn't go away. After the festival, he stayed and rented a mid-terrace cottage close to the harbour, usually rented out to holidaymakers, so the owner had welcomed an autumn lease initially for a month.

Charlie had said the peace and tranquilly of village life would ignite his creativity in order for him to produce more materials for songs.

His agent had apparently said that there was some interest in the band and he felt pretty sure they would get signed by a record company with some good content.

The rest of the band members went back to their homes home and waited for Charlie's masterpieces. They all had additional jobs, proper jobs as Frances had described them, except Jake of course. Charlie though, didn't seem to have any other means of income and it did play on Frances's mind where he got his money from. She tried to find out by throwing hints when she was with him about his source of income, but he never said anything. Apart from the mystery surrounding this, Frances found Charlie to be funny, genuine, honest, and he made her niece so happy. The month turned to two months and then he joined them over Christmas and the New Year. Charlie started to become a permanent fixture in their lives. Maybe he would be the one after all. Time would tell.

10

The Coward

"A person who shows a shameful lack of courage"

"Charlieee." He imagined he heard a ghostly voice say his name. He was still for a moment, trying to decipher whether it was a remnant of his dream or memories of her that were emerging being back in this house. He heard it again. Was she back home? It mattered not. He just needed to get out of the house. His mind was whirling, he was trapped and that wasn't good for him. He started to panic. He looked out of the window. It was far too high to jump out of. The only escape route was down the spiral staircase. If he was quiet, he might make it to the front door without anyone hearing him. He touched his back pocket. The car keys were still there. He was being a coward, he knew that, but he just couldn't stand the claustrophobia he felt. It was as though he was drowning in his own anticipation and fear.

He opened the door of the bedroom; it creaked ever so slightly, and he waited to see if anyone downstairs had heard. But the only sound he heard was what he assumed to be the TV, no sound of the child, nor Fran. Maybe the child was in bed and Fran dozing in the chair watching the TV.

He slowly made his way down the few steps onto the first floor of the cottage. It was dark except for a slither of light coming from the gap of her bedroom. His heart almost stopped. She was home. What should he do? He could knock on that door and see her again. He'd come this far, maybe he should at least say hello, get done with the business that had brought him back and then bugger off. But the coward on his shoulder screamed loudly in his ear, "Just get the fuck out of here!" And then he heard it again, her saying his name, although it was almost a whisper.

"Charlieeee, is that you, are you there?" He knew it was her, not his imagination, the way she always trailed the end of his name. He put his ear to the door. He could hear someone in there. His mind was racing. What should he do? The coward perched on his right should was screaming for him to just leg it, but there was a gentle voice in his left ear telling him to just man up and go in. He knocked ever so quietly on the door, hoping that his knock wouldn't be heard, and he could

pacify the voice on the left before the coward on his right enabled him to leave without guilt.

"Charlieee, it is you, come in," her soft voice almost made his knees buckle. It was her, she was just a few yards away, just the door between him and that beautiful face and with that face came his demons, but there was no escape now, he knew that. He turned the door handle, took a deep breath, and mustered up all the courage he had left, which wasn't much.

He had decided a forthright entrance was the best thing, he would just demand to know why she had dragged him here, and no matter what it was, he would leave that night, no matter how late, he just could not stay there with all those memories tormenting him.

"Yeah, it's me Rosie, just as you bloody commanded," he could hear his voice but it didn't feel as though it was coming from him as his automatic self-protection mode tried to distance and protect him from the impact of the reality he was about to face.

"What's all this bleedin' secrecy? It's like entering the house of riddles..." he continued. He had rehearsed this moment in his head many times over the past few days. He had played out various scenarios, practiced his words, the tone of his voice, his body language.

"Hello, Rosie, how are you? Hello Rosie, what the fuck do you want?" Whichever he had practised, he knew that once again, just like the first time they met, she would have the advantage. She had all the cards, and she hadn't shown any of them until now, this very moment when he opened the door and looked at her for the first time in almost eight years.

His voice stopped when he saw her. His heart literally did stop. His Rosie, his beautiful Rosie, who, as much as he tried to deny it, was still the absolute love of his life. She was the effervescence of life itself. But instead of laying eyes on the Rosie he remembered, a form barely recognisable had taken her place.

123

All that had made her had been sucked out. She looked hollow as though her whole being had been eaten from inside of herself.

"Fuck no, Rosie no, no, no," he whispered. He turned away, struggling to comprehend what he was seeing. Rosie said nothing.

He felt his stomach churn, and he rushed over to the sink in the corner of the bedroom and dry retched. Still, she said nothing. The coward on his shoulder screamed at him to run away, to not turn around and look at that empty hollowed out creature that was laid in Rosie's bed. It wasn't her; he didn't need to stay.

She spoke "Charlieee, my Charlie," the voice was barely audible, "I'm so glad that you came." He looked up into the mirror above the sink and saw someone who resembled her trying to push herself up off the mattress and he heard the winces of pain as she did so. He watched her reflection and tears started to flow. He turned and walked over to her, helping her sit up. The first touch in so long. A touch not filled with love, nor even anger, but of care and compassion, and shock at feeling her emaciated frame and how little was left of her.

He sat on the edge of the bed and took hold of her hand. He looked into her sunken eyes, that still shone and sparkled like he remembered, and his tears kept falling. He couldn't contain his sobs, and he hid his face in his hands. He didn't want her to see him cry.

He couldn't bear that she would see his guilt, the guilt of not being there for her, that she would see the coward on his shoulder and his shame. His cries eventually started to subside. He could hardly breathe. She took hold of his hand and he could see that her face was wet with tears too. She was still so very beautiful. In fact, she looked more beautiful than he had ever seen. How was that possible? Her rosiness had not yet left her.

"It's cancer Charlie, it came so quick," she whispered.

"I'm sorry you didn't know before you saw me. I thought Aunt Fran would have prepared you."

"She was there, your daughter, so Fran didn't say anything and then I came upstairs and fell asleep and I was trying to sneak out, the coward that I am, when I heard you calling. I had no idea Rosie, I should have guessed it was something terrible, I was so caught up in my own feelings, angry that you had written, memories of this place, that there was no space to even consider..." his voice trailed off, "this," and he started to cry again.

He managed to speak. "How long have you known?"

"Not long, just about a month, but it has really taken hold very quickly, so it has probably been growing inside of me for a while." She gasped for air and for a moment Charlie thought she was going to leave them that very second.

"Shhh don't speak just breathe Rosie, breathe," and when her breathing regulated after a few moments, he leant forward, cupped her tiny face in his hands and kissed her ever so softly on the lips, a kiss so gentle that it belied the depth of love he felt. The familiarity

of her soft lips, the smell of rosewater, she always rinsed her hair in rosewater, and all the love he had locked away for so long just flooded back, as his tears started to flow again. They were together again, this time not only connected by love, but by tears and sadness too.

He stayed with her until she fell asleep, which only took a few minutes. He left the curtains open despite the onset of darkness, as he knew she loved to see the sea as she woke. He pulled the duvet up over her skeletal arms; the muscle had almost disappeared and put on a bedside lamp before going down the stairs. The coward on his shoulder had been banished and a huge, heavy feeling of sadness weighed down on him in its place.

11

Trespasser

"Invader without permission"

"I knew he would come. I need to feel his strength and his love to prop up what remaining life I have left in me. It breaks me to see his sorrow and I despise even more, this trespasser that has taken residence in my body. He is now starting to cast shadows on my brightness, devouring my life's energies and dulling my ability to connect to those I love. It drains me, this unwanted, uninvited stranger. He has been there for a long time, I know that now. He was clever, lurking and hiding, always shifting around, exploring every bit of me, but never staying in one place long enough for me to find him.

In those early days he had such patience, waiting there, hibernating until he awoke and decided this was the time. He is no longer patient, he has changed and is no longer content with sharing my body with me, his selfishness has been ignited. He wants it for himself and there is no going back, no reasoning with him at all.

Many times I had felt my body wasn't my own, that someone or something else was there, but it didn't worry me, for I had always felt the spirit of my mother within me and that feeling brought warmth and comfort.

You tricked me into thinking that I had nothing to fear. Even when my instincts had told me otherwise, I ignored you, easily distracted by the joy and love my daughter evoked. You must have been comfortable there inside me as it took you seven years to show yourself, to decide the best place and time to start your battle with me. For seven years I have not questioned the feelings I have had, but I have now worked out the exact moment you found me, when you became a part of me, without asking, just decided to sneak in.

Hindsight is not always our friend in life. We never know when its wick will be alighted, creating shadows over our past until the lightness comes and then we see it. The moment it becomes part of our conscious, never to fade, and despite the regret I have for not seeing it before, I will not allow that to consume me, because if truth be known there is no regret in me, just pure happiness and you will not take that from me, or tarnish my memory, no matter how you try.

29th of February 1988 fourteen minutes into the start of the day when the bundle of cells that had been growing inside, decided she wanted her independence and it was time to leave the security and comfort of me to make her own way in the world, almost 8 weeks early. Whilst the images I recall are blurred, I remember the sounds so clearly.

The ambulance siren, the voices of the doctors, nurses and midwife, their professional and controlled tones, all their experience and training overriding the emotions they have, but I could hear the worry and concern, the way they ended their words abruptly, almost coldly, concealing their care and devotion to life. Even though I faded in and out of consciousness as they tried so hard to stem the flow of blood that ran from me. I remember three things with absolute clarity now.

They are all entwined, connected, and can never be unravelled. The first is the euphoria of hearing my child's sweet birth song as she opened her lungs for the very first time. A beautiful, melodic, and unique note that nature enables all mothers to hear before anyone else, to connect her to the life grown inside, now on the outside. Neave's birth song wasn't a cry, it was just a sigh, but I heard it and I knew she was safe.

The second is a very faint doctor's voice shouting, "three, two, one, stand back," and then a surge so strong I felt my body arch as an electric current ran through me and I heard the deafening monotone of my heart quieten. Then the familiar rhythmic bodoom, bodoom take back hold as life was returned to me.

The third one you do not need me to recount to you stranger, for you will remember it well, when you decided that I was the one, and this was the time as you so silently drifted into me with my first inhale of breath after the shock.

I have wondered why me? Was it because I cheated death and cheats always get their comeuppance?

My family has suffered loss more than most and if suffering were to be shared out equally, Aunt Fran's would have been spent by the time she was far younger than me. There is no fairness in the world, and wasting time looking for answers and reasons is futile. The breaths we are given are precious, and we never know how many heart beats we have been given until the unknown moment we are unable to count them anymore. So you see stranger, I do not look back on your arrival with anger or sadness because it was the time that life was given to my daughter and I was gifted back seven more wonderful years with her.

In my dreams, I have asked for more time. More time to hear my child's voice, see her face and watch her grow.

More time to say thank you to Aunt Fran because no matter how many times I say it or show it, it will never be enough to convey the gratitude and love I have for her. And now my Charlie has arrived. I will ask you once again, despite me promising myself I would not ask you for anything again. I know tonight I will beg. I need more time to fill the years of lost love without him. But I already know the answer. You are ruthless; you are heartless and have no soul, no compassion and I lie here powerless, getting weaker each day until the time comes for your insatiable hunger to consume all of me. The irony of this is your mutilation of me, your greed that will eventually take my life, will also end yours. This is the stupidity and futility of it all.

I have asked myself what was the trigger that activated you? As I have gotten to know you more, to understand your nature, your overwhelming need to be in control, I am now sure it was that day not too long ago when Neave and I were rolling down the dunes, wrapped together, covered in sand with Lou-Lou barking and chasing us.

We laughed that much my stomach hurt and I recall with ease the beauty of those innocent eyes looking straight at me. Her brushing grass from my hair as she cupped my face in her hands, kissing every bit of it, saying "love you Mummy" with every kiss. I felt my heart would break and for a fraction I think it stopped, just like it did all those years ago when you became my uninvited, invisible, unwanted companion. You almost left it too late, didn't you? As you realised the love that had grown between us over the years might just have had the power to interfere with the future plans you had for me.

You thought you had time on your hands to decide when it should start, so you had lain comfy and content exploring my body, believing you had plenty of time to make the decision to turn over the vessel that contained the sand of time on my life to mark the start of my end. Your own sense of importance blinding you from this strength building inside me day by day since Neave's birth song imprinted itself onto my heart. You almost left it too late and had you waited just a short time longer, you would never have been able to break through the protective shield of our love. I imagine you with your feet up in a huge armchair, a glass of port in one hand, foie gras in the other, getting bloated and fatter on your own self-worth.

You enjoyed the comforts of my healthy body, my active imagination, the vivid, colourful creativity of my mind and you watched as a passenger enjoying the experiences, knowing eventually it would all be yours. Fattening the lamb before the slaughter. The more goodness, love, and enjoyment I had, the greater the feast would be at the time of conquest. Acknowledging your complacency in almost losing me is what is fuelling the ferocity of your consumption of me now.

Your anger is your own, stranger. I have none of my own for you, and you do not have me yet. I have realised this is a battle I cannot win, so I will save my strength and my dignity and I have decided I will no longer compliment you with even one ounce of my attention or focus. The energy I still have will be directed away from you, and although you will still rot my body, I will never let you contaminate, poison, or extinguish my light and my love, for they are far stronger than the self-pity, anger and sadness you desperately try to infiltrate into my heart and my soul. You may win the battle but this fight you will never win. I will always deny your darkness, even in my very last breath.

I think of the story I was told as a child at Sunday School. The wind is arguing with the sun that he is the strongest. The sun tries to explain there are many types

of strength, but the wind is having none of it, saying his brute physical strength, ability to control and ultimately use force to get his own way is much stronger than the warmth and gentleness the sun has.

So confident is wind of his strength that he rises to a challenge that sun sets for them both to measure who is the most powerful. Sun sees a man walking through a field with his coat on but unbuttoned. Sun says to wind that whoever can remove the coat from the man will be the one with most power. Wind agrees to this, thinking his blustering would take care of the coat in no time. So off he went, blowing and whirling round the man, looking to catch hold of the coat and yank it from his possession. But no matter how fast and hard he blew, the man just held onto his coat, wrapping it tighter and tighter round his body until in the end the wind was exhausted and had to stop trying. It was sun's turn, and she gently opened her arms to the man sharing her warmth and brilliance with him. Within minutes, without force and of his own free will, the man removed his coat, threw it over his shoulder and continued on his way over the field. Sun tries to explain to wind that sharing what we have unconditionally with others, not forcing or coercing, has a power that has no limits or boundaries. But wind is too angry to listen, just like you stranger.

You will never steal the essence of me and no matter how much you bully me, invade, and consume me, you will never understand, experience, or feel the wonder of unconditional love, nor the strength and power it brings.

Your narcissism and your persistent and unyielding selfishness to be the centre of all things deafens you to my words. In fact, it fuels your consumption of my flesh. I will never give into you, but I am growing weaker each day. I needed reinforcements.

I wait for Charlie to come back to me, to make my disintegrated body feel safe and whole once again.

12

Mara

"The purveyor of anxiety, fear and demons of the night"

"Why didn't you tell me?"

Were his first words to Frances when he entered the kitchen. She was standing by the sink washing dinner pots. Instead of answering the question, she turned around to face him. Putting her finger to her mouth, she looked over his shoulder and spoke to Neave, who had followed Charlie into the kitchen.

"Hello Neave, Charlie is here for the dinner you made him. Charlie, Neave has made you her favourite pizza. We've already had ours, but she wanted to stay up to say goodnight to you."

"What didn't you tell him, Aunt Frances?" The inquisitive little child asked.

"I didn't tell him that Mummy was in bed poorly, Neave, but I think Charlie called in to see Mummy on

his way down here. Is that right Charlie?" He said nothing.

"Do you want a glass of wine with this pizza Charlie?" Frances was already pouring it. "We can talk a lot more after you have eaten and this wee one is in bed." She gave Neave a huge smile as she took her hand and sat her at the table.

Charlie sat down at the table and picked up the large glass of wine that Frances had poured. His hand was shaking so much he had to hold it steady with the other one. Neave, who was oblivious to the non-verbal communication happening between Frances and Charlie, continued to chatter. "It's got three different types of cheeses Charlie, and tomato and basil that I picked myself today from our garden. Do you like it? I think I'll call it Charlie pizza because I made it especially for you and Aunt Frances said you are Mummy special friend so I made you a very special pizza."

Charlie looked into the small face, perfect skin just like porcelain, almost translucent, with pale blue eyes capped by wispy blonde curls that touched her face so very gently, and all he could see was Rosie. He had to look away briefly because Frances had made it clear to him that any conversation about Rosie was not to be done in front of the child.

There was a huge booming voice in his head screaming…I told you, love always ends in pain…and even though he had chosen to put himself in a self-proclaimed love vacuum since he left, believing he had frozen himself to the impact of love and that he had his emotions firmly under control, he had been fooling himself thinking he could eradicate the love he had for her.

He'd just hidden it, lied to himself that she didn't matter.

He kept his eyes averted so Neave couldn't see the mixture of bewilderment and pain, but of course she had seen it. Children are so very perceptive and intuitive.

"Don't be sad, Charlie," she said. "Mummy says we mustn't be sad just because she's poorly and I've made you special pizza. Look, it's got a smile on it. He looked down at the homemade pizza and saw she had made a face on it out of tomatoes and herbs.

This tiny act of thoughtfulness brought even more tears to his eyes, and he quickly wiped them away with the back of his hand before looking back at her and smiling.

"Well how can anybody not be happy having a pizza made them made for them, especially with a happy face on it," he said as he forced a smile, "Do you want some too?"

"I've had mine," she said. "My tummy was rumbling so Aunt Frances said I could eat mine and not wait for you."

The last thing Charlie wanted to do was eat, he still felt sick, but he pulled a piece of pizza off and put it in his mouth. "This is yummy. Did you make this all by yourself? It's really good," he said, washing it down with the remainder of the wine, which he topped up from the bottle Frances had left on the table, taking another huge gulp.

The effect of consuming the second glass of wine so quickly after the first was making Charlie's head spin, and he felt more confused as an image of Rosie as he had just seen her merged with her as he remembered her. In the background he could hear Neave chattering, and he smiled and nodded when he thought he needed to. He heard Frances say it was time for bed and some part of him found a voice and he heard himself say, "Night, night, sweet dreams". The child put her arms around his neck, gave him a huge hug and kissed him on the cheek, which took away any

morsel of control he had left. He wasn't used to outbursts of spontaneous kindness and love anymore.

"I like you Charlie, you have a kind face," was her parting comment as Frances took her hand to go to bed.

Alone in the kitchen with a head full of wine, the memory box that has been so firmly shut for many years just disintegrated and he saw her everywhere.

He needed to have all of her, everything she had ever touched, and he frantically opened the kitchen drawers and cupboards, pulling out contents until he found the one that stored the tablecloths and towels. He threw numerous ones on the floor until he found the one he was looking for, the one she had hand embroidered at Christmas time when he had been there. It had tiny red berries and deep green holly leaves with the date 1984 sewn on it. He put it to his face and breathed in its aroma. He ran his fingers over the stitching, remembering her sat at the table, needle and thread in her hand creating the flowers.

He was so engrossed in his actions that he hadn't heard Frances return to the kitchen. He just felt Frances's hands on his as she rested her head on his shoulder blades. They stayed there motionless, taking solace in the comfort of human touch as they struggled with their emotions and deep pain.

It was Charlie that moved first, putting his arms around her as he looked into the face of this heartbroken, sad woman, pain showing on every inch of her. She was crying, and it occurred to him that she probably hadn't had an opportunity to show her sadness with anyone yet, hiding it from Rosie and Neave, and he felt incredibly touched that he was the one she had chosen to share it with. Her fortitude and love for her girls had given her the strength to push down and hide her emotions deep down inside until now. Charlie held her, sharing in her sorrow and tears until they stopped and her sobs became long sighs.

He took her to the table and emptied the remnants of the bottle of wine between two glasses and offered her one which she took.

"What happened Fran?", he asked softy, "Is she going to get better? What does Neave think is wrong with her mum?" His mind was racing again.

"Too many questions, Charlie, and I don't have answers. The only thing I do know for certain is that she isn't going to get better. You surely know that Charlie, you have seen her. It came so fast, and the doctors can't tell us how long she has left, just that it isn't long.

139

You have lost almost eight years of time together and she wants to make sure you don't miss any more, so she wrote to you when it became clear she wouldn't be able to fight it. She is so very weak, but she still smiles every morning when she wakes, thankful of the oxygen she can still inhale and the time she can spend with Neave. You were and still are a huge part of her living days Charlie, and we all need and owe it to her to remain strong for what short time she has left. Neave obviously knows she is ill, but she doesn't know she won't get better. Rosie will tell her soon, I am sure." She took her handkerchief out of her apron pocket once again and dried her eyes.

"What I do know Charlie, is that it is the most wicked thing, cancer, it is the devil's spores. I really do think it is that. The devil always wants the people who are full of goodness and light. He seeks them out, hunts them. He doesn't pray on those he knows he's going to get, those people who are filled with hate and anger as they are easy fodder for him when they go, so he has to go after the ones that are full of kindness, love, gratitude, and humility, all the things that make humans so special. It's true Charlie, I swear it, I know it and I feel it in me, it's the devil. He is so intimidated by her, her gentleness, her ability to love unconditionally.

In all my years I've never seen Rosie angry, resentful, or jealous. She doesn't have any meanness,

no matter what life has thrown at her.

There's no badness. Sadness, yes, but she doesn't let it eat away at her, change her.

Sadness comes from love and love is the most potent sources of goodness, and sadness is just the ashes of love we have lost, that's all. She had great sadness that stayed with her after you left Charlie, though never any anger, such sadness that it did overwhelm her, and it stayed with her until Neave was born. As that little baby opened her eyes and Rosie looked into them, it was as though Neave just absorbed it from her, pulled it right out of her and filled the void it left with love. She healed Rosie Charlie, she's a healer. She sees things others can't, she's as special as Rosie. She is so intuitive, she just sees the good in people and brings it straight out for them to see for themselves. She saw that in you Charlie. Do you know what the name means? It is Irish, Niamh, only we spell it differently. It means radiance, and she is a little sunshine in all of our lives. Myths say that Niamh was the princess daughter of a sea god and you know our family is so connected to the sea, I mean, with Rosie's father being a Viking god and all that."

She was rambling. It all came out in one go, all her emotions, feelings, thoughts that just needed to come out. Charlie sat listening to her.

"Don't you look at me like that Charlie, I haven't lost it, although there have been times I wished I had, to relieve the responsibility of it all. It's a sad state of affairs when I pray to have the innocence and lack of whatever that Rosie's mother didn't have, to take away the worry and responsibility. Simplicity brings happiness Charlie.

141

She is so special just like her mum and grandmother," she paused again, "and thank you for listening to me, there is no-one else I could have said this to, not even Annie, her best friend because as much as she is a wonderful person and Rosie loves her, it isn't like the love we have for her."

Charlie waited to see if she would continue. She took another bottle of wine from the rack and filled their glasses. She had more to out pour.

"I am so tired Charlie, so weary, it's hard to keep being positive on the outside when you feel as though you are rotting inside, and then I feel guilty as it is my beautiful Rosie who is actually rotting from the inside. I've got to keep going for both their sakes, I am going to be guardian to yet another little orphan whose mother died before her life was lived."

She put her head in her hands and started to cry again. His silence giving her space to just let go.

"You know how slender she always was Charlie but yet she always had so much more energy and zest for life than anyone I have ever met. Her whole life is Neave. She shared her energy with her, her wisdom, her creativity. They were always together. Neave came to the café with her from being a baby was with her every Saturday until Rosie became too weak to work. She helps wipe the tables and all the regulars love her. She natters away with such thoughtfulness and compassion it's as though she's been here before." She stopped to take another mouthful of wine.

"When Neave had gone to bed, Rosie would stay up writing stories, illustrating them, she gets that creativity from Kathleen. There are loads of them in the boxes in the attic where you are staying."

Charlie felt his heart skip a beat as he remembered Rosie writing, and it gave him a just a tweak of calmness as he knew he would be sharing his dreams with some part of her, even if it was just her words. He had an impulse to just run up the stairs, rip open the boxes and let his fingers trace every word she had written. He remembered how she wrote, so expressive, and the words from her letter came into his head.

He was so grateful she bore him no malice and that her forgiving heart had allowed him to spend precious time with her before she…he couldn't bring himself to even think the word, never mind say it even in his head. It was as if he said it, then it would arrive and he couldn't let that happen, not yet, not ever, but he knew it would come and it would come soon.

"In the early days before we knew, her energy levels waned a little, but it was very gradual, totally unnoticeable until you look back and the signs were there, but we missed them. She started to fall asleep with a pen in hand mid story. She would joke about the hills getting steeper and her bones getting old before their time. The walk to and from the café each day after dropping Neave off at school took longer. She even employed Annie to help at the café so she could reduce her hours. She thought it was her asthma playing up.

Do you remember Annie, Charlie? She's the bossy one, she never really liked you. Anyway, the lack of energy and breathlessness got worse and even the increase in her medication didn't take it away and then one day I looked at her, I saw her but she wasn't her anymore. Her vibrancy and vitality just wasn't there the way it used to be and the pink in her cheeks she was born with and why we named her was fading.

So after weeks of nagging her, she took herself off to the doctors who told her to come home and pack a bag as he wanted her to go into hospital for some tests. Even then, she thought it was a fuss over nothing. She even wrote a story for Neave about a princess who'd been so fed up of being a princess she pretended she was sick and went to the hospital for a rest, taking her best friend in a suitcase so they could have uninterrupted play without her having to be a royal for a few days whilst she was there.

When the tests came back, it was a complete shock because although I knew she wasn't well, I just never ever imagined it would be cancer. Initially, they felt chemotherapy might save her life or at least extend it for three years, maybe.

It soon became clear to the doctors as more tests were done, that the cancer had really taken hold and that chemo wouldn't cure it. She didn't want to spend the time she had left making herself more ill, so she told them she didn't want any treatment except for pain relief and she came home. There she was again, thinking about us instead of herself.

144

She did what she'd always done and flipped it, turned a negative into a positive and said she had been gifted time that was even more special because it was running out, and that she intended to spend it taking Neave to places they hadn't had chance to explore yet."

She paused, her eyes darting all over as she relived all of the past few weeks in just a few short moments.

"It became clear quite quickly that she wouldn't have the strength to make the journeys she wanted. Further tests came back and the three years went down to six months, but even that was optimistic. That was four weeks ago Charlie and look at her now. The doctors want her to be in hospital, but she's having none of it. She says she wants to stay with the people she loves in the last few weeks she's got left. She told me she was dying two weeks ago. She told me she hadn't got much time left. I told her she was mistaken, as I couldn't bear to hear her say that, but she took hold of my hand and asked for pen and paper. She told me she needed you Charlie. She wanted you to come, and here you are."

Charlie couldn't utter a word. He was still trying to take it all.

"As much as Rosie bears no anger towards you, Charlie, you have to know that I am not blessed with her forgiving nature. And although I am so pleased you are here with us, it is where you belong, where you've always belonged, I look at you and see the tears she shed when you walked out.

145

So please forgive me in advance if I get short with you and snap, I don't mean too, but I am carrying anger too, not just at you but at God for taking yet another one of my precious babies. I just don't understand it Charlie, I really don't. This is testing my faith more than with my parents or even Kathleen."

She didn't say it to make him feel guilty about the years of absence. She said it because it was true. He had abandoned her, put himself and his feelings before her. She didn't need to press the guilt button within him, he had already done that. But she was right about this place. It was the only place he'd ever felt he might be able to find peace, but he didn't stay long enough to find out.

He held onto her hand and said, "I think I'd like to go back to her now. Would that be okay?"

"You don't need to ask for my permission to see her Charlie. Even a blind man would be able to see the connection between you two. It is like a magnet always pulling you back to each other and no matter how far away you run, or whatever you do to try to break it, it will never stop its pull until you are together. It started the day you two met."

Charlie smiled faintly remembering how she had likened him to Lou-Lou. Lou-Lou!

"Lou-Lou," he spoke his thoughts out loud. "Where is she?" His face starting to fall again as he presumed she was no longer with them. "Is she...?" he couldn't say the word.

146

"No, no, no," Frances said, reading his face. "She's stopping at Annie's. I've not got the time or energy to walk her since Rosie became bed ridden. They say animals are much more intuitive than us and again, with the gift of hindsight, she knew before any of us. Months before the cancer was diagnosed she became her shadow. They were always close, but she wouldn't leave her and followed her around continuously. Lou-Lou is incredibly distressed too. You know how close they are and when Annie brings her round to take Neave on the beach with them a few times a week, we have to literally drag her away from Rosie's side. She just cries as Annie puts her in the car."

"Where is it, the cancer Fran?" he asked.

"It's all over Charlie, her stomach, and guts. It's in her lungs and lymph nodes too. She's got blood clots in her lungs, which is why she gets so breathless and although she is taking medication to break them down, if one moves and reaches her heart or brain, then that will take her before the devil's spore does.

I feel so guilty wanting her to stay longer with us as I know she is suffering, although she doesn't complain. It's torment each day watching her suffer, knowing the only time pain will leave her is when she is gone, and selfishly I pray each night asking God to keep her with us. I pray for her life to be prolonged. That is so selfish when she is selfless, and I feel guilty for it Charlie I really do, because it is only death will take that pain away and it will take her with it too."

Death, that was the word…the word he just couldn't allow himself to say or to think because once out there it would penetrate his head and it would be there always, but Frances had said it, broken down his final defence and it was lodged there unmovable, bringing the true reality of what he had to face.

It would be his new constant companion, loitering in the shadows of mind, in the backdrop of the memories he had, and it would always be there, even though she was still with them. A permanent reminder that the depth and greatness of love is only matched by equal amounts of loss and pain when it is gone. He felt that death was with him now and he had to learn to live alongside it without its darkness stealing what shine his beautiful Rosie still had left. He felt exhausted listening to Frances, so goodness knows how she felt.

They both felt weighed down by the enormity of the challenge they had over the next few weeks. And then what? He couldn't bear to allow his mind to venture there. He kissed Frances on the top of the head.

"Thank you for being her guardian angel. I am so, so sorry for the past, I really am, but I will do everything I can to bring some happiness to her and to support you…and Neave".

He squeezed her hand before leaving the kitchen and heading towards Rosie's room. Selfishly, he hoped she was awake. He wanted to take her in his arms, plead for her forgiveness and tell her how much he was sorry, how much he loved her and that he would never leave her again.

As he opened the door, he could see that she was fast asleep. The full moon was shining through the bedroom window and she looked like Sleeping Beauty laid there waiting for some handsome prince to kiss her and just like magic bring life back into her. How he wished that fairy tale was true. He could see her chest rising and falling and he hoped and prayed that one of the blood clots that her body was struggling with didn't take her from them in the night.

He wanted to stay with her, sleep in the armchair at the side of the bed, but he knew his sleep would be restless and he feared it would make her restless too.

He wanted to have all the energy he could have the next day and all the days she had left so instead he kissed her on the forehead, whispered, "I love you my beautiful Rosie," before closing the door behind him and climbing the spiral staircase to the attic.

That night, Charlie's sleep was tumultuous. Nightmares vivid, dark, and angry, with images from the past like ghosts, as a sea monster rose from the depths of the ocean taking hold of his Rosie, dragging her under as he tried desperately to reach her and pull her back from its clutches. But he too, was being dragged under. He gasped for breath and tried with all his might to stay above the waves. He felt something grab his ankle, pulling him down further. Down into the cold, dark water. He looked expecting to be in the clutches of the sea monster, only to find it was Rosie's hand that had hold of him. Her face was serene, and she was smiling at him.

He felt a calmness and an acceptance to give up the struggle so he could be with her, so he gulped in the water. The sensation of filling his lungs with water was too much. He panicked and as he started to drown his survival instinct kicked in. Kicking out at her shoulder, she released him so he could escape. He looked back at her as the sea monster came forward, swallowing her in its gaping mouth.

Once again Charlie woke gasping for air, drenched in sweat. He was in that state between awake and still being caught in his nightmare and he panicked, thinking he had lost her, that he had let a monster devour her just so he could live. Eventually, the soft light from the lamp he had left on, reassured him that this was just a nightmare and it wasn't real. He wondered what the dream was all about, although he thought he knew - it was his conscience.

Last night he'd wanted to escape and leave her to her own demons, putting himself first as he always had done. He had failed her in the past; he was weak; she had always been wiser and stronger than him, but he vowed to himself that he would never put himself before her for the rest of her days. He looked at his watch. It was 6:15 and he could hear the start of the early birdsong and the distant sea welcoming another day. He opened the window, let some warm air in to soak up the perspiration that had completely drenched his body and the bedsheets. He had no way to prepare for how the day would unfold. His head was overwhelmed with images and thoughts of her, his Rosie.

13

Tapestry

"Interwoven threads of life"

I am grateful for the life that still remains in my body. The drugs dull my pain but it always remains, constantly nagging away and as the days pass, I need more pills to manage it. The drugs take me to a place I am unfamiliar with, and at first it unnerved me.

I find myself there mainly when I sleep, when I am dreaming, but these are not ordinary dreams, the ones that are forgotten when you wake, that are often irrational and random, they are different; I remember them, every detail.

There are also times when I find myself in this same place of in-betweenness when I am not in sleep, I am awake, but I am in the shadows of myself, not quite connected to reality. It is here in this no-man's-land of my mind that I am connected to my memories, and they are clear and lucid. I am able to feel them, relive the moments. I am like a traveller in myself, my past life is the path and I see, feel, hear, taste and touch all of it again but much stronger than the first time.

This is a one way journey and I know there is no turning back if I miss something. I have no idea how long the path is, but I know it will lead me to the end. How incredible of the human body, mind, and soul that it gifts me this opportunity to recall and remind myself of the beauty and wonderment of my life.

When these reveries are offered to me, I am always walking through nature, however there is little order as the seasons interface with each other without the structure of time. Sometimes I feel the coolness and freshness of spring showers that fall to awaken and replenish thirsty, hungry soil after its hibernation from the frost of winter, where its nutrients have been frozen, resting, ready for the moment when it is time to start the life cycle of creation once more. Other times I feel the composting leaves underfoot, softly flexing as I walk over them. Crocus and snowdrops, beautiful blue cornflowers, foxgloves, and wild roses bloom all around me. The sun burns down on my skin and I stretch out my arms and turn my head to the sky to absorb its energy and warmth. Rainbows, rapeseed, barley, oak trees and hedgerows and the sound of bees, bird song and insects, a tiny army of life-givers scattering pollen and seed to ensure the continuation of this wondrous earth.

The cycle of life can come and go so fast in this place I frequent. The rich, multiple hues of autumn, orange, red, magenta, as I watch leaves fall, rot, and then feed the land and restart again. Maybe this cycle signifies the number of years I have been lucky enough to have life, and so I try to slow them down as I know the time is limited before the years run out.

I am in awe of the beauty of mother nature's architecture and form, snowflakes her finger-prints, trees, her lungs and we humans are but visitors and should be more respectful of what she shares. It is truly magnificent.

This place offers me arches, paths, and doorways to choose from. I have come to understand these are gateways to different memories. I always choose the ones that are the most vivid, bright, and colourful, I trust my instincts to take me to the places I need to go to, revisit the times, places, people, and experiences that have shaped my life, made me into who I am today. I am taken back to times in my childhood when I feel again the safety and love that built the foundations for my passage into adulthood, giving me the strength and confidence to be content and happy with who I am. I have Aunt Fran and my mother to thank for these gifts. They have always been with me in life and they are still there, protecting and helping me as I move onto the next.

Sometimes a path repeats and opens up again, and I have an opportunity to revisit a memory. One of these is the night Aunt Frances had held me tight as a small child when my over-active imagination created monsters scratching at the window during a fierce storm. The intensity of the sensation of warmth, security, and comfort I feel again as I relive the memory of her holding and speaking to me reassuringly, must have been a significant moment in my life.

She told me that it wasn't a monster, it was mother nature. That we could hear her every day if we listened carefully. She was usually calm and serene. She could be heard whispering, telling stories, or sweetly singing when the wind blew through the trees, the gentle swaying of grass or when the sea lapped against the land.

A storm was Mother Nature showing she was restless or unhappy just as people needed to share their feelings so did mother nature, otherwise they fester inside. When the lightning and thunder had struck, she told me it was her concert; the lightning to brightening the stage, the roll of thunder announcing the start of the performance and the rain her voice.

I never feared nature's storms after that. In fact, I remember being excited as a storm built, especially on a warm summer night.

I see things here that I only dreamed in my imagination. I have been on the sea in the vessel when the Kraken was slain hundreds of years ago. I have witnessed Hefring herself rise from the sea and with her bare hand pull away at the landscape creating the safe haven for Viking settlers, promising always to keep them safe from the dangers of the sea, so that even when the strongest of storms blew and the gods showed their anger with huge waves to engulf fishermen and sailors, she kept them safe. In all the accounts recording Hefring's history, there are no stories about the storms and sea surges ever encroaching onto the land to cause floods, nor of any disasters or deaths at sea. Unexplainable.

I feel like I am lucky enough to be in the middle of a Hollywood blockbuster movie. An incredible experience as my life becomes yet another thread in this never ending magnificent tapestry of time, layer upon layer of stories and lives, all connecting to our origins, our beginnings and eventually as our thread stops, our ending. Some people are blessed with longer threads. I have not been, but I feel the souls of my ancestors and they bring comfort to me.

14

Neave

"Brightness and radiance"

Everyone was still asleep. There was no sound except for the waking up of the old house as it stretched, its timbers expanding as they absorbed the warmth of the sunlight, exhaling the coldness of the night. Charlie remembered this feeling of security and peacefulness when he was with her. He used to lay resting at the side of her, her blonde hair tangled around her neck, the face of an angel sleeping at his side. It was weird that when he was with her, he always woke early as though he didn't want to miss any moment, but the Charlie without her reverted back to being a night owl, not rising until afternoon, this way he had less available hours to engage with other people. But today he had woken early again, and he recollected how he used to listen for the chatter of the day to start as the house and the world outside awoke, just as it had done today.

This was the time the notes used to come to him. He heard riffs, melodies and notes, and music formed as he listened to the sound of the day waking.

When he was with her, the songs were soft and gentle, whereas for the past eight years they have been hard rock, almost brutal in their composition.

Today, as he lay there, the sounds were sad and melancholic and he reflected just how clever and intuitive the brain was, unconsciously tapping into moods and emotions.

There was light from under her door. This time it was sunlight, but there was no noise whatsoever from the other two bedrooms where Neave and Fran slept. He gently opened the door, hoping with all his might to see her still sleeping in the bed. Her face was turned towards the window. He could see the duvet moving up and down and he sighed with the relief and knowledge she was still with them. He saw that she had taken her medication as there was a half drunk glass of water and an empty packet of tablets on the bedside table. He closed the door and went down the rest of the stairs into the kitchen. It felt strange, empty and quiet.

It was the hub of the house and there was always a kettle boiling, the clatter of pots, and conversations.

Frances had cleared the pots from last night. He automatically went to the cupboard that had the mugs and in and drank two cups of coffee sat before he heard the light patter of feet on the stairs and the kitchen door flung open as Neave burst in.

"Charlie, you had a sleepover!" she exclaimed and once again ran over and annihilated his personal space phobia by flinging her arms around his neck and giving him a huge wet kiss on his cheek.

He screwed his eyes up and automatically went to wipe away the kiss. Neave stopped him, giggled, and said,

"A morning kiss on your cheek is the best way to start the week. Leave it on Charlie."

"It's the weekend," he replied.

"Best way to start the weekend then."

"That doesn't rhyme."

"What's rhyme?"

"Never mind, I'll leave the kiss there." It was far too early for all this activity and conversation.

"Good morning Charlie," Frances was tying her dressing gown cord as she joined them. "How did you sleep?"

"Charlie, what do you want for breakfast? Do you like toast or crumpets?" interrupted Neave.

He put his hands to his ears… "Far too many questions for a man who doesn't usually see this side of noon!!"

"But I want to know if you want dippy eggs," Neave said, "Mummy used to make them for me but she can't because she is still poorly so I want to help Aunt Fran to do them and we could take breakfast up to her."

"I love dippy eggs," he said, "and I am sure Mummy would love a cup of tea in bed even if she doesn't want any breakfast. She was still fast asleep when I came downstairs."

"She still is," Frances replied, smiling at Charlie for keeping Neave chattering.

As the days passed, she could sense Neave becoming more concerned about Rosie. She was such an intuitive child.

Neave had a rabbit that had free run through the house until the pet died a couple of years ago, so she was aware that living things come to an end, and she felt sure Neave was struggling with this as a possibility with her mother as each day went by. They would have to find a way to tell her very soon, but not today.

Neave climbed on Charlie's knee. Fran had never seen her take to anyone the way she had with Charlie, which only reaffirmed in her mind that Neave was aware of how poorly her mother was. It felt as though she was looking for someone to connect to, and Fran felt uneasy that she was choosing Charlie. He didn't have a very good track record on staying power and she just couldn't bear to see her great niece's heart broken by the same man.

Neave continued to chatter the way children do, asking questions and not waiting for the reply before starting the next one. Fran set about making breakfast whilst Charlie tried to keep up with Neave.

""Are you magical Charlie? Mummy is magical, and she says I am too." This time she paused and waited for an answer, looking directly into his face.

"Erm I don't think so. I am not a magical being, but I am a musical being. I make songs, not spells, does that count?"

"What do you make songs out of?" she asked.

"Well…nothing really. I just make them up myself in my head, and then my head makes my hands play notes on my guitar, and that then makes my mouth sing."

She thought for a moment and said, "I can't do that. Is it because you are a grownup and when children grow up maybe we can do that too"

"No Neave, not all grown-ups can do that. In fact, not many at all," he replied.

Her eyes darted from left to right as she processed what Charlie had said.

"Well anyone that can make something out of nothing has to be magical, because only magical people like fairies and wizards can make things out of nothing, waving their wands or sprinkling fairy dust, maybe your guitar is like a wand Charlie!" she exclaimed and her face lit up all excited, "and the notes are the magic spells. You see, you are magical, you are the amazing magical, musical Charlie!" It was as though she had just found a pot of gold, she looked so pleased with herself and once again flung her arms around his neck, "I love you Mr Charlie, you are almost my very best new friend, and you can be in our family as you are magic like me and Mummy."

Frances looked across and saw that Charlie needed rescuing from the Neave hugs, so she said.

"Come and butter the toast, Neave, and what about me? What magic do I have to be part of this family?"

"You have magic to live forever and look after everyone," she said and Fran thought to herself that half of that statement was true, she certainly had been put on the earth to look after people, but she didn't want it to be forever.

"Anyway all these stories and questions, I hope you have remembered your manners this morning. How do we start the day? It's not with magic and wizards is it?" Neave said nothing, so Fran spoke for her.

"Good morning Charlie, good morning Aunt Fran, how did you sleep?"

She didn't repeat the words as Frances expected, but instead said, "It's a silly question to ask, that's why I don't say it Aunt Fran?"

"Why is it silly?" Charlie said.

"Well…how did you sleep?" She opened her eyes wide and put her hands in the air as if to 'say are you all silly' and continued, "Everyone knows how to sleep. We all sleep the same. There is only one way. You lie down, you close your eyes and then you have lovely dreams and wake up and open your eyes. Are there any other ways to sleep Charlie?"

Charlie smiled, the first real spontaneous smile he had had since the letter day. It came from a warm place within him and it surprised him. He had never had much affection for children, never spent much time with them, but this little bundle of joy, perched once again on his knee, with her innocent but curious blue eyes, her endearing smile and infectious giggle was evoking a feeling he had never felt before. He couldn't describe it except it made him feel part of something, something more than he had felt when he had been privileged to be part of this family all those years ago. She was still waiting for him to answer.

"Well now, that is a really good question to which I do not have an answer. Are there any different ways to fall asleep? Mmm tell you what, I'll have a think about that and let you know." He winked at Frances.

"You are funny Charlie, and a bit magical," she giggled.

163

"Time to take Mummy her cup of tea Neave, this is your job isn't it? Eat your dippy egg Neave and then you can take mummy her cup of tea and biscuits.

Neave devoured her breakfast enthusiastically, then took the plate of biscuits as her and Frances left the kitchen to see Rosie, leaving Charlie once again on his own. He so wanted to run up the stairs and hold her, but he was learning very quickly that the world he was in now was not about him, it was primarily about Rosie, then Neave and then Frances, he was way down the pecking order and quite rightly so, he just felt privileged that he was here at all, he certainly didn't deserve to be.

He was on his fourth cup of coffee, having enjoyed the eggs and toast, when he heard a voice shout, "Morning, are we up?"

Lou-Lou ran through the door into the kitchen, her tail wagging incessantly as she bounded over to Charlie, licking his arms and his face as he leant down to fuss the excited dog.

"Wow mate, that is the best hello I have ever had. You remember me, don't you? I've missed you," he said as he fussed her.

"Wow, well that's more than I can say about you," said a voice very frostily. Charlie looked up and saw Annie in the kitchen doorway.

"This is a LOVELY surprise...not," she continued. "Look what the cat brought in Lou-Lou, a big rat."

"Hello Annie, yes, it is a surprise, even for me. Happy to see you."

"Mmm, sorry I can't say the same back," she hissed.

Luckily, Neave had heard Annie arrive, and she had run downstairs to greet Lou-Lou. She ran over to Charlie and joined in the welcome with Lou-Lou.

"She loves you Charlie."

"Lou-Lou does, I am not so sure about Annie," Charlie replied

"Let me clarify any ambiguity that might still be around...I certainly don't love you Charlie boy, and I definitely don't like you," she replied.

"Do you know Lou-Lou and Annie Charlie?" Neave asked just as Frances joined them. She could feel the tension developing.

"They both know Charlie, Neave, they were all friends together a long time ago," Frances shot a glare at Annie and she dropped her eyes knowing full well that all the anger and disdain she had for the man sat in front of her, and there was a large amount of it in her, needed to be kept sealed at least whilst Neave was around as that was what Rosie wanted.

"So pleased you are here, Charlie boy. I really am. Neave, are you ready? Get your wellies on and a jumper.

There is a nip in the air. It's time to take Lou-Lou on her walk, and then you can come back to my house and make fairy cakes for Mummy."

"Aren't I at school today?" she asked.

"It's the weekend, don't you remember Neave? No school at weekends, just fun, fun, fun," Charlie said. Annie rolled her eyes.

"You've got your feet under the table quickly haven't you?" she hissed, still with a false smile on her face.

"What can I say? I've still got it," he replied, unable to stop himself. Frances was not amused.

"When you two have quite finished" she said, "We have a very excited dog and little girl here, so maybe you should say your goodbyes, in fact why don't you both grow up and skip to the end of the story when there is always a happy ending." She glared at the two of them. They both fell silent. Neave put on her outdoor clothes and ran to hug Charlie once more before she left with Annie and Lou-Lou, who really didn't want to leave Charlie's side, which of course Charlie revelled in as Annie looked on with even more disgust on her face.

"I'll bring my fairy buns back for you Charlie," Neave shouted as the front door slammed closed behind them, an indication of Annie's mood.

Charlie smiled to himself. Some things never changed. His and Annie's relationship had always been strained, and despite the sadness of the circumstances that brought him back, he was certainly looking forward to winding her up again. He had always had the ability to get her hook, line and sinker, and this interlude had demonstrated that he still had it. It was game on.

15

Selfless

"Caring for others more than oneself"

"Rosie." Charlie sat on the bed at the side of her, holding her tiny hand in his. The skin was almost transparent. He stroked it gently as she opened her eyes.

"Did I wake you?" he asked, concerned.

She shook her head ever so slightly

"A dippy egg for breakfast," he announced as Frances entered the bedroom with a tray, beautifully prepared with one of the embroidered lace cloths from the kitchen drawer he had emptied the night before, a flowered China plate with a boiled egg and bread and butter on it, a small teapot, milk jug, cup and saucer and a single pink rose in a small crystal vase.

His heart warmed as he saw a small smile appear on the corners of her mouth, a mouth he remembered kissing for the very first time almost ten years ago.

How time flew. He had wasted almost eight years not being able to kiss that beautiful mouth.

He remembered asking her if he could kiss her, something he had never, ever done before with anyone. The softness of that kiss, that very first kiss, its sweetness and gentleness was how Charlie had always imagined a first kiss should be. For him, despite the many that had gone before, it was his first kiss of love and it had exceeded all he had ever read or sang about.

Rosie tried to push herself up to receive the breakfast tray, but she was weak, especially so in the mornings. Charlie helped her and noticed that, as always, she looked to the left to see the sea from the bedroom window.

"How are you feeling today?" Charlie asked.

Followed by Frances, "And how did you sleep?"

"According to your smarty pants daughter…" Charlie continued, "that is a very silly question because everyone knows how you sleep. You just close your eyes and dream and then wake up in the morning. I guess she's right?" He hoped this would spread the smile across her face, and it did.

"Where is she?" Rosie asked.

"She's out with Annie and Lou-Lou," he replied.

Rosie lifted her eyebrows and looked at him.

"So you and Annie have met already? I wish I had been there to witness that, and did Lou-Lou remember you?"

"Lou-Lou still loves me. She tried to hump my leg. Always thought it very weird that a female dog humps…is she bi do you think?" He grinned, "and Annie, she still hates me, but I'm sure it is just a veil for the love she holds for me."

"You delude yourself Charlie," she replied, smiling more as she imagined the encounter.

"Frances here had to step in and stop her from fawning all over me, didn't you Fran?"

"Step in and stop the petty one up-man-ship that was going on, and all in front of Neave," Frances answered, "I was not amused, and I don't want that every time you two meet," she continued still looking upset as she placed the breakfast tray on the bed.

Charlie winked at Rosie even though he felt he was going to break down again, seeing the pain she was in and how ill she looked.

"Breakfast in bed, to whom do I need to thank for this?" Rosie said, looking at them both.

"Actually, me," Charlie said, "Your favourite breakfast and Neave's too."

"Neave certainly seems to have made an impression on you Charlie, you have mentioned her twice already," she said softly, "and if you have made this breakfast, I am left wondering if you have something you need to confess or say sorry for," she continued hoping to keep the mood light.

She wanted her remaining time to be filled with more happiness and she was so pleased that she and Charlie had just picked up their mick taking, tit for tat conversations of old like when they had first met. But she could see from the way the tears welled up in his eyes, and how quickly he looked away from her, that she had inadvertently stuck a sword into his guilt, opening the wound wide open.

She saw the self-loathing he was trying to hide in his reflection from the mirror over the sink. She decided she would pretend she had not seen it and continued, "A rose too! Well Charlie a rose and dippy eggs forgives all transgressions." She squeezed his arm to reassure him she held no grudges, that it mattered not he had not been there in the past, she was just happy he was with her now. The touch of him evoked so many feelings and she felt the excitement of him hit the pit of her stomach as it always used to.

She managed to eat about half of the breakfast and a full cup of tea with a collection of multi coloured pills that Frances counted out for her. He wanted to ask her so many questions, wanted the huge time gap to be filled in. He had nothing of real substance to fill his absence, music, Jake, Rocky his dog, women, which of course he wanted to erase from his mind, none were memorable enough to want to keep, and he asked himself how on earth he could have filled almost eight years with this nothingness thinking it happiness and fulfilment.

After Neave had left earlier, he had started asking Frances questions, and she had told him he needed to ask Rosie, but that he had to give her time, not let his need to know overshadow her desire to share with him. This was Rosie's time, and he needed to remember that, reminding him quite brutally that selfishness was ingrained into him and he needed to think twice before he spoke about anything to her.

He and Rosie had discussed selfishness and selflessness quite early in their relationship. Although he never denied he was selfish, he had argued that this was not always a bad thing, that sometimes you needed to think about yourself first. Rosie had struggled to accept this. It was the word selfish she had been concerned about.

After numerous discussions about it, she did accept he had a point in that taking care of ourselves is essential to have the ability to care for others. Without this, there might be a time when we could break and not be able to look after the ones we love. They had compromised on the definition and benefits of the word and created selfish with a small 's', the type that was needed to self-care for and look after ourselves, and then there was selfish with a huge capital 'S' that Charlie was much more at home with.

He looked at her, knowing full well she had never put herself before anyone, not even for a fraction of a second, because if she had, she might not be lying in front of him with the life being sucked out of her.

Rosie could see his head was not with them, so she squeezed his arm again as Frances continued to chatter about Neave. She could see he was reliving memories, and she did not want him to dwell on the sad ones. She needed his carefreeness and humour to distract her from the stranger within her.

Charlie smiled at her, blinking away the tears before they fell. They were opposites in every way. His dark features against the paleness of her, his selfishness against her selflessness, it was certainly true that opposites attract.

There was nothing Charlie saw within her that was mirrored in him, yet she was Ying to his Yang and this is why they fit so well together. Their life had been a living jigsaw puzzle made up of pieces that on their own were mis-shapes with no story to tell, but as they built their life together and connected more, a picture of harmony and perfection had started to emerge. It had been his actions that had stopped its completion and the happy ending was now lost forever.

They'd had many discussions about behaviours and values and she had brought out all that was good within him, prising it free with her questions, getting to parts of him he never knew existed. Love being the most surprising, but there were others too. He recalled her asking him about his values; they had been laid in the bed she was resting in now, snuggled up underneath the covers as it was a cold February morning. The memory was so strong he felt as though he was there now, living it again.

"I have no idea what you are talking about, the only value I know is the value of the money I have in the bank or in my wallet," he had teased, knowing this was the start of a conversation he was going to feel uncomfortable with and he needed to derail it before it went any further.

"They aren't values and you know that, Charlie."

"My values are love, life and sex," he had said, touching her tiny breasts, hoping to distract her. She had taken away his hand and kissed it.

"I can't deny that those things are important and wonderful," Rosie had answered.

"Even more so since you met me," he continued still trying to deflect the conversation.

"Values, Charlie," she was being persistent, "values are what guide our behaviours, influence how we think and what we do. They are the backbone of what is important to us."

"As I said, love, life and sex."

"OK then, if these are your guiding values, where did they come from? Who taught them to you? Your parents?"

How wrong she was, his parents had certainly not taught him anything about love, life, or sex that he would want to remember.

He seriously needed to curve the ball away from himself. He did not want to go anywhere near the memories of his childhood, upbringing and definitely not his parents. He was starting to feel uneasy.

"So Little Miss Philosophy, why don't you tell me about your guiding values and where they come from first? You know…you show me yours before I show you mine." He had smirked, trying to halt the huge ball of anxiousness that was growing in his stomach.

She ignored the innuendo and continued. "Values Charlie are picked up in our everyday life from people who are significant to us, like parents or teachers or friends. I think they leave an unconscious legacy with us. We often don't know they are there, and the impact of them can be good or not so good as we unconsciously make decisions led by them." She had said with a very serious look on her face.

"I'm not good with all this deep stuff Rosie, it's just not me, honestly I'm not that interested. People are just people and we either like them or we don't. You are the Queen of Hearts and everyone loves you. Doesn't that just get kind of boring or frustrating that you have to live up to that?"

"Whereas me, I don't share my life with many people, they know I'm just a here today gone tomorrow type, and they have no expectations of me so I don't carry that burden of responsibility of letting them down, it's a simple as that."

She persevered with the conversation.

"I'll give you an example. Aunt Fran always used to say...'A liar is as good as a thief' to me when I was little as I had this wide expanse of imagination that sometimes got carried over into real life as lies. She told me that telling a lie is actually stealing the truth. It is taking something from someone that isn't yours to take."

He felt her squeeze on his arm again, bringing him back from his memories to the here and now. He needed to shake free of all this reminiscing; it was taking time away from the present and the precious moments he had left with her.

"It looks like a beautiful September day today." Rosie said. "I love September. It reminds me of when we met Charlie. Such happy days. Do you remember when we first met on that beach?" She was smiling as she said it.

"How could I forget?" He said. "That day changed my life forever." He squeezed her hand. "I have never recovered from the trauma caused by being sexually MAN handled." He looked directly at Rosie to see if she remembered their second encounter too.

"Is this a conversation I need to hear?" Frances said. "I know I am quite open minded but I certainly don't need to hear any details about any sex with anybody on any beach at all!"

Rosie laughed. "Aunt Frances, you brought me up as 'no sex on the first date type of girl', so no stories to tell you and I wouldn't anyway.

They are mine and Charlie's memories, good memories, exciting memories," she continued, teasing her.

"I think I'm going to leave you two. There is probably too much information going to be shared for my ears," she said, collecting the breakfast tray as she prepared to leave the room.

"I want to go to the beach," Rosie said. Charlie and Frances look surprised and horrified.

"Stop looking at me like that," she continued. "I want to go to the beach, and I'd like Charlie to take me."

"If you want fresh air, why don't you go into the garden? It is full of colour still and it is shielded from the sea breeze," Frances replied, imploring her with a look of deep concern.

Rosie shook her head. "I want to go to Mangata beach" was her answer.

"Well then, to the beach you will go," Charlie said. He could hear Fran sigh behind him as she opened the wardrobe, muttering about the need to keep warm.

As Frances helped Rosie dress, Charlie decided to leave the room. He knew every single curve and inch of her, but it had been such a long time since he had gazed up upon her naked body that he felt it was disrespectful for him to stay.

Or maybe it was the guilt or the Selfishness (big S) in him not being able to deal with the reality of seeing the shape and form he adored decimated by the cruelty of cancer. However, he could not avoid that reality as he put his arms under her knees and lifted her off the bed to carry her downstairs. He had tried to prepare himself for the difference in her, but as he lifted her, he was taken aback by her lightness; she felt no heavier than Neave when she had sat on his knee earlier that morning. She was wearing a long cotton, blue print dress, which was literally hanging off her frame, and a huge chunky pale blue woollen jumper on top, which he guessed she had chosen not just to keep her warm but to try to conceal just how frail and thin she had become.

She put her blue woolly arms around his shoulders and nestled her tiny face into his neck. He could feel her shallow breath on his skin and his legs nearly gave way as she ever so gently and softly kissed his face and whispered, "I'm so glad you're here. Let's go to Mangata."

The beach was only a short drive away. Rosie had the car window wide open, her head resting on her arms on the frame and her eyes closed as her soft fine hair blew back into the car.

"You okay?" he asked. "You don't feel sick or anything do you?"

"No, no sickness today," she said quietly. "I'm just feeling nature and a little more alive today because of it."

He reached over and stroked her hair. She looked back over her shoulders to look at him, and all he could see was the blueness of her eyes. He saw they were water filled, maybe tears from the coolness of the breeze in her face or sadness. He did not know; it did not matter. The only thing that mattered was that he was with her, they were together again.

It was only a few minutes before the car was driving into the car park that led to the beach. It was rarely used, and it was no surprise that there were no other cars there. The rough gravel was overgrown with weeds and sand grass that had self-seeded. The sea was hidden from view by a mound of earth and green grass, but the familiar sound and smell of the ocean filled the car as it came to a halt. Rosie shivered.

"Are you sure you are up to this?" Charlie asked, concerned.

She nodded and smiled at him. "I've been waiting for this day, Charlie boy," she replied, "for you and me to be back here."

Charlie got out of the car, went to the boot, and put the brightly coloured flowered rucksack that Aunt Frances had filled with fruit, yogurts, coffee, and juice onto his back. He had joked with her and asked her for some cake and scones, saying he was allergic to all that goodness and vitamins as it made his teeth itch.

Rosie had already opened the door to the car. Her sandaled feet were resting on the gravel by the time Charlie had closed the boot. She held her arms out to Charlie just like a child waiting to be picked up. She looked so very young and so very small. He lifted her from the seat and once again she nuzzled into his neck.

"I love your Charlie smell," she said. "Like clean T-shirts that have dried on the washing line."

Charlie remembered her smell too. Rose and jasmine consumed his senses as the wind flicked her long, wavy hair around his face during the short descent down onto the beach. She didn't look forward towards the sea, instead kept her head rested on his chest as he wove through the large clumps of grass, his

feet sinking into the deep sand. Even though she was feather light, he stumbled a few times, which made her giggle, which in turn made him laugh until he collapsed into the soft dunes with her laid on top of him.

"Don't try your witchy tricks on me again," he said brushing her hair from his face.

"Actually, I was thinking about sexually man handling you," she replied as she gently kissed him on the lips, stroking his hair the same way she had done in the café. "You seem to have some sand in your hair, George Michael," she teased. She felt herself already aching for the intimacy of his touch. He felt it too. The sexual energy between them had not waned. It felt like the first time. It had

181

always felt like the first time every time they had made love.

They lay there in each other's arms listening to the rhythmic breaths of the sea, inhaling and exhaling as waves licked the shore against the distant song of seagulls overhead, evoking feelings in both of them that had been buried away for such a long time.

She was the first one to break the silence as they watched the fluffy white clouds float by. "It fascinates me," she said, "to think that there are probably parts of this enormous coastline, maybe even this beach, that's never felt a human footstep."

"Wow Rosie, I always said you should write lyrics to songs. Where do these thoughts come from? You have such a great way with words. I loved your stories, the ones about Vikings and your mother. I loved listening to your voice, the way it changed as you became excited about a monster or a god from the sea. Your stories were the sweetest songs I ever heard and used to wish I could capture them, but no matter how much I replicated the words and added the notes, they never sounded the same."

"This place holds so many memories, since time began," she continued, "all of them lost to history. Stories of love, of happiness, fun, and stories of bloodshed and hardships too. There is always a balance to life Charlie, and for every good thing there is a counter challenge and it is up to us which side of the see-saw we want to sit on."

"There you go again," he said softly. "Keep talking to me Rosie, I have missed your voice. It brings me peace, it calms me.

When I was with you, when I am with you, I see the world differently. Words of songs that I sang in the past that had no meaning come to life and I feel their emotion. "

"I cried at films that until I met you were of no importance. And when you wrote to me, I swear I felt

your words before I read them. I have been existing in a grey world Rosie, in the pretence that it was full of colour and life."

"Well listen to you Charlie, that sounds like song words to me," she said. "I know we have things to talk about, I bet you have questions and I have things I need to say to you too, so we need to get them out of the way because you are back now and Charlie, I do not want us to dwell on what we missed, I just want us to enjoy this," she waved her hands towards the sea and back towards the land. "And us. I don't want the sadness to take hold Charlie, I want to enjoy what we have left." She shivered again as the sun hid behind one of the huge clouds that were gathering, exposing them both to the coldness of the north wind. He took a blanket from the rucksack and wrapped it around her shoulders, kissing the top of her head as he did so before he said,

"Coming back has opened up things I have hidden away and the fact that it is early September and the village is already preparing for Mabon is like déjà vu. It is quite overwhelming and then finding out about the fuckin' cancer. I am finding it difficult Rosie to even get my head around the shit stuff, never mind make space for us. I feel like I am being haunted by memories. It's not been 24 hours yet, and I have got almost eight years of you to catch up on."

He looked at her and felt heartache. But the male ego that had silently appeared and sat on his shoulder was starting to natter in his head. She had shared her life with someone else, someone she had also loved. Someone who had given her a child to love, something he had failed to do.

Naively, he had thought he had been her only love, and even though it was him she had called out to, to spend what was left of her life with, he couldn't stop the pool of jealously filling up inside him. Images of Rosie and this unknown person laying in the sand, and in her bed together. The other voice on his other shoulder was the voice of reality telling him it was his fault, that he always walked away from anything at all that he found difficult to deal with. She did not need to hear his ego talking, but she did need to hear his apology. He felt his stomach start to churn as he tried to speak. He had to say it; he had to own up to his own failings if he had any chance of giving her what she had just asked him for, what she deserved.

"I am sorry Rosie. I am sorry for leaving. I am sorry for being weak. I just couldn't cope and didn't know what to do, so I ran away," he sputtered out quickly.

"And you thought I did know what to do?" she replied, not accusingly, but really trying to understand

him. "You always seem to know what to do and what to say, and I just felt I was making things worse. I couldn't cope with all the sadness, the anger, not being able to understand why…" he stopped mid-sentence.

"Why what Charlie…why our son died?"

She had the strength to say what he was still unable to talk about. He thought he was going to throw up again, and he hid his head between his bent knees. He wanted to run away, but this time he knew that he could not.

"Say his name, Charlie, please say his name. It's Christopher. His name is Christopher Charles, your son, our son, named after my father and you Charlie," she softly said.

He had never felt so alone, even though she was with him, his shame of leaving her was consuming him. He shook his head. "I can't," was all he could say.

She sighed. "You amaze and disappoint me in equal amounts Charlie."

There it was out, the word, that word, 'disappoint' and it hit him like a fist on his chest. The one word his defences had never managed to deflect.

He heard his mother's words, "You are such a disappointment Charles," she almost had vomited the words at him, "Just like your father, a complete and utter disappointment."

His defence kicked in, "Yeah, that's me, a complete and utter fucking disappointment. You got me in one."

"Stop it Charlie, there you go again, just hearing half of what I said so you can choose to retreat right back into that anger bunker of yours. I also said you amaze me too, but I can't lie, and I hoped you would have been able to acknowledge our son's existence after all these years." She sounded sad.

She should have been angry, but there was only sadness and pity in her voice. She took hold of his hand.

He looked at her as he quietly said, "Christopher Charles Shafton." It felt like he wasn't saying the words. They were coming from someone else's mouth.

"Thank you," she replied softly.

"It's the first time I have spoken about him since I left. I could not accept that the lifeless little baby in the

tiny coffin was my son, the life we had made. He couldn't hear my voice anymore so I didn't need to say his name."

"I needed to hear your voice Charlie, but you stopped talking to me too. None of us know what happens after we leave this world, if we have spirit or presence, but I believe we do."

"This has brought me comfort. I have felt my mother with me all my life and I still feel Christopher too, Charlie. He was beautiful, he was ours for only a short time and I am still able to feel all the love he brought us. Over time, this has proved to be stronger than the sadness."

He did not reply. What could he say to her? He said the only thing he felt he could, and that was to repeat his son's name. He put his head on her stomach, wanting the memory of feeling the life she grew to return to him. She winced slightly as the weight of him was too much for her.

"I'm sorry," he said.

"That is enough sorries for today," she replied, running her fingers through his hair as he lifted his head and laid back on the warm sand.

"What did Aunt Fran pack for us Charlie, wine by any chance?" She needed to lighten the conversation. It had been a huge moment talking about Christopher so that it was no longer the elephant in the room. It was one of the things she knew she had to address, for him to acknowledge their son and the joy he had given them. There were other things too she needed to talk to him about, but not today. As he had said, he'd not been back 24 hours, and he was clearly struggling with a lot of internal feelings and demons from the past, as well as the shock of her illness.

"Sorry, no wine, coffee for me and fresh fruit juice, apparently no coffee for you."

"Cup of coffee it is then," she smiled. "Next time, sneak the wine."

They spent just over a couple of hours on Mangata beach, sometimes sat quietly just watching the waves, but mostly reliving the best bits of the time they had spent together.

He had even managed to speak about his initial fear when he had found out she was pregnant, and how that had turned to excitement and joy. As always, she was right and now he had spoken Christopher's name, the dam of denial he had built inside was giving way and he already felt his anger was starting to trickle away.

He was in awe of her. How could she not be angry with him? He was sure that if she had walked out on him, he could not be so forgiving. He watched her constantly, taking in every bit of her. The way she still tilted her head to one side when she was thinking. How the end of her nose turned up ever so slightly when she smiled and how she still evoked the desire in him. He wished they could make love one last time.

"I'm tired," Rosie said. It was almost 2 o'clock. "I need to go and rest before Neave gets back. But thank you Charlie. I did not think I would ever get back here. Maybe there will be time to come back, but if not, then I have the most wonderful memory that I will take with all my others into the next life."

He found it hard to hear her talk this way, but this wasn't about him, it was her time.

"Your carriage awaits, Queen of Hearts," he said as he lifted her from the protection of the dunes into his arms and carried her back up the hill to the car.

16

Christopher

"A borrowed life"

"I am still feeling the happiness we had on the beach Charlie. The afternoon sun has moved away from my window, but I can still see the sea and as I curl up in my bed, I can still feel your arms around me. I am drifting into the place again. I know each time I go there, it becomes harder to return. Its pull is getting stronger, but I am resisting it as I need my time with you. I wish I could share this with you and you too could experience its wonder and how this passage evokes gratitude and joy at being able to live my life again, albeit a snapshot.

Even those memories that at the time were sad, I am happy I can have them again and talking about Christopher has opened up an archway to our time with him. It is covered in incredible white lilies and I know this will take me back to the time when he was part of our lives. I am still aware of the pain I felt when he left us, pain like no other. Not even the pain I feel now as

my body is being taken away from me compares to that of losing a child. It feels like your heart is being ripped out.

I am back there, the morning I looked into his cot, seeing his tiny lifeless body, still and cold. I reach down and lift him up into my arms but this time I am not screaming and sobbing, crying out for help, I am gently rocking him, telling him I will be with him soon.

If I am honest with myself, I had sensed just the tiny thread of life he had been given. I hadn't understood its meaning until now. That same feeling is strong within me. I was also in denial as no mother wants to contemplate their child not living life beyond 17 weeks, 3 days and 4 hours. I ignored my instincts. If I had acknowledged them, I still could not have saved him and the 17 weeks, 3 days and 4 hours of love and joy we had together would have been stolen by the grief of knowing he would leave too soon. So again, I am grateful for my mind's ability to care for my wellbeing as it concealed the reality of truth to allow time to love and cherish our child.

I touch my stomach as memories of me carrying him flood back. Christopher was so strong whilst he lived inside of me, always kicking, impatient to leave

me, stretching his limbs in the womb, something I watch him doing now as I now see him newborn in your arms Charlie, a mass of black raven hair, just like yours.

Of all the generations of women in our bloodline, not one has ever given life to a boy, always girls, my mother, my grandmother, and those before her too. It is impossible to trace back our very first family name as names are only passed onto males, so ours was lost the day our ancestral mother died at the beginning of our time.

Maybe our ancestral father was a Viking god too. Growing a baby boy inside me was against the natural flow of who we are, but I feel privileged to be the first of us to have felt a son at my breast, even just for a short time.

We pass the seed of life on to our daughters, ensuring our bloodline continues, even if our name has been long forgotten. This I know will never cease until the earth decides it is time for its eternal sleep and every living thing is gone forever.

My daughter and future daughters of daughters will always have the wisdom that has been passed down over many generations.

This wisdom will continue to grow and be inherited by our babies, and the girls and women they will become. Much of this is not given through words and learning. It has become engrained in our DNA, intuition being its teacher. Charlie you called me your white witch and I have no doubt that many of my sisters of time were feared and cast out at best, but more likely burnt. Religion dictating what is wise and good over the natural evolution of my family as we were condemned as evil.

I do hope that in time, the human race stops being fearful and rejecting what they cannot understand. Learned knowledge and science is incredible. Every day our intellect expands our understanding of the world, finding ways to remove pain, suffering, cures to illness, but with logic comes dismissal of the things we do not yet have the means to comprehend because it can't be seen or measured scientifically.

Until the time comes when we can explain the unexplainable and truly accept the incredible power of our bodies and minds, I know my daughter and her daughters to come will never be truly valued, and the world will continue to be a far lesser place because of this.

I know I will connect with our son once more because he was a happy baby; he laughed and enjoyed his short life; he was loved and loved us back.

There had been no time for cynicism to develop loathing, anger, or jealousy and because of this, we will find each other again. I have no concept of the form or structure I will have after I go, but this is not important. I just know I will be connected again with Christopher and that is something that will ease my departure from you, Aunt Fran and, of course, my beautiful daughter Neave.

It is so important that I rid myself of any sadness or anger as I pass over so I do not leave a scar on the world I depart, a scar that will be a breeding ground for hatred and evil to take hold and spread chaos over the world I love so much. We have seen the consequences of too many scars on the world in dark times like the holocaust when one man's evil managed to spread so quickly it almost managed to permanently devour all the goodness we collectively had.

Wise people in our past knew about the importance of this, even though they could not explain it.

Giving last rites, encouraging the dying to ask forgiveness for their sins, renouncing evil was not just

for those leaving to enter a place of peace and goodness, it was to ensure they left no residual negative energy, to breed and multiply badness in the world they left behind - our world. And my dear Charlie, this is why you are here now with me so you can start to understand the damage and harm you will continue to harbour and pass onto the world if you do not change. I love you too much to let this happen because I need to know you will join Christopher and I in the afterlife when your time comes. I cannot leave knowing you will live a life full of unhappiness and rage. We have work to do and very little time left.

17

Mangata

"The night, the moon, the ocean"

That night was very warm and balmy. Charlie had gone to bed early, unusual for him, but he had felt exhausted, however he could not sleep. The attic seemed to have captured the heat from the day and stored it in his room. He opened the window. There was a full moon, a cloudless sky, and there was a calmness that only night time brings as the world starts to sleep. The only sound was the murmurs from the waves. He had an idea. He got dressed and tiptoed down the stairs into the kitchen and filled the empty rucksack that was still on the kitchen table with a bottle of red wine, two plastic tumblers, a half-eaten uncut loaf and a huge chunk of cheddar cheese, the only cheese that he could find in the fridge. With the rucksack on his back, he crept back upstairs, trying to remember which of the steps creaked so as to avoid it and not wake Frances or Neave.

Rosie was awake when he entered the bedroom, which surprised him. He put his finger to his lips to indicate to her to be quiet.

As always, the curtains were open and the moon lit the room. He took the blue jumper she had worn earlier from the chair and helped her put it on top of the cotton nightdress she was wearing.

"Where are we going?" she whispered.

"To Mangata," he replied.

The night air felt warmer than the day and there was absolutely no breeze, no sound of human life as he carried her to the car for the second time that day. He turned the ignition on and they waited for a moment to ensure that Frances hadn't woken before they set off for the short journey to the beach. They said nothing to each other, but her eyes were wide with excitement and her cheeks were once again tinged with pinkness instead of the greyness that had crept into her pallor. The sound of the waves was the only thing that could be heard as Charlie turned off the engine. It was as if the world had pressed pause and there was only the two of them on it. He carried her back down to the spot they had laid in earlier in the day and, before they sat down, they gazed out towards the horizon.

The moonlight was reflecting on the sea and the gentle movement from the ripples gave the illusion of thousands of fireflies dancing on a beautiful iridescent path of light.

"That is Mangata," Rosie whispered. "It is an old Scandinavian word that has no real translation. It means a path of light from the moon on water. There can be nowhere else on earth more magical than being here with you right now Charlie."

He sat her down on the cool sand, opened the rucksack and laid out the blanket he had taken from his bed. As he pulled out the wine and cheese, she laughed and it was the laugh he remembered so well, such a girlish laugh, so sweet. She looked so beautiful with moon beams dancing through her wispy hair. She really did look like an angel, just perfection. He saw no trace of the illness he knew was there, he just saw Rosie as she was almost ten years ago when she had captured his heart.

"Would it be ok if I kissed you?" he said, trying to smile and relive the moment, but in all honesty, he was nervous. She smiled and nodded. She still took his breath away. He stroked her hair so gently and caressed the contours of her face, before tilting her head to let the moonlight flood over her beautiful face as he kissed

her. It was a first kiss all over again, and he felt as though he was floating. His head was spinning. There had never been a more profound moment in his life, and he knew there would be nothing that would ever compare to this. Although he was selfish, he was a selfless and patient lover, and the intensity and passion that stirred inside them both did not affect the gentleness of his touch and her exquisite response.

Charlie did not feel her as she was now, but as she had been before her body had been stripped of its vitality.

Her skin remembered his touch and her heart quickened in anticipation of him, his kisses pausing temporarily as he lifted her clothes over her head and he gazed at her nakedness. Slender arms, tiny breasts and long elegant legs, her sex the same colour as her almost white hair.

He wanted to take all of her in so that he could always remember this night. She took his head in her hands and guided it to one of her nipples. He remembered how much she loved the way he caressed it with his tongue, the way he held it gently in his teeth before taking the whole of the breast into his mouth.

She moaned, her back arched as their excitement and anticipation of each other rose. He felt a little anxious, just like the first time when he had wanted it to be perfect, but this time it had to be beyond perfect.

His nervousness was unfounded as their bodies harmonised, just like a perfect waltz, moving together, breathing together, sharing intimacy together.

As always, he waited for his own pleasure so that he could look down on her and watch the buildup to that moment of complete and utter abandonment on her face. Her eyes were closed, her mouth was slightly opened, but tonight as her moans increased, he was unable to hold back and he joined her in her ecstasy just as she sighed a tiny cry of fulfilment, and whispered. "I love you Charlie," in his ear.

As they laid together in the sand dunes, Rosie thought this must be how her mother had felt in the arms of her Viking prince brought to her by Mangata, the moon beam path on the sea. She silently thanked the gods for bringing Charlie into her life, for their lightning the night he saw her face for the first time, for their life together, but most of all, for this night.

He stroked her back as she wrapped herself around him, the euphoria of their love making also tinged with sadness as they both knew this would be the very last time their bodies would unite. He looked at her and said, "I love you too Rosie, always and forever."

When he carried her back up the stairs to her bedroom, she was almost asleep, nuzzled into his neck, the scent of their lovemaking still on her. He laid her

on the bed, she turned to look out of the window and as he pulled the covers over her, she said, "Stay with me Charlie." There was something about those four words that broke his resolve not to cry again when he was with her. The tears silently fell on his face as he wrapped her in his arms, and with the sound of the distant sea, like a lullaby to children, they both fell asleep.

18

Daughter

"Purity, Innocence, And Beginning"

Frances opened Rosie's bedroom door as she did every morning before descending the stairs. It did not surprise her to see them both curled together fast asleep. She had heard them leave and return. Her first instinct was to stop them, but she knew her niece had very little time left and she could see what a difference Charlie had already made on her, on them all, in the past twenty-four hours. It felt like he had been back for weeks, the way they had all slipped back into familiar ways. Even Neave accepted his presence as though she had known him all her life. Neave had such a way about her that people just warmed to her. Her childhood innocence, coupled with an inquisitive mind and happy demeanour touched everyone she met.

As Frances passed Neave's bedroom door, she could hear her singing to herself. She had always been an early bird, just like all of them, not wanting to miss anything that the day might bring.

"Sshhh," Frances said as the little girl's face beamed when she entered her room. "Mummy is still sleeping. Let's get some breakfast and get ready to go to church without disturbing her." They tiptoed down the stairs, avoiding the creaking one, ate their breakfast, dressed, and it was only when the front door closed that the noise stirred Charlie from his sleep.

Rosie was curled up with her arms around him, and he could tell from the way she was breathing that she was still sound asleep. He slowly unfurled her arms, rolled over to the edge of the bed without disturbing her, pulled on his jeans and t-shirt and went downstairs to make a coffee. He thought it was still early as the house was quiet and he assumed Frances and Neave were still asleep. A note on the kitchen table explained they had gone to church, causing him to look at his watch, surprising him. It was 10.30.

It was an overcast day, the warmth of yesterday and the night forgotten to a cool Sunday morning. His mind played back the memory of their lovemaking on the beach and a tear fell down his face. It felt as though he had been back with her for much longer than the 36 hours he had actually been there. He returned to the bedroom with a pot of tea and two slabs of Frances's homemade date and walnut cake smothered in butter.

"Wakey, wakey queen of hearts, or rather sleeping beauty," Charlie whispered in her ear. A smile appeared on her face before she opened her eyes.

"I had this dream last night that I was laid in the dunes with a Viking prince who came to me on the path from the moon," she said. "Do you know anything about that?"

"Might do," he replied, gently kissing her neck. She put her arms around him and he pulled her up, propping the pillows so she could sit up.

"Tea and cake for breakfast, Frances is at church so I reckon you have about two hours to get as much crap down your neck as you can before the vitamin matron gets back and takes it all away," he said as he gave her a mug of tea and a slice of the cake.

"I need my tablets," she said. "Aunt Fran labels them up in little envelops with the days on. They are in the drawer in the bedside table." She looked very tired but had a radiance about her, almost an aura. He absolutely adored her.

"Last night was the best," Rosie said as she took hold of his hand.

"It was, but what did you expect from the lurrvvv god?" he replied. He was learning fast from her that if melancholy showed its face, it had to be thwarted, and the best way to do that was with their banter.

"I am so glad you are here Charlie. It is the place you belong," she said as she finished eating the cake. Her appetite seemed better today. "There is something I need to talk to you about," she continued. Charlie felt that familiar knot of anxiousness form in his stomach again.

"It's about Neave." He was sitting on the bed at her side. She stroked his arm. She used to do this when she had things to say that she knew he would find hard to hear. Charlie knew that by this action, the conversation was going to be a difficult one. He remembered she had done it in this bed when she had told him she was pregnant. She said she could measure the anxiousness inside him from the feel of him, the temperature of his skin, the way it tensed and how the hairs on his arm involuntary moved. He wanted to take control of the situation. He had decided after last night that he did not care if she had loved someone else, because he knew she would never have done that if he had not left. He had lost count of the women he had made love to.

He really did not want to know anything about the guy, as he also knew that once those images were in his head, they would stay there and mutate, and he just did not want that.

He had managed to silence the little green monster who had been on his shoulder the day before, and he was working hard to banishing him forever.

"Rosie, it doesn't matter. Honestly, I really don't need to know. In fact, I'd rather not. If I had stayed with you," he faltered, wondering how best to say it, "Well, you wouldn't have loved anyone else. I know that for sure. It isn't any of my business and I have no right to know who he is, who Neave's father is. If I had had any balls whatsoever, I would never have left and maybe I would have been lucky enough to have given you another child.

She is such a delight Rosie and I know that is because of you and Fran, but I guess her father must have been pretty special for you to have loved him."

She said nothing. He quietly sighed with slight relief. Maybe for once in his life he had managed to do the right thing and put her feelings before his own, although he did know he was better off without knowing any details of her other lover.

"You know him Charlie," he said very quietly. She was staring at him, taking in every twitch, breath, and motion of him. He felt himself stiffen, his breathing increase as she curled her fingers around his arm, as though pre-empting his gut instinct to flee. He could not look at her. He did not want to know. Why did she say that when he had asked her not to? Now his mind was racing as to who it could be. Maybe the bloke who had come into the café every weekend, he remembered teasing her about him, that she had a secret admirer, especially after a Valentine's card had been left on top of one of the bookshelves. She used to flirt with him without realising it was flirting.

Blokes always thought a friendly smile was an indication that they had a chance, and Charlie knew all too well the predatory nature of men; they would wait forever. As much as he could recall the guy was quiet, quite studious as he was always reading a book, but Charlie had wondered if he was just pretending to read as he knew Rosie would ask him about the book and that would engage them in conversation. It must be him, he was thinking, convincing himself of this when she said,

"It's you Charlie, it is you." His face went from apprehension to confusion in a fraction of a second. He was hearing something his mind could not comprehend

and too many questions were erupting for him to take in and make sense of what she had said. How could Neave be his child? He was recounting the years in his head. She was five, he left almost eight years ago. He just stared at her.

"I was pregnant when you left. I didn't know Charlie. She is tiny for her age, she was eight weeks premature and her little body hasn't caught up yet. I don't think it ever will. Everyone thinks she is younger, and I knew yesterday you hadn't realised she was yours."

"She is my child!" he said. "Mine? Oh, my god. My child!" He had stood up and was pacing the bedroom, running his hands through his hair. If there was a moment he would flee, this was it, and she had been dreading telling him. She needed him there until the end. She had seen the very same behaviour when he left before, and she hoped with every bit of hope left inside of her that he would not bolt again. He looked at the door, but he did not leave. He returned to the bed and took both her hands in his.

"I have a daughter," he said. "We have a daughter. Fucking hell, why didn't you tell me Rosie?" his question didn't come from anger and Rosie inwardly sighed with relief. The toll of telling him had drained

her of energy and the greyness he had seen in her when he first saw her yesterday had consumed her again.

———

208

He remembered Fran's words to not let his 'need to know' consume her right to tell.

"Rosie, we can talk about this later. You look tired and, to be honest, I just don't know what to say to you, I really don't." He pulled her to him and held her. He felt her tension go and her body relax a little and the wetness of her tears on his neck.

"I want to talk now Charlie, I need to do this now," she replied as she sat back and rested against the pillows.

"She was conceived the last time we made love before you left. Do you remember that time, Charlie?"

He did remember, and he put his head down as he did, the memory just too hard to look into her eyes and share. He nodded.

"It was the morning that Christopher left us," she said quietly. "We made love because he hadn't woken early for his feed, and you never got over the fact that if we hadn't been making love, we might have noticed he wasn't breathing, that we could have done something to save him. I have lived with that too Charlie, but I know that we could not have saved him and that many parents who lose a baby to cot death ask

themselves the very same thing, what could they have done differently, filling themselves with guilt. I know this is why you left. All you saw was guilt and shame when you looked at me after he had died."

"How on earth could I tell you that the moment our son died, we were making another child? What would that have done to you Charlie? You wouldn't have given her a chance to love you or you her. Y

ou would have seen the same guilt and shame in her, even resentfulness that she is living and Christopher died. She does not deserve that Charlie. And I loved you even though you left me, and I felt your hurt. I did not want to add to that pain. Why would anyone want to add to the pain of someone they love? You just would not have coped and you would have self-destructed."

"As I said in my letter, I have tried many times to write to you to tell you, to ask you to come back and give her a chance for you to love her, even give us another chance, but I never could. I did not want to spoil the life you had, and why would I even contemplate bringing you into her life if you might not have the capacity to love her? But then this," she pointed at her body, "and I knew the time had come and I had to take the risk for both your sakes."

She was exhausted, her voice was becoming a whisper, and her breathing was shallow and fast. She was not crying, and Charlie held his tears back. What should he do? What should he say? He just let the words flow without thinking or holding back, something that was incredibly scary for him.

"My sweet, sweet Rosie," he said as he held her. "I am so, so sorry. I am always sorry, I am sick of being sorry, but you, as always, fill me full of wonder and I yearn and pray to be just one ounce of the person you are. Neave is a credit to you. She is you through and through and I am thankful she resembles nothing of me. I need to be a better person and I promise with all the love I have in me for you that I will. I will become someone you will be proud of."

"I have always been proud that you are her father, Charlie. I remember what an amazing daddy you were to our son. She will need a daddy Charlie to help her through what is to come. She is so special Charlie, her capacity to understand and to empathise is well beyond her years. She carries my family's bloodline that goes back thousands of years. The gifts Kathleen passed onto me, the ones my grandmother passed onto her, will be Neave's. She will guide and support you in life with her intuition. Do not be afraid of it, trust her. I can see she has already touched your heart and this love will grow inside you until you burst with pride, like I

do when I see her now. She will show you who you are Charlie, and she will help you rid yourself once and for all, of the demons that have stolen you from the life you deserve."

Her voice was barely audible. He didn't really understand what she was saying about her bloodline and demons, maybe it was the drugs. It didn't matter, she had felt it important to share this with him. She had not only given him a second chance to be a father, she was trusting him with the most important thing in her life, Neave. But he also had a sense she was bestowing him the guardianship of something incredibly special, like Excalibur to Arthur. He felt overwhelmed by the belief she had in him. It far surpasses what he had in himself. He didn't understand a lot of what was happening in his life anymore. He just knew that, just as it had when he had first met her, his life would change beyond recognition once again.

Charlie held her until he felt her body give way to sleep, and then he watched her sleep, once again in absolute awe of her strength and her ability to love unconditionally without judgement or demand. He did not cry. Something inside of him had changed.

He felt as though he had at last become an adult. The needy child in him had grown up. He felt uncannily calm, he could not explain it, but for the first

time for as long as he could remember he did not feel angry. He felt as though he was where he should be. He realised that he had never felt the security of a home, that he had always felt displaced without even understanding what that felt like until now.

The feeling of being lost was going. He had a purpose that far exceeded his own needs. Once again, he had felt the magic of her, and he felt both humbled and grateful.

"Maybe you are my white witch Rosie," he said softly as he kissed her on her head before leaving her to sleep.

Frances returned from Church with a very talkative and excited Neave, who told Charlie she had made a stained glass window at Sunday School while Aunt Fran had been singing Jesus songs that were very lovely but not nearly as lovely as her window she had made from tissue paper. She said it was a gift for him for making her Mummy smile a lot. She proudly handed him a very intricate piece of child's art, which he felt even an adult would struggle to do better. He felt so proud of her, his daughter. He felt a warm glow of something inside of him and he just wanted to pick up this delightful child and hug her, which of course, he couldn't, not yet at least.

"Hold it up to the light Charlie, see how pretty it is," she said proudly. Charlie did as he was told. He was taken aback by its beauty, but also because he recognised what she had produced, a very large sun surrounded by an abundant harvest of barley. The detail was incredible.

"Wow, how good is this?" Charlie said, smiling back at her. "Where did you copy this from?"

"I didn't copy it from anywhere. It just came into my head, so I made it for you and it's yours to keep. You can put it on your bedroom wall if you like or on the window so that the sun can make pretty pictures to dance in your room. Can I go out in the garden Aunt Frances? Please, please, please, Charlie, can you come too?"

"I'll come and join you in a minute," Charlie replied as she ran out of the door leading to the garden, the sun had managed to melt away some of the clouds and the coolness of the morning was fading to the warmth of the afternoon.

"What's wrong Charlie, you look…well I am not sure what it is. Is it because Neave gave you her art?"

"It's that yes and the fact that she…she is my daughter," he replied. Frances put down the kettle she was just about to fill.

"So, you know then? When did Rosie tell you, or did you work it out for yourself?" she asked, looking at him to work out how he felt about it.

"She told me this morning."

"She did? How is she? She has been so worried about how you would react, and I have been too Charlie. You haven't got a good track record of dealing with things."

"No, I haven't, you are right." He was very calm and not what Frances had expected. In fact, he seemed far too calm, especially for Charlie, and she wondered if he was in shock. "And we have spoken about Christopher too," he continued.

"When you snook out at midnight and didn't come back until the early hours?" she asked.

"You heard us?"

214

"I hear every noise this house carries," she said. "I feel my bones are part of it."

"Well no, we spoke about it when we were on the beach yesterday. I need you to know I had no idea Rosie was pregnant when I left."

"It wouldn't have made any difference to you going Charlie, we all know that. I pleaded with her to tell you. I thought it might have brought you back, but Rosie was right in keeping it from you. The question is Charlie, what now? Are you going to be a father or just her Mummy's friend?" she was looking him straight in his eyes.

"I am her father. I will be the best I can be," was his reply.

"That is good to hear Charlie, no one can ask for more than that. I hope for that little one's sake that you can be the father Rosie believes you can be. It isn't easy bringing a child up, especially on your own and carrying huge grief at the same time, I can tell you."

"I know and so does Rosie, so do not underestimate how challenging it will be. The sacrifices you will have to make, the range of emotions you will have. But if you can do that, if you can always put her at the centre of your world, then she will bring you indescribable joy and happiness. Can you promise to do that Charlie, because if you cannot, then even though you know she is your daughter, she can never know you are her father. I am serious, Charlie, so help me God, you broke Rosie's heart and I will not allow you to do the same with Neave."

Charlie felt the force of her protection of those she loved, and of her fear that he would walk out again. Of course not now, he would have to be the most heartless person on the planet to do that. But she needed to hear him say that even when the pain of losing Rosie consumed him he would stay.

"Look Fran, I can't imagine just how much you must have, or even still do, hate, and loathe me. It can't be any more than I feel for myself, but I promise you on my love for Rosie, and you must know I have never stopped loving her, that I will be a father to Neave, and I will never walk out on her ever." There was a moment of silence when they both stared at each other, ensuring they both understood the gravity of what each was saying.

"OK then, I will put my trust and belief in you, just as Rosie has. I think I need a sherry," she said as she took a bottle off the kitchen dresser. Charlie could see her hands were shaking as she poured the liquid into two small glasses and said, "To Neave," as they downed its sweetness in one gulp.

"What was all that strangeness about the art, then?" Frances asked, shuddering as the sherry went down, "Was it because you were looking at your daughter for the first time as her father?"

216

"I was looking at her as her father, of course, but the design on it, it is the same design as the stained glass window at my home, well the place where I grew up, hardly a home. Honestly, it's unreal the similarity."

"She is a special little girl Charlie, I sometimes swear she can read my mind, feel what I feel. Maybe it's a design that is in lots of glass windows and she has seen it somewhere else, although it is not in our church."

Neave came running in, a bundle of energy with a handful of flowers held together by garden string.

"These are for you, Aunt Frances, because you looked worried. I could see you from the garden. I am going to make Mummy a special coloured window too," and with that Neave ran upstairs singing 'Jesus wants me for a sunbeam'.

"See what I mean?" Frances said, "Have another sherry."

19

Love and shadows

"Protector in the darkness"

I wake to the muffled sounds of my daughter's giggles. I don't know what time it is, but it must be getting quite late as the sun is casting long shadows of trees through my bedroom window. I am more tired as each day goes by and I know my days in this life are almost over. There is one more thing I need to do, and that is to tell my darling daughter I will not be with her to watch her grow into the wonderful woman I know she will become, but I do not know how to do this. The bond between mother and child is indescribable. It is unique, it is strong, it is fierce, it is warm and loving, encouraging, and enabling; endless words, but none can quite capture what it is, how it feels.

My sweet Neave, as I lay here unable to make out the exactness of your words, just the melody of your voice, I hear deeper tones interjecting that make you giggle, and I know Charlie is with you, your father. I am grateful I have been able to hear and feel this harmony.

It is the distant chatter of love, and it brings me peace until the sadness I store away when I am with you all breaks through in my moments of solace.

219

I opened my eyes today feeling happy and thankful I am still alive, but the sadness quickly consumes my gratefulness, knowing that very soon I will wake no more to hear my child's song or see the shimmer of the sea from my window. Today the tears are plentiful, a salty waterfall dropping onto the bed linen.

It is because of this destructive, relentless dark stranger, who I loathe and despise with every part of me, that all those I love are now together. The irony is that without his existence, my family would not be complete. I have always believed that for every good thing, there is a balance of its opposite, and today I am reminded of this. There is no death without life, no life without death, and I remember the words Charlie said to me many years ago that there is no real love without real pain and I feel both today.

I catch a glimpse of myself in the mirror. I hardly recognise the face that looks back at me. My brightness is being extinguished and the rosiness I was named after is barely visible. I pinch my cheeks to put the colour back just in time before I hear the sound of your feet on the stairs and you burst into my room.

"Mummy, Mummy," I hear you shout as you throw your arms around my neck, squeezing me, covering my face with kisses.

"Yuk Mummy, you don't taste very nice today," you say as you taste the saltiness from my tears and pull a funny face. I gently hold you to me to me so I can smell your hair and feel its softness tickling my face.

"You cheeky thing," I say. "So what do I usually taste of?"

"I don't really know, it's just a Mummy taste."

"It's probably because I've just been on an adventure."

"An adventure, that can't be right. You have been sleeping all day."

"I went on adventure, I really did. I took a small boat, and I went out to the sea so that I could see my reflection in the ocean, and I guess that's why you can taste saltiness from the sea air."

"How did you go on an adventure on a boat when you've been in bed?"

You snuggle into me. You always find a place where your tiny little body just moulds into mine. This

is how we always tell stories, and I have told you stories since life gave you to me. Even as a baby I would chatter away to you and you would always look deep into my eyes as though you understood everything. Words soothe you Neave.

I remember the moment you were born, your tiny, wrinkled face contorting as you adjusted to life on the outside of me.

I remember the feeling of euphoria and love that ignited when I heard your birth song, the sounds you made to let me know that you were alive and connected to me.

Yours was not the frightened, fearful noise of a cry, just gentle sounds, your song. The very first thing you saw when you opened your eyes was my face and when you looked into my eyes, you stretched out your arms.

The doctors say babies are born with an instinct of falling which is why they stretch out their arms, but yours wasn't out of the fear, you reached out to me and touched my heart. My memory tells me it felt like lightning and thunder, but maybe that was the defibrillator that brought me back to you and I was gifted seven years more of life to spend with you.

How do I tell you the story of what is to come Neave so that even when my physical presence in this

world comes to an end, you know my love and protection will remain with you always? I know that even when my body is gone, some part of me will always be with you, just as my mother has always been with me. For the first time since you were born, I am uncertain about what to do. The dilemma I face is that as soon as I find a way to tell you, I steal away from you precious days of innocence and happiness and replace them with bewilderment, sadness, and uncertainty. I cannot bear the thought of extinguishing your giggles and smiles, so I have held on as long as I have been able to, but I know that time has arrived.

"So Mummy," you say, interrupting my thoughts. "Tell me an adventure." I see you smile when Charlie comes into the bedroom and brings us tea, milk, and cake. Charlie sees me wince in pain as you snuggle into me.

"Let's put this cushion at the side of Mummy so you can lay on that Neave," Charlie says.

"I don't want to because I can't feel Mummy and smell her."

I hear the conversation, but it is distant, as though I am disconnected from my body and floating in the room, looking down on you both. I concentrate on bringing myself back and hear myself say, "My bones

hurt today Neave, that's all sweetie. Let's tuck this cushion right under my arm against my chest then we will still be able to cuddle and I'll still be able to kiss the top of your head, is that OK?"

"You are poorly too much Mummy. When will you get better?"

I shoot a glance at Charlie and he sees the anguish in my eyes, knowing I have to tell her. He closes his eyes and turns away to hide his sadness, and makes excuses to leave. My eyes meet his as he is leaving and without any words spoken, I can see they are whispering 'I love you' and this gives me some strength to find the words for my daughter.

Alone and searching for ways to start the conversation no mother wants to have with her child, I feel the peculiar feeling that I am not in my own body returning.

The potency from the darkness of the stranger in me is gripping my heart and pushing down on my lungs. I close my eyes and inwardly and silently scream and plead with to him to give me more time, but I know he is not listening to me. His final act of wickedness is to take me when I am with you, my daughter, to punish me for fighting him. He is strong today and I feel myself being pulled to a place I do not

know that I haven't visited in my dreams. I feel I am in the eye of a tornado of colours. I am not afraid. It is a beautiful place and I feel the physical pain I carry start to disappear. Calmness fills the places the pain has occupied. I have no strength left and I know my time is ending, but then I hear it, just like a lark in early springtime, the distinctive call, my child's song, your voice Neave whispering my name over and over again. It becomes louder and I feel myself coming back to you. I can smell you Neave, you smell like the summer sweet pea flowers in our garden. The essence of my daughter is far stronger than the stranger's darkness and he will not have me today. You, my sweet pea, have given me what he tries to take from me…time and love.

"Mummy, Mummy, Mummy," I am back with you Neave. I feel my fingers squeeze your hand.

"I thought you had gone back to sleep. Will you tell me the story please?"

The little kisses you are covering my face with, once again breathe life back into me and I open my eyes and look into yours. I lift my arms so I can wrap them round you.

They feel so heavy. How can they be so heavy when there's nothing left of them, no flesh, just skin and bone? I hold you tight and even though the pain is

acute. I want to remember this pain as it is probably the last time I will have the strength to hold you, my beloved child.

I do not know how to start a story that ends with my ending. I have to trust my instincts to tell it the way it needs to be told.

"Close your eyes Neave and feel the sunshine from the window on your face. Can you feel it? It feels a little bit like the kisses you put on my face. Now imagine we are laid in a lovely boat. The boat is full of cushions and we have our eyes closed and the sunshine on our faces. Can you feel that?" You nod.

"This is a magic boat. It is a bit like Aladdin's magic carpet and it can take us anywhere we want. But this boat is more special than the carpet because it takes us back into our memories. Memories are the things we remember from the things we have done. But that's not all, because this boat makes memories feel real and we can smell, and taste and touch and hear everything as though we have magically gone back into the memory and we are living it again. Imagine Neave that you have your favourite chocolate with you, those buttons that are covered in the hundreds and thousands of coloured candies. Imagine you are putting them in your mouth and tasting how delicious they are."

"I can really taste them Mummy, this is a really good magic boat," you say.

"This is the special place you can always go to if you want to remember any special times we have had. You will always be able to find me here Neave, even when I have gone, this is where I will be and you can come visit me for cuddles and kisses and ask me anything at all."

"But I don't need to find you on the boat Mummy, I can just come to the bedroom and see you and when you are better, I can just shout Mummy and you will find me."

I feel my heart beat faster, my mouth is dry. I hold you as tight as my arms can and I push back my tears.

"Everything ends Neave, stories end, the flowers in the garden lose their petals and the leaves fall from the trees and end. Can you remember when Timmy, our little white mouse, ended? One morning he just didn't wake up, and we buried him in the garden so that he could give back to the earth all of his goodness because he didn't need it anymore. People too end, if we didn't, there wouldn't be any room for all the babies that are born."

"Are you going to end?" you ask very quietly, I feel the uneasiness in you, the fear that is creeping in.

"Yes, I am going to end Neave and I will end soon." I can hardly say the words. You are quiet and perfectly still.

"Your beginning was right here in my tummy, and my beginning was in my mummy's tummy. My mummy ended just after she made me. She wasn't with me when I grew up to tuck me in at night or read me stories, but I feel her in my heart. I am part of her because she grew me inside of her.

226

Whenever I feel sad, I touch my heart, close my eyes, and imagine her hugging me and I feel better."

"That is why Neave that when we are here, we need to enjoy life, have fun, be happy, explore everything and be kind to people as we aren't here forever. But endings aren't sad Neave, it is just the end of a person's story, their adventure has finished, but other people's stories carry on. If we miss people who have ended, we can see them in our dreams and imagination and that is why I am sharing my special place with you, my boat, so that when I end you can still come and see me and you can remember all the lovely things we have done and you can ask me anything is if I was still with you."

I can hear you starting to sob very quietly and gently and I know I need to keep my tears from falling.

"You are my sweet pea, and you are a very special little girl Neave. You will always feel me with you, and when I am not here anymore Aunt Frances will still look after you and Charlie too. He is going to stay because he loves you very much." I hesitate, wondering whether I should tell you he is your father, but you make my mind up for me as you say.

"But you are my Mummy and that is why you love me," I can hardly hear your words through your sobs. "Charlie is only my friend, he can't love me. I don't want you to go Mummy, please don't go."

I cannot hold the tears back.

"I am not choosing to go Neave, it is just that my time has run out. I would never leave you if I had a choice. And I need to tell you something else too, something very lovely that I know will make you happy." Am I doing the right thing, should I tell you my daughter…

"Charlie is not just your friend, he is your daddy," I whisper in your ear. The words are said and cannot be recanted. The toil of our conversation is absorbing my energy. I need to reassure you now, this very moment as I do not know if I will have the strength tomorrow to finish this.

I sense you trying to understand what I am saying.

"Daddies are with you when you are a baby. Janie's daddy has always been with her and Rachel's too, so he can't be my daddy, because he hasn't been with us forever like their daddies have."

I can hear the angst in your voice, and I feel I have made a mistake telling you. I over estimate you Neave, because you show so much more emotional maturity than the majority of adults I know and sometimes forget that you are still only seven. What can I do? I cannot undo the words that I have spoken.

"He lives a long way away Neave and I didn't know where he lived, so I couldn't tell him when you were born. I told him yesterday when we went to the beach that he is your daddy and he was so happy, and he will be with you always."

"I don't just want Charlie daddy though, I want you too."

I have run out of words to say to you Neave. I feel the guilt of dying, something you never think about when you have life. I kiss your head and hold you until your sobs subside and I feel your body go limp as you fall asleep.

I fall into a deep sleep too, and I see the stranger in

the shadows of my being. I am weak and very vulnerable, and I prepare myself for his darkness to envelop me, but he just stays in the shadows. I would like to think he has a tiny fragment of compassion, but I am not deceived. It is the strength of the love between us Neave that is my protector, at least for tonight.

20

Charles Henry Shafton

"Boy to Man"

Charlie and Frances spent two excruciating hours in silence. Frances was cleaning every cupboard in the kitchen to try to divert her thoughts and Rosie's anguish of telling Neave that her mummy was going to die. She wanted to hold them both and take away their sadness. She would gladly take Rosie's place if she could and let the cancer consume her ageing body instead of her Rosie's. Charlie paced the garden and the house with headphones on listening to music, but neither spoke to each other, they waited to hear movement from upstairs, Neave's voice, or her footsteps, but they heard nothing and at six thirty they both climbed the stairs and went into Rosie's bedroom.

If an artist could have captured on canvas the image of both Rosie and Neave curled up together fast asleep, it would have had pride of place in The Louvre. It was an exquisite vision of beauty and sereneness. It

took Charlie's breath away. Neave was Rosie's tiny double. Their porcelain skin, the white blonde hair falling over their faces.

The image reflected nothing of the sadness and difficulty of the conversation that had taken place. Charlie carried Neave to her bedroom. She opened her eyes and in a sleepy voice she said, "You are my daddy," before she fell asleep again.

He put her in bed, fully clothed. It had taken him by surprise, he had no idea Rosie was going to tell her. Frances had heard her say it to Charlie, and she touched his shoulder to acknowledge the words spoken.

"I'm going to stay with Rosie, so she has someone with her when she wakes. God knows where she got the strength from to tell her …" he still couldn't say the words, "to tell her she wouldn't be with us for much longer and then on top of that, that I am her dad," he whispered to Frances. It seemed to Frances that the last eight years of her life had been compressed into two days. It was surreal and exhausting.

"I'll bring you some food up Charlie. I think we all need a bit of space on our own tonight."

Over the next few days, Rosie's strength deteriorated rapidly. The doctor wanted her to go into hospital, but she was adamant that she wanted to stay at home and so a nurse was assigned to visiting daily. Neave was much quieter and when Frances tried to speak to her about Rosie, she just said she knew her mummy's end was coming and that Charlie was her daddy.

She would lay with Rosie or sit on Charlie's knee on the rocking chair that Rosie had spent much of her childhood on creating adventures about Vikings and their gods. Even Lou-Lou seemed to know that Rosie's time was ending. She no longer bounced into the house, barking and tail wagging, instead she spent much of her time calmly laid at Rosie's side.

Annie's acerbic attitude towards Charlie had gone too. They all tried to keep some happiness in the house for Rosie, but the sadness kept creeping in.

Frances, Charlie, and Annie took turns sitting with Rosie, and Neave stayed away from school to be with her. It was Neave who made Rosie smile the most; she played with her toys, told her mummy stories, and did lots of drawings whilst she was with her. It was beautiful to watch how mother and daughter were connected, and Frances was true in her assessment of

the child, in that she seemed to have an ability to just sense what was happening and how to respond. She seemed to have adjusted to the fact that Rosie would leave them soon, much better than anyone could have imagined. She continued to laugh, giggle, and sing when she was with Rosie. It was when she left her mother's presence that she was different, no skipping or singing in the hallway or playing on the swing in the garden. Although Rosie slept more than she was awake, she didn't seem to be in as much pain. Maybe it was the drugs the nurse administered daily or because she was surrounded by those who loved her and that was the only thing she wanted.

It was over these days that Charlie and Frances became much closer. Frances told Charlie about her childhood and more about her sister, Rosie's mother, and her parents. Charlie had always respected Frances but learning more about the sacrifices she had made to care for Kathleen and then Rosie brought home to Charlie how privileged his life had been in many ways, but barren in others. The saying 'Money doesn't buy you love' was so true. He had learned that it had been Frances who had telephoned his mother Arlene to ask for his address and how she had denied she knew where he lived, which was a lie, but Frances had called repeatedly and eventually Molly had given the address to her.

Frances also told him that Rosie had visited Arlene when she was pregnant with Neave, despite Frances advising against it. Rosie had returned very upset, said she did not want to discuss it and Frances had never asked her again about what had been said. Under normal circumstances Charlie would have probably lost his temper and called Arlene but whatever had been said between them, Rosie clearly did not want to discuss with him, otherwise she would have already told him, and so he had to let it go for the time being. But he was left with an image in his head that he could not shift of the coldness of an unfeeling Arlene and the warmth of Rosie in the same room. It upset him to think his own mother had shunned a woman pregnant, carrying her very own grandchild. But it did not surprise him, nor did it really surprise him that his own mother had known he had a child and had not bothered to contact or tell him.

Charlie told Frances about the day she had come to his boarding school, The Edmund School for Boys, to tell him his father had died. Stood there in the Head Master's office in her signature uniform of very old fashioned dark grey skirt suit, matching hat and gloves and flat brogue shoes, she looked straight out of a 1940s war movie. He had never seen her in anything colourful or casual, even when he was home during holiday times.

He knew her visit must have been something serious as she avoided him at all costs, so to make a special journey it had to have been important.

"Your father is dead Charles." Not even a 'Hello', or 'Sit down I have some bad news.' No compassion at all for a boy of fourteen who had lost the only person he had received any love from, the person who welcomed him home, took him to cricket matches, and encouraged his musical abilities.

Frances learned his father had left him a legacy. Charlie told her he had an annual income that had funded his musician life style. Albeit not an extravagant amount, he always knew that if he didn't have enough gigs to pay the rent, then he had his father's money to help. The inclusion of this in his will had really angered Arlene and to this day Charlie could not understand why, when she was so wealthy, that she begrudged him this. Their solicitor had insisted Charlie was at the opening of the will. He told Frances he vividly remembered the smell of polish from the gloomy dark wooden furniture in the office, and the words on the will that were read out to him by Mr John James Jameson.

"To my son Charles Henry Shafton. I leave the shares in my investments to be managed by J. J. Jameson et al. until he is 30 years of age when will be

given the investments in full. Until that date, dividends from these to be entrusted and distributed to so that he has the means and the freedom to explore and discover himself and find his future path in life."

He recalled how he had had felt her stiffen, her face contorted with disgust and John James Jameson asking her if she needed a glass of water or a sherry. He was eternally grateful to his father, as this meant he had had the means to break free of Arlene and live independently, pursuing his passion for music. His father had probably known that after he had died life in that house with his mother would have been horrendous for him, and Charlie knew that even if he hadn't had this legacy Arlene would have kicked him out at eighteen with no means whatsoever to maintain himself. He said he knew the wealth Arlene still had would not be left to him when eventually she died, although his mother had no other living relatives as far as Charlie knew.

However, he didn't want anything from her ever and she certainly did not deserve to enjoy the company of Neave, ever, not that she would ask for it.

Charlie just let the words flow as though he needed to get everything out, as if he wanted Frances to know all of him and his life history. Maybe sharing with her

he was anchoring himself to her and Neave, showing he would always be a part of their lives and that he wouldn't bolt again.

As they continued to share their life stories, Frances started to understand a little more about the man her niece had fallen in love with. She saw through his arrogant persona, a shield he had developed and held tight to protect himself from anyone getting close to him. He had never experienced love from his mother as a child, and this had certainly affected him. Frances could see there had been love between Charlie and his father, but an outdated social etiquette had prevented his father from demonstrably showing affection to his son. So very sad and emotionally harmful.

Until Rosie, the only other person Charlie had trusted and built a bond with, was Jake. Frances remembered Jake as the lanky, long-haired friend who always looked as though he was stuck in 1966, with his flared trousers and tie-dyed t-shirts. She was glad Charlie had someone else apart from Rosie that he was close to. She learned they had met in boarding school years ago. Frances could not comprehend why anyone would want to send their child away and miss all the special moments of watching them grow up, helping shape the adult they would become, but as she learned more about Charlie's parents she thought it was probably a godsend he had been there. She learned that his love for music had been fuelled by Jake and his father, who had owned a music recording business.

It had been Jake's father who had told Charlie he had the face, talent, and voice to become a 'rock star' after he had heard Jake and him in the recording studio at their house.

Charlie had spent the summer with them after his father had died, as Arlene had told him she would be in travelling in Europe the whole of the summer, such a heartless woman. Jake had asked his mother if Charlie could stay with them and Charlie told Frances he remembered how alive their family home felt compared to the indifference that filled the rooms at his.

Charlie had never seen his parents hold hands or even physically touch each other. There had always been a social distance between them. The first time he had seen a husband and wife showing affection to each other was that summer, and he remembered looking away with embarrassment when Jake's parents put their arms around each other and kissed. He thought this was true love, and it had affected him more than it had Jake when, because of his father's infidelity, they divorced.

Charlie said he hadn't been able to understand that if you had love like that, why you would throw it away.

He resolved he would never fall in love, denied love really existed, it was just a pretence and seeing how much Jake's mother had been devastated by his father's betrayal, he concluded it wasn't worth having even if it did exist.

Jake's father's business had eventually collapsed, probably due to his extravagant lifestyle and, although from very different upbringings, both Charlie and Jake had had to make their own way into adulthood without parental care and guidance. Jake and Charlie's friendship had been a surrogacy for parentage.

Frances saw the confusion hidden beneath the angry exterior on Charlie's face as he told her Arlene had always been unaffectionate towards him and his father, and he had assumed that was how all families lived until he had been introduced to Jake's. Arlene had never comforted him when he had fallen as an infant, nor played games. In fact, she had avoided conversations with him whenever she could.

He spoke of her class snobbery and how much he hated this, her dismissal of anyone whose family line, name and wealth were not on a par with hers.

According to Arlene, Jake's family was crude wealthy. They didn't have the finesse needed to become part of the elite rich classes whose fortunes had been passed down, and the fact his nouveau rich status came from the obscene world of 'pop music' increased her disdain for Jake even more. It was the final nail in the coffin on their strained relationship between mother and son when Charlie had told her he wanted to be a musician. She had told him to find somewhere else to live after he became eighteen. She wouldn't have the shame of him and 'pop music' at her home any longer. Frances just didn't get it. She had lost too many people in her life and that list was about to get longer, and no matter how she tried, she could not understand how a mother could treat a child like that.

Frances's view that Charlie was an arrogant, selfish, egotistical man was disintegrating, and in its place, she saw the lost, confused, and sad young boy that was still hiding in him.

The bonding that took place as a consequence of these conversations was building foundations that would help them through the devastation, pain and loss that was looming as each day passed.

21

Rosie

"Love, beauty, purity"

I spend most of my time asleep. The drugs affect any remaining sense of night and day I have left. It seems like weeks have passed since Charlie arrived, but my logic tells me otherwise. It is sound that brings me back from my deep sleeps, Neave's chatter and singing, I sense her with me even when I am not awake, and I hear Charlie's voice singing along with her. I smell Aunt Frances's soups and even though I cannot eat anything, she still tries to encourage my appetite. My body tells me I need no more nourishment. I have no hunger and no real desire to drink, but I do manage water occasionally.

This state of drifting must be nature's way of helping me to let go and accept the inevitability that my fight is almost over. Acknowledging this brings a calmness that bizarrely life has never given. It is an alluring peace, pulling me gently from everyone and everything I know. It is like falling asleep in the most comfortable bed when I am really tired and snuggling up, not wanting to wake from the slumber.

I no longer feel my pain, and in fact, stranger, I don't see you anymore lurking in the shadows of my dreams, although I know you are still there. I am aware your devourment has subsided as you do not need to work so hard as my body is now closing down.

Now I have reached this point of no return, and your presence is inconsequential, I have decided I will not acknowledge you again; you do not deserve the very last of me. That is reserved for those I love.

My time in this half way place is filled with beauty. It has no structure, just a presence of all the world's most beautiful gifts. I have never seen the aurora borealis, but I imagine this is what it looks like, a celestial ballet of light dancing round me. I walk through rainbows and reach out to touch shooting stars, and trail my hands through the clearest blue waters. I look behind me to see what I have left, but the image is the same as that in front. I realise I am too far down this path now to go back, but I still hear your voices, like lullabies and bird song. These will be my final words to you all and even though I know you cannot hear them, I hope and believe you will feel them in your hearts.

My beautiful, dearest, incredible daughter, I hope you know I will always be with you. You will become a strong young woman, a compassionate and caring soul. One day you will become a mother and you will also have the privilege of feeling the same depth of love that I have for you. Thank you, my sweet pea, for all you have given me. It has been an honour to be your mother.

The last seven years have given me such indescribable joy and pride. It has been you who has given me the strength to fight for the life I have had. I will always be with you. Be brave my child, life has much to give you. I love you so much.

Aunt Frances, there would never be enough time, nor words spoken, to describe the gratitude and love I have for you. You have given your life to us – me, my mother and now Neave.

You are the most unselfish, caring, and strong person I have ever known, and I am sorry that not only did my mother never have an opportunity to live the life she deserved, neither have you. You always say you would never change it for the world, but you were never afforded the choice.

My dearest Aunt, you are the guardian of our hearts, carer of our souls, and the centre of gravitation for our family. Thank you for your love, your strength and devotion. I do not fear my ending because you have given me the most wonderful life and taught me not to be afraid but to embrace everything life offers. Life now takes me to another place. I go there without fear but with gratitude for the life I was gifted. I leave knowing my daughter Neave is in your guardianship.

I do not worry about Neave's future life; she has your protective arms around her and your unconditional love to guide her and with that knowledge I have peace. I love you.

243

My darling Charlie, I know you are struggling and still feel overwhelmed with guilt. It is true we have had almost eight years of famine, without the nourishment of touch and richness of sharing of our lives together.

You cannot influence or change our past, it has gone, but you do have a choice about how you live your future life, and you have the insightfulness and love of our beautiful Neave as well as the wisdom and strength of Aunt Frances to help you find your way.

There is much for you to learn, not about being a father, this will come naturally to you, and I see that you are already bewitched by our daughter and have already opened up your heart to her.

You will learn more about who you really are, and the journey you will take will help you accept the things you cannot change and embrace the possibilities of what you can have – a happy, fulfilled, and wondrous life, even without me Charlie is in your grasp. You have Neave to help you; she is wise beyond her years; trust her instincts if you are uncertain or falter; look into her eyes when you need the strength to forgive; hold her tight when you feel your volcanic anger erupting, she will soften its impact; hold her hand when you feel lost, she will guide you. I will always be with you Charlie, in your heart and your soul and I dearly hope you will find your peace and acceptance.

In this magical place I travel through, I can bring forth any memory I choose to comfort me and cushion me into my next life, and right now I am looking into your beautiful green eyes and running my fingers through your soft dark curls, whispering in your ear that I love you, I forgive you, I believe in you.

The balance of life must always favour lightness over darkness; goodness, optimism, hope and love over selfishness, anger, and hate, so that when our physical body dies the energy and gift of life that is entrusted to us, can be returned with more vibrancy and power, ready to be passed onto the next living thing. This is the circle of life, the opportunity to give more than we take from Mother Earth when she bestows us life. She trusts us to look after her future. Charlie, I need you to find your place of peace and acceptance, for you to value and be grateful for what life is offering you. I need you to do this to not just to repay Mother Earth for what she has unconditionally given you, but so that when your ending comes, you can find my spirit and we can be together again.

My last wish is that you live your life without the darkness that has blinded you for so long, that you find love again because you so deserve this. It will not dilute what we have, it will only strengthen our connectivity in the afterlife. Pure love is all powerful regardless of where it comes from and the more we love, the more we see and feel the goodness in life and this has the power to overcome our darkness.

These are my last words to you in this life. I am feeling the last pull away from you all, and I know my time is finally ending. It has arrived and I feel myself drifting...

I have never feared death. From the moment we take our first breath of life, we know the inevitability of its arrival, that moment of silence, stillness, void of everything, everyone – flat lined.

But now that it is here, I hold on to every bit of life I have left so I can remember, everything, everyone, before I end.

My eyes can't see any more, yet they are full of colours, faces, moments, a kaleidoscope of memories focusing rapidly, then gone just as quickly. My life rewinding fast, so fast, no time to hold on to the images and memories, but I know they are forever etched within my soul.

The smell of freshly cut grass, egg and cress sandwiches, roast beef, new born life, our sweet, sweet lovemaking, and most of all, you… the taste of you Charlie.

I feel your lips upon my face, our last kisses, your soft caresses, the final touch.

My heart fights bravely and valiantly to keep me with you. It is beating so fast and echoing so loud within me that I cannot hear you, and for the first time I am fearful. Faster and faster, louder and louder, until the beat becomes one deafening, excruciating monotone.

And then it just stops, no warning or slowing…it just stops.

As the finality of me diminishes, I hear your voice whispering to me. The last words, "I love you Rosie." and as I empty of life, your voice fills the voids, before death takes hold, cushioning my journey from the life that I had, the life that I loved, onto the next.

Sound is the last thing to let go. I can still hear your sobs. I wish I could still feel the tears that I know are falling from your eyes, onto my face, still connecting us. Your voice fades, the cries are no more, I am already falling, and I know that all that I was has gone, and so has the structure and familiarity that the gift of life bestows.

Where and what am I?

22

Home

"Safe, belonging, peace"

The days after Rosie's death and up to the funeral seemed one long continuous nightmare from which there was no end. When he was awake, he felt lost, and he wandered silently round the house, remembering her, the way she'd sit cross-legged on the rug opposite him when they had their first summer together; the sound of her giggle. God, he loved that sound; it was always there, a distant sound in his ears. However, it was the last memory of her that invaded his sleep night after night as she slipped away from them. The image of her laying there, pale and fragile, her breathing so shallow.

He had held her hand and wrapped his fingers round her faint pulse to feel the last remaining life in her. The awful moment her breathing stopped, her heart must have beat furiously trying to keep her with them because in those last few moments, her weak pulse pounded so fast and intensely…and then just as suddenly, stopped.

He had kept hold of her hand waiting for a miracle to restart it, but if course it didn't and he had turned to Frances

249

and shook his head before placing his head on her quiet, still heart and sobbed.

They were like ghosts, him and Neave, drifting through each day without touching reality.

Neave slept in Rosie's bed and every morning Charlie would lay with her, holding her hand, window open, listening to the sea, feeling the warmth of the September morning sun on their faces. Neave would only wear her mother's clothes, so huge on her tiny frame. Frances thought she would have got used to the emptiness and deep pain after all losses she had lived through, but it just cut deeper.

The house was just full of sadness, it hung everywhere, and she thought it would never go. She busied herself cleaning, cooking, taking Lou-Lou for walks on the beach, but just like Charlie and Neave, she too felt void of anything except sadness. Even the funeral didn't bring any reprieve, no closure. The little church was full of all the people Rosie's beautiful spirit had touched in her short life. Jake had journeyed to be at his best friend's side, even bringing Rocky hoping they would snap him out of his melancholy, but he knew it would be a long time before the Charlie he knew would return, if ever at all.

Seeing him holding the hand of his daughter, the absolute image of her mother, he also knew that Charlie would never return to the life they shared.

He doubted music and song would ever be part of his life ever again. He was a man racked with guilt and torment, a man who felt his failings as a partner, a father, a man, would always rest in him as penance for his selfishness.

Jake hoped that being around Frances and Neave would bring some life back into him, but he feared for his friend. He had never seen anyone so broken.

It was six days after the cremation that Charlie took the call that Rosie's ashes were prepared for pick from the Funeral Directors Rawson and Sons.

Michael Rawson invited Charlie into a room where the urn containing Rosie's ashes was in the centre of a highly polished oak table, a royal blue box at its side. Michael had seen grief so many times before that, although he recognised the physicality of it, he had over the years become impervious to its emotion. He had learned to show sadness, to comfort relatives, to show compassion in his words and gestures, but it rarely touched him inside. He hadn't known Rosie that well, but the whole village knew her story, her mother dying in childbirth, the loss of her son to cot death, and the way the child's father abandoned her when she was pregnant. Even he had to admit it was a tragic story and he thought he would have to work hard not to show disgust and disdain for this Charlie bloke when he came to collect the ashes. But seeing the wreck of a man in front of him, he could not help but feel sympathy for him, something he hadn't felt for many years.

There were stories about Rosie that she had some sort of aged wisdom and powers passed onto her from Viking ancestors, all of which he had thought was just mumbo-jumbo. He had become a cold man, perhaps from the nature of his job, but at this moment he felt a warmth of spirit within him for the first time in years. It was probably seeing Charlie's pain, he concluded.

He touched Charlie's arm before, very gently, placing Rosie's urn into the silk lined blue box, putting the lid on, and handing it over to him. It seemed minutes passed before Charlie extended his arms to take her from him, and oddly, Michael felt a reluctance to let her go. He eased the situation by saying what he always said, "Be careful. You'll be surprised how heavy it is."

"That will be her huge heart," Charlie responded.

He took the box from Michael, held it close to his chest, and closed his eyes. Michael had witnessed this scene so many times. Relatives hanging onto hope that when the remains of their loved ones touched them, they would feel something of them, maybe a rush of love and comfort as though being reunited after a holiday apart. It was folly, this belief that after death, love still has an ability to reach out and physically connect. His business was death, and he knew death meant gone forever and it was only keepsakes and memories that remained. He waited for the painful realisation of nothingness that always came, to consume Charlie's face, add to his misery, like so many before him, but strangely, this did not happen.

Instead, the grooves and lines of tension and pain disappeared and as he softly smiled, he said, "I have you Rosie, I have you, always and forever. We are going home. Thank you, Michael for taking care of her" and with that he turned and left, leaving Michael perplexed at what he had seen and felt.

Strangely, the room felt very empty now the very small urn was no longer present. He shuddered and tried to tell himself it was nothing different to the hundreds of others who had temporarily resided there, but the sweat on his brow and the shake on his hands suggested not, as he quickly left the room and closed the door behind him.

23

Mangata Moon

"The magic of moonlight"

Having Rosie back in the house with them softened the rawness of their pain. The house felt brighter, warmer, less empty. Neave found the basket that Rosie used to use to collect flowers and berries in and lined it with the huge wool blue jumper that was her mother's favourite, the jumper Charlie had lifted from her minuscule frame when they had made love in the dunes. Assisted by Charlie, Neave placed the urn in it, and it was as though the child's light had just been turned up. She smiled at Charlie and Frances and said, "Mummy's home," before skipping into the garden humming a song, the first sign of any happiness since Rosie had died.

The basket held Rosie's essence, her unique smell, a mixture of roses and the sea. Neave would pick flowers from the garden every couple of days and place them round the urn. The basket had its own place at the side of the kitchen door during the day as it had been Rosie's favourite room. It led to the garden.

Depending on the weather, the kitchen or the garden was the place they used to sit every day over evening meal sharing what they had done, alongside tales and stories handed down over generations of Vikings and princesses, princes, and sea monsters.

In the evening, the basket went upstairs and was placed on the floor in Neave's room and Lou-Lou would curl up at the side of it, protecting them both.

Since bringing her home Charlie had seen her in the shadows of the house, heard her laughter and he was sure he had felt her touch on his face when he laid each night with Neave until she went to sleep, reassuring her that daddy would always be there. Memories of her grew stronger, he started to recall the ones he had locked away because they had been too painful – laying in the grass in the dunes, kissing her belly swollen with their son Christopher, the pride and overwhelming love he had felt when the midwife had handed him over and he felt his tiny little breaths on his face. As much as he welcomed the memories, they only served to compound his self-loathing. They were bittersweet.

Charlie had taken to sleeping in her room once Neave was settled back in her own. He took comfort from being surrounded by her things and the view from the window of the North Sea, where he watched the sunsets and sunrises. It was a sacred space where Rosie had spent her last few days in the living world.

He'd wake in the early hours and in moonlight his imagination would see her in the rocking chair feeding their son, singing sweet lullabies to him in a long lost language that even she didn't know where the words and melodies came from. Sometimes the harshness of his pain eased, but he willed it back as he felt he should always suffer for his selfishness. He was a non-believer of the afterlife and spirits, but he started to whisper to her before he slept, telling her what Neave had done, that he missed her and loved her so much, that he was sorry.

Autumn approached and the warm summer air was replaced by the chill from the sea, the days tuned into weeks, all pretty much the same as a sense of regularity took over their lives, a survival rather that living. He couldn't say normality had returned, as nothing was remotely normal without Rosie. Charlie functioned, helping round the house, filling in at the café that Annie was managing for them and trying as best he could to be happy when Neave was around.

Weekends were the best and worst time as he spent the full days with Neave, walking on the beach, Mangata beach. She seemed so content there, playing amongst the dunes, finding shells and debris that the tide had washed up. It was all treasure to Neave. She collected weather beaten rotting pieces of wood, shells, pieces of coloured glass that had been smoothed by the ocean over many years. She took them home and with the help of Fran, they made objects out of them, just like Rosie had done. They made strings of glass they hung at the side of Rosie's bedroom window that cast beautiful colours over the room when the sun shone.

One day she was sitting digging in the sand, whilst Charlie was doing what he always did, thinking about the times with Rosie on the beach, when he became aware that her chatter and singing had stopped. His heart skipped. Where was she? She always chattered. Panic set in.

"Neave...Neave, where are you?" He could feel the pressure on his chest as he started to run towards the ocean, thinking a wave might have taken her.

"I'm here Charlie Daddy, are you OK?"

The low winter sun blinded him as he looked towards the voice.

A small shape with wild hair blowing in the cold breeze was jumping up and down and it took him back to the first time he had met Rosie, the very same spot he had been laid in the dune. Relief and happiness flooded through him as he ran over to her and held her so tight.

"I couldn't hear you Neave, you always sing, and you stopped, and I thought I had lost you!" Tears were falling down his cheeks.

"I'm sorry Charlie Daddy," she replied, touching his cheek with her tiny hand, wiping his years away. "I have found treasure and I want to give it to you. I stopped singing because when I picked it up I heard Mummy's voice. She told me that I was a clever little girl and that I had to give the treasure to you."

Composing himself, Charlie calmly said, "Well what is this treasure then?" he ignored the comment about Rosie speaking to her.

"Look, it is proper treasure. I am going to ask Aunt Frances to make it into a pendant for you. This way you have something that Mummy helped me find just for you. She said to tell you that it will help you find your way."

Charlie looked at the object that Neave had put in his hand. It looked old, made out of iron. It was octagonal in shape and from each of the eight sides there was what resembled an arm, with a hand holding a heart in the centre. It was battered from time, but it was still clear what it was…eight hands holding a heart.

"Wow, this certainly looks like proper treasure Neave, maybe we should take it to the museum and see if anyone can tell us where it came from."

"It came from Mummy, and she says it is for you. Don't take it anywhere you've got to wear it always because it will take you home."

Charlie hugged Neave again and whispered in her ear,

"Thank you Neave, I will wear it always. You do understand that Mummy isn't with us anymore and that it is wonderful you still hear her, but it is your incredible imagination and memories holding onto her." She had spoken too many times about hearing Rosie, and Charlie was starting to get a little concerned.

"It's not imagination or memories, Charlie Daddy, I go to those in the boat that Mummy told me about before she left us. She talks to me every day now we have her back home with us. She tells me bedtime stories, sings to me when I am starting to feel sad and she always tells me to help you find your way home, but I don't really understand that as you are home with us. Maybe this is a map or a compass? That would be wonderful to go on an adventure with you."

It unnerved him, the thought that Neave was hearing voices, he had no idea what he should do and hoped that as time passed, the voices would stop. Yet he also yearned to have the faith that he too could hear Rosie each day. That night Aunt Fran threaded a leather lace through the pendant and Neave put it round his neck and made him promise to never take it off.

The coolness of October and November passed without Charlie feeling as though he had really lived a day since Rosie had died. It was all one long, painful existence that he knew he had to move on from. Winter had crept up on them and the coldness of the wind from the North Sea took your breath away, but despite this Charlie always left the bedroom curtains and window slightly open as she always did.

His nightmares did not haunt him every night as they had done before he had brought her ashes home, but he felt they should never leave him, to remind him always of his failings to her. He would always wish for them to be his companion in sleep, as he needed to suffer as she had done.

One very cold night, Charlie stood as he always did before sleep and looked out over the sea. It was a calm night with a full moon. His view of the sea was uninterrupted over the tops of the trees that had lost their summer leaves, giving clear sight to the huge expanse of water. There it was. It took his breath as he gazed in wonderment at the beauty of Mangata. He finally understood the magic of the stories that had been told by Rosie and her foremothers for centuries. Although he had seen this before when he had had a life with Rosie, he just hadn't felt the power of it until now.

He watched transfixed as reflection of the moon on the dark velvet water created an illusion of a silver bridge connecting the sea to shore – Mangata and he thought for a moment that he could see the image of a beautiful woman walking across the water towards the beach. This is the story Rosie had told him, how a Viking Prince had come to her mother from the sea, made love to her in the dunes and created her. He had laughed at her, but she was adamant that the story was true, and she wouldn't have him mocking her and her family's ancestors.

He thought he saw her shadow again, gliding across the luminous water moving towards the beach. He rubbed his eyes to clear the vision and when he opened them, a cloud had passed in front of the moon and taken Mangata and the illusion away.

He climbed into bed and pulled the quilt up over his shoulders. The night air was cold and he started to shiver.

Half-awake and asleep, he had the feeling that someone was with him in the room, and then he felt her hands run through the tangles of his hair. He felt her warm breath on the nape of his neck and he froze, unable to move. He held his breath. His imagination was in overdrive. Those damn stories. She was gone, it was his head tormenting him, taunting him, reminding him of what he had lost. But then she spoke. Her voice seemed to be everywhere, filling the room.

"Charlie. Do not be afraid, my love, I am here with you. I am always with you. I miss your touch. I miss laughing with you, but know that I am safe. I am at peace."

He turned and stared into the darkness, his heart beating so fast, his mouth so dry that as much as he tried to say her name, nothing came out. He sat up just as the cloud that had blackened the moon shifted and a soft white moon beam gently lit the room.

And there she was, sat on the side of the bed, his Rosie, silver and translucent in form, but it was her, she was smiling, she resembled the shimmering moon on the waves of Mangata. He gulped and managed to whisper, "Rosie…is that really you? Am I dreaming?"

"It's me," she said gently and reached out and touched his face. He closed his eyes as the tears started to well up.

"I have watched and waited until the Mangata moon came. It showed me the way back to you.

I have felt your pain, anguish, and guilt Charlie. I sense your deep and unconditional love and protection for our daughter, but I also know you feel lost and that anger of yours lays dormant just waiting to explode."

He reached out to touch her and although she wasn't of human skin and matter, he could feel the warmth and softness of her.

"How?" he asked.

"It is just the way it is Charlie. We can choose to stay for a little while in the in-between before our energy is returned to the universe if there are unsettled things that need our help. You need to find your peace Charlie. These feelings you have of guilt and unworthiness are just adding fuel to your anger and I am afraid Charlie that if you do not find a resolution to this, I might lose you to the dark side, forever lost to me and those who love you when yours and their endings arrive. You need to find your light. You have a deep kind heart capable of such love, but your anger is suffocating it and it will break you despite your promise to always be there for Neave. You just won't be able to endure the torment."

"I don't understand. I don't understand any of this. All I know is that you are here. I feel you as though the essence of you is running through my blood and my heart feels the comfort of you. Tell me what to do Rosie. Tell me what to do so that I can always have you with me.

Can you come back to us, this magic and power you get from your mother and her mother and the mothers of all time? Can you use it to come back to us?"

"That just isn't possible in the way you want it Charlie, and I can stay a little in the in-between for a while. I promise you we will be back together, but only if you find peace and rid the demons from you."

The tears were rolling down his face.

"But how Rosie? Please tell me how? I am lost without you. I feel like I am drifting, that I have no roots, no foundations."

"You gave me stability and unconditional love. I never had that before you and I threw it all away. I don't know what to do." He was sobbing. He felt her kisses on his face, the gentleness of her fingers as she wiped away his tears.

"You need to find who you really are Charlie, and connect with your kin, find your place of being. You have always felt lost, that you don't belong, and that is the cause of your anger, your instability, your vulnerability. That is all that I know. You need to start to trust your feelings, be led by your instincts and you will find your place, and this will bring you peace. I have to go now Charlie. It is hard to maintain this state for long, but I will stay with you on this journey for as long as I can, before I fade and Mother Earth asks me to give back my energy to her."

"Will I see you like this again? I need to Rosie, please."

"Even if you can't see me, you will feel me and remember that I will always live on within Neave. My ancestral spirit lives in her. Her instinct is strong, she has the strength of all of our mothers in her, far stronger than I ever had. Look to the treasure she gave you…it will guide you. I love you Charlie."

The image of her started to dissolve, particles drifting into the air. He tried to grab hold of it, hold onto her, but a cool wind blew into the room, capturing the tiny speckles of her in its force and just like that, she was gone. He clutched the pendant Neave had given him and called out her name, but all that was left was the quietness of the room and a moonbeam casting shadows where once she was.

24

In the Shadows of Life

"Watching, waiting, wishing"

This form that I have is hard to explain. A place that runs parallel to the living, in the shadows of life where I can sense you all, like watching a movie, and I watch the scenes unfold, but erratically and intermittently. I follow you all when I can and search for an opening, an opportunity to reach out to you. Mangata shone bright and brought me to you last night Charlie. I do not know how long I can maintain this state before I drift into the final place, but once again I am eternally grateful to Mother Earth for allowing me this time.

I have sensed how much sadness eats away at you all, that overpowers the love in our home, but this has to stop before it consumes you Charlie, you are dangerously on the edge of a life full of hate and anger and with whatever life form and energy that I am now, I will not allow that to happen. You are the guardian of our daughter. You need to find a path out of this…listen to me, be guided by love Charlie and you will find peace.

But hurry, my love, as I already feel myself drifting and the energy I use to be with you reduces my time. Look for the signs Charlie, and have the courage to follow the path.

25

Sons and Daughters

"We will always need love"

He had slept soundly and deeply for the first time in so long. He could hear Frances and Neave downstairs and Annie too. What time was it? It was his job to take Neave to school, he was failing already. He pulled on his joggers and ran downstairs just in time for Neave to throw her arms around him before Annie took her hand and left for school.

"That was a much needed sleep," Frances said as she handed him a coffee, "You look five years younger than yesterday Charlie, think you need a few more of them."

"I had a weird dream about Rosie. I swear she was sitting in the bed with me Fran. She told me to find who I was, where I'd come from otherwise…well otherwise I'm doomed and damned forever," he joked.

"It doesn't surprise me," she said. "After my mother died and then Kathleen, I used to have such vivid dreams about them. At times I couldn't tell if they were real or not, and they always left me with wise words that helped me through the dark times. So maybe take heed Charlie.

I have never really believed in all the spirit stuff that Kathleen and Rosie did, because I have never carried life in my body, and I have had to deal with the reality of loss."

"The one who is left behind has to hold everything together, keep going, and it is tough. Rosie believed life only gives you what you can manage, and I have been given a lot of life for sure. And you too Charlie, have so much life ahead of you and you have responsibilities now. From what you told me about your childhood, I know you want to be the best father you can to Neave, fill her life full of love. That so-called monster medusa mother of yours has a lot to answer for, but do not let her turn your heart into stone. Break free from her once and for all. I am sure she's the cause of all your bloody anger and maybe you have to go face her and your demons, to take control of them and not let them control you."

Charlie said very little, just listened to Frances and remembered what Rosie had said to him; follow the signs and maybe, just maybe, going back to see his mother might help to ease the volcanic anger, resentment, and confusion he felt about everything. He found himself unconsciously holding onto the pendant Neave had given him.

"I think you might be right Fran…I think that is what Rosie was telling me last night."

When Neave came home from school, Charlie told her he would be away for a day or two, that he had to go on a trip.

270

She howled and held onto him, sobbing, asking for him not to leave her, that she felt frightened he wouldn't come back. It was Frances who suggested they go together, that they make it an adventure. The idea didn't sit well with Charlie; he felt Arlene didn't deserve to set her eyes upon Neave. He knew the encounter wouldn't be pleasant, and he didn't want Neave to witness that. But he felt he had no choice as Neave became excited about her first trip with Daddy and Mummy, as she was insistent that Rosie's ashes came with them.

He also thought about what Rosie had said, that she would guide him and maybe he would control his feelings more if his daughter were with him. They would go Saturday. He reckoned it would take just over 3 hours to get there and they would do the round trip in a day if they set off early. He didn't think the conversation with his mother would be long and he knew he would want to get away from the place as soon after as the encounter as he could.

The week went fast, and he was pleased he had decided to go that weekend otherwise he might have ducked out of it. Frances had checked the weather and insisted they pack some overnight clothes and put blankets, drinks, and food in the car as snow had been forecast on the west of the country. The blankets and food were just in case they got stuck anywhere. Charlie could see the worry in her face as she hugged Neave tightly before the little girl climbed into the back of Charlie's car to sit alongside her beloved basket with her mother's ashes in.

Frances told Charlie to stay calm and concentrate on the road, whatever emotions his mother evoked in him. She said she just couldn't cope with any calls from the police to say her only two remaining loved ones had been in an accident.

The first hour or so of the journey was easy, with very little traffic on the roads and Neave fell asleep just after they had set off. She hadn't gone to bed until late the night before with the excitement about their journey, to help Charlie Daddy find his other home before this home. Music from the radio kept Charlie in good spirits and distracted him for a while from his dark thoughts, keeping his demons soothed. But the further behind Hefring was, the more his mind filled with questions...why was he an angry man? Why was he selfish? Maybe the root cause wasn't Arlene, maybe it was inherent in his makeup, in his DNA, that he was a monster.

Maybe his ancestors were descendants of Jack the Ripper or some other deviant, maybe less vicious because, despite his anger, he wasn't a violent man, well not physically anyway. He turned his hurt and anger inwards onto himself, not others.

He recalled images of his father and memories of them laughing came flooding In. He remembered the photos his father kept of them both, photos he kept locked away in the right-hand drawer of his desk in the study. Every time he was home from boarding school, they would take more photos, look at the old ones, and reminisce. It was their secret, hidden away from Arlene.

When he returned home from boarding school to attend his father's funeral, he had gone to the drawer to find the photos, but they had gone. He was so angry, in fact, this is the first time he recalled that volcano of anger erupt uncontrollably within him. He had shouted and screamed at Arlene to give them back to him, but she told him that his father was no longer part of their lives and any memories of him would be erased from her life. She said she had burned them. The rage he felt was indescribable, and it was Molly who had held him until his sobs stopped, took him downstairs to the kitchen and made him hot chocolate. He'd never really understood why Molly had remained the live-in cook, cleaner, nanny, whatever Arlene had wanted, Molly was there to make her life easy. He wondered if she was still alive; she had always seemed old to Charlie, even when he was a boy. Well, he'd find out very soon.

His thoughts returned to his father. Why had he married Arlene when clearly they were mis-matched, so very different? He hardly ever stood up for himself either. He let Arlene push him around, never said anything that was remotely unkind about her, never challenged her hurtful words or ways.

The more the memories came back, the more he thought his father resembled a robot when Arlene was around…the same conversations,

"How was your day dear?"

"How are you feeling, has your migraine gone?"

"Would you like to holiday this Summer?"

And no matter how much she spat her replies at him, if she even bothered to reply, he always smiled at her and said "Whatever you want my love" or something so equally benign.

Charlie certainly hadn't inherited his father's character for sure. He had felt betrayed when his father had agreed to Arlene's plans to send him to boarding school. He had questioned his father's love, but he came to the realisation that it was the fact he loved him so much that he agreed to her request.

Life at boarding school was much more enjoyable than time at home. He had learned about friendships, kinship, what it felt to be wanted, to be liked. It had actually been a great experience for Charlie. The strict disciplined life at home, where appearance and pretence were everything, was replaced by structure, respect and yes discipline, but not at the expense of fun, laughter, and care. It was here that Charlie has his first cigarette, his first spliff, heard rock and pop music in place of classical. Lazy days laid looking up at summer clouds discussing Slade, Free and Status Quo, swearing... He remembered how liberated he felt when he shouted FUCK OFF for the first time, it seemed to release the pressure cooker that continually brought his anger to the boil.

His first kiss, the subsequent discussion in the dormitories, whether you'd reached first base or second.

He suddenly felt an overwhelming surge of love for his father, as he remembered the sadness in his eyes every time he dropped him at school and said goodbye. Having Neave made him realise the strength of a father's love.

It all felt too much. He slammed on the brakes and put his head in his hands, questioning if he could make this journey, whether it would bring answers or just more pain. He felt her small arms around his neck as Neave lent over and hugged him.

"It's OK Charlie Daddy…Mummy has told me to tell you she is with us and it will be OK."

He wiped the tears welling up in his eyes on the sleeve of his jacket, smiled at Neave and nodded before turning the ignition on again.

Neave's chatter helped him focus. She was now sitting on the front seat in full flow.

"So, we are going to see your mummy Charlie Daddy? That means I have a grandma, doesn't it? Everyone at school has a grandma and grandpa…they have a daddy too and I always wondered where all my family was until you came to live with us. What is she like? I hope she likes me."

Charlie looked across at her innocent face and his gut instinct was to protect her from the wickedness of Arlene. He likened it to Snow White meeting her evil stepmother, he just hoped there would be a happy ending to his story, although he didn't hold out much hope.

He needed to put some reality into Neave's expectations, as he couldn't bear to see her disappointed face after she had met the witch.

"Yes, I hope we will meet my mother, that is, if she is at home." Arlene rarely left the house and he anticipated she would be at home. He should have called beforehand, but he knew he couldn't have done that, as she might have chosen to leave if she knew he was coming. He'd never called her mummy or even mum because she had never been one. She was just the body that he was unfortunate enough to have gestated in.

"Wow this is amazing...my mummy is going to meet your mummy. I think Mummy will like this." His stomach churned as he pictured Rosie's visit to Arlene when she returned home upset. His hatred of Arlene for hurting Rosie surpassed the loathing he had for her multifold. He could never forgive her for turning Rosie away.

"Not all mummies are as kind as yours Neave. Your mummy was a very special lady. I think she was the kindest and wisest, most beautiful person that ever lived. My mother, on the other hand was very different. Something is broken inside of her and she doesn't have an ocean of love to give, in fact, she is a bit like the Ice Queen in your story. She doesn't know how to be kind."

"So doesn't she love you Charlie Daddy? Mummies are made to love their babies and look after them, aren't they?"

He wanted to tell her that she was the most uncaring evil bitch in the world, because in his eyes and heart she was, but he knew he had to find a way to explain it better to Neave so she could try to fathom an explanation about why not all mothers behave in a motherly way.

"You know Neave, I actually don't know. She never cuddled me or helped me feel better when I was sad, so I guess I thought she didn't love me. And I think this is why I am sometimes very sad and angry. I think this is why your mummy has told us both that I need to go on a journey and find out if she does love me, but she just can't show it for some reason."

Neave remained silent for a while and he thought she was contemplating and deciphering the words he had said about mothers being different, but it was the other words that had stuck with her.

"So, Mummy speaks to you too? You said she told us both," she asked. "Does she tell you stories and help you feel better just before you go to sleep so you have good dreams not bad ones?"

Such a perceptive child, Charlie thought.

"She has spoken to me, but only once Neave, she told me she keeps her energies to speak to you. But it was her who told me to find my home as she thinks it will make me happy, not that I am unhappy with you and Aunt Fran, but to help me understand myself better.

I know that sounds like grownup talk and I do not expect you to understand, but I have to try."

"If it makes you happier Daddy, then we have to do it. Are we nearly there yet? I'm getting hungry and Aunt Fran said we couldn't eat her food on the way. It is there in case we get hungry on the way home."

It was almost 11 o'clock. They had made the trip from east to west in less than 4 hours, with only a short stop at a garage to fuel up and for Neave to have a toilet break. He was getting hungry too. The air had become distinctly cooler throughout the journey and there was a sense the snow was coming. Probably a good thing Fran had packed a bag. He wouldn't risk a 4 hour journey back at night if snow did fall. He became aware that he was clutching the steering wheel tighter, and it felt like there was a noose around his heart the closer he came to his past.

"I'm hungry too, let's find somewhere to eat before we visit shall we?" He felt the tightness ease a little as he put back the encounter with Arlene and he headed towards the little town of Hepton, about 5 miles away from his childhood home. It was a town he vaguely remembered visiting with his father when he was young.

Hepton had once been a thriving little town, a home for the wealthy Liverpudlian traders, bankers and merchants in the 18th and 19th centuries. Many of the houses were grand in their design, and it still had an air of wealth and class.

Today it was more of a town for visitors and for historians, but it remained the home for more wealthy people rather than the working classes.

The port of Liverpool used to be of great importance, bringing in all sorts of different spices, fruits, silks, just about anything, including people. Slavery is a slur on the western world and he did wonder if this was where his ancestors came from. Maybe his great, great, great, great grandfather had been a slave. Arlene was not only an upper class snob, she was also a true racist. If she had found out his father had black ancestors after they had married, this would explain her disdain for them both. She was such a hypocrite, she feigned compassion and care when she helped organise fund raisers for 'those poor ignorant people living in squalor' in other parts of the world. The more the memories came back, the more he hated her. He needed a pint to ease the volcano getting ready to erupt inside of him.

26

Iris

"Rainbow, wisdom and hope"

They parked up in the centre of the town. There was a busy Saturday market, and the pubs and cafés in the town square looked packed. Neave wanted to take her basket with Rosie in, but the urn was heavy and Charlie convinced her to leave it on the back seat, covered with the blankets Frances had given them to keep her warm. A reluctant Neave accepted, and they wove through the busy crowds, looking for somewhere to eat. Rosie held Charlie's hand very tightly, and he knew she was anxious. There were never crowds like this with people packed together at home. He decided to try the side streets away from the town centre. They were narrow cobbled streets that absorbed the sounds of the busy market, which seemed to help Neave relax a little. The sunlight didn't get through the streets and it felt much colder. Neave started to shiver just as Charlie saw a sign extending from the side of the building – The Bay Horse Inn. It was the place he used to come with his father, how weird they had found it, but uncannily, as he pushed open the weathered heavy green wooden door, he felt a sense of calm come over himself.

The smell of the old furniture and beer was so familiar.

A flashback image of his father stood at the end of the bar chatting away to working men, tired and dirty at the end of the day, and Charlie sat on a bar stool, with his bottle of dandelion and burdock, legs dangling brought a sudden rush of happiness. It seemed nothing had changed at all; the décor was the same, the tattered seats and stained tables remained. This was his father's bolt hole, his escape from the stifling world he endured with Arlene.

He stood for a while, just transfixed on the spot his father used to stand, and he could see his happy face, the lines where he smiled, heard his laugh as he joked with the men. He had forgotten his father like this, and it was such an incredible memory to have back. Maybe this trip might be worthwhile he thought to himself as they walked over to the bar.

"Good day to you both," a woman's voice greeted them. "What can I get you?"

"I'll have a pint of John Smith's please and a glass of orange for Neave here."

Neave waved at the woman behind the bar. "Can we have something to eat please too? We are really hungry. We have been in the car for ages and ages and we need some food before we go and see Daddy's mummy."

The woman smiled such a genuine homely smile at Neave and said, "My, my…a little chatterbox as well as a pretty little girl too. Of course you can. My name is Iris, what is yours?"

"I'm called Neave, and this is my Daddy Charlie. Do you live here too?"

Iris smiled at Charlie before returning her gaze to Neave. "Well Neave, that is a very beautiful name, and I think it is Irish, is it daddy… Charlie?" she asked.

"No idea actually, Neave's mother gave it to her, daddy wasn't around for a long time so I can't take much credit for Neave's name or any of her loveliness." Strangely, he didn't feel anxious saying this to the stout, middle-aged woman he had only met a few minutes ago. Guess he would have to get used to explaining his shame about being an absent father.

"Well, all that matters is that you are here now and have brought this little bit of sunshine to brighten up my rather gloomy bar. Look, you've brought its rays in with you," she continued, pointing at the wall where the sun had created a prism of colours as it streamed through the window, creating a rainbow on the dingy beige wall.

"You saying we are dreary Iris?" a deep voice joked from behind Charlie.

"Dreary no, a pain in the…" she stopped remembering Neave was close by.

"But we need the pain and darkness to make us appreciate the love and light, you know that George," she continued.

283

"You're digging a deeper hole there Iris," he laughed. "Ain't she lads?" A group of men sat with George the Pain, laughed and joined in the banter.

"Take a seat over there, away from this rabble, and pick something from the Food Board. We don't have an extensive menu but it's all home cooked food. I'll bring your drinks across and you can tell me what you fancy."

Charlie and Neave sat at the far end of the room. He felt very calm and at ease. Neave was chattering, but he wasn't really listening, he was preoccupied by the memories of his childhood that came flooding from the recess of his mind; people, scenarios, like watching an old black and white movie. The men that always sat in the same places, had the same beer, ate the same food; the banter, the jokes, the laughter, and most of all, the sound of his father laughing. His eyes welled up for the second time that day. What was happening to him?

"You ok dearie?" Iris's words, so full of what seemed like genuine concern.

"Erm, yes, yes, sorry, I have just realised I used to come here as a child with my father, and I am having loads of flashbacks."

Iris looked concerned, "Bad memories are best kept locked away."

"Not bad ones…I am not sure what is wrong with me today. My bloody eyes can't hold back tears. It is just that not a lot has changed in here and I could feel the old place's heartbeat as I walked in, the walls whispering conversations from long ago and such wonderful memories came flooding back to me."

"Lad, has anyone ever told you, you have a way with words? That is like poetry the way you spoke, a true gift. Maybe you should be a songwriter or poet." She touched Charlie's shoulder and continued, "There is something special about this place, I felt it too when me and my husband first walked in. We'd been looking for a tenancy in the area for a while and none of the places felt right to me. Jim thought I was mad when I decided this was the place. I know I should update it, but… I am just not ready to do that yet. Feels disrespectful for some reason."

Charlie felt part of something here. He felt connected to the woman stood in front of him, that he had known for all of 10 minutes, far more than he did his mother and his childhood home. He didn't understand, but he had given up trying to understand what was happening to him. Three months ago, he was a single musician, idling his days away, self-absorbed with his own importance, and now look at him… a father, his Rosie was dead and he was about to meet his mother.

"We are going to see Daddy's mummy today," Neave chirped in, "Daddy says she is like the Ice Queen and she is a bit broken.

She didn't love Daddy when he was little, and we are going to visit her to see if she loves him now." Charlie gently touched his daughter's face and smiled.

"No secrets here is there Neave?" he smiled, "Sorry you are getting my life story, but I am coming to realise you can't hide from your past because it eventually catches up with you. Just like King Canute, you can't hold back the tide, it engulfs you and either you sink or swim."

"Lad, if this place brings back happiness from a past that seems to me was filled with sadness, you can stay here as long as you want. We all have heaviness that weighs down on us, each of us wrestling with the decisions we have made with no understanding of why God handed us the life we have been given, the good and the not so good. But we have only this life and I try my hardest to not let the past steal from my today by dwelling on it, because a second, a minute, an hour, day, week spent with anger, hurt, sadness could have been full of joy and happiness," she nodded towards Neave as she said it.

"What is your tummy saying it wants to eat Neave?" she said, changing the subject matter, aware the child had been listening intently to their exchange.

"Fish fingers and chips please."

"And for you Charlie?"

He inhaled as though breathing in the oxygen of her words, "Pie, peas and chips please…I always had this when I came before…with mint sauce if you have it."

Iris smiled at Charlie. "Be about twenty minutes," she said as she turned and returned to the back of the bar.

"Daddy...where's your daddy?" She had clearly been listening to everything.

"With Mummy Neave. He died when I was little, not as little as you though. This place was the special place my daddy brought me, and I had forgotten just how happy I used to be when I spent time with him."

"He loved you then." It was more of a statement than a question. "That is good, because you had some love when you were a child, even if your mummy didn't have any in her to give you. Do you think someone put a spell on her to make her unkind? I think Mummy brought you here, don't you?"

She was so very wise this child, just as Rosie had told him. Maybe Arlene just didn't have any love in her as Neave had said, and you can't give something away you don't have. For a miniscule moment he felt sorry for her, living a life without love. Now he realised just how sad that was

Iris's thoughts were full of the troubled young man and his daughter sitting in her pub as she prepared their food.

He reminded her of her own son Adam, well in earlier years. He always had a troubled look on his face, never quite settled in with the world. No matter how much she tried to guide, support, and love him, he couldn't quite find peace.

Turned to drugs at an early age, cannabis, then the harder ones, until eventually heroin had him. It would always have him. Even though the past few years he'd been in prison for theft to feed his habit, which should take him off it, she knew drugs were smuggled into prison. It was hard to reconcile that when she went to see him, he looked more settled and at home there than ever he had done living in freedom, with choices and opportunity to shape his own life and future.

The reality of reality had always been too much for him. It wasn't that she had given up on him, she had just accepted she couldn't fix him with her love. He found accepting love so difficult; it was as though it stung him, and so he barricaded himself inside himself, with drugs as his nourishment. She was his mother and she would always love him, be there for him, but she had put a line in the sand and worked hard, so hard, not to feel the failure she had done for most of his life. Failure as his mother and his protector. Her son too had something broken in him, just as the child had said Charlie's mother had. She had done her best and all she could do was continue to be there for him and not let the sadness and disappointment for his lost and unlived life eat away at her, like a cancer. Jim, her husband, had gone from her too in a way. He had never visited Adam, written to him, or spoken to him since he had been sentenced three years ago, and they had just drifted apart. Even though he still lived with her, well he had his own bedroom above the pub, she knew he had a lover, someone who didn't remind him that he too had failed as a father.

Iris didn't feel lonely though. This place with its whispering walls, as Charlie had described, the warmth and friendships she had with the regular customers who shared their lives with her, filled the void that once was full of love from her kin.

She remembered she had found an envelope with lots of photographs in when she was sorting through old wage slips and other paperwork left by the past managers. She hadn't disposed of them when she found them, just left them as it seemed to Iris her that nothing had ever been taken away from the place and she wasn't the one who would start devouring it of its past by throwing the memories of the lives of people who had been there before. Her heart lifted as she wondered if the stash contained any of Charlie and his father. She would find them out whilst they were eating.

She watched, waiting for the moment they had finished their meal. She approached Charlie clutching the large brown envelope to her chest. The excitement and anticipation must have shown on her face as Charlie looked at her with a semi confused look.

"My turn to ask if you are OK now," he said.

"If you think I am interfering, just tell me to bugger off, but I remembered that I found a number of old photographs…" she paused for a moment as she held the envelope out to Charlie, "and I had a thought that perhaps there might be a photo of your dad amongst them.

If you don't want to look, that is OK, I just didn't want you to leave and disappear forever and me regret not showing them to you."

Charlie just stared at her. It seemed like a long stare to both of them when it was only moments and before he had a chance to say anything, Neave had pulled the envelope from Iris's grasp. In doing so, the tattered paper tore and the photographs fell onto the table.

"Sorry Daddy," Neave said, not sounding sorry at all as she shuffled through all the photos, that in the main were black and white and captured images of working men. Hard work, poverty and graft was etched into every groove and line on their faces, callouses and cuts on their hands and grime and dirt on their clothing. Some of the photos had names and dates on the back of them. As Neave continued to shuffle through them, he saw it. It stood out like a bright rainbow against a stormy sky. His father's name in beautifully written handwriting on the back of one of them. No date, just his name: Henry Joshua Shafton. He heard Rosie's whisper in his ear.

"Turn it over, Charlie, take the gift." He looked up at Iris as his hand plucked the photograph out of the pile. All she could see was a lost little boy desperate to find his father. As he turned it over, she saw the tension in his shoulders and arms subside and she knew that she had been right to share them with him.

"Your dad?" she asked, but she knew without asking. For the second time, she saw tears form in his eyes as he nodded.

"You've found my grandpa?" Neave shrieked with excitement, "Can I see him, please Daddy, please." Charlie put the photograph on the table and all three of them stared at the image of a very proper gentleman, in his three-piece suit, tie slightly loosened, looking to the right so you couldn't see his full face, but you could see he was smiling.

"He doesn't look like you Daddy, but he looks very kind. I bet I would have liked him. I think Mummy will be holding his hand now you have found him, so he never leaves us again."

Charlie took hold of her hand and said, "I am sure you are right Neave, and shall we thank Iris for being a detective and helping us find him?"

Iris looked at Charlie with sadness in her eyes and Charlie nodded as if reading her thoughts, yes Neave's mother had died. She put her hand over her mouth and turned away to stop either of them see the tears forming. Neave sensing her distress as she had a knack if always doing said, "It's OK Iris, Mummy still comes to talk to me and Daddy and so we still have her. It was her that brought us to you. What is grandpa looking at? He looks so happy. I think he's looking at that little boy drinking his pop."

Charlie and Iris looked at the photo and, sure enough, the observations of a very perceptive little girl took their eyes to a small boy in the photo, almost lost from view, leaning over a table with three men playing dominos.

"That's me." Charlie exclaimed, "I know that is me. I remember, I used to play dominos in here. My Dad used to tell me that I was the lucky one, because boys weren't allowed in the bar and I always used to win. Oh my God, fuck…" oblivious of his daughter at the side of him.

"I can't thank you enough Iris. I feel this hour I have spent here with you has given me the strength to go to see my mother after all these years and get some answers about my childhood." He then touched his right shoulder and whispered ever so quietly, "Thank you Rosie."

Neave continued to browse through the photos, looking for more photos of grandpa and Charlie.

"Who is this pretty lady?" she asked as she pulled out a photograph of a very young woman. It had been taken in a studio. It had the name of the studio on the back. T.J. Housley, Photographer, Kilmady, Ireland.

Underneath it had the words Brigid, sixteen years old. "Can I have it Iris, you said my name was from Ireland and this lady is from there, so I think I should have it. Please, please, please and she is so pretty."

Charlie observed the photo. It was older than the one of him and his father.

The woman had long dark curly hair, pulled up at the sides, held in by slides or combs. Long dark lashes, dressed in a very plain and simple dress."

"You can have any of the photos you want. Seems to me you have more claim on them than me," replied Iris.

Neave hugged Iris. It took her by surprise, but the rush of love and warmth that ran through her body from that simple hug meant as much to Iris as having a luck on the Premium Bonds. It had been many years since she had felt a child hug her.

"As much as I know I would prefer to spend the rest of the afternoon with you Iris, we need to be on our way. I'm not sure if it is the John Smith's, the pie, this place, the photos or meeting you that has quelled my anxiousness and given me a little calmness and confidence that I am doing the right thing going to see Arlene, my mother. So thank you from the bottom of my heart." Charlie said as Neave eased her little arms from around her large soft tummy.

Iris felt overwhelmed. Her life and existence meant something to someone. She didn't want them to leave either, but they weren't hers. She was grateful they had fleetingly touched her heart, and she had repaid that by helping him have the courage he needed for the visit to his mother.

"Come on Neave, we need to get going. Look at that sky. It looks like snow is coming and we need to get back home after our visit tonight."

Iris looked out of the window. The snow was certainly coming.

"How far away is home?" she asked

"Northumbria," Charlie replied.

"I don't think you will be making that journey today. Look, this place used to be a B&B. I have a room you can stay over in. I will make the beds up just in case you decide to wait until tomorrow. That journey across country can be treacherous, especially in winter."

Her heart beat a little faster at the thought of them coming back and staying over. Jim hardly ever slept there anymore and the chance of hearing a tiny voice in the morning, making breakfast for them, filled her full of joy.

"Thank you Iris. We might have to take you up on that."

Neave's ears, as always, heard everything.

"A sleep over with Iris...woohoo. And we can bring Mummy to sleep over too and meet you Iris, can't we Daddy?"

Iris was puzzled, she had presumed from the earlier exchange that Neave's mother had died.

"Of course Neave," Charlie replied.

"So sorry Iris but we have Neave's mum, my beautiful Rosie in the car with us...she is in a basket in an urn and before you think that is weird or unacceptable, it is only a few weeks since Rosie died and having her with us at the moment, takes away some of the pain. Do you mind? If so, we will find somewhere else."

"Who am I to comment on what is weird? Whatever brings happiness, peace, and comfort to folk, in my eyes, is

OK. We are open until eleven, so if you decide, which I hope you do, to stay over, just come back later. Even if we are closed, just knock on and I will let you in. I'd enjoy the company to be honest and the nosiness in me will be ever wondering how it went with your mother!"

27

Mother

"Giver of life and unconditional love"

It was nearly two o'clock by the time they were back in the car, journeying out of Hepton. The sky was heavy with snow and the temperature had dropped. Neave was in the back of the car talking away to herself, recounting the encounter with Iris to her mother. Charlie could see her little face through the mirror, and for a moment he saw Rosie, sat at the side of her, stroking her hair. She looked up and smiled at him. He glanced back to the road and when he looked again, she was gone. He wasn't spooked anymore, he just wished that she was with them more.

The closer they came to his family home, the more his head was full of thoughts about Arlene. Why didn't she love him, maybe she did but couldn't show it, but when he looked at his own daughter, a daughter he had only had in his life for a few short weeks and felt the uncontrollable rush of unconditional love and fierce protection of her, he just couldn't fathom why his mother could not love her own flesh and blood the same way. He had to know.

They were close. He could feel every part of his body stiffen as the car drove down Smithson Avenue, the memories of returning from boarding school filling his head. It was a wide road with leafless sycamore trees lining it.

It was getting dark, there was no-one around, the trees looked dead and he felt like he was driving straight into his own horror movie. The road was full of large, detached stone built houses, homes of wealthy people, people who, from memory, were very polite private people who never really connected with each other, or knew each other, unlike Hefring where the community was strong and the people were kind and supportive. The houses suddenly stopped and gave way to a long gravel pathway.

Neave looked up at a very weathered, dilapidated wooden sign and read out loud "The Chapelfield House. Is that your home Daddy?"

Charlie didn't reply and slowly drove the car up the driveway. A gentle right turn exposed the house to them. It was at the top of an incline it appeared to look down on them as they approached it.

"It was never a home Neave, it was just a house. Love makes homes and there is no love in this house."

"It looks a bit scary and very cold," said Neave, clutching the basket and the urn.

The heavy wrought-iron gates, that were now covered in rust, were open, which was a surprise. They had always been kept closed, keeping coldness in and life out. He eased off the accelerator and stopped the car in front of the house. He knew Arlene was home as a very old but immaculate dark green Jaguar MK2 was parked there. Her car. No turning back now. She might have already seen him approaching.

Despite his dislike of the place, it was a very grand house. A stone archway leading to double oak doors with two very large bay windows at either side.

They looked like the eyes and mouth of Medusa, the wild thick bare branches of honeysuckle that clutched to the stone arch that hadn't been pruned for years, resembled the snakes upon Medusa's head, and made Charlie physically shudder.

Directly above the two downstairs windows were two bedroom windows, equally as drab. In between them was the only bit of colour the house had. A long stained glass window. Even with the gloominess of the day, its vibrance and colour couldn't be subdued. Purple, blue, green, orange, red, yellow, all depicting a beautiful sunset against a hilltop. Just like the stained glass window Neave had created and given him. His father had told him the window was there to pay homage to the fact that the house had been built on the site of a chapel, where Vikings had converted to Christianity many years ago and a unified community had learned to live together.

His anxiety began to take hold again, weighing him down as though the house itself was falling down and crushing him. He felt arms around his neck, pushing away the darkness and heard Rosie whispering, "It's only a house. Your heart is stronger."

He looked up at the coloured glass window just as the sun broke through the clouds and a path of golden sunlight reflected from it and touched the steps that led to the door.

"Look Daddy, it is just like my stained glass window and like Mangata, but it's the sun. That must be Mummy telling us it is OK," Neave said excitedly as she jumped out of the car, climbed the three stone steps, reached the heavy door knocker and standing on her toes, she marked their arrival with three loud knocks before Charlie had chance to stop her. He took hold of her hand just as one of the wooden doors open.

The figure of a small old woman stood in the doorway, peering out at them with a confused look. Who would visit on a late winter Saturday afternoon? The silence was interrupted by a gasp from the woman in the hallway.

"Charles…is that you? Is that really you? It is," she answered her own questions. "I hardly recognised you. This is such a happy day. I never thought I would see you again."

She looked down at Neave, who had a huge smile on her face, feeling very happy and relieved that her grandma was no longer The Ice Queen she had been expecting.

300

The woman put her arms around Charlie and he hugged her back.

"Hello Grandma, I am Neave, I am so excited to meet you," and she too joined in the hug.

"Hi Molly," Charlie said, "Neave, this isn't your grandma, this is a lovely lady who helped to look after me when I was a boy. Molly, this is my daughter Neave."

Molly had her hands over her mouth, a mixture of shock and delight as she bent down slightly so that her eyes met Neave's and said, "Hello there Neave. I am very pleased to meet you," and then placed her hand on her head, gently stroking her hair.

"This is a complete surprise. Does Arlene know you are coming and just forgot to tell me? She's a little forgetful these days."

"No, sorry we didn't call, we were just, erm…in the neighbourhood and thought we'd drop by and introduce Arlene to her family," replied Charlie with a hint of sarcasm in his tone, which Molly heard but ignored.

"Mmm…well then you had better come in, it is cold outdoors, having said that it isn't much warmer in here as you well remember Charlie."

They followed her into a wide hallway, the walls were covered by dark oak panels and its unique smell evoked more memories. A huge staircase in the middle of the hall, a small landing where it curved back on itself to the upstairs.

The only light and colour in the room came from the blue, yellow and orange sunbeams that were on the stairs from the stained glass window, but they disappeared as the sun became hidden by clouds.

"Come into the parlour, there is a fire lit and I will get you some tea and biscuits. I will let Arlene know you are here. She was in the study reading, but I suspect she is asleep, otherwise she would be shouting out about who is visiting. Probably good that I tell her. No doubt it will be a surprise." Molly said as she looked up over the top of her glasses at Charlie as she spoke.

Molly left and Neave sat down on an armchair at the side of the open fire. The room was silent except for the sounds of the fire crackling and the ticktock of a clock on the mantelpiece. The faded green velvet curtains were open and the view out of the window was quite spectacular across open fields and woodland. He remembered how beautiful it was in the summer when colour filled the view. Hanging on the wall above the fireplace was a wedding photograph of Arlene and his father. She had taken away all memories of his dad after he had died, except this one.

"That is your daddy, isn't it? He looks nearly the same on our photo. Is that your mummy?"

He nodded. Arlene was dressed as usual in a smart suit, although this one was a pale colour. She had a hat with a small veil that had been lifted and rested on top, and they were both smiling. They looked so happy, in love. What had happened to her?

As the clock struck 2.45, the door opened and a very thin elderly woman entered. She was the opposite of Molly in every way. Molly was round and cuddly and had an aura of kindness and happiness, whereas the person who came into the room seemed to bring an icy chill with her. It might have been the cold from the hall, but Neave instantly knew it was The Ice Queen, her grandmother Arlene. That moment seemed as though it was on slow play as Charlie observed her walk into the room. She was even thinner than before, and had a fragility about her gait, but the steely disposition and rigidity of frame remained. She was like a mannequin, stiff, unfeeling, inhuman.

"Arlene," said Charlie to break to the awkwardness of the situation and aware that Neave was staring at them both, holding her breath.

"Charles," she almost spit the words out as though his name was poison in her mouth. "What brings you here?"

No… how are you? What has been happening in your life? Who is this little princess here? Absolutely no warmth whatsoever. He really shouldn't have been surprised, but he had been hopeful that when Molly had said her granddaughter was visiting, she might have melted a little bit. It was a red rag to a bull to him.

"Nice to see you too…mother," he spit the word out and continued, "How are you Charles, so lovely to see you after all this time, what's been happening to you these last 10 years…oh you have a daughter, how wonderful." His face was turning red as his anger rose.

"I do not approve of sarcasm, Charles, you know that."

"Yeah, I do remember there was nothing you did much approve of."

"Would you like to meet your granddaughter? This is Neave."

Neave forced a smile at Arlene, who said nothing but stared at her. Fortunately, the tenseness was interrupted by Molly as she pushed open the door with her backside carrying a tray with a pot of tea and biscuits.

"Nothing like a nice cup of tea to make everyone feel happy," she said, sensing the tension as she placed the tray down on the small table in the centre of the room.

"Please sit down Charles," Arlene said. It wasn't really a request, more of a demand. "It has been over ten years since I last saw you and you just turn up and expect to have a happy homecoming, I don't think so. The last words you screamed at me were that you despised me and you would never set foot in this house again. What reception did you expect?"

Molly could see the hatred in Charlie's eyes and she knew from days gone by that he would not be able to hold his tongue. She could see Neave going white and she looked as though she was going to cry.

"Neave, do you like to make buns? I am planning on baking today. Would you like to come with me and let the grownups have a talk? It'll be much more fun."

Neave nodded and Molly took hold of her hand and gave a disappointed look at both Charlie and Arlene. "Seems to me there is more than one child in this room," she muttered as she and Neave left, closing the door behind them.

Charlie knew Arlene would not concede and be the first one to start any civil conversation, and he needed to have this conversation with her. He could hear Rosie's voice in his head. "Don't take the bait, Charlie, you can do this." He felt his heart and breathing calm a little and said,

"I apologise, Arlene, I should have called beforehand…but you might have said no, or made sure you were out, and…well can we just be civil to each other for a short while at least, please?" He was surprised the words came out as they did. It wasn't easy for him to apologise to anyone, never mind her. It was Rosie, she was with him, and it gave him courage and calmness.

She sighed, sat in the chair that Neave had vacated, and in a slightly less aggressive manner said, "So why are you here Charles?"

He looked at the small old woman sat opposite him. She is my mother, he reminded himself. She must have some feeling and compassion. I need to find the words to ask her why she hates me. Rosie help me, he pleaded in his thoughts. He thought he would break into the harder conversation gently by firstly talking about Neave.

"You have a granddaughter, Arlene, and she has been really excited to meet you. Aren't you curious about that, who I fell in love with, who her mother is?"

"I know who her mother is. I could tell the moment I saw her. She is the image of her."

He felt as though a thunderbolt had hit him as an image of his Rosie, probably seated on the same sofa he was sitting on, pleading with her to tell her where he was, heavily pregnant, crying. Calm, Charlie, keep calm…he heard Rosie whisper to him.

"I know she came here Arlene, I know you couldn't find it in you to tell her where I was, a pregnant alone woman asking for help and your cold heart couldn't help her…"

"She found you though, didn't she? She didn't need my help. Where is she, and I will ask you once again, why are you here?"

"I am here now because I don't know where else to go. You should know it would be the last place I would ever come to and ask for something from you. Over the past three months my life has been turned inside out. Until three months ago I didn't even know I had a daughter I have missed out on seven years of her life and seven years of being a father, being a husband and now it is too late, because she is dead Arlene…SHE as you called her is dead, my Rosie fucking dead.

Twenty-seven years old and I watched death take her, her beautiful soul, her kindness and rob the most incredible little girl of her mother's unconditional love. But I guess that isn't something you can't even start to comprehend because you are loveless, you have never been my mother, but I need a mother now, I am lost and broken and I need to know why you didn't love me, because I need to make sure the thing that made me unlovable isn't still there. How can I keep my daughter's love if I am unlovable?"

Arlene said nothing, just looked at him.

"I left her Arlene, you know that I left her. I wasn't there for her. I deserted her. What sort of person can be that heartless? Do I get that from you? I didn't know she was carrying Neave, I just upped and left because it was easier than dealing with the pain and anger I had, because before Neave we had a son and he died too. I feel I am jinxed and those around me I hurt, and I just cannot do that to Neave. What is wrong with me? Rosie was the only person who ever loved me, I thought I was unlovable, and I was cold, just like you and incapable of love, but she showed me I did have the capacity to love and be loved and I walked away from it. What sort of nutter does that?" He was rambling, offloading thoughts that troubled him constantly. Tears were running down his face.

There was no compassion in her voice when she spoke, they were just words.

"She…Rosie, came to see me. You are right. At first I thought she was going to try to get money from me. It was

Molly who had pleaded with me to listen to her. She wanted to know about you. Why, as she said, you were like Jekyll and Hyde. She told me she had thought her love for you was enough to overcome your darkness."

Charlie was looking at her. He looked like a small lost boy desperate to be loved, and it affected her. She didn't want it to, but she felt sad for him.

Her voice was much softer when she spoke next.

"As I recall, she seemed a very gentle person, almost too gentle to be human. She told me you had left an angry man, that she was pregnant but she felt no malice towards you, she didn't want to add to your woes. She told me she knew the fear you would have of losing another child and that she didn't want to give you that. The cynicism in me couldn't really take in that someone could be that selfless, and if I am honest, I didn't like her for that. She pleaded with me to reach out to you, to help you work through the past and eradicate the demons in your head. She said she knew they were born here. She asked me why I didn't love you, said she couldn't understand how a mother couldn't love her child. I remember feeling angry at her selflessness. And just as she could not comprehend how a mother couldn't love her child, I could not comprehend how she could not feel hatred and anger when she had been deserted and wronged by you."

Charlie just listened. This was the most she had ever spoken to him. She was telling him about her feelings. She did actually have some.

308

He didn't like what he was hearing, and he was working hard to keep his rage down. Rosie was with him, helping him to listen with an open mind, not fill the space with his anger.

"Over the years, I have thought about her many times. I do not like how I behaved with her and how I felt. I think it was envy, envy that someone could love another person that much she could forgive you when she was hurting so much. I was incapable of that. I am sorry she has died Charles, I really mean that. I am sorry I didn't write to you to tell you she had visited. She kept asking me why I didn't love you and so I had to tell her…"

Charlie waited. He needed to hear why his mother couldn't love him. He felt nauseous, light-headed, wanted to scream, but he stayed composed.

"Did you tell her you didn't love me? Did you tell her why?" His mouth was dry. He could hardly get the words out.

"I told her I am not your mother." He heard the words, but he could not take in what they meant.

"What did you say?" he quietly said.

"I am not your mother Charles."

"What does that mean…do you mean you have disowned me, disinherited me?"

"No, I do not mean that. I am not your biological mother."

That was not what he had expected to hear. It felt like his whole childhood was fast forwarding in his head, momentary pauses when it stopped at a time when he had felt the coldness from her, and now it all made sense. She didn't love him, he wasn't her son. He had so many questions.

"Was I adopted? So, Dad wasn't my dad either? He loved me though, I am sure of it. Why did you adopt? Couldn't you have children?

Why did you choose me and why did you adopt me if you knew you couldn't love me? Who am I?"

Charlie was now on his feet, pacing the room. He could hear Rosie's voice telling him to take deep breaths, that he was safe, that he was loved. She loved him, Neave and Aunt Frances did.

"I am not your mother, but your father was your father?" she said very quietly with sadness.

"I still do not understand. Was Dad married before, did my mother die?"

"No, he wasn't married before. He was a philanderer. He was unfaithful to me. He took a whore whilst we were married." Any softness that had been in her voice before had been replaced with a hiss as she spat the words out in anger.

"Your father was lucky to have married me. There were plenty of suitors. But I loved him. I loved him with all of my heart." She looked up at the wedding photo and Charlies saw tears well up in her eyes.

"I loved him. I just could not abide all that fornication. I had no idea what it was all about. No-one ever spoke about it when I was young, what to expect. I hated it, all that..." screwed her face up as she spoke.

"My mother told me I had to be a good wife and grin and bear it. But I couldn't stand it and after we returned from our honeymoon, I told him I wasn't going to give him my body again. I hoped he wouldn't take lovers. I never asked. He was never angry with me and I couldn't understand that. He continued to tell me every day that he loved me until the day he died. But he brought shame to this house and I could never forgive him for that."

"I was that shame, wasn't I?"

"Yes, well, you were the result of the shame. They did that you know...all the young pretty things came over here from Ireland, flashed their wares to wealthy men and trapped them."

This all felt so unreal. He was in the middle of a film. This wasn't really happening, was it...maybe he was dreaming?

"You cannot imagine the embarrassment when he brought her home with you in her. Expected me to understand, to take her in."

"Who is my mother?" Charlie interrupted.

"I do not know, some Irish whore. I had to keep her here, hidden away in the attic until she had you. Your father convinced me to keep you, take you as our own. It meant we would have someone to inherit. He said it gave us a child without me having to do it again with me. He convinced me that I would learn to love you."

"What happened to her?"

"I shipped her back to Ireland with a tidy sum of money and told her never to come back."

"What was her name?"

"Mary, that is all I knew. I didn't want to know anything about her. I never spoke to her when she was here, I couldn't. She made your father laugh. I could hear them talking. I had to endure that. She made him happy, she gave him a child, all the things I couldn't do, and I was reminded of how much of a failed wife I was every day she was here.

I did try to love you, but every time I looked at you, I just saw her, your mother, and it became unbearable. I tried to forgive him, too, but I just couldn't and the more time passed, the more resentful I was of you. He loved you more than me.

My heart turned to stone to stop the pain and shame. I told no-one, not even my closest friends and family. I even went to live in Europe for a few months so that people couldn't see that I wasn't pregnant. I came home just before you were born. The secret was only known by me and your father, the doctor and Molly."

"You told Rosie all this?"

"Not all of it, but enough."

"Why didn't you tell me Rosie?" Charlie muttered.

"She said it was not her story to tell. She begged me to tell you, but I couldn't. I wouldn't be told by another woman what to do."

They were silent. Both were consumed by a tornado of thoughts, memories, and emotions, causing havoc with their feelings. Arlene broke the silence.

"When your father died, I thought it would become easier, that if you weren't in my life, then I would be able to rid myself of the hurt, shame, and anger.

All it has done is given me time and space to look back on everything, how unhappy I was, but also how I failed not just as wife but as a mother to a small child that didn't ask to be born. I am not very proud of myself, how I treated you Charles. You asked me if I loved you and the answer is no, but ask me if I wished I could have loved you, then the answer is yes. It wasn't you Charles, it was never you, it was me. Age brings with it not just maturity of our bodies but our consciousness and although I thought I would take this secret to my grave, you know what? I am relieved I do not have to."

Charlie felt a sense of relief too. It explained so much about his childhood. There was so much to take in. His father being unfaithful, a false mother who hadn't loved him and a mother who had chosen to give him up for a few quid to start a life without him, forgotten forever.

Did this mean she hadn't loved him either? He thought about her imprisoned in the attic, her baby taken away from her.

Did his father's heart break when Arlene had paid her off? Had he loved two women? So many other unanswered questions, but he just couldn't deal with them right now.

He looked across at Arlene. For the first time in his life he actually saw she was human. Gone was the stiff statue of pretence, and in place was an old, broken woman. His compassion kicked in, as much as he tried to keep it away, as she did not deserve anything from him.

He felt he should reach out and touch her hand; she looked a broken woman, and he felt her pain. He could understand why she sent Rosie away, he could never forgive her, but he recognised that Rosie was everything Arlene couldn't be, kind, forgiving, selfless, a mother.

"Thank you Arlene," he said. "Thank you for the truth. I feel sadness and sorry for you, I really do. Rosie taught me many things which I chose to bury when I left her, but they were gifts from her, and they are still here in my heart. I learned that forgiveness is not about cleansing the souls of those that have hurt us, it is actually a release from the anguish and pain they still hold over us, stealing time that could be spent on happiness, love, and kindness. Forgiveness is not really an act of selfishness, it is a selfish thing to do, a good selfish thing to help heal yourself. I now understand why you treated me so cold and uncaring, although I cannot yet forgive you, because I was a child, and no child should ever feel unloved. But what you have told me today will, I am sure, help me to start to heal."

"I do not want your forgiveness Charles, I really couldn't cope with that."

"Well I haven't given it yet. It isn't yours to give. It is mine, and maybe sometime in the future I will learn to forgive you and let go of my self-loathing and anger."

"When that time comes, you can decide whether you want it. I hope you can, as I think it would help you rid yourself of a lot of pain and create some space for some love and kindness, maybe help you to start loving yourself too."

Arlene said nothing. She just sat looking at the photo of herself and his father.

"Time for us to go. I think we are both exhausted and ready to see the back of each other," he tried to lighten the mood.

As they left the room, she said to him very quietly just as Molly and Neave came to greet them from the kitchen, "I hope you find peace Charles". The sound of his daughter's chatter and giggles filled him with love.

"I have made us butterfly buns, Daddy. You have been such a long time talking, but you and Grandma look a bit happier than earlier. Did you tell Grandma we have some photographs of you and Grandpa? Can I show them to her?"

She pulled out the ripped envelope from her coat pocket and Charlie tried to stop her, not wanting to reopen their wounds. But the old paper gave way and a number of photos fell to the floor, including the image of the pretty young woman Neave had been so drawn to. Charlie felt Arlene start to wobble. He caught hold of her arm to steady her. Her eyes were fixed on the photograph and she was gasping to get her breath. He picked the photograph up. He felt his heart stop.

"Is this her Arlene? Is this my mother?" he asked incredulously. Arlene nodded, and she pushed past them both as Molly took hold of her to make sure she didn't fall.

"Is this my mother?" he repeated. With tears rolling down her face, Molly nodded as she sat Arlene down a chair before she collapsed.

"I've found my mother Rosie, I have found her," he whispered as he held the photograph to his chest and the heavy oak door closed behind them.

28

Brigid

"Wisdom, strength, protection"

Snow had started to fall whilst they had been inside the house and a white blanket had already started to wrap itself over the fields and woodland. There was something magical about standing in it, putting your face upwards to catch the snowflakes. It seemed to stop the world for a moment. Neave wasn't talking.

"Is it my fault Daddy? Did I upset Grandma and I don't understand why you have another mummy?" Her voice was quivering.

He knelt down in the snow and took her little face in his hands. "My sweet Neave. No, it isn't your fault Arlene is upset. You have actually given me the key to finding out who my real mummy is."

She looked confused. "This lady, the lady you insisted we keep the photo of, is actually my real mummy and I didn't know. If you hadn't dropped the photographs, Arlene wouldn't have seen her and I would never have known who she was."

"But I don't understand. How can you have two mummies?"

"I will explain later Neave, it is getting late, and the snow is settling fast. We need to try to get home. But it isn't a bad thing having found out I have another mummy, so do not worry. Come on, let us get in the car."

Poor little thing, he shouldn't have exposed her to all that, but if she hadn't come with him, things wouldn't have unfolded the way they had.

"Brigid, or is it Mary?" he whispered. "Rosie, I have seen my mother. Thank you."

A small flurry of snow curled up in front of them both and Neave said, "Do you see that Daddy, it's Mummy".

As the snow formed into the shape of a wispy woman, Charlie replied, "I do see her Neave, I do. She's always with us. She keeps us safe."

He bent down and rolled some of the snow into a ball and gently threw it at Neave, who squealed with delight as the soft snow fell on top of her head.

It soon became clear they would not be making the journey back to Hefring that night. The roads were full of cars skidding out of control, some abandoned as people took to the streets to make their way home. All this chaos whilst simultaneously seeing the joy as children were out making snow men, pulling sledges.

Charlie reflected on the saying his father always had, 'There are always two sides to a coin Charlie.' He could hear the words as clear as anything being said to him whenever he had complained or been upset, particularly with Arlene. He hadn't understood until now that there is always more than one way to tell the same story depending on which character is telling it. Snow wreaks havoc for some but brings joy to others. Always two sides to a coin.

His thoughts rested on his father. His story was not one dimensional at all. He didn't know how he felt about him. He still loved him, respected him even more for insisting he kept his only son. The thought that his father had an affair with a very young, probably lost and lonely woman, though…that was going to take some time to get his head around.

Charlie had turned the car round and was trying to make his way back to Hepton. The roads were chocka, and the snow kept falling. He wondered if they would make it back to Iris. He was glad Frances had packed the food and blankets, and the wellingtons he had found tucked away behind the driver's seat. Whilst they were immobilised they picnicked on the crisps and cakes Fran had packed, Neave snuggling in a blanket whilst she chattered away to the ghost of her mother, telling her what had happened in the afternoon. By early evening they had managed to reach the town centre, which was uncannily quiet. Cars had been abandoned, people had got home, children, cold from the snow, were probably having cups of hot soup to thaw out their frozen fingers and toes.

He remembered these days from his childhood. He thought perhaps he had drowned the happy memories in the darkness he had created. They were starting to show themselves again, moments of happiness breaking through and with each one, a speckle of peace rested on his heart.

They too abandoned their car, not far from the town centre. He parked it as best he could at the kerbside, put on their wellies, wrapped up and with Rosie's basket covered in the blanket in one hand, the bag of clothes on his shoulder and holding tightly onto Neave's hand with the other, they trudged through the snow which was almost at the top of Neave's wellingtons. The town did look beautiful, very picturesque, like an oil painting hanging in a museum. The odd person nodding hello as they too walked through home. The snow had stopped falling, but it was hard work walking the half mile or so to The Bay Horse. They were both happy to see the shabby sign gently swinging over the pavement. Lights were still on, the door was unlocked, Iris was still open, unlike most of the other pubs.

They welcomed the warmth that enveloped them, thawing them out as they entered the bar. A roaring fire was casting shadows across the dimly lit room.

"Hello," Charlie shouted, because he could see no one in the room at all.

"You back then," said a voice from the corner of the room. It was George the Pain. "She's in the back rustling me up some food. Iris, Iris," he shouted, "the wee one is back with her dad."

Charlie heard a clatter from the back and out came Iris, full of smiles.

"Well just look what the snow brought back. Take your wet coats off and go get a warm by the fire. A cup of tea?" Charlie gave her a look. "Pint is it then and I will get some hot chocolate for Neave."

"Can't get home?" George asked.

"Nope, but Iris said we could stay over if we wanted. She has been so kind to us, even though we have only just met her."

"A diamond, that is what she is. Her bloody husband doesn't know what he's got, flouncing around with that bit of totty in front of everyone when he's got Iris. Well all I can say is what goes around, comes around and he will get his comeuppance for sure. I have tried to convince her to kick him out and let me look after her. She is such a good cook as well, you know, but she won't.

Charlie pulled off Neave's boots and popped on her slippers. Why would Fran pack slippers, the minds of women he would never understand, but Neave was thankful. His mind rested for a moment on the women who had recently come into his life. They were by far the stronger sex, for sure. Men, on the whole, he thought, were much shallower and more selfish than women, weaker for sure when it came to working through the difficult stuff, although his father wasn't like that. Or was he?

Charlie used the phone in the pub to call Frances to let her know they were OK and that they were staying at The Bay Horse due to the snow. He said he couldn't go into all the details on the phone but told her they had met with Arlene and things were starting to make sense. He reassured her they were both absolutely fine.

Iris brought out a huge cottage pie with a bowl of peas and carrots and a jug of hot gravy, and they all sat at the side of the fire, George included, and tucked into the food. George was right, Iris was a good cook. Charlie watched them both, Iris and George, as he teased her, and she berated him. There was something lovely about them both together. They looked like they were married and Charlie felt a little sadness for them both as clearly they enjoyed each other's company and liked, maybe loved, each other. Relationships were never easy. Feeling needed and loved was what most people wanted in their lives, and you do not get that by being alone.

Neave snuggled up on one of the benches and Charlie put the blanket over her that had been in the basket. Before long she was fast asleep. Charlie introduced Rosie to them both. He felt as though he had known them both all of his life, they were such genuine, kind people. Neither seemed perturbed by the urn. Iris was eager to hear about their trip to see Arlene, and Charlie told her almost everything. He placed the photograph of Brigid on the table.

"So this young woman is my real mother. Arlene said she was called Mary but the note on the back said Brigid, so I don't know which is her true name."

322

"It is Brigid," said George. "I remember her. She used to work here many years ago. She was such a shy, polite, pretty young thing and all of us young lads fancied our chances with her, but she wasn't interested at all."

"She kept herself to herself, was always very pleasant. She worked the kitchens and cleaned the bedrooms when it was a B and B. She wasn't here long if I remember correctly."

Charlie felt his hopes start to rise.

"Did you know my father then?" Charlie's voice was almost pleading a yes from him.

"Dunno lad, what was his name?"

"Henry Shafton," Charlie replied

"I do remember him. He used to come here after work and have a couple of pints before going home. A proper gent he was. Always dressed in his suit, polished brogues, and an overcoat, regardless of the weather. He used to stand at the end of the bar…" Both their recollections about him were the same.

"I remember coming here with him when I was a young boy. He dressed the same then," said Charlie.

They hadn't noticed that Iris had left them to chatter between themselves. It was when George said that the woman had worked there, there was something niggling in her head.

All the old paperwork, wage slips and letters she had found in a box in the cellar, the stuff she felt she couldn't throw away, she was sure there were letters that were post marked Ireland. Iris pushed through boxes of crisps, packets of cigarettes, till receipt rolls, toilet paper that were stored in the cellar and, peering to the far corner of the room, she saw a large cardboard box. Just what she was looking for. It was covered in dust and she sneezed as she lifted it from the shelf and carried it up the stairs to the bar.

"Wondered where you had nipped off too. Thought you were bringing us some of the trifle you made the other day, but I can see I was mistaken," said George, "Here lass, let me help you. What have you got here? Not a trifle for sure."

"I'll get you some trifle George, just help me put this on the table." The dust was still wafting in the air and it smelt very fusty.

"Is there a body in here?" he continued to joke.

"It was when you said she worked here, Brigid. I remembered this old box of papers and I have a notion that we might find something to help find more out about that mother of yours, whatever her name is."

"I told you it is Brigid, not Mary. Maybe that was her middle name. Go get us some trifle and another pint love, think we will be here for a while."

"George, I am sure you have a home to go to and it's getting late and with all this snow," said Charlie

"Don't you want me to help you then?"

"No, I didn't mean that at all. It is just that this is my problem, and I don't want you and Iris feeling obliged to spend your evening up to your elbows in old paper."

"Nothing better to do lad, no-one at home waiting for me. She buggered off years ago with the bloody coal man, and besides, I only live round the corner, so it is a short walk back to my cold little house. I'd much prefer to be here, at this fireside with Iris, feeling useful, and you know Iris just wants to help everyone. You and the little 'un are a bit of welcomed company for us lonely folk."

"Cheers then," said Charlie, not knowing how to respond to kindness. Iris returned with a bowl of half-eaten trifle, two pints of John Smith's and a gin and tonic.

They emptied the contents of the box onto the table and started to work their way through the correspondence and papers. Iris found a large pile of small brown envelopes held together by string that were old wage packets.

Some even had old currency on them, pounds, shillings, and pence. George became preoccupied with reading sheets of old newspapers that had lined the box, reading out local news and gossip from the sixties. Charlie found more photographs and searched to see if he could see his father or Brigid in them.

"I've found something!" exclaimed Iris, so loudly that Neave stirred, and opened her eyes briefly before falling fast asleep again.

"It has been a long day for her," said Charlie, "But what have you found? Detective Ironside Iris," he eagerly asked. He could feel anticipation spread through his body like a fever taking hold.

"Wage packet, Brigid O'Callahan dated 1962. That must be her."

Charlie took the small buff envelope and held it between the palms of his hands. "My mother once touched this," he softly said. He examined it. Written on it was the amount she had earned that week. The only other information was an address, but that was The Bay Horse.

"They lived in until they found somewhere else. It must have been when she first came here, but as I said I only recall her being here a few months, then she just vanished," George said. "We all thought she must have gone back home. I remember asking your father about her because he'd taken a bit of a shine to her. Not like that though, I can see what you are thinking. He was too much of a gentleman to take advantage of anyone. He always had a whiskey before he left and toasted his wife. "To Arlene, my love," was what he used to say."

If only you knew George, Charlie thought.

"There were times when I saw him give her his handkerchief to wipe the young lasses tear away.

He'd ask old Joe, the landlord, if she could have a break and he'd buy her a sherry, even though he shouldn't have done as she wasn't of age.

———

326

They'd talk quietly, and he'd reassure her. None of us lads would question him, your dad, we had too much respect for his position and for how he treated us. He'd always buy a round of drinks at Easter, Whit Sunday, and Christmas for us. After she disappeared, I did ask him if she knew where she was, as we were all a bit concerned. He just said she had told him she was going back home as things hadn't worked out as she had wanted, and that was that. Well obviously not, was it?" he said, looking at Charlie.

"It was very gracious of your parents to adopt you and then say nothing to anyone about her having an illegitimate child. You have got to admire them. It's all a bit like a grown up Famous Five, trying to resolve a mystery except there are only three of us," continued George.

Charlie felt too ashamed to tell George and Iris it was his father that had made her disappear, who had locked her away in an attic to hide the shame he had brought upon her. They both assumed that Arlene and his dad had adopted him and he wasn't ready to share that he was the result of his father's infidelity.

"She, Arlene, wasn't kind though. She was a cold-hearted bitch to me, George. If she had been a loving mother, then I wouldn't be sitting here with you all tonight. I would have lived my life oblivious to the fact Brigid was my mum."

"So who is your father then Charlie, did Arlene give any clues?"

Before he got the chance to formulate an answer that wasn't a lie but wasn't the whole truth either, Iris has turned to George and said, "Maybe it was one of you or one of your mates that got her in the family way," winking at him as she spoke.

"She was out of my league Iris, and I would have known if it had been one of my mates. I guess your father found her somewhere to stay until she had the baby and then adopted you. Did your mother tell you anything at all Charlie? Why would they adopt you and then her not love you?"

"She never loved me, she told me, said she thought she could. Instead, when she looked at me, it reminded her that she hadn't been able to give Dad a child. She's a twisted and cynical woman who, despite all the wealth and privileges she has, feels life handed her a cesspool instead of riches." He actually felt he needed to keep his father's reputation intact. What good would it do to displace that? He wanted to find Brigid and discover from her what had happened. He owed that to the memories and the love his father had given him, and in a way to Arlene. She had kept up the pretence to protect herself too and as much as he still did not like her, he had no desire to make her suffering any worse.

There was a silence between them as though they were all contriving their own story about what had happened, how Charlie had come to be.

"I think we are all a little tired, don't you think Charlie? That wee lass needs to be put to bed and George, you need to get yourself off home, it is almost 10 o'clock. There's no-one else that will come in tonight so am going to lock up and have an early night myself." Iris brought their detective work to an end for the night. George said his goodnights, gave Iris an overlong hug, put on his woolly hat and donkey jacket, and set off through the deserted streets back home.

The room that Iris had made up for them was straight back to the fifties.

A dark wooden wardrobe, with a key in the door to fasten it, stood in one recess of the chimney breast, the other side had a smallish table, acting as a bedside table with a lamp on casting a dusky pink light over the bedroom from its shade. It was a double bed, with a thick candlewick deep pink bedspread covering it. To the foot of the bed was an ottoman, this reminded him so much of home. All the beds at Chapelfield House had huge ottomans containing bed linen and towels, each colour co-ordinated to match the room décor. Straight opposite that was a dressing table with three mirrors, one large oval one in the centre with a smaller one at each side. A few trinkets adorned the surface.

"It's err…well it is very homely Iris. It reminds me of my childhood if I am honest."

"You are being more than polite Charlie. It hasn't been used in years, but I always keep in clean, just in case, and you are the first just in case since I have been here.

He gave her a hug, it seemed the right thing to do, and he saw that she had tears in her eyes. He left Neave dressed, just took off her slippers and covered her with the thick pile of blankets on the bed. She hadn't woken at all when he carried her up the stairs.

He asked Iris to bring the box of papers up with them. He knew he wasn't ready to sleep, and he wanted time to look through them all on his own. Iris had given him a bottle of whiskey that was three quarts empty. She said it would make him sleep. He filled the glass and sat on the ottoman, looked at his image in the mirror, "To you Charlie boy, whoever you are," and took a large gulp of the spirit. As it warmed him from inside out he tipped the contents of the box onto the bed.

Putting the box down he noticed something sticking out of the folds at the bottom. He had to unfold the box to release whatever was stuck in it. It was a plastic bag, an old one for certain, discoloured and creased. Inside were two unopened letters. They were addressed to Miss B O'Callahan. The post stamps were blurred but Charlie made out that they were dated February and August 1963. His hands started to shake, and he had another mouthful of whiskey as he mustered up the courage to open them. It felt totally wrong, reading words that were not meant for his eyes. It felt like voyeurism, but he knew he had to open them. He opened the one dated February 26th.

"57, Fishankle Street,

Dingle,

County Kerry

26th February 1963

My dearest sweetheart Brigid,

I hope my letter finds you well in the circumstances. You are lucky to have found a kind English couple to look after and care for you in your condition. I always thought the English looked down on us Irish, so it is a welcome surprise that not all we hear in our little town is true. As hard as it will be, I do think you have made the right decision to let them adopt the little one as soon as he or she is born. The house you are staying at sounds very grand, maids and gardeners and everything. I don't have the address, so I am sending this letter to your place of work, hoping they pass it onto you.

Your mammy and da know nothing and they won't hear anything from me. They are disappointed you aren't coming home for Easter, but they are proud that you are doing well in your career.

They have told the whole street and church that you are already an assistant manager at a fancy hotel. Ignorance is bliss, so they say.

You know I have always loved you Brigid, from the very first day I laid my eyes on you in the school playground. I know you don't love me that way. I know you love me, but not in the way a wife would love her husband, but that doesn't matter that much to me.

331

You say that you can't marry, that you have sinned before God carrying a child out of marriage and you have to carry your sins as a spinster for penance for the rest of your life, but that isn't true. I will marry you Brigid and share the burden. If God wants to punish a kind, gentle spirit like yourself, then I think I will stop believing in him because there are far meaner, so called God loving people that sit there in church confessing their wrong doings then back out repeating them. They aren't good Catholics and they will not get through the pearly gates when their time comes.

Being so pretty, Brigid has been a curse as well as a gift. All the plain girls at school were jealous of you and even the wives in the village as you blossomed into a beauty. You did right to get out of the village. I am just so sorry your dream hasn't gone the way you wanted it to. And them boys and men, always drooling over you. I wanted to punch them; I did a few. They used to laugh at me, Pignose Sheehan they called me. But all that name calling has given me a thick skin and taught me not to care what people think. A disrespectful man took advantage of your innocence and loneliness Brigid. He had his way with you and if he wasn't dead already, I'd be offering to stick a knife in him and dig his grave myself."

Charlie re-read that line…If he wasn't dead already. But his father wasn't dead at the time. Why would his man think he was? Just when he thought the fog that hung over his past was starting to clear, another dark cloud appeared.

Maybe Brigid had said the father of her child was dead, as it made it an easier story to tell. Getting pregnant was one big sin, but the baby being a married man's? That must have been too much to tell, too much shame. This made sense, she had lied to protect herself and his father. He continued to read the remainder of the letter.

"Well Brigid, I do hope that you will reconsider my marriage proposal. I know I am not much of a looker, but I would always provide for you, treat you with respect, and my love would be enough for both of us. I have almost finished my apprenticeship and old man Murphy reckons I have a real talent for carpentry, so I am sure I could find some decent work in England. You could keep the baby too if you wanted to. I'd bring it up as my own and never tell anyone. It is always an open offer Brigid.

I won't ask you again, well not until after the baby is born. But if you change your mind, write to me and I will be over in a shot.

Yours lovingly

Patrick   xxxx"

He felt quite sick. He had just read a letter that never got to his mother. What would his life had been if Brigid had received the letter and accepted Patrick's offer of marriage? So different, full of love he was sure, but none of the wealth and privileges he had had. He would have taken the love over money in a shot, but the choice had never been his.

It made him think about the decisions he was making for Neave. She had not had any say in her life. It wasn't her decision to not have a father in her life for seven years, not in her power to have a mother that would be with her to support and guide her through her life.

The decisions he would make as an adult would mould the person she would become and how she would live her life. All this rested on the adults she had in her life, she had little choice on who they were and so, as her father, he had to take responsibility for the value legacy he would impart on her. He would never abandon her, always love her unconditionally and try as hard as he could to instil the values that Rosie lived her life by. Flip the coin and his life would have been so different.

The second letter was dated after he was born. He knew the story though, he had lived it but he still needed to know what happened to Brigid, and he hoped that this one would help him find her.

"57, Fishankle Street,

Dingle,

County Kerry

8th August 1963

Dearest Brigid

I hope my letter finds you well. Thank you for yours letting me know that you have given birth, and that all went almost to plan (your words not mine) and that everyone is healthy and well. I am unsure if you received any of my other letters; I know I said I wouldn't contact you but I couldn't help myself writing more. I haven't heard from you so unsure if you got them or you just thought it better to do this on your own. Silence and distance affect the mind, and in place of facts, we create stories about what is happening. I have had the worst thoughts that you had died and then the very best of them with images of you taking afternoon tea on a finely cut lawn playing croquet. So just hearing from you, even without an address of where you are living, brings some peace to me.

I still write to The Bay Horse in the continued hope that your benevolent employer will pass these on. I hope you will be able to resume your position there in the near future.

I cannot imagine what you have been through though. Going through the trauma and pain of childbirth only to pass your bairns over to others for their care, not being able to celebrate them with your family and friends must have been heartbreaking. You mentioned nothing about how you are coping, how you are feeling, and I have to hope that you are managing the separation from the kindness of the family and not having your wee ones with you.

335

You have done well with your mammy, she doesn't suspect a thing. It must be hard though living a lie, especially for you.

My offer of marriage remains Brigid. I will never love another. I am always here for you. I am planning a trip over to England in the next few weeks. I need to see you and make sure you are ok. My only contact to you is The Bay Horse, so I do hope that I will find you there.

Yours lovingly

Patrick xxx

"Wee ones…bairns", he said out loud, that implies more than one. The handwriting wasn't very good, and he wondered if he had misread it or Patrick had made a grammatical mistake. But doing it twice? What did it mean? If correct, it could only mean one thing. That Brigid had given birth to two babies. He had a brother or sister somewhere. Could his life be any more of a lie? My God, what happened? Maybe one died? Maybe not, so what happened to Brigid and her child? Did his father and Arlene arrange another adoption on the quiet…or did she keep the baby? She couldn't return to her family in Ireland. He felt sick.

"What happened to you Brigid?" he said to himself softly. "Where are you?" The whiskey had gone to his head, and he was unsure if it was the alcohol or just that he was feeling overwhelmed with the day, but he felt the room spinning and he laid down on the bed with the letters still in his hand and fell into sleep.

His dreams were horrific. A young woman, her hands in chains pinned to a wooden bed in a sparse, cold room, screaming in pain as a doctor who looked like he'd been dug up from a grave, cut her open and pulled and pulled until a creature was dragged from her belly. But it wasn't a human, it was a gargoyle, and it jumped out of his arms and tore at the woman's neck, her blood dripping from its mouth. He was in the dream, looking in from the shadows. No-one could hear him scream and shout. The doctor picked up the monster, wrapped it in a blanket and gave it to a couple, his father and Arlene. The doctor then took a huge knife and continued to cut into the stomach of the dead woman and pulled out another child who was screaming. He placed the second, perfectly formed child on the bed at the side of the dead woman. The baby was kicking and screaming, covered in the mother's blood. He was shouting and crying, but no sound was coming out of his mouth. The doctor, the couple and the gargoyle child left the room, leaving the child alone with the dead woman.

In his dream, and he did know it was a dream, he couldn't wake himself up from the nightmare he was in. He was trapped, couldn't break out. He started to hyperventilate, his oxygen was running out, he felt he was dying. A little girl was stroking his head, it was Neave,

"Breathe Charlie, breathe, you need to come back to us, just breathe." He took an enormous gasp, and he woke, holding his neck with his hands as though he had been strangled.

337

"Breathe Charlie, breathe," It wasn't Neave's voice, it was Rosie, she was whispering in his ear. He could sense her, smell the roses and jasmine.

"Rosie." That was all he could say. He could feel her hands on his shoulders gently pushing him back onto the bed. She stroked his hair, and he felt her kisses on his face. Was he still dreaming?

"Sleep, Charlie, you need to sleep."

29

Rosie

"The balance between the light and the dark"

I watch over you both. I try to bring some peace and calm to this traumatic place you find yourself in Charlie. I have sensed that I have cried when you have been hurting, but this form I have is very confusing. I feel the same as I did when I lived in your world, but the physicality of me doesn't allow me to hold on to the feelings. They seem to drift through me, as though they are not mine to hold on to. But I have been with you every moment of your journey. I think you have felt me there when you have needed me. I am tuned into you Charlie, and I am holding some of the pain you have, because there is too much for anyone to carry on their own. The strange and unexpected thing is that when your anger, anxiousness and darkness consume you, I am at my strongest, which is why I am here now.

The letters, your nightmare. I so wish my body had lived just a little longer to have been at your side. But the other side of the coin is that as your darkness starts to recede, the volcano of rage starts to ease, then the weaker I become.

I am realising Charlie, that my stay in the in-betweenness of our worlds will fade the stronger you become. What an irony, I can only be with you whilst you find the peace you so desperately need, but I will be gone as soon as you find it.

If I was a selfish soul, I would lead you astray so that I could remain, but the forces of life would know I am not being true and I would still lose you anyway. I can't tell you this, that your happiness means my ultimate demise, as it would haunt you forever. I am proud of you, my love. Sleep well, recoup and re-energise for what is to come.

30

Siblings

"Brothers and Sisters"

"Charlie Daddy, are you awake? I am hungry. I dreamed of Mummy last night. She came to me and cuddled up with me. She says she is still with us and to keep going. So where are we going today?"

He felt as though he had been hit many times by a sledgehammer. His head hurt. He saw the empty whiskey bottle on the floor and the opened letters lying on the bed. He groaned, turned over and buried his face in the bedcovers. Neave immediately jumped on his back and started to tickle him. This was the reality of being a father, having to be alert the moment your eyes opened, not to drink whiskey ever again, pretend you do not have a hangover and just be eternally joyful. God, parenting was going to be far more difficult than he had ever thought.

"I don't feel so good Neave, maybe you could go down and see what Iris can cook you for breakfast," and with that she was out of the bedroom, shouting to Iris as she ran down the stairs.

He could hear their muffled conversations, Neave shrieking with laughter and then music started to play. It got louder and louder until Charlie knew he had to rouse himself. He caught his reflection in the mirror.

Christ, he looked rough. His hair was sticking out in every direction and no matter how hard he tried to it pull it down, it would not be tamed. His eyes were swollen and his face was the colour of stone. In fact, he thought he looked more like Medusa than the bloody house had done the day before. He needed coffee, lots of it, and fast. He still had all his clothes on, even his shoes. He would try to keep some breakfast down, then ask Iris if he could have a shower. He opened the curtains and winced, closing his eyes to shield them from the brightness of the sun reflecting off the thick, white snow.

"Wow Charlie, you look like the walking dead," Iris greeted him as he joined them in the bar.

"Never thought I would ever say this…but do you think you could turn the radio down? I have a headache from hell."

'Don't stop Believing', by Journey was blasting out.

"Guess that is the motivational anthem for today," he murmured under his breath as Iris brought him the first of the many cups of coffee he would consume before the morning ended. Neave came running over and gave him a big hug.

"Watch the head Neave, it is a bit sore. What time is it?"

"Almost half-past nine. You must have both been shattered." Iris replied. "I have bacon cooking, think you need a good breakfast to start the day."

"I found some letters last night," he said as he sat Neave back down at the table where she was drawing and colouring.

Iris looked excited. "Oh, let me get you a coffee and breakfast and you can tell me. You don't look that pleased though, Charlie, or is it the hangover?"

"The hangover is because of the letters," he said.

"Right then, let's get Neave her breakfast, you some coffee and you can tell me whilst she is happy colouring. I get a sense it isn't something you want her to hear," and she scuttled back into the kitchen. The smell of bacon actually made him feel better. He sat with his head back, eyes closed, listening to the music in the background. Music had always been his faithful companion, brought him peace and escapism.

"Just a small town girl livin' in a lonely world

She took the midnight train going anywhere…

A singer in a smoky room

A smell of wine and cheap perfume

———

343

For a smile they can share the night

It goes on and on and on and on....

Some'll win, some will lose

Some are born to sing the blues

Whoa, the movie never ends

It goes on and on and on and on..."

It was one of his favourite songs, one he had covered many times himself. Strange though, how the words of songs start to mean different things when your life changes. He'd always felt himself inside the words, the one that was in the bars, finding comfort in the arms of the many women he had met just for a night, then moved on, but now today he felt the words differently. Brigid leaving her small town to find a better life. He was the result of...wine and cheap perfume, for a smile they shared the night...the movie never ends...he was born to sing the blues.

His life was a crock of shit. He felt the waves of self-pity flood over him and then he heard Neave hum to the song and he instantly felt ashamed of himself. His life was full of hope and love, and she was his salvation, his future.

He needed to get his shit together, find out who he really was, and then live his life with his daughter. Rosie was right, Neave would always lead him to the light.

Charlie placed the photograph of Brigid on the table and was staring at it as Iris brought over his breakfast.

"You are the image of her Charlie, same eyes, and hair. Your dad must have helped her find somewhere to stay until you were born. Arlene must have been part of it all, the planning. I am assuming it was much easier in those days to go through adoption. Can you get sight of your birth certificate? Maybe that will help you find out who your father is if he was named on it. What did the letters say?"

She watched his brow furrow and the pain that washed across his face. Maybe she was being too invasive. She shouldn't ask questions. It was his story.

"Lad, I am sorry, I shouldn't pry. Some things as meant not to be shared."

"It's OK Iris, you aren't prying, it is just that in the past twenty-four hours the person I always thought I was, that the last twenty-nine years of my life, have actually been a lie and it is taking some getting used to. And the thing is I have seen my birth certificate as it was needed for boarding school. It says that Arlene and my dad are my parents, so even that is a lie. How did they do that? Even twenty-odd years ago, I am sure that wasn't legal."

"And there is more intrigue too Iris. The letters were from a guy called Patrick, who offered to marry Brigid. She never read the letters. They were unopened. Who knows what my life would have been like if she had received them and married him?"

345

"The impact of adult decisions on kids' lives is quite overwhelming if you stop and think about it. All the big and little things we say and do without even thinking about them, all change children's lives. This experience has brought home to me the huge responsibilities we have as adults. I mean babies don't ask to be born. In my case and Neave's as well, well neither of us were planned additions to the human race, accidental life that is what we are." His voice went to a whisper when he mentioned Neave."

"I never, ever want Neave to think that I didn't want her. I want her life to be full of certainty and love, the things I didn't have. What a mess. I am beginning to wonder if I should have left everything dormant. But I can't be the father I want to be unless I find some sort of resolution."

Iris reached out and touched the back of Charlie's hand. Mothers don't have to carry life to love, she wanted to say to him. But Arlene wasn't the best example of adoptive love. Iris had been raised by her grandmother. She had never known her mother, who too had carried a child out of wedlock. Iris's mother had abandoned her, just walked out when she was born. She had never seen her mother. Photographs were rare in those days, but her grandmother loved and cared for her, and she never pined for her birth mother ever. Not even now, when memories were being evoked by Charlie's story.

"There's more," he said in a hushed voice. "The letters refer to bairns, not one child, but two. At first, I thought it was a mistake in the grammar, but it was repeated. I think I have a brother or a sister Iris."

He looked like a lost boy again, so needy and confused.

"Charlie, oh my. I am not sure what to say to you. But maybe this is a good thing that you have family, if we can find more out?" It was a question more than a statement.

"Having family, someone you are connected to, brings comfort and a sense of belonging, and I so want you to find them," she continued.

"Well they never wanted me when I was born, so maybe it won't be the happy ending you are thinking Iris. But you know what? I deserve to know why I was given away and my sibling wasn't, or if he or she is still alive. I am not giving up until I know." His face had changed, and she sensed anger rising in him again.

"I know where she was born in Ireland, there is an address on the letters of where Patrick lived, but he said she hadn't gone home, the shame and all that, and if she kept the other child, she would never go back. Maybe there was another adoption. The only person I know that was part of all this is Arlene. She would have known two babies had been born. She said they had paid her off. I need to go back there and try to get her to tell me what really happened. She owes me that."

31

Arlene

"The purveyor of untruths"

Charlie made his way back to his abandoned car. It was a beautiful, crisp, sunny winter day, and the church bells were ringing. A few cars were on the roads, which were much clearer as the morning sun had already started to melt the snow. He had asked Iris if she could look after Neave. He did not want to her to return to the house and Arlene. He had to do this on his own. Iris had, of course, jumped at the chance of building a snowman in the pub garden, and she even put a note on the door to say she was closed for the day.

"Are you with me Rosie…" he said out loud as the car crunched through the unbroken carpet of snow that led up to the house. For sure they would be in as there were no footsteps or tyre marks at all. The house looked quite beautiful in the morning sun, not The Munster's Mansion, it had seemed yesterday. Even Medusa's head looked pretty covered in snow.

He knocked on the door. Everything was so quiet, a Sunday and snow brought temporary peace to the busy world. He hoped the day would show him the way to inner

349

peace. He felt his heart pounding as the door creaked open and Molly once again stood before him. This time she didn't look surprised to see him, more that he felt like an expected guest.

"Morning Charlie. I thought you might come back to see us. Come in. We are in the kitchen. It is the only place I have lit a fire. It was very cold here last night and Arlene isn't too well this morning. She led the way to the back of the house.

Charlie's memory box that had been nailed shut for many years opened a little more as the smell of steak and kidney pie wafted into the hallway as Molly opened the heavy wooden kitchen door. The room hadn't changed at all since he last visited. He scanned the room. Pans and utensils hanging from the walls, plates and other crockery stacked on wooden shelves, and a huge wooden kitchen table in the centre. It was warm and homely, and an image of him sitting in his pyjamas, at the side of the fire on a three legged wooden stool with a cup of hot cocoa and home-made biscuits filled his head. It was as though he was reliving it and the memory of the love he had received from Molly as a child, a love he had forgotten, now flooded his heart. He reached out and touched her shoulder as tears welled in his eyes. His childhood had had love in it, it had been suppressed by all his anger.

Arlene was at the kitchen table. He was shocked when he saw her. She looked as though she had aged 10 years overnight. She looked so frail and vulnerable. Gone was the iron woman, dressed in her signature suit, hair drawn back in a tight knot. Gone was the red lipstick and the steel rod that Charlie imagined had been welded to her spine to keep her posture so upright. Instead was an old woman, her fine grey hair unbrushed and long, resting on her back and shoulders, hunched forward as bony fingers clutched a cup of hot tea. He had opened Pandora's box to her past too and the physical impact of that was hard to look at.

He wanted to remain angry and indignant with the woman who had lied to him all his life, the woman who was the root cause of his anger, the woman who had never offered him one ounce of compassion or love in his life. The rehearsed dialogue he had prepared in his head on the journey over, his demands for information and truth, started to slip away as very unexpected feelings of pity and sadness crept over him. She didn't acknowledge him, said nothing, and didn't lift her eyes from where they were fixed on a photograph on the table. Charlie could see it was a smaller print of the one hung above the fireplace, the one of her wedding day. He could see how much Arlene needed Molly. He also realised he knew nothing about Molly. How could that be? How could someone spend 18 years of their life with someone and know absolutely nothing about her, not even her surname, how old she was, what family she had? Taking someone for granted because they are always there is something he vowed he would never do again.

The silence was overpowering, just the crackle from the coal on the fire and the sound of Molly's slippers shuffling on the stone floor. He didn't know how to start the conversation. It was Molly who broke the silence.

"Arlene, Charlie is here. We did wonder when he would return, didn't we?"

She looked up, quite startled to see him there. It was as though she had been in another dimension, transfixed on the photo.

"Hello Charles." Her voice wasn't soft and welcoming, but the tone was less acerbic than the day before. "I guess you have more questions for me."

"You think?" his sarcastic reply.

"I don't know where to begin," he continued. "All I want to know is who I am without having to second guess or find things out from unopened letters hidden away in a box in a pub. I don't want any more surprises, no more layers of lies to uncover. I just want the bare, honest, raw truth and you are the only person I know who can help me. I know you won't fluff it up and soften the details, so please, will you give me some answers?"

"What more do you want to know? I don't know anything about any letters."

"I want to know what happened to my brother or sister for a start?"

She took a sharp intake of breath and Molly took hold of her hand.

"How did you find out?"

"The letters I found were from a man called Patrick from my mother's hometown. He had written to her to ask her to marry him and then again after I …we, were born. He spoke about not one child but children. The letters were unopened, so Brigid never saw them."

She just stared at him.

"Come on Arlene, I deserve to know. I really do. You must have some compassion in you somewhere."

"We didn't know she was carrying twins. The doctor we trusted her health and pregnancy with was an old man. He was a retired GP. He didn't know much about pregnancy as it turned out, but he was the only person we knew who would keep the secret, and he received a generous pay out for his silence."

"Every night your father called into that pub, The Bay Horse, after work before he came home. I soon began to understand why as he told me that he was sorry but that he had had a very short affair with a woman and that she was with child."

"He said he still loved me, he didn't love her and he was apologetic to the fact that he had given in to…well his sexual needs.

I was livid. How could I live with the shame of the affair? People would have known that I was incapable of keeping a husband happy. I just couldn't live with that. I also knew deep down that I had contributed to the situation by me not sharing a bed with him, and as much as I was angry with him, it also was a reminder that I wasn't a true woman, a proper wife, and that is all that I had been trained for all my life."

It was as if she had been waiting for years to unload all that she had bottled up. Charlie didn't need to ask anything, she just kept talking. He watched her face as the details started to unravel and he could see how much emotion was still living inside her. Time had not healed at all.

"She said she would not get rid of the baby. She said that God would never forgive her. I told Henry that neither he nor her would get forgiveness from God, so why keep the baby? As I said yesterday it was his idea that we keep you. You gave us an heir and kept up the illusion that we had a full married life."

"She came to live with us when she was about four or five months pregnant. We couldn't risk anyone seeing her and as much as I detested her being here, it was far better than someone finding out about your father's sins. Your father knew the landlord at The Bay Horse well, Jo Daley, and he said he would send any mail to us for her to make sure her family didn't start to suspect anything. She didn't have any friends as far as I could tell as she hadn't been here long enough. Long enough to seduce a married man though."

"We told my family and friends that I was expecting but that the doctor had advised rest and a warm climate so I went to the South of France for a few months on my own, and returned in late July, what we thought would be a few weeks before the birth."

"Where did she stay?" Charlie asked and did you see her at all before you left for France?"

"Oh yes, I saw her. I wanted to look into the eyes of the harlot and let her know that I despised her and not to think I was being benevolent for her, but to ensure our standing remained in the community. When your father brought her home and I saw how young she was, how…" she paused for a moment before continuing "…how pretty she was, it made me feel sick to imagine your father, a man in his thirties, almost old enough to be her father, fornicating with someone who was practically a child. But also it made me feel even more inadequate as a woman. She was everything I wasn't. It made me question why your father married me and continued to tell me he loved me, even though I scorned his words. How could he fall for her seduction if she was the absolute opposite of me? You cannot imagine Charles how utterly difficult this was for me. We put her up in the attic bedroom and that is where she stayed whilst I was in the house."

"And how difficult do you think it was for her? She was vulnerable, alone and was reliant on the benevolence of you both, and then being locked up in an attic?"

"I didn't care about her at all. You asked me for the truth and here it is Charles. I have no doubt that even though

I gave strict instructions for her not to leave her room unless absolutely necessary, that your father and Molly did not abide my wishes when I was in France."

"Henry did keep to your wishes Arlene and the girl rarely ventured out of the room," Molly responded.

"But that didn't stop him spending time with her did it?" she spat back at Molly. The Arlene he knew so well was still in there, despite her different demeanour.

"The day I arrived home, expecting a least for your father to pick me up, well Jo Daley was there, driving our car! How utterly disrespectful for him not to pick me up from the dockside, but instead his partner in crime was there. It was utterly deplorable to have to share time with him, the shame of it all. All he said was that your father had asked him to help out as Mary or Brigid, whatever her name is, wasn't well that day. Your father had put her above me. As I walked in the door, I expected to hear them laughing and imagined she was still trying to get her hands on your father. I regretted going away."

"Turns out she wasn't ill, but she had started in the early stages of labour which your father, in fact none of us, hadn't considered, as her due date was still weeks away. But when I saw how big she was, I told Henry I suspected he wasn't the father and that he had been taken for a fool.

He insisted that was not the case and that he knew she hadn't been with another man. I didn't ask for the details of how he knew."

Charlie's mind started to race. He remembered the words on the letter, "…and if he wasn't dead already I'd be offering to stick a knife in him and dig his grave myself."

He said nothing as Arlene was in full flow and he just didn't want to stop her.

"She went into full labour the following day. The doctor came and Molly helped him. I felt nothing for her pain, whereas your father, of course, paced the bloody hallway like any expectant father you see on the TV."

"The only thing I felt to be honest, was relief that I wasn't giving birth and it firmly cemented any notion that I had considered whilst I was in France, to grin and bear it and have sex with him in the future, and give him a true-blooded heir. I most certainly was not going to go through that."

"It took a day and a half for you to be born and hearing her screams give way to a baby's cry. I knew life would never be the same again. Your father ran upstairs and shouted down that we had a son. We…well, he had a son, there was no we at all. Then it started all over again, the screams and wailing. I did fear at this point that she was going to die and how on earth would we deal with that? It was one thing keeping the birth of a child a secret but a secret burial. That could never happen."

Charlie listened in disbelief at just how selfish and callous she was. But he had asked for all the details and this is what he was getting.

"Then the second cry. Simultaneous crying. I initially could not fathom what was happening until your father came downstairs and told me there were two babies. His face was ashen, and he ran to the kitchen sink and vomited.

"Twins born 31st July at 11.50 and 11.55, four weeks early, a boy and a girl," said Molly."

"I have a sister…" Charlie said very quietly.

"All our careful planning, gone. I remember thinking she was such a spiteful thing to have two children, and what would we do? Your father, of course, wanted to keep both the soft-headed man that he was, but I was adamant we would only keep the boy, you."

"What did she look like? What was her name? Why keep me, not her?"

"I have no idea what she looked like. I never set eyes on her. It was hard enough for me to take you into my arms and hope that mother's instinct and love would eventually reside in me."

"She did look like you Charlie," said Molly. "You were both incredibly beautiful babies. A mass of dark curly hair with big bright eyes.

We had to separate you after the first day, as we could see your mother was getting too attached to you both. She stayed with us for a few weeks after the birth to recover and she spent much of the time crying and looking after your sister. It was very sad. It was Arlene that said it wasn't fair on her, or anyone else to have her in the same house as her child and her not be able to hold him."

Charlie puzzled on this and was unsure whether Molly was adding a bit of gloss to the story in which Arlene's reputation as a cold-hearted bitch certainly hadn't disappointed. But Arlene did squeeze Molly's hand as she said it.

"What was she called?" he asked.

"We never knew," replied Molly.

"What happened to them both?"

"Believe it or not Charles, it wasn't easy on any of us and as much as I despised her, I could not help feeling upset for her, albeit in a small way. I do have a heart, it is just that it was broken by what your father and her did together. And I had to protect myself, so I stopped myself from feeling. But seeing her sobbing, holding your sister in a blanket close to her chest as she was leaving would soften anyone. She turned and thanked me for my kindness, for looking after her and said she knew her son would be loved. Her words spun round my head whilst your father put her and the baby in the car, with her belongings and £750, and drove her somewhere."

"I never asked where, and he never told me. Her gratitude did touch me, I have to say, but I knew I could not weaken otherwise what life would I have had, knowing we had taken a child away from his mother. I did what I always do best to protect myself. I twisted her words of thanks and appreciation, so I did not feel any pity, sadness, or concern for her, which had started to creep in. Instead, I told myself she had said those things maliciously, to punish me for keeping her child."

She paused for a moment. "It is strange what the mind does to protect us. As I am telling you all this, I am finding it difficult to comprehend that even I could have been so wicked to turn her compassion into hatred, but I did, and that hatred spilled out onto you. It had nowhere to go except the part of her she left behind. I tried Charles, as I said yesterday, but the truth is that I became narcissistic to survive. I put myself first at the expense of other people. I felt so utterly worthless and unloved that it was the only way I could make sense of life. I knew at some stage in my life a mirror would be put in front of me and I would have to face the reality of the person I had become, relive moments of my life that would no longer have the protection of my coldness and here you are Charles, the very thing that made me cold, the mirror revealing the horrors of my life."

Tears were rolling down her face. It was hard to take everything in and process it at the same time as seeing the woman he loathed and hated break down in front of him.

His frightened and distraught mother leaving her child behind. His father hiding his emotion and saying goodbye to his daughter, knowing he would never see or hold her ever in his life…and Arlene forever living through the consequences of her husband's infidelity, knowing she had agreed to live a lifetime of lies to conceal her own humiliation.

It was the tragedy of it all, and seeing the burden Arlene had carried all her life wasn't easy to witness and not feel some compassion for her, just like the fleeting moment Arlene had felt compassion for his true mother. He felt a sadness consume him for all of them, for everyone, including himself, that had been part of the lie and heartache that had lasted almost thirty years and it was time for it all to stop. Rosie's death had taught him that life is too short to let anger and resentment steal the potential of happiness from the future. He hadn't really understood that until now. He closed his eyes, and he felt her with them all in this room. He could smell her, hear her soft voice and gentle laughter. When he opened his eyes, tears were rolling down his face too.

Molly was dabbing her eyes with a handkerchief and she said to Charlie, "There is more than us three in this kitchen."

Charlie smiled and nodded to her. She felt Rosie's presence too. He wanted to reach out and take Arlene's hand but that was too hard to do, too big a step, but he wanted to acknowledge that he understood why she had been cold towards him.

He still could not forgive it because a child had suffered through no fault of his own and for Charlie, this was still unacceptable.

"I am sorry," he said eventually, "I am sorry for all your pain, suffering and loss Arlene. It must have been very hard for you, and I see now why you have been so cold and unloving. For a child to grow up feeling unloved by a parent leaves the deepest of scars, and I have questioned why I was unlovable so many times. I became so angry, filled with hatred and shallowness, not having the ability to be considerate of other people's feelings."

"I thought I had inherited your coldness and inability to love, but I was fortunate enough to meet Rosie," his voice started to break as he said her name. "She showed me that I was capable of love. I have Neave and in the short time since I have become a parent, it has already changed me, and because of my own childhood experiences, I have vowed never to put my own needs before hers and to always love her unconditionally. As I said yesterday I cannot yet forgive you. But I am going to work on that, and whether you want us to continue to be part of your life or not in the future, I will, I know eventually, be able to let go of any residue of the resentment and disdain I have felt for too many years. I am not wasting another moment that could be filled with joy, love, and happiness. I really do hope you can also get a sense of closure and fill the rest of your days free from the pain. You have suffered too. Let go of the narcissist and see what treasures life still has for you."

Arlene's tears continued to flow. The person sat opposite her who had been a permanent reminder that she had never been enough had just given her a key to rid herself of the self-loathing she had carried. The irony of it.

"Are you going to try to find them?" she said through her sobs.

"I think so, but I have no idea where to look. What happens now with us? I am not your son. You no longer have any responsibility for me. There is no reason why I need to be in your life. I will understand if you want this to be the final time you see me."

"Oh Charlie, please do not say goodbye," Molly pleaded. "I have missed you so much and Neave is such a wonderful child. If Arlene wants to say goodbye, then please keep in touch with me."

"I am sorry Arlene, I have always put you first, not because you pay me, because I really do care for you, but I just need to keep Charlie and Neave in my life. I hope you understand."

Arlene nodded. "I think that I would like that too. I do not hate you anymore Charles. I see now the hatred I had was for myself, and I turned that on you. I would like a chance to get to know you and Neave and see if we can build some sort of relationship. I feel as though the weight and burden of the last thirty years is starting to lift. I never realised just how much I was carrying. And for what it is worth Charles, I am sorry too."

She smiled at him, and he realised he had never seen her smile ever. It changed her whole face.

"You need to smile more Arlene, it actually suits you," he joked, breaking the seriousness they all felt.

They all made their way to the door to say goodbye. Molly gave Charlie a huge hug. Arlene held out her hand to him and when he took it, she wrapped her other on top and said, "Please let us know if you find them. I would help a lot to know that they have a happy life. I do not really believe in the afterlife, despite my faith, but I know it would have been important to Henry to know they are well. He never spoke to me about them after they left, but it must have been hard to say goodbye to his own flesh and blood, knowing he would never see his daughter again."

It made Charlie recall the words of the letter again, stating the father of Brigid's children was dead. He wondered if he should share that with them, but felt it best not to. Much had already been revealed and a sense of peace and acceptance was taking hold. Why add something that might not have any relevance whatsoever and rock the foundations they were starting to build.

"I will Arlene," and kissed her on top of her head. "I will keep in touch and when you feel ready, I will bring Neave to see you. You have got to decide whether she calls you grannie, nannie or just Arlene," he joked once again. It was all getting a bit too much to handle.

As the door closed behind him, he fell to his knees and sobbed.

"Thank you Rosie, thank you for loving me, for believing in me and for staying with me. I miss you."

364

32

Rosie

"Faith and Instinct"

"Charlie, I am still with you. I am so proud of the man you are becoming. I know you will be the most amazing father to Neave. That you will love and guide her, always make her feel secure and safe and encourage her to follow her own path in life. I can feel the calmness weaving its way through your body. A silver thread that is reaching, connecting and soothing all of your misunderstood feelings.

I shared today with you, and Molly felt me as well as you. I grow weaker as you grow stronger. But that is OK. I know there is more to discover, I feel it and I am still with you. Have faith in yourself, follow your instinct, and let Neave guide you."

33

Himinborth

"Heaven's Mountain"

It was mid-afternoon by the time Charlie returned to The Bay Horse. Neave greeted him with a huge hug and excitedly showed him the family of snow people she and Iris had made. Daddy, Mummy and Neave.

Whilst they were packing their belongings, Charlie updated Iris on what had happened earlier. He said there was much more to discover but that he needed to get Neave home for school the following day and he needed a bit of time to recoup. He felt emotionally and physically exhausted.

She had packed them some food for the journey home, and he had promised to keep in touch and felt he would be back soon to continue to unravel the mystery of his family. She hugged them both as though they were her own. Just the thought of them not being around was already making her feel lonely.

But she did believe that a deep friendship with them both had been forged over the past couple of days and the magic of it had made her think about the shortness of life and the need to be around people who are kind to you, and not those who suck and hoover all the good from you. Maybe she should spend more time with George and just let go of the life she had had with her husband.

The roads were much clearer as they set off on their homeward journey. It was turning cold as the sun started to set against the cloudless blue sky. Charlie reckoned they would be home by eight o'clock. He had phoned Frances to let her know they would be home later. She was so eager to find out what the weekend had revealed as Charlie still hadn't told her much as he said he didn't want to run up Iris's phone bill, they were already indebted to her. She wouldn't take any money for their stay, saying that Neave had paid the bill times many just with her smiles and giggles.

Neave had snuggled up on the back seat covering herself and Rosie's urn with a blanket and within ten minutes, she was fast asleep. God, he loved her so much, he felt his heart would explode. The golden light of the setting sun was starting to cast long shadows over the road. There wasn't much traffic at all, and Charlie was feeling relaxed about the journey ahead of him. The contrast in feeling from when he was driving there was just incredible. What a difference a day makes, he thought and started singing the words to the Dinah Washington song.

"What a difference a day makes

24 little hours

Brought the sun and the flowers

Where there used to be rain

My yesterday was blue, dear

Today I'm a part of you, dear

My lonely nights are through, dear

Since you said you were mine

What a difference a day makes

There's a rainbow before me

Skies above can't be stormy…"

He stopped mid verse as he slowed down seeing the flashing lights of an ambulance, police car and fire engine on the road ahead. A Policeman was waving his hands and Charlie stopped the car and wound the window down.

"Accident, I am afraid sir. The road will be closed until we have got these folk to hospital and the cars cleared. It's the reflection of the low sun on the snow and ice, blinds people's vision."

"I hope they are all OK," said Charlie.

"In safe hands," replied the Policeman. "You are going to have to turn round and find a different route home."

The commotion caused Neave to wake and ask what was happening. The Policeman hadn't noticed her in the back until then, and he advised Charlie to take extra care, because there was lots of black ice forming on the roads and still snow on many of the 'B' roads. Charlie turned the car round and, with the engine still running, took out a map to find another road. It would add another half hour or so to their journey and it would take them on some of the minor roads the Policeman had mentioned, but he felt sure that it was still the right decision to get home and not stay another night. Frances was desperate to see them and Neave had school, too.

"Do you know the way Daddy?" she asked.

"Sort of with the maps. Looks like we are going to have to go onto a higher road and cut back down onto the main road. It shouldn't delay us too much."

The roads were still snow covered, and it was turning crunchy as the coldness of night started to set in. The road wove upwards and Neave had now taken the front seat, with map in hand, trying to decipher its multitude of blue, green, and red roads.

They came to a junction where they needed to turn right to start the descent, but the road was closed. It said due to heavy snowfall.

Charlie started to wish he had turned round and had another night at Iris's. He was getting anxious. There were no lights on the road, which was becoming more slippery the higher they climbed. He had no idea where they were, and he had a seven-year-old child to protect and get home. The scenery, though was quite breathtaking and the snow that rested on the trees and hedgerows looked as though it had been sprinkled with gold dust as the last rays of sun rested on the branches.

But his nervousness was becoming evident and Neave, sensing it, said confidently, "It is this way Daddy, I know we can get home going up this road."

He had no choice to be honest, as it was the only road open. They continued to drive up the hillside, with its any bends and twists.

"Look Daddy I can see some lights," shouted Neave very excitedly.

"Civilisation at last," Charlie murmured.

It was almost 4.30 when they saw a sign that said, 'Welcome to Himinborth'. It was a small town that seemed to be perched at the very top of the world, on a plateau so that it could look down on life, watch what was going on, but not really have to bother getting involved with it. The main road was literally a circle that went around the town and eventually took them back to where they had joined it.

Off the road, Charlie had noticed a number of straighter and narrower roads that all seemed to lead to the same point in the centre of the town. For some reason Charlie touched the pendant that they had made from the artefact they had found on Mangata beach.

"Guess we need to choose which road to go down Neave, otherwise we will be driving round in a circle all night," he said, trying to joke off the trepidation he was feeling.

"I have counted them Daddy. There are eight roads and I think we should take this one."

Charlie took a sharp left onto the road. There appeared to be very little traffic or any activity at all as he entered the small town. It was Sunday though, Charlie thought, and a cold evening too.

"Look how pretty the Christmas lights are Daddy. Much better than at Iris's town."

It was certainly a very picturesque town. As they were approaching the end of the street that led to the centre of the town, Neave squealed with delight.

"Look Daddy, it is Father Christmas."

Charlie parked the car on the street. There was some sort of festival and market taking place for sure and this place of nothing and nobody was now a hive of activity with a massive crowd of people.

372

Neave was so excited as she put on her gloves and hat and headed towards the crowds of people that were meandering through a variety of Christmas stalls, selling everything from Christmas tree decorations to home-made cakes, brandy snaps, and Christmas punch.

Neave was off. He called for her to wait for him, but she disappeared into the crowd. Charlie tried not to panic as he pushed through strangers, apologising for knocking them, explaining he was looking for his daughter. He found himself at a large stone cross with a number of steps circling it. He stood on the top step, and it gave him an elevated view of the marketplace. All he needed to do was spot her bright red coat. So long as there weren't hundreds of girls wearing red, she should be easy to spot.

He scanned the mass of people and was starting to really worry when he spotted her jumping up and down, talking to a woman at a stall. He tried shouting her name, but his voice got lost in the noise.

He leapt off the steps and dashed over to where he had seen her, hoping she didn't wander before he got to her. He could hear her giggles cutting through the Christmas noise, like a homing beacon. When she eventually came into sight, he ran over and scooped her up in his arms, trying not to berate her for running off but telling her she need to stay with him. She hugged him and told him that she was sorry but that she had found a puppet she so needed and wondered whether Father Christmas might bring it her. She said it looked like her Mummy as it had such a happy face and long hair and she loved it so much.

373

"She's a cracker, isn't she? Such a bundle of energy. We kept her here knowing that her daidi or mammy would find her." Charlie heard a soft Irish voice speaking as a woman's hand touched the top of Neave's woollen bobble hat.

"Thank you so much," Charlie replied. "I have only just come back into her life and being a new parent, well I am still learning and had no idea just how exciting Father Christmas was. Thank you so much for keeping her safe."

He put Neave back on the ground and she pulled his hand to look at the array of beautifully carved wooden toys on the stall.

"Look Daddy, this is the one I want. Do you think it looks like Mummy?" Charlie couldn't really see Rosie in the puppet's wooden face, but it was certainly happy with two red, rosy cheeks painted on and two plaits of hair made from yellow wool. The man behind the stall was making the puppet come alive by pulling the strings. Neave giggled. Charlie nodded to the man, leant over, and whispered for him to bag it up incognito as Neave still believed in Father Christmas and he need to find a way to conceal it.

The woman had overheard the conversation and said very quietly to Charlie, "Why not have a wander and buy something for her mammy, get a large bag and then we can pop it in when you come back?"

"That is a great idea and once again, thank you for keeping her safe."

Charlie turned to the woman, who was certainly wrapped up for the winter evening. A rainbow of knitted colours wrapped around her neck, gloves, and hat to match. She smiled at him and for a moment she looked vaguely familiar, but it was hard to make out her face properly as it was wrapped in a scarf and the light was dim. The woman stared at Charlie and the smile that had been on her face dropped. She looked confused for a moment and then took a step back with a deep intake of breath, holding onto the stall as she started to wobble. Charlie instinctively grabbed hold of her arm to steady her.

"Are you OK?" She continued to stare at him, but all the colour had gone from her face. He thought she was going to faint.

"Charles." He thought he heard her whisper his name, but there was still so much noise he must have been mistaken. But she repeated this time a little louder.

"Did you just say Charles? How do you know my name?" Charlie's heart started to pound and the anxiousness that had just subsided after he had found Neave rocketed again. He raised his voice and asked her again.

"How do you know my name?" The man who was still entertaining Neave with the puppet dashed round to the front of the stall and took hold of the woman's arm.

"Hey there, young man, what's the problem?"

"She knows my name. I want to know why?"

Neave had become aware of the conversation and took hold of Charlie's hand.

"Charles Henry Shafton," the woman said this time not in a whisper and the word were very clear.

"Do I know you?" Charles replied, feeling incredibly vulnerable and a little frightened at the same time.

There was a pause and then the woman said, "I am your mother," as she put her gloved hands over her mouth, turning to the man saying, "It's Charles, Patrick, it is really him."

Charlie was trying to process what he had just heard…'I am your mother' the words were spinning round his head. Patrick, he knew that name, but where from, he couldn't focus properly. She removed the scarf from her face and her hat, and a mass of dark curly hair peppered with sprinklings of grey fell and he instantly saw this was the woman, albeit much older, from the photo. It was Brigid.

Over the past twenty-four hours, he had wondered if this moment would ever be in his life and if so, where would it be? What would they do? Now it was here, he just froze. The version he had created was that she would pull him to her arms, tell him she loved him and that she was sorry she gave him away. It wasn't on a market stall in a place that he stumbled across by accident.

"Brigid?" was all he could say.

"Yes, I am Brigid," she replied and took a step closer to Charlie, who instinctively stepped back. He felt he wasn't in his own body.. Neave clutched Charlie's hand harder. Something was happening, and she didn't know what it was. She was feeling anxious.

"My mother Brigid?" he asked. The man, was it Patrick, from the letters? The pretty face, much older but still the sparkle in her eyes. The eyes were green, just like his. The photograph was black and white, so he hadn't seen that her eye colour was the same as his.

"Is this the lady we have been looking for Daddy, she looks a bit like the lady in the photograph," Neave said quietly. Charlie just nodded and tears started to well up. The emotion he felt was something he had never felt before in his life. He started to feel his body shake, his mouth was dry. He felt totally out of control.

"How did you know?" he stammered. "How do you know me?"

"You are the image of your sister Charles. How could I not know my own son."

Charlie felt like the world was spinning. His brain just could not comprehend what was happening. Was this a dream that Rosie had conjured up? He couldn't work out if it was reality. He must have looked as though he was about to keel over as he felt two strong hands steady him.

"Lad, take a deep breath. You look like you are going to pass out". The words floated around his head as the hands guided him to a chair.

Brigid looked at the grown man in front of her. He looked like a lost boy. He was a lost boy, her boy. She tentatively took a step closer to him. Taking off her gloves, she knelt down to look directly into his eyes, and cupping his face, said, "Child, my son. I have prayed for this moment every day of my life, but I never, ever thought it would come. I have never stopped loving you, thinking about you, and the sadness that lodged itself in my heart the day I left you has never gone. I carry it each moment of every day."

He was in total shock. How on earth could this have happened? They were lost in the snow, the accident that diverted them, Neave finding their stall, that could not be coincidence, he just could not believe that. He could feel the pendant on his neck, warm against his cold skin. The pendant. A circle with eight arms leading to a heart in the middle. It was this town! The circular roads they have navigated, the eight roads that Neave had counted, the stone cross he had stood on to look for her at the centre of it.

"Rosie," he whispered. Neave heard him say her mother's name.

"Mummy helped you find your mummy didn't she Daddy. I knew she would."

"Feckin hell," he heard the man say said in a much louder voice.

Charlie looked into the woman's eyes, and he knew. He felt it in every cell in his body. This was his mother.

"Feckin' hell," he repeated

Neave threw her arms around Charlie's neck and the woman stood up and buried her head into the man's chest, softly sobbing.

"Feckin hell for sure, sorry Neave," he said again

"What does feckin hell mean Daddy?"

He hugged her so tight.

"I love you so much, Neave. Thank you, you brought us here," he whispered in her ear.

"It was Mummy. She told me to come here."

He wiped tears with the back of his hand and looked up into the darkness of the two people looking now down at him.

"Feckin' hell," Charlie repeated and smiled slightly. The tenseness that was carved all over the woman's face eased a little.

She looked up into the man's face and said, "It is him. It is him. It is my son."

That moment, those few minutes in time compared to all the minutes he had lived, all the experiences he had had, he had never, ever felt so vulnerable, so fragile, so needy, yet so safe at the same time. Neave was hugging him so tight. He needed to let her know that he was OK, he could feel from the strength of her tiny arms around his neck that she was worried.

"Meet Neave, your granddaughter," Charlie said proudly.

"We have a granddaughter, Patrick. God has blessed me this day, bringing me my own son and a granddaughter. Thank you," she whispered, looking towards the dark velvet black sky.

"Pleased to meet you properly, Neave," Brigid said. "I am so happy that you stumbled across us. What a clever little girl you are, an angel from God himself." She smiled at them both.

"She told me that she was on an adventure to find her grandma with her mummy and daddy..." Brigid's words slowed and she looked questioningly for Neave's mother.

"Mummy is still in the car," said Neave. She was on Charlie's knees, swinging her legs, much calmer now that Charlie had stopped crying. Brigid looked back at Charlie for clarification.

"It's a bit complicated. She is not with us anymore, she..." he hesitated.

He had never said the word out loud before. He stood and picked Neave up.

"She died a few months ago."

His lips started to quiver, and Brigid instinctively hugged them both. The first hug from his mother. The power of maternal unconditional love and this was the first time in his entire life he had felt it. It was so different from the love he felt for Rosie and Neave, which was a fiercely protective.

This one tore away at all the anxieties he had, the insecurities he had hidden for years, masked by anger and rage. It calmed him; it obliterated the darkness that fed the demons that lurked inside him. He felt whole for the first time in his life. It wasn't just the strength of the hug she gave him, that belied the tiny frame she had, this it was something that nothing else could equal or surpass, the purity and power of a mother's love.

"You are my grandma?" Neave questioned. "Do I have two grandmas, Daddy if you have two mummies?" Neave's innocence and endearing ways softened the acuteness of the situation.

"You have a much nicer face that the other one, doesn't she Daddy?"

"She certainly does have a much kinder smile, for sure."

"You have a fine Irish name, did you know that child?" said Brigid

"I didn't choose it," Charlie said. "It was her mother's choice. She is …was called Rosie." Charlie just wanted to sit down in the dirty, slushy snow and sob. He thought he would be more reserved, even angry when he met her. But it seemed to him the volcano of hot molten lava that he had little control over when it erupted was finally gone. He felt strange without it. Without anger, he didn't know who he was. Just like Arlene, he thought.

Brigid put her hand on Charlie's arm and squeezed it, acknowledging his sadness.

"I am pleased to meet you Charles," said Patrick, holding his hand to shake Charlie's.

"It's Charlie. Everyone calls me Charlie, well except Arlene, that is,"

"Your mother?" quizzed Brigid. Charlie just turned his nose up.

"Aye well, I am finding that mothers come in all shapes and sizes," he responded.

"And your da?" enquired Brigid. "How is he? Such a gentleman. I owe him so much."

"Sadly, he died whilst I was in my teens."

"So much sadness, Charlie," she replied, squeezing his arm again.

"Why don't you two go and get some hot chocolate from Dougie over there and come back in ten minutes? We will get this stall packed away in the car, and maybe you'd like to come back to ours and have a proper drop of something. We have so many toys at our house for you, my sweet young girl," Patrick said. "It is what we do, we make toys, help Father Christmas out all year. It is a grand job Neave."

"Sounds like a very good idea, don't' you think Neave?" replied Charlie. Neave was jumping up and down in excitement. She had never met Father Christmas's helper and, by her reckoning, he was her grandpa too!

They left the loaded car and trailer parked in the town centre. They only lived a short walk from the marketplace and they all walked together down another one of the eight streets in the town. Patrick walked in front, holding onto Neave's hand. Charlie could hear snippets of a story he was telling her about making toys for Santa. Brigid had put her arm through Charlie's. He just couldn't take it all in. Two days ago, he thought his mother was Arlene, a cold hearted witch, who in the end turned out to be just a hurt and sad woman who actually wasn't his mother, and now he was walking with his true mother, back to her house, oh and he found out he had a twin sister.

What the heck was going on? Was it real? He felt breath on his neck and heard her words, "I love you Charlie," and he knew it was all real. It had been Rosie who had led them here.

He hadn't realised her instructions to follow Neave could have been to lose her first, but how on earth the child had found Brigid and Patrick out of all the people there was a miracle. Brigid said it was God, Charlie, well he knew it was Rosie.

They walked for only about 5 minutes, but the noise from the Christmas Fayre was quickly left behind. The street was a mixture of small shops, butchers, haberdashery, general grocers, and houses, some of them small terraced ones, some a little larger, set back off the street with driveways and gardens. It did feel all very unreal. Even the town looked as though it was part of someone's imagination, a Christmas pop-up book.

"There is so much I want to ask you," said Charlie. "For starters, what is my sister's name? Is she at home?"

"No, she isn't at home, Charlie, she is in Paris. She works in the fashion industry and is out there for some sort of show with the company she works for. She will be back for Christmas and her name is Caitriona, Cat as she likes to be called. We have all of our lives to catch up, Charlie, but I just thank God for bringing you back to me. It is a miracle for sure."

"And I thank Rosie. It was her that led me here, of that I am sure. She was the most beautiful, kind, and unique woman on earth. And Neave is just like her, in looks and ways. They saved me from myself."

Patrick stopped outside of a small shop front. O'Callahan's Toy Shop was above the window, painted on a wooden board. The shop window was full of beautifully carved wooden toys, train sets, cars, garages, doll's houses, with teddy bears, rag dolls, cushions, and much more scattered all over. It was laid out to look like a child's bedroom.

"This is yours? It is amazing."

"We mainly do commissioned work, customised pieces. We have people from all over the world who are customers, but mainly from the UK, Ireland, and America. Just by fluke to be honest, an American tourist saw some of our pieces in a small shop my sister has in the town me and Patrick grew up in. My sister sells some of our things over there. She comes over a few times each year to get stock and this American couple saw our things and they now advertise us in their toy shops and soft furnishing company. Those Americans they must have so much money Charlie. It changed our lives. It enabled us to fund Cat's degree in fashion. And now you are in our lives, too. God must have forgiven me for my sins, he surely must have," she said.

They entered the building through a door at the side of the shop window that took them into a small room that was set up like an office with a small settee and a couple of chairs. There were toys all over the floor and photographs on the wall of people receiving the gifts that Patrick and Brigid had made.

Charlie peered at one of the photos that caught his eye.

"Is that Steve Tyler...Steve Tyler from Aerosmith?" he asked incredulously.

"It is," Brigid said proudly. And that is Livvy, the doll I made for his daughter. Can you see her name embroidered on the back of her hand?"

"Could this day be any more bizarre? I sing. I was in a rock band until recently and I just love to cover their songs. He started to sing Dream On...

Half my life's in books' written pages. Storing facts learned from fools and from sages. You view the earth...

Dream on

Dream on

I dream on

Dream a little, I'll dream on."

Brigid stared at the handsome young man in front of her. Her son, her beautiful, talented son. She was filled with overwhelming pride, for what she wasn't too sure, because she hadn't been with him to guide and support him, but she did create him, he was part of her and that was something to be immensely proud of.

"No, you don't know that one?" Charlie asked.

"One of my faves, but not everyone knows what it's about."

"So I took a big chance at the high school dance

With a missy who was ready to play

Wasn't me she was foolin'

'Cause she knew what she was doin'

And I know love is here to stay

When she told me to

Walk this way, walk this way

Walk this way, walk this way"

"Now I know that one," laughed Brigid.

"Is there a rock concert happening in the shop?" Patrick shouted from another room.

"That is quite a voice you have there Charlie. Not sure where that comes from, although your father did play the fiddle and sing Irish jigs>"

Charlie looked at her. Henry hadn't a musical note in his body. Charlie certainly had never seen a fiddle in the house…so it was true? Was Henry not his father?

"I have so much to ask you. I lost the person I thought I was just a couple of days ago and I have no idea who I really am."

"You are Charlie, my handsome son and you are a wonderful father, just hold on to that for a short while, I will tell you our story over time as we have the rest of our lives to finish the book, or maybe it's a song waiting to be sung," she laughed.

34

The Truth

"Will set you free"

They lived in the rooms at the back of the shop. It was one of those buildings that was a bit like a Tardis, much larger than it seemed. The kitchen was huge with homemade cabinets and a really large oak table with six chairs. Charlie assumed these were all made by Patrick and Brigid. The letters had said he was a good carpenter. At the end of the room were two French doors that led into a garden, which was lit up by moonlight reflecting off the thick piles of snow. A very worn green chesterfield type sofa and two upholstered armchairs were at the back of the room. Patrick poured a generous amount of whiskey into two glasses and gave one to Charlie, taking a sip out of the other himself.

"She doesn't touch the stuff, do you Bridge? Do you want a cuppa?" said Patrick. Brigid shook her head. "I'll get some juice for Neave and take her outside to play in the snow for a while whilst you two talk."

"Thank you Patrick. We have the stew and pancakes for tea. Charlie, you and Neave have to stay for food. You must be getting hungry."

"I am not hungry at all at the moment, but thank you. There is some pack up here in this bag that Neave might want?"

He gave the bag to Patrick, who took hold of Neave's hand and said, "Shall we have a picnic in the snow?"

Neave was delighted, and they were gone into the garden, leaving Charlie and Brigid alone for the first time. So much to say, so many words, but they were stuck in Charlie's throat. What do you ask your mother the first time you meet her? She took hold of his hand and he could see tears welling up in her green eyes.

"Is that the Patrick who wrote to you when you came over?" Charlie started the conversation.

"It is. How do you know that?" She looked puzzled.

Charlie pulled out the letters he had found at The Bay Horse.

"I found these at The Bay Horse. They were unopened. They are from Patrick. He offered to marry you. I am sorry I opened them…" his voice trailed off as he gave them to her.

She hesitated before taking them, holding them in her hands as though they were precious stones.

"He told me he had written. I never got them. Maybe…maybe things would have turned out differently if

…" her voice faded. She carefully placed the two envelopes on the cushion at her side.

"That is the past, and I will take some time later to revisit it. What is more important is now. How did you find us? Charlie, I am so, so sorry. I never, ever stopped thinking about you. At birthdays we always celebrate you and Cat. She knows she has a brother. You have always been part of our family, even though you haven't been here. We have wanted to reach out and find you, but we didn't know if you knew about us and didn't want to cause you any anguish. We thought you would have had a wonderful life, full of the luxuries and opportunities we could never afford and with loving parents. I have often thought about Arlene and the images I conjured up were of you bringing warmth and love to her."

"I could see, even at the young age I was, that she was a troubled woman. When my heart felt as though it was breaking from missing you, I consoled myself by telling myself that God had given me two babies so that you could heal her suffering. But how did you find us? We love it here, but it is so isolated, people have to come here specifically. Folk do not just stray upon it by accident. It must be God's will. Maybe he has finally forgiven me for letting you go."

"To be honest…" he paused, he didn't know what to call her. "Brigid," he eventually said, "I can't answer that with any sort of reason or logic.

You believe it is God. I am sorry I just don't have the faith you do, even though Arlene and Dad brought me up as a Christian, I have had that many demons in me, I just couldn't accept that God who is supposed to love us all, could love someone like me, someone unlovable, that is until I met Rosie. She changed my life, and she brought me to you. She is here with me now, her spirit. I know this. Neave, she has her mother's spirit. She senses and feels things, and her intuition and emotional maturity are far beyond many adults I have known. The roads were closed and the only road led to here. Is that a coincidence? I don't think it is." He held his pendant, it felt warm again, and he took this as a sign that Rosie was with him.

"Look at this. Neave found it on the beach where I first met Rosie. It looks like a map of the town. Rosie believed her ancestors were Nordic Vikings. Her colouring, the white-blonde hair and pale blue eyes, just like Neave's and just like Rosie's mum too."

"This place was first occupied by the Vikings and its name, Himinborth roughly translates as Heaven's Castle or Mountain. That pendant you have certainly looks like our town," said Brigid. "I felt a pull to this town."

"I have always felt that this is the place I needed to be. There is so much history about the town captured in old books, tapestries, and paintings that are in the old church. I am Catholic. Our church isn't Catholic, but it was the only place I could go to reach out to God. Our minister, although Church of England, says it is a place for faith, regardless of what that is. It is a place of sanctuary, of healing, of love.

Did you know that Vikings and Christians spent many years living together with their different faiths? There are tapestries in the church so old that you can hardly see the images. But they portray different people working together, living together, loving together.

I think this place is very special, and I have come to accept that my God is not everyone's, but most people need some sort of faith to bring them peace. I do believe your Rosie brought you here. I believe that this place is my destiny, a place I needed to be. I never understood why until today. It is the place where God, the spirits, whatever they are that guide us come together. It is Heaven's Castle. It is the place that brought you back to me."

There was a sense of calm and acceptance, as you would expect to feel in a place of prayer, and it helped the conversations that flowed between them.

"I don't really know who I am," Charlie said. "Forty-eight hours ago, I was the son of Arlene and Henry Shafton, and now I am not. I feel lost but …found at the same time. I knew I wasn't right. Everything was always a struggle. I never felt as though I belonged and I didn't know why. Thought it was me, that I was a bad person, unlovable until I met Rosie. But I screwed that up too. We had a son, and he died as a baby. I was so angry that the love and peace I thought I deserved had been taken away from me, that I just upped and left."

"I put any thought of Rosie to the back of my mind, well the best I could. She was always there though, I just locked her away. I played my music and drifted through life, angry, apathetic, uncaring, never unkind, but not having the capacity to really care about anything anymore."

Brigid reached out intuitively and held his hand. She had tears in her eyes.

"You are my son and I have never stopped loving you, thinking about you and feeling so heartbroken for giving you away. You must be angry with me." The tears were rolling down her face.

Charlie was moved. This was his flesh and blood, the woman who had given life to him. She was the only living person he had any family connection to. He must have been getting softer because he felt nothing but sadness for them both, no rage or disappointment. Maybe, just maybe that part of him that had finally been quelled.

"I am not angry with you. I didn't know you existed until a couple of days ago. I think I am still in shock. I have so many questions. I just want to know the truth of who I am and why I was left with Arlene and my Dad. I am sorry I opened the letters. They were private, but it was from these that I discovered I was a twin. Weird, isn't it that of all the places we went to, it was the Bay Horse? The land lady had saved a whole load of photos and papers from the previous managers, and the clues of who am I were in it all."

The effects of the whiskey were starting to take effect and the tenseness he had unconsciously been holding onto started to diminish.

"I have this too," he said, pulling out the photograph of her.

Brigid took it and stared at it, "It was a long time ago," she said. "Many more lines and grey hairs these days."

"Tell me my story please," Charlie said softly. "Some force or energy I do not understand has brought us here to you today. I cannot really get my head around it all, but I need to know before I leave."

"You found me after two days and you must be wondering why in almost thirty years I haven't sought to find you." She sounded very sad, and her face was etched with guilt. "And you do deserve to know the truth Charlie. You tell me what you know as clearly you know and I will fill in the details."

He could see she was nervous. Her hands were shaking, and she was fidgeting with her wedding ring. "I am not sure how much we will get through before that wee one gets fed up with Patrick's stories out there," she continued.

"This is what I think I know. That you came to Liverpool as a very young woman. You got a job and lodged at The Bay Horse. My father took advantage of you as a young woman seduced you…" He looked at her to confirm or deny it, but she remained silent and continued to listen.

"You wouldn't have an abortion and you wouldn't go home to your family because you felt ashamed and would be shunned by them. Arlene and my father would never have had children together, so he convinced Arlene to adopt me, pretending Arlene was my mother. But you had two babies, and they kept me and sent you away with my sister. I grew up knowing nothing about this. I thought my mother, Arlene, hated me. She never showed any love or compassion. I called her a stone hearted witch."

He was rambling. An outpouring of facts, suppositions and emotions that were overwhelming him.

"They shipped me off to boarding school at seven so that she only had to be in my presence during holiday times."

"When I was fourteen, she came to the school and told me my father was dead. Life was even worse after that. At least I knew my father loved me and my memories of him are that he was a kind man, a gentle soul who continued to be loving towards Arlene even though she was such a bitch to him. After Dad died, I spent holidays staying at my friend Jake's family home. She hardly saw me and when I was eighteen, she told me that I was an adult and she didn't want to see me anymore, that I was an embarrassment to the family, especially as I wanted to be a musician. Me and Jake have remained friends and until Rosie, we were inseparable, playing in bands, living the life of single men. But deep down I felt I wasn't in the right place."

He paused to take a breath. He shook his head as though still not believing what has happened over the past few days, took another sip of whiskey, and continued.

"I put my energies into writing music, and when I met Rosie, everything changed. She showed me I was capable of loving someone and was lovable in return. I was so happy. When I left her, our son had died, cot death, and I didn't know she was pregnant with Neave. I am ashamed. I was callous and selfish and I missed out on seven years of my daughter's life. I have found out Rosie went to visit Arlene, but she sent her away. How can a woman do that to another woman, especially carrying a child? I knew nothing of this until a few months ago. I was living my selfish life with Jake when she sent me a letter saying she needed me. I was angry at her for disrupting my life, for opening up all the sadness and rage I had boxed away. But she knew I would come."

Charlie paused for a moment, reliving the moment he saw her laid, a shadow of herself, in the bed they had once shared.

Brigid was taking it all in. She felt sick to her stomach. Her gift of love, the gift of her son to a broken woman to heal her, hadn't been the happy ending she had wanted and hoped for all these past years. That thought that had just been shattered, had helped justify her decision to leave her son. She felt broken. But this wasn't about her, this was about him.

"I had to return to the place that had been our home. Home should be a place of security, a place full of promise, hope, and love. I thought I was responsible for destroying our home because I was never meant to be loved. That is what I believed. I went because I wanted to show myself that if I met her again, I wasn't still in love with her. I wanted to show myself that the love and happiness between us hadn't been real. It was just a pretence because deep down below my 'couldn't care less exterior', I was so desperate to be loved I had made it up. And then… I saw her, broken, dying and I will never ever forgive myself for leaving her. Maybe if I hadn't left her, she might not have got cancer?"

He looked at Brigid for some sort of confirmation. She was looking at him with such sadness in her face, shaking her head.

"I had no idea that Neave was my daughter. She is so small. I thought she was much younger and Rosie had loved someone else."

Charlie started to sob, uncontrollably. Brigid instinctively put her arms around him and waited until his sobs subsided.

"All she wanted was for me to find myself, find the source of my demons, find peace and be Neave's father. She said that if I lived my life and then died an angry man, then we would never be together in an afterlife. It was all too much for me to take in."

"I was, and still am, riddled with guilt. But she came to me in my dreams, and I know Neave still feels and hears her and she helped me find the courage to visit Arlene to find out why my mother never loved me. We found the photograph of you at The Bay Horse before we called on Arlene and Neave wouldn't let it out of her sight. Arlene saw it and well, the weekend has been so crazy, but it has all led me to you, here." He sighed as though he had just unburdened himself, made his confession.

"That is so much to take in Charlie, a life nothing like I imagined for you and for that I am deeply, deeply sorry. I too am wracked with guilt. I should have been braver, but I wasn't. I thought I was giving you a better life, but Charlie, if I had taken you then you would not have met Rosie. You would not have the beautiful child you have and so there is some goodness that has come out of your life. Do you see that? And that isn't me relinquishing any responsibility I feel for your unhappy childhood," Brigid said.

"You have many of the pieces of the story, Charlie. I did come over to England at such a young age. I was adventurous and didn't want to settle down and get married and live my life planned out for me, have children, stay at home, be a good wife and so on. I thought England would give me opportunities I didn't have in Ireland. Turns out that I was meant to have children and be a wife at a young age in the end. The thing I had been running away from followed me. It was my destiny."

She took a deep sigh before continuing.

"Charlie, never think ill of Henry. He was a very kind and wonderful man and I knew he would take care and love you as if you was his own."

Charlie looked up at her, he had been staring at the floor. So, was it true that Henry wasn't his father.? He felt numb.

Brigid continued, "Henry, he wasn't your father. Well, what I mean is he wasn't your biological father. He sounds as though he was a wonderful dad to you. I met someone before the ship sailed for Liverpool. I had gone to Derry a few days earlier. My da had hoped that living away from home for a week without anyone, I would surely have changed my mind before the ship sailed and I'd be back home. I knew I wouldn't, but in that week I met Tommy O'Donoghue. Turns out he was from the next village to me, and he too wanted to escape from the rural, poor life he would have had there. He was a handsome and cheeky man.

He was full of life and energy. I had never met anyone like him. He was staying in the same B&B as me and the first night I was there, eating my evening meal, he spontaneously jumped on the table, started playing the fiddle and singing. The landlord tried to get him to stop, but the laughter and joviality brought people off the streets, and they bought ale and food, so he let him sing every night until the ship sailed.

He took a shine to me; I was innocent and naïve and I thought we were madly in love and that we would have a life full of adventure and fun in England. We vowed to stay

400

in touch. I had already got the position at The Bay Horse, lots of places in Liverpool advertised for staff in Ireland. They knew they could pay us less and we would work twice as hard as we didn't want to go back. He didn't have a job but said that there would be loads of navvy work round the docks. He said there were many places for people to sleep on the docks until they found work and he would find his cousin who had made the journey a couple of weeks before us."

"Told me as soon as he got settled, he would write to me or come visit. I waited for a month and heard nothing, so on my day off, I took the tram to the docks. It wasn't a good place. I felt scared and the men there were not polite at all, very intimidating and rude. But by chance, one of the men heard me speak his name. It was Tommy's cousin. He told me that Tommy was also a bare knuckle fighter, supposedly a good one, and that he had started to fight in the docks, as he hadn't managed to get a job and needed the money. There were fights arranged by bookies, illegal ones of course, but it was good money. The first two fights he won, but the third he took a blow to the head, fell unconscious with blood coming out of his ears. There weren't any medical people at the fights and by the time someone had managed to get a nurse to him, he had died."

"A pauper's grave and no one, not even his cousin, knew where he had been laid to rest. I don't know if Tommy would have been good to his word. Come and found me, like he said he would. I tell myself he would have. He was the first man I laid with. I was sixteen. I was heartbroken and Mr Daley, the pub landlord, could see I was upset when I got back. That was the first time I spoke to your dad, Henry. He bought me a sherry, shouldn't have done as I wasn't old enough. But I told him my heart had been broken. He told me that I had my whole life ahead of me and that once I had got over the shock and grief, then I would see that if Tommy hadn't died, then the life I had left behind, the life I wanted to escape from would have caught up with me. I knew he was right, as for sure I would have wed Tommy and settled down with bairns. Your da told me that a much more adventurous and wonderful life was ahead of me, with great possibilities."

"The irony is the thing I longed to escape from was actually my destiny, becoming a mother and a wife is what I got in the end, But I wouldn't change anything about the life I have had…except of course if I could rewind, I would have kept you, that would be the only thing I would change. Despite the harshness and challenges of my life, it has been a good one, for which I am eternally thankful." She paused for a moment to recall her memories.

"Henry was such a wise, kind man, a proper gent. I didn't know I was carrying at that time and tried to see the tragedy of Tommy's death as a second opportunity to have a different life, just like Henry had said.

Of course, that wasn't to be because within a few weeks, I knew I was in the family way. I could never have got rid of my babies, and back then it was an illegal backstreet procedure. Mr Daley thought I should consider it and because I didn't have the money, he asked Henry, who said he wouldn't give me the money but had an idea of how to make it OK."

"And that is where the lie started," said Charlie.

"I never thought about it as a lie, more of an untruth. No-one ever asked me if Henry was the father, only Mr Daley knew, and God bless him, he never told anyone to the contrary. So, I just went along with the untruth, the story Henry concocted. Henry told me that Arlene would never carry a child. I didn't ask why. To help me justify it to myself that I gave you away, I told myself God had given me two babies so that I could make another woman happy. For my sin of laying with Tommy I would always carry the guilt and shame as punishment of giving one away as penance for my actions."

Charlie was listening and, in a way, it wasn't really a shock that Henry wasn't his father.

The letter he had read from Patrick had said bairns, but it was all so much to take in. His head was full of questions. Why would his father make something like that up?

Why would he take the rap for some guy he had never met, help a woman he hardly knew and then have a life full of scorn and anger from the woman he married, the woman he supposedly loved, and then go to his grave not telling anyone?

"Why though?" Charlie asked, "Why would he do that? I do not understand. I need to ask you Brigid, is this the truth? You aren't making it up because you gave me away, are you?" He looked full of anguish and confusion.

"Why would he do that? Not tell the truth. He was a good loving father to me, and I have missed him so much since he died. He was the only thing in my life that was stable, that I felt safe with and now you are telling me that isn't the truth either. My whole fucking life has been a lie."

He felt the tingling of anger start to return to his fingers, but a strange thing happened, and he knew that Rosie was with him still. The pendant started to heat up.

"Charlie, look at the pendant…it is changing colour!" Brigid exclaimed. It was a myriad of different colours, almost translucent. Charlie put his hand on it. It was so hot. He felt a bolt shoot through his whole body, just like he did when Rosie had reached out to him, sent him the letter. Was that only three months ago? It was a lifetime away.

He felt a rush of energy fill his body, but this time he didn't feel the uncertainty, the anger rising, but a feeling he could only think was how people describe when they have been baptised, born again.

He was filled with a sense of euphoria, love, and belonging. He knew Rosie was there with him. She had brought him home. She had quelled his demons once and for all and crushed the darkness that had consumed him most of his life. He felt exhausted. Brigid looked on as she watched her son's demeanour change from tense and uncertainty to calmness and acceptance. She closed her eyes and took hold of his hands.

"Thank you God, for bringing my son back to me. Thank you for delivering him from the darkness into the light. I ask for your forgiveness for all of my sins so that my son can live his life full of hope, happiness and love. Amen."

Charlie didn't know what was happening. He didn't believe in Brigid's God, but he believed in Rosie, and he knew she had helped him finally rid himself of the chains and rot that had suffocated and imprisoned him. In its place, a feeling he had never felt before, freedom.

"Thank you Rosie, I love you…" he whispered.

35

Endings...

"Are just beginnings"

It was Christmas Eve. It had been three weeks since Charlie had returned to Hefring. It had been three weeks since he had last felt Rosie with him and even Neave hadn't mentioned her since they got back home. Home. There is a word he never thought he would ever say. Chapelfield House had never felt like home, and even when he had lived here in Hefring, with Rosie, it still hadn't felt as though he truly belonged, and belonging somewhere was such an alien feeling to him. To be content, to not be at odds with himself, to constantly question himself and to feel the exhaustion of keeping his anger within, had made him weary. But the absence of it was something he was adjusting to.

It is strange, he thought, you never know something has been missing in your life if you have never felt it. It is invisible; you are unaware of its existence. But there is a void you are aware of but don't understand and you instinctively fill the hole with anything and everything, even if it is destroying you and it takes you further away from the thing you really need.

You can't miss it until you know what it feels like. For the first time in his life, he knew what it felt like to belong somewhere, to be loved unconditionally, to have a sense of purpose and reason for being.

He hadn't been back to see Arlene, but he had telephoned her. She had deserved to know the truth, just like him. He had no idea whether it had made things worse or better for her, but what he did know is that truth brings answers, might not be the answers you wanted but the gut feelings you have that something isn't right, that something is off kilter, that somehow you are on the wrong path, is instinct and it shouldn't be ignored. For him, the truth was liberating, and although there were many questions still unanswered, it didn't seem to matter as much anymore as you can never change the past, you can only look forward and be responsible for your future. His future was to be a father, a good father, a biological father to Neave. He had been given a chance to make his life meaningful and have purpose. It was something he had never felt before.

Arlene hadn't said much at all when Charlie had told her that Henry wasn't his true father. She had been very quiet, hadn't asked any questions and thanked him at the end. Although that meant that in reality, she had absolutely no legal or moral obligation to him at all, she asked him to keep in touch. She said it would break Molly's heart if he and Neave didn't visit them. Charlie felt that actually it was Arlene asking them to visit, but she just couldn't admit it, so used Molly as the reason.

He had pondered much about why Henry (could he still call him his father now?) had kept the secret. Henry had loved him as though he was his proper father and Charlie would not let those memories be overcast by the lie. Looking back, he guessed that was why his father never hit back at all the names Arlene had called him, the accusations she had spit at him.

It was because he had nothing to reprimand himself for, in fact, quite the opposite. In his eyes and heart, he had done a good deed.

He had hoped that he had given a young woman a second chance at escaping poverty and the shame of being an unwed mother, whilst giving him and Arlene an heir. Charlie knew his father had loved Arlene, but never understood why. They were so very different, but then again, he and Rosie were so very different too. He knew his father would never have forced himself on Arlene and wouldn't purposefully do anything to make her unhappy. He must have thought that having a child would soften her, release her from her self-loathing and demons. It is strange that when you have had demons yourself, and you rid yourself of them, how attuned you become to other people who are living with darkness, that previously you were impervious to.

It must have been so difficult to work through what to do about the lie when Brigid had two babies. Brigid didn't have a bad word for Henry or Arlene. She had said the house confinement during pregnancy was a life of luxury, something she had never before, or since experienced.

Food, warmth, security and compassion from Henry and Molly, things she wouldn't have had if she had been on her own or had returned to Ireland. The decision for Henry to keep Charlie not his sister, Brigid had said, was because he was the firstborn and he was a boy. She had said it was heartbreaking to hear Charlie cry and not to be able to console him, but she knew he was being looked after and cared for by loving people, Molly and Henry for certain. She had really hoped that her baby boy would have melted the ice queen's heart.

It is hard to unravel a lie, to tell the truth and hope that by revealing it will make life better for all of those affected by it. Henry probably knew the truth might lead to Charlie being put into care or risk Arlene hating him even more for lying in the first place.

He also considered that if Henry had exposed the lie, then maybe his soul would have felt a little less troubled as carrying a lifelong untruth is a heavy cross to bear, but by lightening his load, he knew the darkness and heaviness would be picked up by the people he loved so dearly, Arlene and himself. Was it right to keep the secret? Who knows, but what he did know is that his father's intentions came from a place of love and compassion. He had done it for all the right reasons, a perfect storm, a happy ending he had envisaged for two women.

Little could he have known that a life born out of lies builds its foundations on sand and, over time, the sand shifts.

There is no stability. It is as though the energies of life know they aren't in the right place and constantly try to pull you back to where you should be. Charlie felt lucky that Rosie had taken him by the hand and, at times dragged him through his journey. Many people live their lives unhappy, unsettled, unloved without ever getting an opportunity to find out why, never mind being given a second chance to realign, readjust and live the life they were meant to have. Charlie believed everyone deserved to be happy, to live the best life they possibly can. Children don't ask to be born, he remembered being told. Adults, consciously or by accident, create life and it is an adult's responsibility to ensure that children feel loved, safe, secure and have the best possible shot at a good life. That is what his life would be, to ensure his daughter had enough stability and love from him.

He hadn't met his sister yet, and that was something to look forward to in the new year. Neave had called Nannie Brigid and Grandpops Patrick numerous times on the phone and Frances had invited them over during the holiday period.

Jake, the only person he had had in his life that he felt comfortable with until meeting Rosie, was also planning a trip. Charlie had been so wrapped up in his own feelings he hadn't given thought to Jake and, of course, his beloved dog Rocky, so he was really looking forward to spending some time with them both. He wasn't sure how much Jake had taken in about everything that had happened when Charlie told him on the phone, as Jake was almost permanently stoned.

411

There were good and not so great things about his new self. Before, his selfishness would have protected him from the feelings of others, so remorsefulness and empathy were new to him and at times he found himself crying, sometimes out of guilt, but sometime out of pure love when he looked at Neave. But these days, the feeling of sadness and regret did not open the gates to his resentment and anger as it would have done before. He had come to see them as stepping stones that had taken him through turbulent times.

It seemed to Charlie that life was a little bit like a river and we all have our own. The flow of water is like the energies of life, never stopping, and always flowing forward. We can't control the flow of energy, but we can affect the curves and directions of travel to ensure we get to where we want to be, but we can't do that for other people's rivers and lives. They have to carve their own, make their own decisions about the direction of travel. We can build bridges to join them or boats to visit to share love, compassion, sadness when they need us to be with them. But it is their journey, their decisions to make and their responsibilities to carry, not ours.

He would never know why Henry made that decision. He would never know what his life journey would have been if that lie hadn't been made. What he did know is that you can never go back upstream, against the flow, because if you try, life becomes a permanent struggle, because you cannot change the past you can only navigate the future, until eventually your river comes to an end, and you reach the ocean, and its vastness absorbs everything.

The person you were once is gone, but your legacy and energies become part of something bigger, something stronger and more permanent than life itself. Was it God, was it Heaven, was it Mother Earth or Valhalla…no-one would ever know, but he knew he would meet her again, his Rosie, and Christopher, wherever or whatever it was. But not yet. He had a life to live and a daughter to share it with.

He missed Rosie. But he also knew the final goodbye was edging closer, and he knew the time to say goodbye was near. He also knew she had stemmed the flow of her energies into the next life, built a temporary dam to stop her from her ultimate destination, as she wanted to help him. She belonged in her ocean and she needed to be released.

The full moon would be in the sky tonight and Charlie's idea to sail out and scatter Rosie's ashes onto the sea was welcomed by Frances and Neave. They had the small sailing boat and if it was a still sea, they intended to row just beyond the shore and say goodbye to Rosie, and if the sea was too choppy, which would be likely on a December evening, they would drive to the harbour, and scatter her from the safety of the harbour wall.

It was five o'clock and they put on their warm coats and wellingtons, gloves, and hats. The evening was uncannily calm and warm, no wind, and no clouds, which ordinarily would have meant a very cold frost in the air, but not tonight.

It was quite balmy. Charlie, Frances and Neave decided to venture down to the Mangata beach to see if it was safe enough for the boat. The sea was like a lake, a few ripples washed up onto the soft sand, and there in front of them was Mangata. A silver road from the reflection of the moon showing them the way to go. Charlie rowed out only about ten yards, aware that the sea can suddenly change, but none of them felt any sense of danger. Quite the opposite. It felt the right place to be.

They carefully removed Rosie's urn from the jumper Neave had wrapped around her. The night was silent. Not even the sound of people celebrating Christmas Eve in the village could be heard. They all took it in turns to say their final words to her. None were sad, there were no tears. Charlie removed the lid that had been holding her in one place. They all lifted her and watched as all that was left of her fell from the urn and was picked up by a gentle breeze. It looked like fairy dust, golden and silver as the moon lit it up.

As the tiny particles landed on the sea, what appeared to be thousands of hands came up from the water, caught her, held her gently before taking her down into the deep. All that was left was a silver lining on the calm, dark water. It looked like the shadow of Rosie, and Charlie and Frances stared as it lifted from the ocean and wrapped itself gently round Neave. Neave was smiling. She held out her arms. A small dark cloud passed over the moon and momentarily there was darkness and when it passed and the moon opened up Mangata again, Roise had gone.

Charlie took out his guitar that he had taken with them and whilst Frances and Neave huddled together with tears on their faces glistening in the soft light of the moon, Charlie said his final farewell to her.

It was his song that had brought them together and it would be his song that was their final goodbye…until the next life, until they would meet again.

"Forest trees that gently sway with rivers deep and wide,
This would be the perfect place if you were by my side.
Mountains topped with soft white snow and waterfalls so blue,
This would be a perfect place if I had not lost you.

For the world to be a perfect place, I'd wake each day and see,
The beauty of your angel face always smiling down on me.
Caressing strands of flowing hair, and see those eyes so blue,
But that's all that left is dreams we shared, my Rosie I love you.

Diamonds sparkle on ocean seas and soft white beach of sand
This would be my perfect place if I could hold

your hand.
Memories of a September sun, the sky a
Summer blue,
This would be my perfect place if I had not lost
you.

For my world to be a perfect place, I'd wake each
day and see,
The beauty of your angel face, always smiling
down on me.
Caressing strands of flowing hair and see those
eyes so blue,
But all that left is the dreams that we shared, my
Rosie I adore you.

Cold dark nights all alone wondering where you
could be,
Always remembering my perfect place when you
were here with me.
Stars don't sparkle anymore, ours a love so
strong and true.
Trying so hard to make a perfect world, now that
I have lost you.

For my world to be a perfect place, I'd wake each
day and see,
The beauty of your angel face, always smiling
down on me.
Caressing strands of flowing hair and see those
eyes so blue,

But that's left is the dreams that we shared, my Rosie I miss you.

I have to make a perfect place, for the father I need to be,
I see you in our daughter's face, when she's smiling down on me.
She brings me lightness in darkened days, care and compassion too
For she is you in all her ways, my sweet Rosie, I will always love you.

"Goodnight, goodbye, God bless my Rosie, I love you."

36

To Charlie

"You made it Charlie, I knew you would. I sense the calmness within you, the forgiveness and most of all the peace. No residue of the explosive anger nor the selfishness that had fuelled your life for so long. I am here now. I am at peace, no pain, and ready to say my final farewell to the beautiful life I have had. I am ready to give back the energies Mother Earth bestowed on me.

I left you the moment your peace came. Ironic that isn't it? That I have to go to make way for your peace. But my life has been rich, full of love and opportunity. I am sad to not witness our daughter's life and to see you flourish and grow and become the man I saw hidden away behind the cocky young musician all those years ago. But I know with all my heart that you will care for her and be at her side throughout her life. Part of me lives on inside her, but you know this.

I give myself back to Mother Earth, I am grateful for my life, all the love I have felt and for being your heartbeat even for just a short time. I know you cannot hear me and sense me anymore. These are my final thoughts and words as I wait for my ancestor to take me.

Until we meet again Charlie, live, laugh and love every minute of every day until you reach the end. I love you…

"ROSIE."

"Mummy," whispered Neave as she put her tiny hands on her heart…" You're still here…"

Acknowledgements

Where do I start to acknowledge and thank all the people who have influenced, contributed and supported me in writing this novel? Everyone we meet in our lives leaves a little imprint on us. Sometimes it is apparent, and we consciously acknowledge its influence and impact. Others stay in the recesses of our minds, not quite as visible, but nonetheless, they shape our views of the world, our values, thoughts, and actions. The ideas, characters and plots in this novel must have come from all of my life experiences, what I have read, been taught, experienced, and people I have met and lived my life with. I thank the life I have had for allowing me to write and enabling my creativity to develop.

There are many people I am indebted to for their support and encouragement, without whom I would never have finished the book, never mind getting it published. Here are a few fantastic people who have been the wind beneath my wings.

To my wonderful friend Lisa Pogson, who has held my hand, shared her wisdom and her networks with me. Thank you for our late-night texts and early morning chats and being just one of the most generous people I have ever known. Thank you. I would not have reached the end without you.

To my incredible circle of friends who believed in me, read copies of the many drafts and gave me valuable feedback, Gill and Jill, Janice and John, and Malcolm in particular.

To my husband, Terry, thank you for your patience, your nagging to complete the novel, and the endless supply of coffee and red wine when I found the time to write. And, of course, your love and absolute belief in me. To Wayne Miles for the music and vocals to my lyrics, A Song for Rosie.

To my children, the indescribable love I have for you as a mother has helped shape the characters in my book. It is such a privilege to be your mum.

To the people who are no longer with me: my mum and dad, who always spoke with such pride about my writing long before I contemplated a novel. Family and its importance are grounded in every bit of me because of you. To Pete, my first husband and father of my children. Dying too young and how our blended families coped and continue to love and care for each other has been a huge influence in the story.

To Sharon Brown, Publisher at The Book Chief, Laura Billingham, Editor at The Book Chief and Danielle Crossley from Deearo Marketing, who have shared their knowledge and expertise in getting Mangata Moon to print, I could never have done this without you all. You are a fantastic team. Thank you.

And finally, thank you to all of you who have bought my book. I hope you enjoy reading it as much as I have writing it. Let me know!

www.jacquelinefreeborn.com

The Author

Jacqueline is a trained counsellor and hypnotherapist and has spent most of her working life working in the not-for-profit sector supporting communities and organisations helping people achieve their potential. She was 'The Custodian of The Rotherham Story', building a network of advocates and positive storytelling about her hometown.

Although this is her first novel, she has always written for herself to help work through challenging times, as well as creating poetry for family and friends. Jacqueline is a wife, mother and nannie and her family are her life.

Jacqueline is a recipient of The Athena International Award for Leadership in recognition of her values driven leadership.

Preview of Book Two in this Trilogy

The second book of the trilogy finds Charlie settling into his new life as a father and provider, adjusting to the responsibilities and unconditional love he has for his daughter. Just when he thought he knew the trajectory his life journey was on, when he should feel at peace with himself, an unsettledness inches its way into him.

There is something about Neave that bothers Charlie, but he cannot fathom what it is.

*****

I hear their cries in the distance. Are they calling for me to return? It's hard to determine if they are songs of love and sorrow, or growls of anger because I left. But I had no choice.

I lose their calls for a while and I wonder if I am mistaken, and it is the howling of the wind that mocks me, as it tears through the trees, stripped bare of life by the harshness of winter.

I try to search for them, but the snow blinds me, piercing my eyes and face with needles of ice as I struggle to see what is out there. The blizzard is mesmerising, and I feel myself being pulled into it, as it entices me to surrender myself to its conjuring. I feel the adrenaline that gave me the courage to leave, turn into fear, its consumption of me rapid. I need to ground myself. I kick off my boots and the freezing stone beneath my bare feet jolts me back to you.

I pick you up, my sweet, dear child. You do not look afraid. Your eyes fix on me with absolute faith that I will always keep you safe. That's what a mama does, and I hold you tight to keep you warm.

Nature is angry tonight. She is raging. Is it because I have taken you? I was so sure this was the right path for us. Did I make the wrong choice? I question my judgement and I call out to our earth mother for help and guidance. The cold is numbing, anaesthetising me from my panic and fear. I wrap my shawl around you to offer shelter from the rage of the night.

The sounds of the storm dissipate, and I feel the warmth return. All becomes silent. She has answered us, and she will protect us. I look down and lock onto the calmness in your eyes, like sapphire stars in the night, guiding us to where I do not know. But I am with you and that is all that matters.

Forgive me, my child. I love you."

A SONG FOR ROSIE

Listen to Charlie's final song for Rosie

Q&A WITH

JACQUELINE FREEBORN

Why did you want to write a book?

I just love the power of words and how they evoke imagination, feelings, and memories. The combination of the same words conjures up different things for different people.

Does writing energise or exhaust you?

Writing energises me. I love it when my imagination takes control of my hands, and something creative appears on the page. I think in a world where being logical, sensible and doing what is expected or needed, writing brings me freedom.

What message did you want your book to convey to the reader?

This is the first novel of a trilogy I want to write. A few people who read draft copies said it was like getting gentle therapy in a story, which made my heart smile. Story telling has always been an essential part of human life, inspiring, learning from, and passing on morals and values. It's a story about relationships and love in its many forms, the power and potency of love, and the insecurity and emptiness when it isn't felt. The old adage, 'Build a House on Sand, and it will fall down, ' is the same if life is built on lies or untruths. I hope that readers assimilate and absorb some personal learning from the characters, which helps them reflect on their own lives in some small way.

What is the first book you read that had a real impact on you, and why?

I loved The Borrowers as a child. Studying Wuthering Heights in O'Level English Literature made me love reading more. It is hard to pinpoint the book that had a real impact on me, but My Sister's Keeper by Jodie Picoult stands out for me. I love all of her books. I love the way that, through a fictional story, she challenges me to think about everyday dilemmas, the choices we make, and the impact those decisions have on other people. Philosophy in a novel.

How did it feel to hold your book in your hands for the first time?

I am overwhelmed, emotional, and proud. I finished the draft novel while my mum was still alive, and she was so proud. I wanted her to hold an actual copy in her hands before she read it, but sadly, she passed away before it was published. Holding my book makes me think about my parents and the life they gave me.

How many other books do you feel you have in you?

Mangata Moon is a trilogy, so I have at least two more books. The process of writing and having a book published fuels and energises me, and I have already started the sequel.

How much time did you dedicate each day/week to writing your book?

My writing journey reflects my life, which is chaotic and opportunist. I needed to be more organised and write when I had free time, which wasn't very often! Sometimes, it was when I was sitting waiting in the hospital; other times, it was at the end of a working day or when I was on holiday. I find routines and structure quite tricky, and I think my brain becomes rebellious when told what to do and when, so being organised and dedicated to a particular day or time doesn't work for me. When I do write though, I lose all sense of time and it's midnight before I notice the day has passed!

How would you deal with a bad review?

I will probably feel rubbish, but I have dealt with many times in my life when I have had to work through not being everyone's cup of tea. Writing and reading are very much personal tastes and preferences. I am proud that I have finished my first novel and that it has been published, and I have and will continue to learn from the whole process.

Did you suffer from writer's block at any point during the writing process? If so, how did you overcome it?

I didn't get writer's block. I have learned that if I apply a logical approach to my writing, in that I plan too much and add detail in that planning, then the words don't flow. I must find a starting line and see where the words take me. I write quickly, and then I read and tweak. It will be interesting to see how I approach the subsequent two novels and if this haphazard way continues.

What are your favourite genre of books to read?

I like novels rather than factual books. When I get time to read, I want escapism, not reality; I have far too much of that. Novels, I like historical ones that enable me to learn about history and how people lived, but through a story. I also like books about relationships. I don't know how I would classify my preference. I love fantasy and sci-fi films, but not books...how weird is that!

Did you find writing a therapeutic experience?

Absolutely. I have always written during difficult times, just for me. What comes out of my head onto paper is often reflective of the things I am dealing with but in a story form. I have also written poetry, and people have asked me to write for special occasions. Story-telling and poetry enable us to tackle things that are challenging and sometimes difficult to talk about.

What advice would you give to someone considering writing their book?

Just start it. You might change the beginning later, but get going. Don't overthink things or be too methodical about the process; do what feels right. Go with your gut. Once the words are out, you can change them, move them around, delete them and add more; get them out of your head onto paper or the screen. It becomes quite addictive, and the adrenaline kicks in when you start. Don't be afraid to cut chunks out; take feedback from others and talk to like-minded people to encourage and support you. Most of all, believe in yourself.

What would you have done differently, if anything, in writing your book?

Lots. I free-handed the book. I then had the mammoth task of typing it up. Next time, I would still probably free hand as when my head starts going, I can't type quickly enough, and I don't want to lose the words. But I would type up each chapter before I began the next. Also, I need to be more organised where I leave my draft writing so I don't forget where it is! I would also give myself a time frame for writing a trilogy; I do not want a considerable time lapse between books.

Are you planning on writing more books similar to your current one, a completely different genre, or is one enough?

There are two more books that continue the characters' stories, so I am sticking to the same genre at the moment. I can't plan any further ahead than that, and I guess it will all depend on how a story starts to develop in my head.

Printed in Great Britain
by Amazon

INTRODU
New Zealand birds

Alina Arkins
Photography by Len Doel

REED

ACKNOWLEDGMENTS

Many thanks to Geoff Moon for commenting on the manuscript and contributing photos. The authors also gratefully acknowledge the assistance of Auckland Zoo Educators and Otorohanga Zoological Society during the production of this book.

Reed Publishing
Te Karuhi tā tāpui o Reed (Aotearoa) **(NZ) Ltd**

Established in 1907, Reed is New Zealand's largest
book publisher, with over 300 titles in print.

For details on all these books visit our website:
www.reed.co.nz

Published by Reed Books, a division of Reed Publishing (NZ) Ltd, 39 Rawene Road, Birkenhead, Auckland 10. Associated companies, branches and representatives throughout the world.

National Library of New Zealand Cataloguing-in-Publication Data
Arkins, Alina.
Introducing New Zealand birds : a guide identifying common birds
in New Zealand / Alina Arkins ; photography by Len Doel.
Includes bibliographical references and index.
ISBN 0-7900-0981-1
1. Birds—New Zealand—Identification—Handbooks, manuals, etc.
I. Doel, Len. II. Title.
598.0993—dc 22

ISBN 0 7900 0981 1
First published 2005

Edited by Carolyn Lagahetau
Designed by Sally Fullam

Printed in New Zealand

Contents

Part 1
THE PAST

TWO HUNDRED MILLION years ago the Earth was a very different place to the world we know today. Land in the southern hemisphere consisted of a vast supercontinent called Gondwana. At that time a small area at the edge of Gondwana, which would one day become New Zealand, lay under the sea. As the nearby land eroded sediments in this area slowly built up, becoming rock over time. Then, around 130 million years ago, movements beneath the earth's crust elevated this new land above the sea surface, and ancient New Zealand was created.

At this stage the young New Zealand was still attached to the edge of Gondwana. Most of this great southern land was covered in forest, with a canopy of conifers and an understorey of ferns and mosses. Birds and mammals had not yet appeared. Life on land was dominated by dinosaurs and other reptiles, plus amphibians and insects.

Around 100 million years ago convection currents in the hot liquid rock beneath the earth's surface began to push and pull at the Gondwana landmass. Very slowly, over millions of years, Gondwana split up into fragments that would one day form the southern continents of Africa, Australia, Antarctica, and South America. Some northern hemisphere countries such as Turkey, Arabia, and India, as well as numerous island countries, were also formed from fragments of Gondwana.

Via the process of continental drift, these fragments began slowly moving towards their present-day positions around the globe. A small fragment drifted away. New Zealand's journey into isolation had begun.

The ancestors of many modern trees grew in the lush forests of Gondwana.

Islands adrift

AROUND THE SAME time as Gondwana began to break up, flowering plants had appeared. Birds were beginning to diversify into myriad forms. Early mammals, restricted to small, insect-eating animals during the time of the dinosaurs, also began to diversify and disperse across Gondwana.

By 80 million years ago the land that would become New Zealand had completely separated from Gondwana. At that time the New Zealand land area was much greater than it is today. In fact, it was more like a small continent, stretching north to include what is now New Caledonia, south to the Campbell Islands and east to the Chatham Islands. With sea level fluctuations the land has been repeatedly submerged and uncovered. At present only about 10 percent of this original land area remains above sea level.

Unique wildlife

As it moved further from Gondwana, New Zealand carried with it the wildlife that had colonised it before it broke away from the supercontinent. This included the ancestors of the modern podocarp trees such as rimu and totara, and other conifers such as kauri. Many ferns and fern allies were present, as were some of the early flowering plants, including the ancestors of southern beech species.

A giant kauri tree, descendant of Araucarian pines that flourished during the Jurassic period.

Peripatus, **or velvet worm.**

A kauri snail, one of New Zealand's giant carnivorous land snails.

The tuatara has survived in New Zealand almost unchanged from Gondwanan times to the present day.

Animal life included species such as tuatara, land snails, weta and the velvet worm, or *Peripatus*. Many of these animals have survived to the present day, almost unchanged from their ancestral forms. For this reason they are sometimes popularly called 'living fossils'.

Skinks, geckos and frogs were also part of the early New Zealand fauna, as were the predecessors of such birds as the kiwi and the moa. It is thought that these birds were already flightless at the time they colonised the land that would become New Zealand.

So New Zealand moved away from Gondwana with a selection of flora and fauna that was now geographically isolated from the rest of the world. But new species that were capable of crossing the seas continued to arrive. The seeds of some flowering plants were carried on the wind and took root in New Zealand. Able to fly across the widening seas, the ancestors of birds such as the kokako and the rifleman, and more recently the fantail and the pukeko, made their way to the New Zealand islands.

One major group of animals almost entirely missed out on colonising New Zealand. By the time any land mammals reached the nearest edge of Gondwana, New Zealand had severed its last land links with the supercontinent. Only two species of bats later managed to migrate here and survive to the present day. Birds became the dominant terrestrial vertebrate animals in New Zealand, evolving into a variety of forms, most of which were found nowhere else on earth.

Flightlessness

ONE OF THE features of New Zealand's avian fauna is the high proportion of flightless species. One such group is the ratites, represented in New Zealand by the kiwi and the extinct moa. The name ratite is derived from the Latin word *ratis* (raft), a reference to the flat sternum that does not have a 'keel' to which flight muscles are attached in other birds. Other ratites are the ostrich, emu and cassowary.

In contrast to the ratites, which are thought to have already been flightless at the time they reached New Zealand, the lack of mammals here left the way open for many other birds to revert to life on the ground with little fear of predation. These birds lost the ability to fly and took up many of the ground-dwelling ecological niches occupied by mammals in other places.

In addition to our national bird icon, the kiwi, New Zealand has, among others, a flightless parrot (the kakapo), a flightless rail (the weka), and a flightless swamphen (the takahe). A number of other species are poor fliers and spend much of their time on the ground or hopping among tree branches. Many more flightless species once existed here, but became extinct after the arrival of humans and the introduction of predatory mammals.

Bird evolution

THE ORIGIN AND evolution of birds has been something of a mystery. Because they are light and hollow, bird bones often do not fossilise well, so in many places the early bird fossil record is comparatively poor. At first most scientists believed that birds evolved directly from reptiles. But fossil discoveries in the last decade or so lend support to the theory that birds evolved from a group of dinosaurs called theropods.

In 1861 the first bird-like fossil was found in a quarry in Germany. It was named *Archaeopteryx* ('ancient wing') and was dated at 150 million years old. With its long tail and clawed fingers (reptilian), and wishbone and feathered wings (bird-like), the creature was thought to be a transitional form between reptiles and modern birds. Today, scientists know that *Archaeopteryx* most closely resembles a small theropod dinosaur.

In the 1990s a well-preserved fossil of a small dinosaur that had long, filament-like growths on its body was found. Scientists think these filaments are an early form of feathers. This fossil, and others found since, share some skeletal characteristics with modern birds, supporting the theory that birds evolved from a group of small meat-eating dinosaurs. Although most scientists now accept this theory, there are still many more questions about the evolution of birds that are yet to be answered.

The arrival of humans

A feral cat, one of many species of mammalian predators brought to New Zealand by humans.

FOR MILLIONS OF years New Zealand carried its cargo of wildlife in isolation from the rest of the world, with the occasional arrival of new species by air or sea. Evolution in New Zealand continued at its own pace. Climatic changes, rising and falling sea levels and other changes to the landscape generally occurred over very long time periods, allowing most of the flora and fauna time to evolve and adapt to the new conditions.

However, around 1000 years ago this abruptly changed when humans first set foot on New Zealand shores. Polynesian immigrants arrived and colonised the land. Like all colonists do, they began altering the landscape of their new home. Vegetation was cleared to make way for settlements and gardens. Large areas of forest were burned, and birds were hunted for food. Many bird species were unable to cope with this new threat, and became extinct over the next eight or so centuries.

Around 200 years ago the second wave of human settlement in New Zealand began. European settlers arrived, bringing with them a large number of species new to New Zealand. Some species were intentionally released in an effort to make New Zealand more like the settlers' homelands, or to provide a source of income. These included European trees and food plants, and sheep and cattle. Others, such as rats and mice, were not deliberately brought here but nonetheless arrived via ship. Within a few decades feral populations of predatory mammals such as cats, stoats, weasels, possums, and hedgehogs became established in New Zealand. This was to have a further devastating impact on the remaining bird fauna.

Extinct birds

Many more species of birds once existed in New Zealand than the ones we see today. There are more than 50 species of birds we know were once found here but are now extinct.

Some of these birds disappeared before humans arrived in New Zealand. For example, several species of penguins no longer exist, including the New Zealand giant penguin. At 1.5 metres in height, this is the largest penguin known to have lived. There were also two species of false-toothed pelicans (so named because of the serrated edges of their bills), and an albatross. We know very little about these birds and how they lived, and the reasons for their extinctions will probably never be known.

A much greater number of species have become extinct since the arrival of humans

A mock-up of a giant moa.

to these islands. This event was to spell the end for a significant proportion of New Zealand's bird fauna. New Zealand truly was a 'land of birds' and many species had become flightless and lived their entire lives on the ground. Their only predators were other birds, such as raptors (birds of prey) and owls. This made them extremely vulnerable to hunting by the first Polynesian immigrants, and later to the many mammalian predators that Europeans brought into the country.

The most famous of New Zealand's extinct birds is the moa. There were around 11 species of moa, all herbivorous. At three metres in height, the giant moa was the tallest bird known. Moa took flightlessness to the extreme — they are the only birds known that possessed no wing bones at all (or at least the remains of wing bones have never been found). Hunting pressure and habitat loss are thought to be the main reasons for their extinction.

A number of other bird species are extinct on the three main New Zealand islands, but small populations continue to exist on some of our smaller islands. Without intensive conservation management, a considerable number of living species are still at risk.

Other pre-European extinctions include a pelican, a swan, and a crow. There were also two goose, two wren, and four duck species, as well as three raptors, including the New Zealand giant eagle, the largest known bird of prey. The adzebill, named for its large, strong bill, was the sole member of a family of birds unique to New Zealand. Also extinct is the New Zealand owlet-nightjar, a nocturnal bird related to the frogmouths of Australia and New Guinea.

G. COX

New Zealand eagle.

W.L. BULLER

Huia were last seen alive in 1907. The white-tipped tail feathers and the long, curved beak of female birds were prized as ornaments by Maori. Many huia were shot and sold to museums and collectors for display.

The arrival of Europeans brought a further threat. In the last 200 or so years of European colonisation, approximately another nine bird species and six subspecies have become extinct. Further forest clearance took its toll, as did the shooting and trapping of birds for sale to museums and collectors overseas. However, the most detrimental effect, which continues to this day, was that brought about by the introduction of mammals to New Zealand, against which most birds had no effective defence strategies.

Post-European extinctions include the laughing owl, New Zealand quail, Stephens Island and bush wrens, New Zealand thrush, and the huia.

Part 2
THE PRESENT

FOR A SMALL COUNTRY, New Zealand has a remarkable diversity of habitats, from coastal to lowland forest to high country tussockland to wetlands and pasture. Many of the more accessible areas of the country have been highly modified over the last several centuries by human activities, whereas other areas remain relatively untouched and are often refuges for some of our now rare native wildlife.

In considering the kinds of environments in which different birds live, it is important to note that many species occur in a range of habitats, and are not neatly divided into one or another. Some birds have been able to take advantage of the landscape changes brought about by people, and now live in urban areas as well as their traditional habitats. Others have always naturally occurred across a range of different habitats, and many move from one habitat type to another according to the season. This following information is arranged in chapters relating to habitat types in order to give an idea of the kinds of birds that are most likely to be encountered in each of the major habitats described. The majority of the most common birds are included, plus a few of the less common species. At the end of each chapter, there is an 'Also seen' box that lists birds that may also be found in that habitat, but which are described in another chapter.

Australasian gannet colony.

Sea birds

OF ALL THE world's oceanic bird species, over half may be seen in the New Zealand region. This, plus its island nature and ease of access to the many kilometres of coastline, makes New Zealand a great place to observe sea birds.

Sea birds include the tube-nosed birds, penguins, gannets, and skuas. These are birds that feed at sea, coming ashore only to roost or nest.

Before humans colonised New Zealand, large numbers of seabirds would have nested on the mainland islands. Today, however, most species nest mainly on offshore islands that are free from the mammalian predators that have devastated the bird populations. Despite this, a few seabirds such as gannets and royal albatrosses, still have nesting colonies on the mainland.

Only the more common species that are most likely to be seen have been mentioned here. Many more seabird species may be encountered. When birdwatching, particularly at sea, a good field identification guide is essential. However, many seabirds look similar to each other, and even with a good guide book it can still be difficult to identify the different species.

Tube-nosed birds

Many seabirds, including albatrosses, mollymawks, shearwaters, petrels, and prions, belong to the large order Procellariiformes, or tube-nosed birds. All the members of this order have characteristic external nostrils in a tube along the top or sides of their bill. Excess salt that builds up in the bird's body is excreted in solution from these nasal tubes.

The endemic northern and southern royal albatrosses are locally common in New Zealand waters. The **southern royal albatross** breeds on Auckland and Campbell islands, and may be seen off the southern coasts of New Zealand in winter. The **northern royal albatross** breeds at Taiaroa Head (near Dunedin) and on the Chatham Islands, and is

Wandering albatross.

Albatross taxonomy has been under recent revision. Results from genetic studies have led researchers to suggest that some subspecies should now be classified as species.

regularly seen in more northern waters outside of the breeding season. Both species are similar in appearance.

The **wandering albatross** is found throughout the southern oceans of the southern hemisphere. There are four subspecies, three of which breed on New Zealand subantarctic islands.

Mollymawks are small albatrosses, and several species are found in the New Zealand region, including the **shy mollymawk**, **black-browed mollymawk**, and the endemic **Buller's mollymawk**. They breed on subantarctic islands and can regularly be seen in New Zealand waters, although more commonly in the south.

Significant numbers of albatrosses are killed each year as a bycatch of fishing vessels, in nets or by baited longlines. Researchers are trying to find ways of reducing this bycatch by developing new fishing methods.

Shearwaters and petrels make up the largest number of species of other tube-nosed birds. They may be seen in coastal waters all around New Zealand. A few nest at high altitude on the three main islands, but many are now restricted to offshore islands, particularly those free of mammalian predators.

Common shearwaters are the **flesh-footed shearwater**, **Buller's shearwater**, **fluttering shearwater**, **little shearwater**, and **sooty shearwater**. The latter are sometimes harvested by southern Maori for food.

Petrels found in the New Zealand region include the **common diving petrel**, **northern** and **southern giant petrels**, **grey-faced petrel**, **Westland petrel**, **mottled petrel**, **black-winged petrel**, **Antarctic fulmar** and **cape pigeon**. The populations of several endemic species, such as **Cook's petrel**, **black petrel**, and **Pycroft's petrel** have been severely reduced since the introduction of mammals to New Zealand, and these species are now rare.

Within the same group are the smaller prions and storm petrels, such as the **fairy prion**, **broad-billed prion**, **Antarctic prion**, **grey-backed storm petrel** and the **white-faced storm petrel**.

Shy mollymawk.

Buller's shearwater.

Fluttering shearwater.

Giant petrel.

Grey-faced petrel.

Westland petrel.

Cook's petrel.

ABOVE: **Little blue penguin.**

RIGHT: **Yellow-eyed penguin.**

Penguins

Penguins are flightless birds found only in the southern hemisphere. Of the 16 known species, 13 are found in the New Zealand region, although some of those only rarely. Penguins have short, waterproof feathers and webbed feet. They are agile swimmers, and feed on fish and other marine invertebrates. Penguins come ashore to breed and to moult, and some species roost ashore each night.

The **blue penguin** is the smallest known penguin. It is commonly seen in coastal waters throughout New Zealand. Some blue penguins make their nests on or near the shore, while others may travel several hundred metres inland to find a suitable nesting site. Their loud, sometimes eerie cries, given as they come ashore at night, are a familiar sound in many coastal areas.

The endemic **yellow-eyed penguin** is found only in the southeast of the South Island, and around Stewart Island and other southern islands. It comes ashore in the evening to its nest or roost. Yellow-eyed penguins are endangered, and research programmes are under way to try and understand more about their ecology and behaviour.

Three other penguin species are endemic to the New Zealand region. They are the closely-related **Fiordland crested penguin**, **Snares crested penguin**, and **erect-crested penguin**. All are found only around the South Island and subantarctic islands.

Gannets

The **Australasian gannet** is a common native bird around New Zealand coasts. These large birds are well-known for their spectacular feeding behaviour, which involves plunge-diving into the water at speed to catch fish and squid. Gannets breed in colonies on rocky islands and clifftops around New Zealand.

Skuas

Skuas are a small group of seabirds, and only a few species are likely to be regularly seen in New Zealand. The most common is the **Arctic skua**, which breeds in the Arctic then migrates south for the southern hemisphere summer. This species may be seen in coastal waters and occasionally on the shore throughout New Zealand. Arctic skuas are similar to a large gull in appearance. Their colouring varies, ranging from dark brown all over, to brown with a pale neck and underparts. Arctic skuas have been observed chasing gulls and terns on the shore, forcing these smaller birds to surrender fish they have caught or disgorge their last meal.

Also seen: terns, gulls, shags (coastal birds)

Forest birds

BEFORE THE ARRIVAL of humans, approximately 80 percent of New Zealand was covered in forest. Today, forest clearance has reduced that figure to around 20 percent, with coastal and lowland areas being hardest hit. Despite this there are still significant large areas of forest throughout the country, much of it protected as national parks and reserves. In recent years many landowners with fragments of 'bush' on their properties have shown an interest in protecting these, sometimes enhancing and extending them with supplementary planting.

Many visitors to New Zealand are surprised at the apparent lack of birdlife in our forests. Loss of habitat and the introduction of predators has substantially reduced the populations of many species, with some now found only on offshore islands or as the subject of intensive mainland conservation programmes. This loss in turn endangers the forest itself, as many plant species depend on birds for pollination and seed dispersal.

On the other hand, some species, such as the fantail and grey warbler, have adapted well to, and in some cases benefited from, these changes to their environment. They have been able to expand their home ranges into scrubland, rural and urban areas.

Most New Zealanders will have experienced being in the forest at some time in their lives. Tramping or 'bushwalking' is a national pastime, and there are many excellent walking tracks and routes available that allow access into forest areas.

Successful birdwatching in the forest varies a great deal from place to place and from season to season. With few exceptions, most New Zealand forest birds are small and not

View inside a lowland forest.

brightly coloured, making them difficult to spot in the dim light beneath the canopy. You may often hear more birds than you will see. The best way to observe birds in the forest is to find a place to stop and sit quietly for a while. During the nesting season (usually spring–summer) male birds defend their territories, and this may afford you a chance to see the birds as they respond to your presence within their territory.

Most of New Zealand's forest birds are endemic, that is, they are found nowhere else in the world. A few, such as the fantail, grey warbler and bellbird, originally came from Australia, and have close relatives in that country.

Perching birds (passerines)

As a group, perching birds make up about 60 percent of all bird species. Most of the more common native New Zealand forest birds are passerines. The smaller perching birds include the fantail, grey warbler, tomtit, rifleman, whitehead, brown creeper, and silvereye. Larger perching birds include the New Zealand robin, the wattlebirds (kokako and saddleback) and the honeyeaters (tui, stitchbird and bellbird).

Fantails are one of the most easily recognised forest birds. They have a long tail, often held up in a fan-shape, hence their name. These small birds catch much of their insect prey on the wing, displaying highly manoeuvrable flying ability. Fantails are common throughout New Zealand, and have adapted well to human modifications of the landscape; they are often found in rural and urban habitats as well as in the forest. New Zealand fantails originally came from Australia, where they are known as grey fantails.

The **grey warbler** is another common perching bird, found throughout New Zealand in forest, rural and urban habitats. These small birds are named for their distinctive, soft warbling call.

RIGHT: **Grey warbler at nest.**

BELOW: **Fantail.**

GEOFF MOON

ABOVE: **Male South Island tomtit.**

RIGHT: **Female North Island robin.**

The **tomtit** and **New Zealand robin** are two closely-related species. The tomtit, which is smaller than its relation, is more common than the robin, being found in forest throughout most of the country. Both birds have a colour difference between male North Island and South Island birds, with the latter having a brighter yellow colour on the breast. Their diets consist of insects and other invertebrates, at times supplemented with fruit. Tomtits glean most of their prey from tree trunks or other vegetation, whereas robins take most of their prey from the forest floor.

The tiny **rifleman** is New Zealand's smallest bird. It is a member of the endemic family of New Zealand wrens. Riflemen are locally common throughout most of New Zealand. Their high-pitched, short call is out of the hearing range of some people. Their diet consists mostly of invertebrates, which they glean from the trunks and branches of trees.

Whiteheads and **brown creepers** are two closely-related species. Whiteheads are found only in the North Island, whereas brown creepers are found only in the South Island and Stewart Island. Both are small, mostly insectivorous birds. They are locally common in forest and scrub areas. Another related species, the **yellowhead**, is now rare. It is found only in the South Island, mostly in beech forests of the southwestern part of the island.

The **silvereye** (also known as white-eye or waxeye) is self-introduced to New Zealand from Australia. Silvereyes are common throughout most of the country, and are also found in parks and gardens in urban areas. They are usually seen in small flocks moving through trees and shrubs in search of invertebrates, fruit and nectar to eat.

ABOVE: **Brown creeper.**

LEFT: **Rifleman.**

BELOW: **Silvereye at nest.**

Wattlebirds

The entire wattlebird family, consisting of two living and one extinct species, is endemic to New Zealand. They are characterised by the fleshy 'wattles' that grow at the base of their bills.

The last official record of the extinct huia was in 1907. Of the two remaining living species, only the **kokako** still exists on the mainland.

The kokako is a large, blue-grey forest bird. The North Island subspecies has blue wattles, whereas those of the South Island subspecies are orange. The latter subspecies is now thought to be extinct. Kokako feed mainly on fruit and foliage. Poor fliers, their main mode of transport is to run and hop among the branches of trees.

Although rarely heard these days, the haunting call of the kokako is arguably one of the most beautiful of all our bird species. Loss of suitable habitat and predation are the two main threats facing the remaining North Island birds. In some areas, conservation programmes aimed at reducing predation of eggs and chicks have helped to increase the breeding success of kokako.

Kokako.

Honeyeaters

Birds of the honeyeater family have a brush-tipped tongue, used for lapping nectar from flowers. The New Zealand members of this family are the tui, bellbird, and stitchbird. In addition to nectar, they will also eat fruits and insects. All three species are endemic to New Zealand. Only two species remain on the mainland islands today.

Tui are among our most easily recognised birds, adults possessing distinctive white tufts at the throat. They are common throughout most of New Zealand. As well as forest, they also inhabit farmland and urban areas where sufficient food resources are available.

Tui.

The olive-green **bellbird** is smaller than the tui, and not as widely distributed. It is more common in the South Island than the North. The bellbird's melodious song is similar to that of the tui, but without the distinctive clicks, coughs and other unusual sounds that form part of that bird's repertoire.

The honeyeaters play an important role as plant pollinators. As they insert their bills inside flowers to sip nectar, pollen rubs off onto the feathers of their head or throat. When the bird moves to another flower, the pollen is transferred to this flower and pollination may occur. Honeyeaters thus play a significant part in the life cycles of many plants.

Bellbird in flax flowers.

New Zealand pigeon

The **New Zealand pigeon**, sometimes called the woodpigeon, is New Zealand's only endemic pigeon. Found in forest and scrub throughout the country, its diet is mainly fruit, occasionally supplemented by foliage. New Zealand pigeons are important for forest regeneration because of their role as dispersers of plant seeds. They are in fact now the only forest bird large enough to swallow the seeds of some large fruits, such as those of taraire, karaka and tawa.

New Zealand pigeons are threatened by predation and illegal hunting. The effect of these threats on the species is compounded by the fact that they have a naturally slow reproductive rate, with only one egg laid per clutch.

New Zealand pigeon.

Forest parrots

The **kaka** is a large forest parrot, distributed throughout much of New Zealand, but only locally common on the mainland. There are two subspecies, the North Island kaka and the South Island kaka. The largest numbers of North Island kaka are now found on offshore islands such as Little Barrier and Kapiti islands, where the islands are free of introduced mammalian predators and competitors.

Kaka eat nectar, fruit, foliage, and insects and their larvae. They often feed high in the canopy, where they are not

Kaka.

Red-crowned parakeet.

easily seen from the ground. They use their strong bills to pull apart rotting wood in search of grubs, and also to help them climb up tree trunks and along branches.

Kaka nest in tree hollows, therefore areas of mature forest that provide sufficient nesting sites are important for the long-term survival of this species.

Red-crowned and **yellow-crowned parakeets** are so named for the coloured patch that extends from above their bill to the crown of their head. Red-crowned parakeets are higher in number than yellow-crowned, but their habit of feeding on the ground has made them very susceptible to predation, and they are now rare on the mainland. Most live in forests on predator-free islands. Yellow-crowned parakeets are still found on the mainland, but are uncommon. Both species are omnivorous, eating a wide range of plant and invertebrate foods.

Yellow-crowned parakeet.

Birds of the night

As night falls in the forest, a different set of animals emerge from their daytime hiding places. Darkness provides protection from visual predators, and the opportunity to forage with reduced competition from other species.

The **kiwi** is undoubtedly New Zealand's most famous bird, and one of the most unusual. It is the only bird in the world to have nostrils at the end of its beak, and it has a remarkably good sense of smell. This enables it to sniff out its prey of worms and other invertebrates as it probes deep into the soil with its beak.

Female great spotted kiwi.

Kiwi are flightless; their tiny vestigial wings are hidden beneath their feathers. A kiwi's long, filament-like feathers are more like the fur of a mammal. Female kiwi lay one, or sometimes two, huge eggs that may weigh up to 20 percent of their body weight. Chicks are fully feathered when they hatch and are able to feed themselves. In many areas chick mortality is high because of predation, mainly by stoats. Adult kiwi, with their larger size and strong legs, are better able to defend themselves against attack by these mammals.

You are more likely to hear a kiwi's call than to actually see one in the wild. Male kiwi have a repetitive, high-pitched crescending call, and the female may answer in a similar pattern but with a more hoarse voice.

Based on genetic studies, changes to the classification of kiwi have recently been proposed. However, there are two main types of kiwi: **brown kiwi** and **spotted kiwi**. These are further divided into species and subspecies, but all belong to the same genus (*Apteryx*) and family (Apterygidae), and are found only in New Zealand.

North Island brown kiwi.

Brown kiwi are found on all three main islands, but are most common in the North Island. The **great spotted kiwi** is found only in the South Island. The rarest species is the **little spotted kiwi**, now thought to exist only on a few offshore islands.

Another nocturnal bird, the **morepork**, is New Zealand's only remaining native owl. The name 'morepork' is an approximation of the sound of one of the bird's calls. Common throughout New Zealand, moreporks may even be found in gardens and suburban parks. Moreporks roost in trees during the day, and become active at dusk.

Like most owls, moreporks are birds of prey. Their large eyes give them excellent vision in low light. Their main prey are insects, but they will also catch small birds and rodents, and in some areas, bats.

Morepork.

Cuckoos

Two species of cuckoo are commonly found in New Zealand. These migratory birds spend spring to autumn here, where they breed, then fly to the Pacific Islands for the winter. Like most cuckoos they lay their egg in the nest of another species. The cuckoo chick evicts the other nestlings, and the substitute parents raise it as their own.

Shining cuckoos may be found in forest, scrubland and gardens throughout the country. They lay a single egg in a grey warbler nest. **Long-tailed cuckoos** are less common, and are found mainly in forest areas. In the North Island the host species is the whitehead; in the South Island, the brown creeper or yellowhead.

Shining cuckoo.

Rails

The **weka** is the only rail species likely to be encountered in mainland forests and scrubland. Weka are common in only a few areas, such as East Cape in the North Island, the west of the South Island, and Stewart Island. They are also found on some offshore islands.

Also seen:
introduced passerines
  (town and countryside birds)
kea (high country and alpine birds)
kakapo (rare and endangered birds)

Weka.

Coastal birds

Sheltered coastal habitats, such as this one at Miranda on the Firth of Thames, attract large numbers of waders.

NEW ZEALAND HAS around 15,000 kilometres of coastline — a vast length for such a small country. It is a diverse coastline, with habitats ranging from long sandy beaches and dunes to rocky shores and near-vertical cliffs. New Zealand's only species of mangrove tree grows in sheltered coastal areas in the north of the North Island.

Nobody in New Zealand lives further than 130 kilometres from the sea. Most of the country's major towns and cities are built on or near the coast. New Zealanders have a long tradition of association with the coast, either as an access way to the sea, or for recreational purposes.

Because of the relatively open nature of most coastal habitats, the birds that live there often tend to be more conspicuous than birds living in other kinds of habitats. In some places flocks of hundreds or even thousands of birds gather on the shore, where they can be easily observed while roosting at high tide.

Few of the birds that may be seen on the shore are found there exclusively. Many are also found in inland habitats, such as rivers, lakes and wetlands, particularly at certain times of the year. For example, the pied stilt, pied oystercatcher and wrybill spend autumn and winter at northern beaches and estuaries, but migrate to South Island rivers and pastures for the spring–summer breeding season. White-faced herons are just as at home in pasture and wetlands as they are in coastal habitats.

Estuarine mudflats are important feeding areas for many shorebirds.

Waders

Waders are a group of birds found in shore habitats, particularly harbours and estuaries where their food of intertidal worms, molluscs, crustaceans and other invertebrates is most plentiful. More than 60 species of wading birds have been recorded in New Zealand. Many of these are migratory birds that breed in the northern hemisphere then fly to New Zealand to spend the summer here. Of the species that breed and live in New Zealand throughout the year, oystercatchers, dotterels, pied stilts, and wrybills are the most common.

Pied oystercatchers are usually seen in large flocks at northern harbours and estuaries during the winter. In spring they migrate to their South Island breeding grounds. The **variable oystercatcher** is less common, and remains at the coast all year round, in pairs or small flocks. Their colouring varies: some birds are black and white, some are mostly black with some white patches on their underparts, while others are completely black.

The endemic **New Zealand dotterel** is a rare species, usually found on sandy beaches in the North Island. A second subspecies lives on Stewart Island, nesting above the treeline. The **banded dotterel** is more common and found throughout most of New Zealand. Banded dotterels mostly nest on shingle or braided riverbeds, returning to the coast after breeding.

The **pied stilt** is a common native bird, easily recognised by its long legs and black-and-white colouration. Pied stilts are found throughout New Zealand in a wide range of coastal and wetland habitats.

The **wrybill** is the only bird in the world with a bill that curves to the side. Each bird's bill curves to the right. Wrybills are endemic to New Zealand. They exhibit seasonal migration, spending the summer nesting on South Island braided riverbeds, then flying to northern harbours and estuaries for the winter.

Southern pied oystercatcher.

Variable oystercatcher.

New Zealand dotterel.

Banded dotterel.

Pied stilt.

Wrybill.

Eastern bar-tailed godwits.

Migratory waders

Each year in spring, around 200,000 migratory waders arrive in New Zealand. Of the many species that have been recorded here, the three most common are **eastern bar-tailed godwits**, **lesser knots**, and **turnstones**. These birds nest in the Arctic Circle during the short Arctic summer, then fly to their southern hemisphere wintering grounds. In New Zealand they can be seen at harbours and estuaries throughout most of the country between September and April, although the largest flocks occur in the north. Here the birds spend the summer feeding on the rich food supply found in harbour mudflats, building up reserves for their journey northward.

Lesser knots.

Gulls

New Zealand has three species of gull. The **black-backed gull** is the largest species. Black-backed gulls are widely distributed throughout the southern hemisphere. Juvenile black-backed gulls are a mottled brown colour. Besides coastal shore habitats, they are also found in towns and cities, near rivers and lakes, in pasture, and occasionally in the high country.

The smaller **red-billed gull** is found near the coast all over New Zealand. These gulls nest in large colonies of up to 6000 pairs.

In spring and summer, **black-billed gulls** are usually found inland, near rivers and lakes and on farmland. They feed on pasture and aquatic invertebrates. Most nest in large colonies on riverbeds, mainly in the South Island. In winter they move to coastal harbours and estuaries, where they add marine invertebrates, fish and shellfish to their diet. Gulls eat a wide range of foods, both plant and animal. Black-backed and red-billed gulls will often take food scraps offered to them by people and may gather in city parks and at picnic areas.

Terns

There are three species of common native tern in New Zealand. The largest is the **caspian tern**, a species also found in many other countries around the world. Caspian terns are mainly seen at sandy beaches and estuaries, where they nest in colonies. They can be easily recognised by their large size (slightly smaller than a black-backed gull), and orange-red bill.

White-fronted terns are New Zealand's most common tern, usually seen in large flocks or nesting colonies on the coast all around the country.

Black-fronted terns are endemic to New Zealand. During spring they are found mostly in the South Island, where they nest on the shingle riverbeds. In the non-breeding season, black-fronted terns disperse to eastern coasts of the South and North islands, as far north as the Bay of Plenty.

Terns feed mainly on fish that they catch from inshore waters. They rarely venture very far out to sea to feed. Black-fronted terns also take insects and other small prey from riverbeds, lakes and farmland.

Shorebird nests

Waders, gulls and terns make their nests on the ground. Wader and tern nests are very simple, just a shallow depression in the sand or shingle, called a scrape. Gulls build a nest out of twigs, seaweed, grass, feathers and other materials.

Usually both parents take turns to incubate the eggs. When the chicks are born they are able to see and walk almost straight away. This helps them to survive, as nests on the ground are vulnerable to predators such as cats, dogs, stoats and ferrets.

Shorebird nests are also at risk from people using beaches. Eggs and chicks are well camouflaged, making them difficult to see, especially from a moving vehicle. Each year nests on New Zealand beaches are trampled or crushed, and in some areas this is a significant threat to the survival of shorebirds.

Black-backed gull.

Red-billed gulls at their nest.

Black-billed gull.

Caspian terns and chick.

White-fronted tern and chicks.

Black-fronted tern at nest.

Reef heron.

White-faced heron.

Herons

The most common heron in New Zealand is the **white-faced heron**. Although often found in estuaries and coastal lagoons, they are also seen inland near rivers, lakes, wetlands and farmland throughout the country. White-faced herons are self-introduced from Australia, and are also found in Indonesia, New Guinea and on Norfolk Island.

Our largest heron is the **white heron**. This species is found worldwide, but it is not common in New Zealand. Here white herons breed only near Okarito, on the west coast of the South Island. Outside the breeding season the birds disperse to estuaries and coastal wetlands throughout the country.

The much less common **reef heron** mainly inhabits rocky shores and coastal inlets. It is most often seen in the north of the North Island, becoming rare further south.

White heron.

Spoonbills

The **royal spoonbill** is a large white bird, easily identified by its flattened, spoon-shaped black bill. Self-introduced from Australia, spoonbills are now common in many estuaries and harbours around New Zealand. They feed in shallow water, sweeping their bills from side to side to catch aquatic invertebrates and small fish.

Royal spoonbill.

Shags

Shags (known elsewhere as cormorants) are a common coastal bird, although they can also be found near inland waters. Shags feed mainly on fish and aquatic invertebrates, which they catch by diving beneath the water surface. Their webbed feet allow them to swim underwater. Shags nest in colonies, usually on cliff ledges, small rock islets or in the top branches of trees.

The **black shag** and the **little shag** (largest and smallest species respectively) are common throughout New Zealand. They can often be seen standing on a rock or a post, holding their wings out to dry.

Little black shags are common at North Island harbours, estuaries, and lakes, but rare in the South Island. The **pied shag**, with its black back and white face and underparts, may be seen on the coast throughout much of New Zealand. **Spotted shags** are endemic to New Zealand. They are a coastal species, rarely seen inland.

Little shag.

Pied shag.

Also seen:
penguins (sea birds)
black stilt, New Zealand pipit (high country and alpine birds)
introduced passerines, cattle egret (town and countryside birds)
fairy tern (rare and endangered birds)

High country and alpine birds

MUCH OF NEW ZEALAND'S landscape is dominated by mountains. Both the main islands have mountain ranges where the tops remain covered in snow for much of the year. Skiing and mountain climbing are activities enjoyed by New Zealanders and visitors alike.

The Southern Alps in the South Island contain New Zealand's highest peak, Aoraki/Mt Cook, 3700 metres above sea level. In the North Island, the highest peak is Mt Ruapehu, 2797 metres above sea level.

'High country' is a general term used to describe high-altitude habitats, which may include forest, shrubland, grassland, and wetland habitats. The term 'alpine' is more specific, and refers to the area above the treeline, and below the highest snowfields. Alpine vegetation consists mostly of tussocklands, herbfields, mosses and lichens. Below the alpine zone we find subalpine vegetation made up of shrubs and grassland, and below that montane (high altitude) forest.

A few shorebird species migrate to high country areas in the summer. Wrybills and some banded dotterels nest on South Island braided riverbeds, and some pied stilts and pied oystercatchers nest on high country riverbeds or farmland.

High country habitat near Mt Ruapehu.

Very few birds known as alpine species are found solely in high altitude areas. During the colder months, most birds retreat to lower altitudes. The endemic **rock wren** is in fact the only New Zealand bird that remains in alpine regions all year round. Rock wrens live among rocks, scree, and scrub in alpine and subalpine areas of the South Island only. They eat mainly invertebrates, but also the small fruits of some shrubs.

Rock wren.

Kea.

Takahe.

One of the alpine birds most familiar to many New Zealanders is the **kea**. These large parrots are now found only in the South Island. Closely related to the kaka, kea prefer habitats around the treeline, sometimes coming down into the forest for food. They are mostly vegetarian, eating seeds, fruits, leaf buds and other vegetation, but will occasionally eat insects, worms, and grubs. The kea is the world's only alpine parrot.

Studies have shown the kea to be

one of the most intelligent of all birds. They have a reputation for getting up to mischief around areas of human settlement, sometimes causing great damage to vehicles and other personal belongings left unattended and within their reach.

The **takahe** was thought to be extinct until 1948, when it was rediscovered in Fiordland. These endemic, flightless birds look similar to the pukeko, to whom they are closely related. Takahe are endangered, and conservation management programmes are under way to try and increase their population size. Some birds have been transferred to islands, such as Kapiti and Tiritiri Matangi, as part of this programme. The takahe's natural habitat is tussock grasslands and high-altitude forests in Fiordland. They eat mainly grasses and fern rhizomes.

New Zealand falcon.

The endemic **New Zealand falcon** is now relatively rare. Although it does live in some forest areas, it is more commonly seen in the high country, particularly in the South Island. Falcons mostly prey on small birds and mammals, and large insects. Unlike the

Blue ducks.

somewhat larger Australasian harrier (now common throughout New Zealand), falcons rarely scavenge dead animals.

The **blue duck** is also endemic to New Zealand, and is now rare. These birds inhabit fast-flowing streams and rivers in high-altitude forests of both the North and South Islands. Their diet consists mostly of aquatic insects and insect larvae. Adults remain in their breeding pairs all year round.

The **black stilt** now breeds only on high country shingle riverbeds and wetlands in South Canterbury in the South Island. Black stilts have suffered a severe decline due to loss of habitat and predation by introduced mammals. They sometimes interbreed with the more common pied stilt, producing hybrid forms. Black stilts are the subjects of an intensive conservation management programme aimed at protecting remaining habitats and increasing the population size. After the breeding season some black stilts migrate to North Island harbours, where they spend the summer and autumn.

The **New Zealand pipit** is a small bird that prefers open country, often seen in high altitude areas, but also found near the coast. They are usually seen on the ground, where they feed on invertebrates and sometimes seeds. Pipits can be recognised by their habit of flicking their tail up and down when on the ground.

New Zealand pipit.

Also seen:
Australasian harrier, introduced finches, hedge sparrow (town and countryside birds)
pied oystercatchers, pied stilt, banded dotterel, black-fronted tern, black-billed gull (coastal birds)

Wetland birds

IN THIS BOOK the term 'wetlands' describes habitats such as lakes, rivers, swamps, saltwater marshes, and mangroves. Since European colonisation, the majority of New Zealand's lowland swamps have been damaged or destroyed by activities such as draining to provide land for farming, or by fire, or by the harvesting of peat, gold, sphagnum moss and kauri gum. Rivers and river banks have been damaged by pollution from farm run-off, stock trampling, removal of native riparian vegetation, planting of exotic trees (such as willows), water weeds, and introduced fish species. The resulting changes to the water quality, substrate, and flora and fauna of many rivers has made it difficult or impossible for native aquatic plants and animals to survive.

However, in recent years increasing recognition of the ecological importance of wetlands has prompted many people and organisations to become involved in restoration projects. Today there are places where it is possible to visit wetlands and observe the birds that make their homes there.

Lake Taupo is New Zealand's largest lake. Like many North Island lakes it was formed by volcanic activity. Most South Island lakes are glacial in origin, deep and surrounded by steep land.

New Zealand rivers vary from small, fast-flowing mountain streams to wide, slower-flowing rivers in lowland areas. The Waikato River in the North Island is New Zealand's longest river, beginning at Lake Taupo and reaching the sea on the west coast just south of Manukau Harbour. Many South Island east coast rivers have wide, gravelly beds, and the water flows in small rivulets or channels, separating and rejoining many

Wetland habitat of mangroves (foreground) and swamp vegetation (background).

Female paradise shelduck.

New Zealand scaup.

Brown teal.

Grey duck.

times. These are called 'braided' rivers.

Swamps are characterised by their vegetation of grasses, sedges, reeds and flaxes, which provide cover for many birds, especially when nesting. This can make swamp birds difficult to see in the wild.

Waterfowl

Waterfowl are ducks, geese, and swans. They are aquatic birds, with webbed feet for swimming.

The endemic **paradise shelduck** is found throughout the country on lakes, ponds, and farmland. Males and females have distinctly different colour patterns. The paradise shelduck population increased markedly throughout the twentieth century as forest clearance and construction of farm ponds provided increased areas of suitable habitat. Large flocks often gather during the moulting season (December–March).

New Zealand scaup are widespread but relatively uncommon. These small endemic ducks dive to the bottom of lakes and ponds to feed on aquatic plants and invertebrates, sometimes remaining submerged for longer than a minute.

The **brown teal** is a rare species, now found mostly on northern offshore islands such as Great Barrier Island. Once widespread, their numbers have seriously

Grey teal.

Male mallard duck.

Black swan.

declined due to predation and loss of habitat. Conservation programmes have seen captive-bred birds released on other islands such as Kapiti and Tiritiri Matangi in an attempt to secure the population.

The native **grey duck** and **grey teal** are common species. The grey duck sometimes interbreeds with the introduced **mallard duck**, which is also abundant throughout the country, and is the most common duck seen on ponds in city parks. The **Australasian shoveler** is found in lowland wetlands and estuaries throughout New Zealand. This duck can be recognised by its large, spoon-shaped bill, with which it sieves small aquatic plants and animals from shallow water.

The **black swan** is common on lowland lakes and lagoons. This large bird, native to Australia, was introduced to New Zealand in the 1860s. Two introduced geese, the **Canada goose** (from North America) and the **feral goose** (from Europe) are also common in wetlands and on farmland.

Canada geese.

Feral goose.

New Zealand dabchick.

Grebes

Although they may appear outwardly similar, grebes are not closely related to the waterfowl. Their large feet are lobed instead of webbed, and they spend almost all of their time in the water. While relatively clumsy on land, grebes are excellent divers. They build floating nests, anchored to nearby vegetation.

Four species of grebe have been recorded in New Zealand, but only two are likely to be seen in the wild. The **Australasian crested grebe** is a large bird with a distinctive head crest of feathers. To date it has only been seen on large South Island lakes. The smaller endemic **New Zealand dabchick** is found only on North Island lakes.

Australasian grested grebe.

Other wetland birds

The **pukeko** is a large native bird, very common in swampy areas and farmland. Self-introduced to New Zealand from Australia within the last 1000 years or

Pukeko.

Australian coot.

so, the pukeko is also found in many other countries, where it is known as the purple swamphen or purple gallinule. Also self-introduced from across the Tasman Sea, although much later, is the **Australian coot**, now well-established in many areas.

The **banded rail** is found in mangrove forests, coastal swamp habitats and some freshwater wetlands in Northland, the northern tip of the South Island, and a number of smaller islands. They were once common throughout the country, but like so many of New Zealand's native birds, their range and population size have been restricted by habitat loss and predation by introduced mammals.

The **spotless crake** and the **marsh crake** are locally common, the former mostly in the North Island, and the latter in the South Island. Marsh crakes are similar to the banded

Banded rail.

rail in appearance, though smaller. Spotless crakes are dark blue-grey on the head, neck, and underparts, with dark brown upperparts. These birds live among wetland vegetation such as sedges, reeds, and rushes. Due to their shy habits it can be very difficult to see them in the wild. Also found in this type of habitat is the equally secretive **fernbird**. These endemic birds have a long tail that appears frayed. Fernbirds are most common in the northern half of the North Island, and the west and south of the South Island.

The **Australasian bittern** is widely distributed throughout New Zealand, but is now thought to be rare due to loss of habitat. When startled, the well-camouflaged bittern 'freezes' in a characteristic posture with its head and neck stretched up and bill pointing skyward. This makes it extremely difficult to see among the reeds and other vegetation in which it lives.

The native **kingfisher** is common throughout New Zealand. These strikingly-coloured birds are found in a wide range of habitats, but usually near water. They eat a variety of prey, including small crabs, aquatic animals, insects, lizards, mice, and sometimes other small birds. Kingfishers watch and wait on a perch, then dive to the ground or water to catch their prey.

LEFT: **Fernbird.**

BELOW: **Kingfisher.**

Also seen:
herons, shags, gulls, pied stilt, black stilt, pied oystercatcher, banded dotterel, black-fronted tern, black-billed gull (coastal birds)
blue duck (high country and alpine birds)

Town and countryside birds

THE CONVERSION OF most of New Zealand's lowland forest and wetlands into pasture meant the loss of large areas of habitat for many native birds. However, the urban and pasture landscapes of today have also created habitats for birds. A large number of the species seen in towns and cities, in parks and gardens and on farmland were deliberately introduced from overseas, but a few native species have been able to take advantage of the opportunities offered by city living. Buildings provide roosting and nesting spaces, and parks and gardens provide a wealth of different plant types for food and shelter. Birds that prefer more open habitats find a home in the rural pasturelands that characterise many areas of New Zealand.

Passerines (perching birds)

This large group of birds includes most of those commonly seen in urban and rural areas. Most are native to Great Britain and mainland Europe, and were introduced to New Zealand in the mid- to late-nineteenth century by the Acclimatisation Societies that existed at that time. Larger passerine birds include the **blackbird**, **song thrush**, and **starling**, abundant in parks, gardens, scrubland, orchards and forest margins throughout New Zealand. The **myna** is found mostly in the north of the North Island. The **magpie**, introduced from Australia, is now common in parks and farmland throughout most of New Zealand.

A New Zealand pasture landscape.

Blackbird.

Thrush at nest.

Starling.

Myna.

Magpie.

House sparrow at nest.

Greenfinch.

Skylark.

Welcome swallows.

Smaller passerines include the **house sparrow**, **dunnock** (or **hedge sparrow**), and the four species of finches that have been introduced to New Zealand: the **chaffinch**, **goldfinch**, **greenfinch**, and **redpoll**. Another common small passerine is the **yellowhammer**, seen mainly in farmland, scrub and other open country areas.

New Zealand's only lark, the introduced **skylark**, is a familiar bird in open rural landscapes. This ground-nesting bird is often heard singing while flying high over pasture or other open country. Adult birds have a small crest of feathers on the top of the head, a useful characteristic to help distinguish them from the similar-looking native New Zealand pipit.

Welcome swallows are a more recent arrival in New Zealand, becoming established here in the middle of last century. They are now common in many parts of the country, and are often seen sitting on powerlines or flying over water to catch insect prey. Their mud nests are usually attached to the outside of buildings or other man-made structures.

Rock pigeon.

Other birds

As in many other towns and cities around the world, the **rock pigeon** is a common sight in some New Zealand urban areas.

The introduced **Australasian harrier** is frequently seen in open country areas, particularly pasture, throughout New Zealand. The harrier is a familiar sight in many areas, soaring over the land searching for prey. They are also commonly seen on roads and roadsides scavenging dead animals.

About 20 gamebird species have been introduced to New Zealand since European colonisation, and around half of these have become established in the wild. All gamebirds feed on the ground, and male birds are usually more brightly coloured than female birds. The **ring-necked pheasant** is one of our most common gamebirds, found in farmland and scrubland, mainly in the North Island. **California quail** were first introduced to New Zealand in the 1860s, and are now found in pasture and scrub habitats throughout most of the two main islands.

The **spur-winged plover** belongs to the shorebird family Charadriidae, and is related to the dotterels and wrybill, but is included here because it is commonly seen on farmland. Spur-winged plovers are self-introduced to New Zealand. They first bred here in the 1930s, and are now common throughout most of the country.

The **cattle egret** is a member of the heron family. It is a widespread species, occurring in North and South America, Asia, Africa and Australasia, and was first recorded in New Zealand in the 1960s. Cattle egrets do not breed in New Zealand, but spend the winter here, arriving in April/May and departing in October/November. Initially they stay in western coastal areas to feed, then they move inland, mainly to pastureland where they are usually seen in association with cattle and sheep. They occur in small groups or larger flocks.

Australasian harrier.

Also seen:
fantail, grey warbler, morepork, NZ pigeon, silvereye (forest birds)
gulls, white-faced heron (coastal birds)
waterfowl, pukeko, kingfisher (wetland birds)

A caged pair of pheasants.

Male californian quail.

Spur-winged plover at nest in pasture.

Cattle egret.

Rare or endangered birds

North Island saddleback.

Male stitchbird.

MOST OF THE birds featured in this section are ones that you will only see in wildlife centres or bird sanctuaries. All are endemic to New Zealand, so the small populations that remain are the last of their kind in the world. They have all been severely affected by the changes to their former habitats brought about by human colonisation, and for many their only chance of survival is on predator-free islands or sanctuaries.

The **stitchbird**, one of our three honeyeater species, was relatively common in North Island forests until the mid- to late-nineteenth century. After this time its numbers declined rapidly, until the only remaining population was on Little Barrier Island. From this population some stitchbirds were translocated to other islands such as Tiritiri Matangi and Kapiti islands, where it is hoped that they will survive.

GEOFF MOON

Kakapo.

The decline of the **saddleback**, one of our two surviving wattlebirds, followed a similar pattern. These striking birds were once common throughout New Zealand. During the nineteenth century, however, as introduced rats, cats, and mustelids spread across the country, saddlebacks gradually disappeared from the mainland, until only one small population remained on Hen Island in the north. Successful transfers of some of these birds to a number of other islands has resulted in the population increasing once more.

Saddlebacks are handsome birds, with their orange-brown 'saddle' and bright orange-red wattles. They eat mostly invertebrates, but sometimes fruit and nectar also. They feed at all levels of the forest, from the floor to the canopy. Saddlebacks use their bills to probe beneath bark and into rotting wood, searching for prey.

One of New Zealand's most well-known conservation stories is that of the Chatham Islands **black robin**. The survival of this species today is testament to the dedication and innovative efforts of conservation scientists and wildlife officers. From just five individuals in 1979, the population now numbers over 150.

Several factors were responsible for this success. Initially the birds received supplementary feeding, and their nests were protected from predation by seabirds and starlings. Black robin eggs were removed from their nests and placed in tomtit nests. This encouraged the black robin pairs to lay more clutches of eggs. Meanwhile, the black robin chicks were successfully raised by their tomtit 'foster parents'.

The flightless, nocturnal **kakapo** is the heaviest parrot in the world. Kakapo have a 'lek' mating system, where individual males set up a system of tracks and 'bowls' (shallow depressions) in the ground. During the night, a male bird sits in one of these bowls and produces a loud, low 'booming' sound, which may carry for several kilometres. This sound attracts females, who mate with the dominant males. As in other lek-mating species, the male birds play no further part in raising the young.

The fossil record shows that kakapo once lived throughout New Zealand. Today, however, the known population consists of less than 100 individuals, all of which are confined to islands. The kakapo's flightlessness, strong scent, and ground-nesting habit makes it extremely vulnerable to mammalian predators, a fact that contributed to its rapid decline during the late nineteenth and early twentieth centuries. Kakapo are now the subject of a Department of Conservation recovery programme to try and increase their population size.

The **fairy tern** is one of New Zealand's rarest shorebirds. Previously widespread, they are now found only in the north of the North Island. Fairy terns nest on the ground on sandy beaches and estuaries. Like other terns, they eat mostly small fish caught in inshore waters. The main threat to their survival is nest disturbance by people using beaches, and mammalian predators of eggs and chicks. Environmental events such as storms and floods can also devastate nesting attempts.

Fairy tern at nest.

Threats to
New Zealand birds

ALTHOUGH TODAY WE recognise the uniqueness of New Zealand's wildlife, and conservation efforts are under way to protect our remaining birds and other animals and plants, there are yet threats to the survival of many species. The major threats are habitat loss and introduced animal and plant pests.

Offshore islands, such as the Poor Knights Islands in Northland, have become sanctuaries for many species of endangered native wildlife.

Part 3
THE FUTURE

Mangroves are an important habitat for birds, but are at risk from land reclamation and development.

Habitat loss

Since the middle of the twentieth century the widespread logging of native forests has largely ceased. Most remaining large areas of native forest are now owned by the State and managed by the Department of Conservation for the benefit of all New Zealanders. Many smaller forest blocks on private land have also been protected under covenants by landowners.

However, continuing urban sprawl and the demand for land and utilities (such as roads) continue to threaten some habitats, particularly wetland and shore environments.

Australian brush-tailed possums eat native vegetation, birds, and eggs.

This is a worldwide problem, especially in under-developed countries with large populations. Many of our migrant bird species are threatened by the loss or degradation of suitable 'stopover' sites during their migration journeys.

Animal pests

Collectively, introduced animal pests pose the biggest threat to our native birds. Our population of around 70 million Australian brush-tailed possums chews through tonnes of vegetation each night, damaging native forests. Possums were introduced to New Zealand in the nineteenth century for their fur. Not only do they

Ship rats eat native birds and their eggs and chicks, and can reduce forest regeneration by eating seeds on the forest floor.

compete with birds for plant food, it is now known that possums will raid birds' nests and eat the eggs.

Predation of eggs, chicks, and even adult birds is a major threat posed by mammals such as cats, mustelids (ferrets, stoats, and weasels), dogs, and rats. Evolving in isolation with only other avian predators to contend with, many New Zealand birds developed excellent visual camouflage tactics to protect themselves and their eggs. When mammals were introduced to the country, the native birds were completely unprepared for and largely defenceless against such predators, which hunt mostly at night using their sense of smell.

New Zealand birds have not had enough time to evolve new defence strategies against these pests. The only chance of saving some species from certain extinction is to remove or reduce the threat from mammalian predators.

Competition for food between birds and pests is also a significant threat to many species. For example, introduced wasps feed on the sugary 'honeydew' secretions produced by scale insects that live in the bark of beech trees. Honeydew was a major food source for many forest birds, such as kaka, and the competition with wasps for this resource is thought to have contributed to the decline of kaka and other birds. Another threat to native birds is competition for food and nesting sites with introduced birds.

Plant pests

Plant pests have become a major problem in some areas. Some species introduced to New Zealand as garden plants have found their way into natural areas, where they become pests due to their vigorous and prolific growth, which may strangle native species. This may result in loss of habitat, food sources, and nesting spaces for native birds.

In eastern parts of the South Island, large 'braided' rivers are a feature of the landscape, and an important habitat for birds such as wrybills and banded dotterels. However, plant pests such as gorse, lupin, and willow now cover large areas of some riverbeds. As the birds prefer open environments for nesting, this reduces the number of suitable nesting sites. The plant cover also encourages rabbits into the area, which then attract predators such as stoats, increasing the risk of predation to the birds.

What are we doing to help birds?

Although we have a relatively poor record in terms of species extinctions over the last few centuries, New Zealand has recently developed some innovative techniques to aid bird conservation. Several world-famous conservation projects have been carried out in recent decades where species have been brought back from near extinction, in some cases where only a handful of individuals remained. Through successes such as these, and also by learning from mistakes where failures have occurred, new techniques for bird conservation can continue to be developed.

Traps like these are used in many native forest areas to catch predatory mammals such as stoats.

Sanctuary islands

Most successful bird conservation projects to date have involved relocating (or 'translocating') small groups of threatened birds on to islands. Through the use of this technique, the number of 'safe' populations of many bird species (such as saddleback, kakapo, and stitchbird) have been increased. This reduces the risk of extinction, as although a species may be or become extinct on the mainland, there will still be populations surviving on islands.

Once a population of birds has been established on an island, further work to improve their chances of survival can take place. Pests may be controlled or removed, either by trapping or laying poison baits, or a combination of both. The island's vegetation may be restored by supplementary planting of species that will benefit the resident native wildlife.

Hope for the future

There are many ecological restoration projects currently under way in New Zealand, ranging in size and scope from large areas of public land managed by the Department of Conservation, to smaller blocks of private land. Schools and community groups have become increasingly involved with restoration projects, encouraged by the successes that have been achieved elsewhere, and by the opportunities such projects offer to educate and involve local people, especially children.

By studying the ecology of our native wildlife and that of introduced species, we are learning more about how species interact with each other and with their environments. The information gathered can be used to help devise better ways of controlling pests and enhancing native species' populations, so that we can continue to enjoy the sight and sound of New Zealand's unique birds in their native habitats.

Tiritiri Matangi Island

Tiritiri Matangi is an island sanctuary which lies four kilometres off the coast of the Whangaparaoa Peninsula, north of Auckland city. It is the site of a successful ecological restoration project.

The island's original forest cover was cleared, first by Maori and later by European settlers, and for much of the twentieth century the island was leased from the government for farming. Since 1865 the island has been home to a lighthouse, which guides ships into nearby Auckland Harbour.

After the farming lease expired in the 1970s, scientists and conservationists proposed that the forest be allowed to grow back on the island to provide habitat for birds and other native wildlife. The farm animals were removed, and in 1983 a nursery was set up on the island to grow the many native plant seedlings that would be required to replant the island. Between 1984 and 1994 volunteers planted over 280,000 native trees. The resident kiore (Pacific rat) population was eradicated by dropping poison baits on to the island from a helicopter.

With its regenerating forest and lack of mammalian predators, the island became a safe haven for birds. A number of species, including kakariki, takahe, saddleback, stitchbird, North Island robin, kokako and little spotted kiwi, have been introduced to the island.

Tiritiri Matangi is classed as an 'open' sanctuary, which means anyone can visit and enjoy seeing and hearing birds, some of which are now extinct on the mainland. If you visit Tiritiri Matangi, please take care that you do not inadvertently bring animal or plant pests to the island.

Why are islands used?

Besides the three main islands, New Zealand has hundreds of smaller islands and rock stacks dotted around its coastline. Around 220 of these are managed by the Department of Conservation. Islands continue to play a large part in current native species conservation.

It is unlikely that it will ever be possible to completely eradicate plant and animal pests from New Zealand's mainland islands. This is not the case with smaller offshore islands, however. Their small size means that it is often feasible to remove pests, and the surrounding water makes it difficult for pests to reinvade the islands.

Because islands can be difficult to access, many of them have suffered less human modification, and there are often fewer pest species present. Such islands are usually safer places for native wildlife, and it is for this reason that they are chosen for conservation projects.

Mainland island examples:
Trounson Kauri Park and Rotoiti Nature Recovery Project

The term 'mainland island' has been coined to describe an area of land undergoing ecological restoration. It involves taking the methods of pest control, revegetation, and translocation of native species used on offshore islands and applying them to an area on the mainland. Places like peninsulas and bush blocks surrounded by pasture are often chosen as they have a natural boundary line to define the area and help minimise the risk of reinvasion by pests. Trounson Kauri Park and Rotoiti Nature Recovery Project are two of a growing number of places being managed as mainland islands in New Zealand.

Trounson Kauri Park in Northland has been managed by the Department of Conservation as a mainland island project since 1995. It consists of an 'island' of kauri forest surrounded by farmland. Predators such as rats, stoats, possums, and feral cats are controlled through the regular use of bait stations and traps spread throughout the park. This has allowed natural forest regeneration to occur, and provides a safer habitat for birds such as kiwi and New Zealand pigeon. North Island robins have also been successfully reintroduced to the park.

The Rotoiti Nature Recovery Project consists of an area of beech forest near Lake Rotoiti in the South Island. The project was started in 1997, with the goals of controlling pests to allow native species populations to recover, and to reintroduce species that were historically present but have now disappeared from the area, such as kiwi and yellowhead.

Trounsoun Kauri Park and Rotoiti Nature Recovery Project can be accessed via well-maintained tracks, and education displays enhance the experience for visitors. As well as providing safer environments for our wildlife, mainland islands also help to teach people about our natural history and inspire them to take steps to help protect it for the future.

A boardwalk through Trounson Kauri Park allows visitors to experience the beauty of the kauri forest without damaging tree roots and seedlings.

Glossary

Arctic	an area of ice-covered sea around the North Pole, also including the northern parts of Canada, Alaska, Russia, Greenland, Iceland, and Scandinavia.
Avian	of, or relating to, birds (Class Aves).
Conifer	cone-bearing plant, for example, pine.
Continental drift	process by which the plates (pieces) of the earth's crust slowly move, carrying the continents with them.
Convection current	currents in the magma (liquid rock) beneath the earth's crust, caused by convection; hot liquid rising, cool liquid descending.
Endemic	found naturally nowhere else in the world.
Foliage	collective term for the leaves of a plant.
Gondwana	name given to the vast southern continent that the southern hemisphere continents of today were once a part of.
Habitat	the place or type of environment where an individual or species lives.
Herbivorous	plant-eating.
Intertidal	between the high-tide mark and low-tide mark.
Invertebrate	animal without a backbone.
Larva (pl. larvae)	juvenile stage of some insects (also known as 'grub'), for example, caterpillars are the larvae of moths and butterflies.
Migration	the mass movement of animals from one place to another.
Nectar	sugary liquid produced by some flowers to attract pollinators such as birds and insects.
Nocturnal	active at night.
Podocarp	a type of conifer found predominantly in the southern hemisphere, and prevalent in New Zealand native forests.
Pollination	the act of transferring pollen from the male to the female parts of a flower.
Predator	an animal that preys upon (eats) other animals.
Taxonomy	the study of the classification and naming of species.
Territory	a defined area that is defended against intruders by the resident individual or pair.
Theropod	small meat-eating dinosaur.
Treeline	the point on a mountain at which trees can no longer grow, usually giving way to other vegetation such as shrubs and grasses.
Vestigial	referring to an organ or body part that is present but no longer functional, for example, vestigial wings in flightless birds such as the kiwi.

Index